TWISTED MINDS

RICHARD S. JOHNSON

Brilliant Books Literary
137 Forest Park Lane
Thomasville, North Carolina 27360 USA

How long, oh Lord must I call for help, but you do not listen?
Or cry out to you, "Violence!" but you do not save?
Why do you make me look at injustice? why do you tolerate wrong?
Destruction and violence are before me; there
is strife, and conflict abounds.
Therefore the law is paralyzed, and justice never prevails.
The wicked hem in the righteous, so that justice is perverted.

Habakkuk 1 vs. 2-4 NIV

ACKNOWLEDGMENT

Many thanks to my wife Sandra for reading, editing, and other support for this book.

Thanks to the people who read earlier copies of this manuscript and made suggested changes.

Thanks to the mountain people of the Allegheny Mountains who make excellent examples of how country folks live and support each other.

Thanks to Jay Williams, Andre Morgan, and the many people of Brilliant Books Publishing for their patience and most helpful support in getting *"Twisted Minds"* published.

PROLOGUE

Somewhere near the middle of a mind-numbing nightmare, Jake Brewer and his wife Jeanne drove north along the Susquehanna River. Gravity sucked them into a black hole of disastrous consequences. Tonight their enemy would discover life became a two-sided war. There would be no turning back. Jake planned it that way. People could die. They earned it.

Thick slabs of river rock rearing through the shallow Susquehanna River spoke of the drought hanging over the land; the red strapped sky foretold another day of hot, dry weather. After crossing the river on the Clark's Ferry Bridge, Jake pulled into a truck stop, stopped away from buildings, and carefully surveyed his surroundings. Blast furnace heat struck him as he ducked out of the truck. Jake pulled a small box from under the truck seat and closed the door without making eye contact.

Friends love Jake Brewer, a man who usually carries a ready smile that draws people to him. Combat Marines who served with him know an intense, take-charge leader who asks no quarter. This night he is neither; his face wears worried lines. Doubt creeps in. He hesitates briefly, breathing deeply, surveying his surroundings before marching across the parking lot, leaning forward as if into a stiff wind, hating what he must do but resolute in completing his mission.

"Vengeance is mine, saith the Lord." Jake glances skyward as thoughts thunder through his mind. "It's not vengeance, Lord. They declared war."

Jake walks on cats' feet for his muscled frame, a slight limp evident. A tall man of chiseled good looks, baby blue eyes, and a body that suggests action, Brewer can be a dangerous man. Usually easygoing, apprehension engulfs him as the "what ifs" rampage through his mind. Since his problems exploded early last winter, he's been drawn ever deeper into a personal hell. Now he's on the attack. There is one way out. Winning. That's his intention.

Stopping at the payphone, Jake massages the tenseness in his neck, his eyes darting furtively about as he mentally runs through the plan one last time, disliking each ugly possibility. Running his tongue around to work up saliva, he pulls change from his pocket and the voice-changing device from the box. Jake placed the gadget over the mouthpiece and adjusted it toward the high end, where experimentation proved it sounded like a husky feminine voice. He retrieved a paper from his wallet, swallowed hard while dialing the first of two numbers, and then dropped the requested change into the machine. Clearing his throat, he worked through a short conversation and hung up.

Drawing a deep breath, he searches for the strength to make the second call, an action that will start a chain of events bordering on the outposts of insanity. A bout of stomach flutters accompanies the realization that he has no choice; the second call is mandatory. Resolved, he places the call, holding his breath while it rings in. After what seemed like an eternity, the phone rang once and died. "Please hang up and try again . . ."

Jake returned the voice changer to its box, anxiously surveying the premises. He mops nervous sweat from his brow with a handkerchief before wiping the phone and immediate area free of fingerprints. Apprehension accompanies the realization of the events now set in motion. Turning to leave, he bumps into a weasel-faced woman crowding the phone station, craning to see what he's doing. Gut sick, he brushes past her, wondering how much she witnessed. Hurrying into the men's room, he heads to an empty sink in the rear, cupping handfuls of cold water on his face. A stare grabs him, and he shoots a return. The gawker glances away. Concern rising, he dries off and checks himself in the mirror.

Running his comb through graying chestnut hair, he notes the pinch-faced stranger slip one last glance in his direction as he turns to leave. How in the world did I get here, Jake questioned, but he knew. "Oh Lord, help me out of this mess, and I'll never . . ." He paused, knowing to finish the thought could be a lie. His attack was well planned. He shook his head in disgust, surveying his surroundings as he walked to the truck.

"Jake, what's wrong?" Jeanne asks as he climbs into the truck, her dark eyes searching his face for answers.

"Jake?" she questions as he starts the truck and heads toward the highway.

"I heard you."

"You didn't answer."

"If anyone asks, we ate dinner and drove straight home."

"Do you feel well?"

"Shouldn't I?"

"You're not yourself."

"How am I supposed to be?"

"We hardly talked over dinner, and you have that look. Besides —"

"I get the picture," Jake snaps, glancing at the love of his life. Tears slipped down her high cheekbones; her mouth turned sadly downward. Fear drained the color from her face, matching the pearl earrings she wears. Jeanne is beautiful. She's also insightful. She knows him.

Frightened eyes beg for an explanation. None would be forthcoming. He squeezes her hand. "I'm sorry."

"Sorry about what, Jake?"

Without answering and lost in worrisome thoughts, Jake exits route 322 and heads south on highway 15. Sweating himself fast to the seat with bile burning his throat, he flipped the air conditioner to MAX AIR. "Harumph." He cleared his throat again.

After he unknowingly sighed aloud several times, Jeanne said, "Sorry's not good enough! What am I mixed up in?"

"What?" Jake snapped.

Looking at her man, the set of his strong jaw, she softly answers, "After all these years, I know my husband. You're acting like – "

"Like what?" Jake interrupts, not seeking an answer.

"Like the last few days before you left for Vietnam the second time. Detached. Edgy. You're rubbing your head and neck. Something's eating you."

"It's nothing," he snaps back.

"Tell that to someone who doesn't know you. We're in trouble."

"What gives you that idea?"

"You, Jake. You're angry. Hell's about to boil over."

*   *   *

Meanwhile, 170 miles to the northwest in the Allegheny Mountains big woods country, smoke hung about the green shaded pool table, shrouding players in flickering shadows. A neon sign in the Pandemonium Bar's window flashes "Straub Beer." A bullish man with broad shoulders bent over the table sighting his shot, his low-slung jeans exposing half-moons. Others look on; some hold cue sticks or long neck beer bottles hanging at arm's length. A collection of baseball hats smother unkept hair - John Deere, CAT, a green Skoal cap, Stihl Chainsaws, all evident. Whisker stubbled faces, tattooed arms, and beer bellies more or less covered by an assortment of rough-looking T-shirts signify tribal membership. With the clack of balls, the shooter applied hard body English, jamming his cue against the floor when the ball refused to drop.

The next shooter, taller than the others and skinny, hat on backward, spits a stream of Red Man toward a badly stained coffee can and steps forward to line up his shot. Two women stand watching the game. One has a cigarette dangling from her mouth with her head tipped sideways to keep the smoke from her eyes. She's wearing stained sweat pants and a too-tight blouse, revealing a fat roll. The other woman is an attractive, well-groomed redhead in tight Levis and a form-fitting blouse covering ample breasts. The first fits the crowd; the second appears drastically out of place. Guttural laughter and ribald humor interspersed with expletives run competition with two huge speakers issuing nonstop country music from a severely abused jukebox.

The bartender, a slight, prematurely balding man with a wavy ponytail, bloodshot eyes peering out of a pitted eggshell face, catches the phone buzzing and answers. "Pandemonium Pleasure Palace. Ivory at your service."

"Link Coleman, please?"

"He know you?"

"We're friends. The name's Grim."

"Damn lady, you must be at a loss for friends." Holding the phone away from his face, he boomed across the room, "Hey Link, phone."

"Who is it?"

"Some woman named Grim."

"I don't know no friggin' Grims," the thickset man with massive arms snarls, grabbing the phone. "Hello."

"Hi Link," the voice says softly. "It's Grim. Shark there?"

"Yeah."

"Swifty?"

"Everybody's here," Link snarled, "everybody 'cept Rusty."

"Where's Rusty?"

"Moved out."

"Punk there?"

"What would that idiot be doin' in town?" Link growled. "You gonna tell me what ya want?"

"Grim Reaper comes bearing a message of grave importance."

"Gimme the message. I got a pool game goin'."

"BOOM," the caller barks into the phone.

"Boom?" Link asked in an angry yet puzzled voice.

"Yes, BOOM, big boy. It's part of the big bang theory. Listen closely, Linkie. The hill country will hear your big bang in exactly thirty minutes."

The phone went dead, and Link slammed it down.

"Who's the chick, Link?" Ivory asked as he pulled another draft.

"Claims she's the Grim Reaper."

"That's death. What did she say?"

"Something about the big bang, whatever that is."

"It's an explosion theory scientists use to define the start of time."

Whattaya make of this Ivory?" Link asks, now more concerned than angry. "Yer the college guy."

"Sounds bad, Link," Ivory solemnly stated. "I'd be scared. Sounds like a death threat."

"Screw that. Nobody threatens Link Coleman."

"Link, be careful. Grim knows where she can find you," Ivory said. "She could walk in here and empty a gun into you. Maybe the last thing you'd remember would be the white-hot pain of bullets tearin' you apart. I wouldn't open any packages. Tear off the paper, and blam, you're pushin' up daisies."

"Bull."

"Be careful, Link. A package bomb could blow you to smithereens. They send 'em for birthdays. Maybe Christmas. When's your birthday?"

"Damn," was all Link could manage in a worried voice.

*   *   *

On a mountain top outside of town, a young, bored state trooper slumped over the steering wheel of his Jeep Cherokee police vehicle, half asleep, watching the tar paper shanty and mobile home below as darkness slips in. Newly assigned to the hill country, this is not his idea of Saturday nightlife. Given a choice, he'd let these hillbillies fight it out to the last man. This might be his job, but it isn't his war.

As darkness descends over the mountains, the bored trooper laid his binoculars aside, checked his weapons and the door locks once more, then leaned back against the seat waiting for his shift to pass. Crickets ply their rhythmic beat, a lonesome whippoorwill calls for a friend, and the pleasant smell of nearby pines sweeps in on the evening breeze. Closing his eyes for what he promises himself will only be a moment, the trooper slips into a peaceful slumber.

"BAHWOOOOOOM!"

A horrendous explosion slammed through the hill country accompanied by a massive fireball.

The confused trooper jerked awake, wondering what happened, fearing he knew the answer.

CHAPTER 1

Unknown to Jake and Jeanne Brewer, a difficult time in their lives was beginning as Jake fastened the last tire chain, climbed into the truck, and headed down the mountain to their home - the Hill Place. With the engine temperature gauge pegged in the danger zone, Jake barreled through the last hundred yards of drifting snow and swung uphill into the turnaround. When the truck spun out, he snapped into reverse and wheeled to a stop in front of Hill Place. Jake popped the hood release, jumped out, and threw up the hood. A sharp blast of Arctic air slapped him, and he grabbed his flying hat. After scooping handfuls of snow away from the plugged radiator, he climbed into the truck, shivering, rubbing his hands together to alleviate the bone-chilling cold.

Two choices existed if they wanted to depart this desolate place; they could get the road plowed or wait for spring.

"Thought that last drift had us," an old voice cracked.

Looking at Pappy, his father-in-law and friend, Jake nodded, "Me too."

The old man sat hunched over, pulled by eighty-eight years of gravity, but sparkles in those dark eyes were apt indicators of a clear mind and a strong sense of humor. "Jeanne's looking at a lot of shoveling to get us out of here."

"Won't mind shoveling. I'm still alive. The way we flew in here, I thought we were hunting a place to slide into eternity."

Pappy chuckled nervously. "I saw trouble when snow pushed up over the hood."

The beginnings of a brutal winter slammed the Allegheny Mountains in early December 1993. Jake realized disaster often breaks with dumb decisions. Instead of turning back when they saw the snow's depth, he chose not to ruin their plans and prayed. Oh well, he thought, we're here, and climbed out, shrugging into his coat. His lifelong home, hand-built by his father, stood before him. The big log cape cod with green shutters and tall fieldstone chimney suggested the peace he so badly needed. A glance caught Jeanne looking at the place in a way that said, "I second that." She turned and smiled, her even white teeth showing, her dark eyes flashing "I love you." She owl winked sending Jake's heart fluttering.

"Better stay here until I get the fires going," Jake said, closing the truck door. Heading toward the house, he sensed that "being watched" feeling bred in from combat patrols. He saw nothing amiss as he scanned his surroundings. No tracks in the snow. No movement. Nothing.

The watched feeling grew more intense, a sense that never betrayed him. Stomping his boots clean on the porch, he stiffened. The entry door stood ajar and lights were on. Anger clashed with worry as he retreated to the truck for his revolver. Opening the cylinder, he checked for loading and snapped it closed. "Can you give me that flashlight?" Jake asked his wife, urgency in his voice. "Keep the doors locked until I get back."

"What is it?" Jeanne asked, her voice strained.

"Stay here," Jake ordered quietly. Old Gus, their black cairn terrier, protested with a piercing howl as he closed the door. Deep snow prevented travel in the truck, and Pappy couldn't walk out. Taking the house was their only choice. Stomach knotted, Jake steeled himself. His mind flashed back to another conflict. Kelly and Wright were dead; Fanelli lay dying. Others were injured. Automatic weapon fire rode the night wind. Jeanne must never know. Realization stabbed home. God remembers!

His gun barrel tracked his eyes as he inspected the living room. A scraping noise drew his attention to the dining room. Jake tensed. It sounded again! Expecting a shot, he warily slipped across the room, easing gun first around the dining room corner. Windblown Venetian blinds scratched across a broken window. Glass lay scattered about. Old tracks partially covered with snow lay outside the broken window. Drawers and cupboard doors hung open in the kitchen. Empty cake mix and spaghetti boxes lay on the floor.

Jake locked outside and cellar locks preventing anyone from entering while he searched upstairs. Oh Lord, help me, he silently prayed, scanning the bathroom before warily climbing the steps. He carefully placed his feet on the step sides to prevent squeaks. The lookout was clear, but the adjoining closet door stood open. Shining the light inside and seeing nothing, he locked the door. Standing to one side in case someone fired, he quietly turned the door handle to the master bedroom. A sound alarmed him. Was someone waiting? His heart pounded. Hearing nothing, he eased in. He knelt, shining the light under the bed, then in the closets. Nothing.

Stealthily, Jake moved to the small bedroom, searched it, then turned his attention to the front bedroom. The door stood open. The room shouted danger. Double beds and two closets could hide several people.

Jake hesitated. Was there more than one intruder? He paused long enough to hold the big magnum with his left hand and wiped the sweat from his gun hand.

Wham. Something slammed below. Carefully retracing his steps to the first floor, Jake opened the cellar door and flipped on the lights. Nothing happened. He eased in, nerves raw. Musty smells greeted him as he slowly maneuvered down into the cellar. Ominous shadows cast by bare light bulbs increased his uneasiness. They were here. Where and how many?

Gripping and releasing his hand on the revolver, he slowly cleared the steps and eased around the furnace, gun first, followed by one eye, displaying a minimum target profile. The outside cellar door hung open, banging in the breeze. Someone was waiting. "Come out of there!" Jake ordered. No answer. "I said come out of there." Nothing.

WHAM. The cellar door slammed.

The truck horn summoned. They're after Jeanne! Jake eased around the furnace. Nothing.

Scrambling across the cellar, he paused to look outside. Fresh tracks led away from the cellar. A lone figure was disappearing into the darkening forest. The intruder's back filled the Colt's sights. Jake began to squeeze off a round, then slowly down the gun. "Oh Lord, help me," he muttered. His killing days were over.

Jeanne called from the truck, "You okay?"

"Yeah."

After studying the tracks, Jake retreated to the cellar, closed the doors, and cautiously moved to the room that held the water systems pressure tank. Finding no one, he flipped on the switches for the pump and furnace, then returned to the truck.

"Did you see that guy?" Jeanne asked excitedly. "Moved like an orange penguin."

Pappy added. "Had a black bag in each hand."

"Tracks duck-footed," Jake said, "Punk Coleman." He had come upon those tracks while hunting.

"Jake, we can't stay here."

"No choice. We can't get out."

"We'll be all right," Pappy assured her as she climbed out and began laboring through the thigh-deep snow. At the house, she grabbed a shovel and started clearing a path to the truck.

Jake discovered the undamaged storm window lying in the snow outside the broken dining room window and replaced it. Returning inside, he turned up the thermostat and listened until the fuel oil furnace kicked on. He knelt by the woodstove, placing sheets of wadded newspaper inside, topped it with pine kindling, and added pieces of split oak. Jake grabbed the jug holding the sawdust and kerosene mixture, distributed a double handful in the stove, and lit it. Flames built quickly.

Jake returned to the cellar to check the water system. The pressure gauge read zero. "Damn," he muttered. Turning off the pump, he struggled down to the spring house in waist-deep snow. The door stood open, and the pump's discarded insulation cover lay in the snow, freezing the pump and busting out a piece of the cast-iron housing, destroying the pump. Angered, he laboriously climbed the hill and explained the situation to Jeanne.

"Might as well get water in," he said, grabbing four of the five-gallon water buckets from the pantry and heading back down to the spring. Quickly filling the buckets, he climbed through the snow with the first two.

"Jake!" Jeanne screamed from the porch.

Jake dropped the buckets and struggled up through the deep snow. Bursting into the house, lungs on fire, he saw Jeanne disappear through the front room, heading upstairs. She threw back the bed covers in the front bedroom. Rancid odor hit. The intruder had messed the bed. A blood-caked pillowcase and towel indicated he was suffering a severe head wound. "See that?"

"Couldn't this wait until I had the water up?" Jake asked, fighting back anger.

"I thought you'd want to know!"

Upset with himself for his shortness, Jake pulled Jeanne to him. "I'm sorry, Honey."

"Forget it!" she snapped, pushing him away, "We have work to do."

Jake folded the bedding inside the mattress pad and balled it on the floor. He opened the windows to air out the place, turned over the mattress, and headed for the garage to stash the soiled mess. Done, he helped Jeanne clean up the mess and then carried water while she cooked supper. When Jake struggled to the house on his fourth trip with forty gallons of water in, his arms ached from holding the buckets out of the snow to prevent spilling them. He filled the large metal canning pot and placed it on the top of the woodstove that served as their winter water heater.

Jake added wood to the stove while delicious smells of a country supper fueled appetites. His stomach was growling when Jeanne called them to the table where pork chops, boiled potatoes, steamed vegetables, and applesauce greeted them. Holding hands to say grace, Jake slipped a glance at Jeanne. The years had added to her gentle beauty, naturally colored cheeks, the lips he loved to kiss, the olive complexion inherited from the Indian ancestry of her mother's family.

With grace over, the natural smile and dark eyes flashed, I love you, Jake.

CHAPTER 2

Dinner over and the dishes done, Jake gathered materials to stop the air leaking around the storm window. After locating the staple gun, he couldn't find staples. Accustomed to his problems finding things, Jeanne explained they were in a black bag, but he couldn't find that either.

Shaking her head in mock disbelief, she entered the pantry. "Men! You never put anything away, and you can't find things that are put away for you. They're hanging behind the door."

Jeanne stepped into the pantry and closed the door. "Jake, the bags are gone!"

"What?" Jake muttered disgustedly, remembering Pappy reported the intruder had a bag in each hand. "Wonder what else he took." They set about creating a list of missing tools, food, a gallon of windshield washer solution used for cleaning black powder rifles, a quart of denatured alcohol, and D-Con rat poison. "Man, Jeanne, he might think that poison is a snack. Poison or the alcohol could kill him."

"Not our problem."

"Come on," Jake protested, "no one should die like that."

"Something good could come of this."

"Like what?"

"When you misplace something, you can always blame it on Punk."

"I don't need Punk. I'm married, remember?"

Jeanne smiled. "How could I forget?"

Jake cut clear plastic to size, fastening it over the broken window with duct tape and reinforcing it with the staples remaining in the gun. Done, they settled into the front room. The conversation centered around the

Colemans, a fourth-generation family who called these mountains home. They were as tough as this land that birthed them and had grown out of control since their father, Old Clyde, suffered a heart attack the previous summer.

"Wonder why he broke in here?" Pappy asked.

"His brothers beat him," Jake answered. "He's severely retarded."

"He might get worse," Jeanne retorted. "I'm not a good victim."

"They had you in mind when they created the 'Don't Tread On Me' flag."

"Their lives mirror the crude redneck stories people tell about them," Jeanne snapped, obviously irritated.

"It isn't easy being poor with a houseful of kids."

"The world should suffer because they can't control their sexual appetites?"

"No, Jeanne, it shouldn't," Jake said. Aggravation edged his words. "There's a lot more. Clyde's first wife died in childbirth with their third kid when she was nineteen. Clyde went to Buffalo and brought home a woman with three kids. They had his kids, her kids, and their kids living in the old Coleman house until it burned. Those kids never stood a chance. Their grandfather, Harley Coleman, was a moonshiner who many claimed made the best shine going during prohibition. Word was the congressman, district attorney, and sheriff were all boozers, and they protected old man Coleman. It seemed like the Colemans always got off light for the stunts they pulled."

"Bet it got exciting with all those Coleman kids raising Cain," Pappy said.

"It did," Jake agreed. "One day, Dad and I stopped by to talk to Colemans about a logging road they wanted. We parked at Clyde's house where kids were running wild among junk cars and stuff. There was an old dug well covered with half-rotten boards in the middle of the yard. Clyde was sitting on the steps, and Dad suggested, 'You better put something over that well before a kid falls in and drowns.' Clyde thoughtfully looked at him, spit some tobacco juice off to the side of the steps, and drawled, 'Well, Jackson, ya can't expect to raise 'em all.' One of his hunting dogs fell in and drowned, so he pulled a junk car over the well. Thought more of those hunting dogs than he did the kids."

"Maybe he knew how they'd turn out," Jeanne said.

"They aren't all bad. Chance was an honor student, a fine athlete, and a friend. He spent a lot of time here when he was a kid."

"Yes, and your mother said his brothers robbed your henhouse while he ate with you."

"Do they work?" Pappy asked, politely changing the subject.

"Clyde can't since his heart attack. Most of the boys are loggers or work at sawmills. Rusty works on the highway department and lives in the trailer with Clyde, Lu, and their youngest, Butch. He's a senior in school. Punk lives in that chicken coop with a little wood stove, and the rest live in the shanty, which is a replacement for their grandfather's five-bedroom house that burned. Link's in prison. Shouldn't be eligible for parole for another three or four years? He beat the rape charge. The woman was afraid to testify, but they sent him up for assaulting the cop and carrying drugs."

"Wonder who beat Punk?" Jeanne asked.

"Probably Shark or Swifty," Jake replied. "Both are snake mean."

"They sure have wild names," Pappy said.

Jake knew the stories behind most of them. "Some smarty decided Lester might be the missing link. Link stuck. Swifty got tagged Swifty because he isn't. Shark owns a double row of pointy lower teeth. One of the kids couldn't say George, so he became Gore. Mousey's natured a little mouse-like, Punk is retarded and happened into that name, and Rusty is short for Russell. Chance joined the Navy and never came back. Bob got hung at the stone quarry."

"They have all boys?" Pappy inquired.

"Nine boys and three girls, Mary, Josie, and Garnet. The girls didn't have nicknames. Mary was the oldest girl and got pregnant in high school. She told someone she didn't know if the baby's father was her father or brother. Child welfare folks got wind, and the girls disappeared."

"Wasn't one of the boys married?" Pappy inquired.

"Rusty married a Miller girl who lived just over the hill from the Coleman's place at that farm on the left. It didn't last long. The talk was some of the other Coleman boys hung around Rusty's wife when he was working, and Link raped her. They split. It's hard to sort facts from fiction.

One wild story was that Rusty was sitting on the Coleman porch the morning after the wedding. Clyde asked him what he was doing home, and

Rusty answered, 'The marriage won't work, Pa. Why she's a virgin.' Clyde reflected a bit and then agreed, 'Yer right, boy. If she ain't good enough for her folks, she ain't good enough for ours neither.'"

"What happened to Punk?" Pappy asked after laughing at the Rusty story.

"Some say incest. Talk is men stopped by to see Lu while Clyde was working. Shark supposedly resulted from one of those liaisons. Clyde told my dad, 'I'd a throwed her out fer screwin' everybody, but I can't take care of all them kids my damself.'"

"They need a lifeguard on their gene pool," Jeanne said. "Wouldn't be so many of them."

They soon ran out of things to talk about, and Pappy turned in. Jake retrieved snowshoes and dressed for a trip to the Vance place, the nearest phone where he could call in a police report. His steps crunched like potato chips in the crusting snow. The clear mountain night saw the Milky Way stretched to the horizons. Light pollution surrounded even towns of modest size, blocking out the majestic beauty of the night, but not here; not where the only light was from the few hill country houses that turned off their lights when the people turned in. "Man and some folks believe this happened by accident," Jake said to himself as he marveled at God's creation.

Lights sparkled in Vance's windows, indicating someone was up. Jake was removing his snowshoes when King howled, and the door opened. Misty saw who was there and gave Jake a flirtatious smile, then a hug. Her emerald eyes explored his, searching for a corner where lust might lurk. "My, you came courting late tonight."

Jake felt red rising in his face. He wasn't good at this kind of play, and Misty knew it, always enjoying his discomfort. "I need a favor."

"Oh," she teased, "and what might that be?"

"Dean home?"

"Does that make a difference?" she softly asked.

"Come on in, Jake, tell us a lie," Dean yelled, ignoring his wife's hassling.

"Let me tell you my problems instead? Someone broke into our place, and I need to call the cops."

"Punk get your place too?" Dean questioned. "He broke in down at our homestead."

"He did. Different problem. We're in, and there's no way we'll get out without help. I prayed you'd be around to plow, for a price, of course."

"Of course, for a price. Friendship isn't worth much, but bucks talk," Dean said sarcastically.

"You have to buy fuel," Jake said, offering him two fifties. Dean finally took one, protesting that it was too much. Jake phoned the police, explaining the break-in and the problem with the missing poison and alcohol. When he was off the phone, Misty brought them coffee, and bending low over the table, showing cleavage; she smiled at Jake.

"What'd he do at your place?" Dean asked, regaining his friend's attention.

"Took off a storm window and broke the inside window to get in. Tried to get water and ruined the pump, so I'm carrying water early this year."

"My goodness Jake, all you'll get done is carrying water," Misty said.

"We always pull the pump after Christmas and get along fine."

"I bet Jeanne doesn't like living like that. I wouldn't."

Dean shook his head. "Jeeze, Misty, we all lived like that until they ran power out here in 1958."

"I guess Jeanne's just another one of you hillbillies," Misty said without thinking.

Dean was embarrassed for his wife and changed subjects. "The law has to do something about the Colemans," Dean complained bitterly. "Swifty assaulted a woman at the Handee Mart. The speculation is they're on drugs. Some say they're connected to the drugs coming into the county along with some county officials. There's talk of folks taking care of the Coleman problem ourselves if the law doesn't soon do something."

"Have to think hard on that."

"Sleep on it. I'll have your road plowed about daylight. Just in time for a seat at Jeanne's breakfast table. We'll talk on it then."

Dean plowed in on his old D-4 Cat dozer just after daylight. It was a gift from Jake's father, Jackson, when they moved off the hill. It came with the stipulation that Dean would plow the road as needed, and he always held up his end of the deal. Bacon, sausage, and a swarm of other breakfast scents greeted Dean and stood appetites at attention. Warm conversation attended breakfast until Jake rebuffed another call to arms against the Colemans. "That's fine, Jake until someone's killed up here," Dean snapped, slamming his fist on the table. "You can leave, but we live here full time." His anger ended the friendly conversation; his departure a few minutes later left a foul taste on the morning.

Trooper Hanratty arrived mid-morning. Might be too soft for police work, Jake thought as he looked over the fair-skinned, apple-cheeked officer who carried an all-business attitude. After basic introductions, the investigation began. Jeanne informed him this wasn't their first Coleman-related problem, and their patience was wearing thin. Hanratty scanned the place with a practiced eye, noting the plastic covering the broken window. "Is that where the intruder entered the premises?" he asked, recording information in a small notebook, turning it over for privacy when he wasn't writing.

"Yeah," Jake answered, thinking Hanratty sounded more textbook than necessary.

"We watched a man come bustin' out of the cellar carrying two black bags," Pappy began. "He wore old hunting clothes and walked funny."

"Hunting clothes, Mister . . ." the trooper paused, searching for Pappy's name.

"Phillips," Pappy answered. "An orange coat and hat like hunters wear. His left sleeve was coming loose, and the lining was hanging out."

"He walked hunched over and moved like a penguin," Jeanne added. We believe it was Punk Coleman," Jeanne said.

"Did you get a good look at him, Mrs. Brewer?" the trooper asked.

"A side look as he struggled away."

"Then can we be sure who it was?"

"If it looks like Punk and walks like Punk, it might be Punk," Jeanne snapped.

"I'm sorry if I offended you, but I can only use facts, ma'am."

"Please call me Jeanne, and I understand what you can use in your report. But, if it looked like Bung, it could be Bung."

"I can't let suppositions cloud facts," the trooper hedged.

"Trooper Hanratty, we have snowshoes. Let's follow those tracks," Jake suggested.

"My shift ended at eight," Hanratty said, blushing as he glanced at his watch. "I'll get another trooper up to help you."

"I don't need help," Jake replied, an edge riding his voice. "I know where those tracks go."

"You followed them?"

"Check the tracks. They'll tell you who made them and where he was headed!"

Easing away from the conversation with Jake, he asked Jeanne, "Anything missing?"

"Two shopping bags full of stuff," Jeanne answered testily. "Here's a list of some items we believe are missing, but only time will tell what he took. Things we think he stole could turn up later, and we won't miss some things until we need them."

Hanratty nodded and copied Jeanne's list into his report.

"Someone better check Punk soon. The poison or the alcohol could kill him," Jake suggested.

"Poisons are clearly marked. I wouldn't think he'd ingest them," Hanratty muttered.

"That could be a deadly mistake," Jake annoyingly retorted. "Punk can't read."

Hanratty was nervous. "We can't say for sure who the intruder was, but —"

Jake's eyes narrowed. "Friend, if you don't plan on checking Punk, say so! I'll do it myself."

Sensing his seriousness, Hanratty consented, "We'll stop. Is there anything else I should see before I go?"

"You can get fingerprints where his filthy hands were all over my cupboards," Jeanne said.

"Fingerprints are important in some cases, but a camp burglary is hardly —"

Jake interrupted sharply. "Let's get something straight. This place isn't a camp; it's home. I was born and raised here. We pay a lot of taxes, some of which goes toward police protection."

"I wasn't putting down your home; I was sharing my experience concerning previous cases. Rest assured, we'll do everything we can to wrap this up." With tension building, Jake led him to the master bedroom, where Hanratty saw Jake's revolver lying on the nightstand. "That yours?"

"It is, and I know how to use it," Jake replied in a thin voice, looking the trooper in the eye.

Hanratty discovered Jake's cold eyes held a fierceness that said he faced a dangerous man.

"Got a pistol permit?"

"Want to see it?"

"Should be in the report. What kind of gun is it?" the trooper asked.

"Colt Trooper Special .357 magnum," Jake replied as he dug out the permit.

"Hmm, self-protection, 6'3", 223 pounds," Trooper Hanratty said as he read the permit. He handed back the permit. His actions said he wanted away from this man and now. Relief came when they completed the inspection, and Jake headed downstairs. At the door, Hanratty paused, "Thanks for your cooperation, Mrs. Brewer. I hope we can clear this up for you."

"Somebody better and soon. The problems are long past getting old."

Jake showed Hanratty the tracks leading from the cellar to the woods. Hanratty added the duck foot walk to his notes at Jake's insistence. Walking to the garage, Jake retrieved the soiled bedclothes and handed them to the trooper. "Here's DNA evidence that might help solve this problem."

"My gosh, what is he?" the trooper questioned in disbelief as the odor rose when he rolled out the contents.

"Severely retarded and beaten. The pillowcase blood came from the beating that drove him here. His brothers keep him around for his social security checks. He sleeps in that old chicken coop, just surviving. He needs your help."

"I'm not sure what I can do," the trooper apologized.

"For starters, you can check on him. Might find him poisoned or frozen to death. Stop at the top of our hill on the way out. Snow's deep but passable. His tracks come up a hundred yards down the dug road and head west. You'll find the same tracks crossing the road just past the Colemans by the spring run. You might ask the Coleman boys who belongs to those tracks."

"I'll have to call in backup," the trooper reluctantly agreed.

"Backup?" Jake asked, noting the trooper quickly wished he hadn't mentioned it.

Hanratty's face reddened. "It's better if there are two of us when we stop at the Colemans."

"I see," Jake said with a cold smirk. "When armed lawmen trained to handle bad guys need backup, ordinary citizens are in deep trouble."

Hanratty nodded agreement, yet those hardened eyes suggested Jake Brewer might be anything but an ordinary man.

CHAPTER 3

Hanratty glanced at his watch, cursing his dilemma. The odor rising from the bedding Brewer stuffed in the back seat grew his anger. "Damn! Brewer expects me to look for tracks, and he'll check. This is nuts," he told himself.

The trooper grumbled as he struggled through thigh-deep snow, "So what if I prove Punk did it? He isn't competent to stand trial. And I'm fooling with idiots in this godforsaken place while my wife and kids worry because I'm late coming home. I must be nuts to do this for a living."

"Damn," he yelled in frustration, and then feeling foolish, he looked around to see if anyone heard him.

A hundred yards out the dug road, duck tracks heading west met snowshoe tracks that paralleled them. Returning to his vehicle, Hanratty radioed for backup as he drove to the Coleman shanty and parked where he was no longer visible from their windows. The same tracks viewed earlier disappeared by the spring heading for the Colemans. The left print now appeared to be barefoot with blood in it. Snowshoe tracks had followed to this point and then returned up the mountainside.

The previous week he investigated the break-in at the Vance homestead. If Rusty hadn't arrived, they would have had to use their weapons to leave. Someone could get hurt and maybe killed before the law got serious about the Colemans. He worried it might be him.

Soon, a snow cloud followed a rapidly approaching vehicle. Hanratty felt relief when he recognized Elvis Johnston in the Cherokee. He was a big black man with the reputation of being a tough hombre, state wrestling champ, and marshall arts expert who wore a smile well. A solid choice to go the Colemans, Hanratty thought. He won't start trouble, but he'll be ready if it comes.

"How'd you get here so soon?" Hanratty asked.

"I was at a wreck down where this road intersects route120 to Parker. A car slid into the ditch. Couple guys in a log truck stopped. You should have seen the size of those guys. The driver was a gray-haired, man-mountain kind of guy. He just kept coming out of that Mack. A big guy with a black beard climbed out the other side. Hardly labored with the car. The driver spit tobacco in the road, tipped his hat to the woman driver, and they roared off."

"Any name on the truck door?" Hanratty asked.

"Yeah. Brewer Logging."

"You met Jackson Brewer and Bear Mihalovich. Tough men." Getting back to business, Hanratty said, "We'll park in front of the Coleman place. Stay in your vehicle until they chain their dogs!"

"What if they don't?"

"We don't go in."

"They'll see cops and chain their dogs so we can hassle 'em?"

"They aren't afraid of us. Be careful. You can't trust them."

"I can take care of myself," Johnston assured him as he climbed into his vehicle.

Slowing to a stop at the Colemans, Trooper Johnston noted the multiple tarpaper patches on the roof, the smoking stovepipe tipped at an obscene angle, and places where the fake brick siding hung loose. There were no windows in the front, just one slab door, but he could see a window on one end. Perched on cement blocks, the place didn't look substantial enough to stand against the winds that tore across these mountains. A pile of split firewood lay outside the front door. Two decrepit sheds, a partially collapsed barn, and what appeared to be a chicken coop stood off to the side.

Johnny forgot the dog warning and opened his door. Five of the meanest dogs he ever saw swarmed about, growling and snarling, climbing along the vehicle on their hind legs. He jerked the door closed and slid toward the middle of the seat as a big shepherd put his feet on the door with his teeth clicking against the glass.

The shanty door opened, and a scruffy-looking man came blinking into the sunlight. He wore untied boots, filthy pants, and an unbuttoned, food-stained flannel shirt. One knee was out of his pants, and he carried a pick handle. With two crusty fingers in his mouth, he whistled at the dogs. When they paid no attention, he fought through the snow, cursing loudly, swinging the pick handle with both hands. One of the dogs grabbed at him, and he knocked the dog rolling. The dog's painful scream garnered attention as it tucked tail and ran.

Another occupant, dressed in a like outfit and sporting a multi-day beard with long greasy hair hanging out from under a ragged orange cap, came out of the shanty to assist Shark. When they succeeded in chaining the dogs, Shark raised the handle over his head, gesturing for the troopers to come down. Hanratty stopped to get Johnston. He remained seated and in no hurry to get out.

"C'mon," Hanratty coaxed. "Stay on the path. They can't reach you."

Dogs lunged wildly, struggling against their chains to reach Hanratty, but he never hesitated.

Johnston pulled out his sidearm before walking hurriedly past the dogs, their teeth clacking, springing against their chains. Recognizing the trooper's discomfort, Shark held a delighted grin. His brother stood with a blank look, staring, maybe at the troopers, or perhaps somewhere beyond.

"Ratty, ya lose somethin'?" Shark smiled.

"Problems," Hanratty answered. "This is Trooper Johnston."

"Yer a big nigger," Shark said as he looked over the black man, "but yer 'fraid a my dogs," he added with a yellow-toothed grin. "Crapped yer pants, didn't ya?" He laughed heartily, exhibiting tobacco-stained shark teeth that gave him his nickname.

"They could scare you," Johnston admitted, his words coming softly.

Shark agreed, pulling up his sleeve to show ragged purple scars that healed without stitches. "That pit bull bitch done this. Got two 'Merican pit bulls, a rotwyer, a cop dog, and a junkyard dog," he said, beaming with pride. "Mean dogs."

Johnston nodded, staring at the ugly wound, then back at the snarling dogs. His face told the world he didn't need a warning to stay clear. Until now, he was tough enough to handle most anything that came down the pike, but his eyes exhibited fear of these dogs.

"Nuff a that. Let's get coffee," Shark said, turning toward the door, nodding for the troopers to follow. Johnston stepped around the yellow holes in the snow where men had relieved themselves. He shook his head, unable to accept the scene unfolding around him.

"Two coffees?" Shark asked as he picked up dirty cups.

"I'm coffeed out," Hanratty replied, "but Trooper Johnston needs one. He's had a rough morning."

Inside, Johnston hesitantly closed the door, totally unprepared for what lay before him.

Sweltering heat from the wood stoves exaggerated the stench. Unbelieving, he looked around, exploring creative ways to breathe without taking the defiled air into his lungs. A filthy Mr. Coffee sat on a wooden crate; dirty handprints and coffee stains hid the original color. The carafe was half-full of a black substance that looked more like road patch than something fit for human consumption. A beer bottle half-filled with cigarette butts, a nearly empty gallon wine jug, and a deck of cards littered the table. The smell of urine was overpowering. Following his nose, Johnston noted a hole in the floor that served as a urinal.

Shark handed Johnston coffee in the cleanest cup. "Drink," he commanded the trooper.

Johnston saw no way to refuse and took the filthy cup, holding it away from his body.

"Why ya here, Ratty?" Shark asked, grinning widely.

Without commenting on the name he detested, Hanratty studied Shark's face. "Somebody broke into the Brewer place. Tracks lead here."

"Ain't us," Shark said, his grin gone.

"Whoever was over there left with enough D-Con rat poison and alcohol to kill a man."

Shark thought about this revelation with a mean glare replacing his smile as he pondered what to do. "Go!" he said, grabbing the cup from Johnston and pointing to the door.

"No, Shark, we're checking out this problem," Hanratty said.

Shark saw no use arguing and walked toward the door with the troopers washing in the overpowering odor that clung to him. Gore never looked when they passed but walked in their direction as they neared the chicken coop. Shark cracked the door and peeked in, blocking Hanratty's view. Hanratty pulled the door wider, and in the dim shadows, he spotted a partially covered form sprawled on the loose hay. Two black bags and several open containers lay beside the still form. A lake of technicolor vomit contained pieces of pickles, cheese, and still frozen sausage. Johnston turned away, his stomach rebelling.

"What the —?" Shark asked upon discovering his brother.

"Got a flashlight?" Hanratty asked.

"Damn thing broke."

Hanratty found Johnston standing away from the coop fighting the urge to heave. Understanding, Hanratty said, "Toss down a flashlight. Then stand by your radio."

Relief flooded across Johnston's face, but the feeling of deliverance only lasted until he saw the dogs. He broke a new path through snow-covered berry briars to his vehicle with dogs straining against their chains, snarling and wildly biting the air.

Hanratty grabbed the light Johnston pitched to him and stepped in to examine the pitiful sight. Punk's missing shoe exhibited the foot bled earlier but now appeared frozen. Hanratty felt Punk's throat and found a weak pulse. An open box of poison lay nearby. Holding the light on the regurgitated mess, he recognized pieces of partially digested D-con. Stepping outside, he called Johnston, "Call an ambulance. He ate poison and has a frozen foot."

Shark began cussing. "Damn, Brewers. Cops too. We'll get even. Ya can bet yer fannies on it."

Almost an hour passed before a siren screamed in the distance. A red and white rescue vehicle arrived, sliding sideways as it skidded to a stop on the icy road. The driver and an attendant jumped out, retrieved a stretcher, and followed Johnston's trail to the chicken coop.

Fred Collins moved in and took his pulse. "He's barely alive."

Punk was loaded, and the EMTs whipped the ambulance around and, with siren wailing, tore off toward the hospital. After the ambulance departed, Hanratty told Johnston, "Let's gather that stuff in the coop for evidence."

"Leave it be. We bought it," Shark snarled.

"The poison too, Shark? You can't have it both ways."

"Up yours," Shark growled.

Hanratty walked into the coop, and when Shark tried to follow, Johnston prevented his entry. "Careful Nigger, I'll feed ya to them dogs," Shark threatened.

"Hold it!" Johnston ordered. Shark flipped him the bird and kept walking. Johnston grabbed him, "I said, hold it!"

Spinning in one continuous motion, Shark slammed a fist into the trooper's face, breaking his nose. Blood sprayed. Shark pounded him like a jackhammer, raining blows, stunning Johnston. Years of contact sports guided the trooper's reactions. He caught Shark's fist coming in, jerked down, and jammed Shark headfirst into the snow. The big trooper pounced on Shark, pinning him and pulling his arms behind his back; he snapped on cuffs and yanked him to his feet.

Shark came up spitting snow. Twisting out of Johnston's grip, he turned sharply and kicked his leg, knocking the trooper down. Shark dove into him, knocking the wind out of him. He spun, kicking at the trooper's head. Disbelief crowded the trooper's face as Shark butted him in the jaw. Pain watered his eyes. Johnston took a glancing blow, grabbed Shark's foot, and jerked him down into the snow.

The clamor of snarling dogs prompted Hanratty to look. He saw Shark's head jammed in a snowbank. Blood streamed down the trooper's face and onto his uniform jacket. "You okay?" Hanratty asked, noting his nose hung sideways.

"Yeah," Johnston snarled, fighting for air as he struggled to his feet. "Shark attacked me." The trooper grabbed him by the neck and crotch of the pants. Jerking Shark up over his head, he ran toward the dogs.

"No! No!" Shark screamed, knowing his fate. Angry dogs snapped in anticipation. The trooper pulled up, tossing Shark in the snow just out of reach of the dogs. Fear rode Shark's face.

"You're afraid of the dogs too, Shark."

Shark stared pitchforks, spitting at the trooper. "Damn big lipped nigger. Go back to Aferca. You an' Brewer are gonna get it bad."

Hanratty grabbed ankle cuffs, "Snap these on. I'll see if I can find a coat." Gore had been watching and headed for the shanty, returning with a filthy blanket. He threw it over Shark's shoulders and went back inside without saying anything.

Trying to stop the blood, Johnston pressed snow against his upper lip and nose. With snow in his other hand, he wiped clotting blood off his jacket. Pain throbbed through his face making it difficult to concentrate. A pair of shiners would follow the swelling in his eyes.

With evidence collected, Hanratty called in a report. "We ran into a problem at Colemans.

Johnston's hurt, and we're bringing Shark in. Send troopers out here to pick up Johnston's vehicle. Can't tell what might happen if we leave it here."

"Roger, 3 4. Is Johnston hurt bad?"

"Broken nose and his pride's suffering."

"I can have people up there in 30 or 40 minutes. Best I can do."

"Okay," Hanratty agreed and signed off just in time to see Johnston drag Shark up the hill by the ankle cuffs. Snow funneled under his shirt and over his face. "He tried to butt me in the nuts," Johnston explained. "I fought back the urge to pistol-whip him."

Hanratty shook his head, understanding Johnston's frustration. Realizing he couldn't allow Shark to lie there in the snow, he pulled him to his feet, brushing the snow off his clothes. After shaking snow off the blanket, he wrapped it around the shivering prisoner. Hanratty opened the rear gate of the Cherokee and sat Shark down. "Behave yourself, and you can sit there."

Shark spit at Hanratty without saying anything, glaring at him with dark, hateful eyes. Johnston asked, "Can't we just lock my vehicle and leave?"

"We should wait if you can handle it. His brothers might destroy the Cherokee."

"I can wait," Johnston returned angrily.

"Hey, nigger boy," Shark called defiantly. "Ya got yer black butt kicked. Hah, hah. You blackies never could fight. Hah, hah."

"You better record charges so we can go over them with the Corporal. He'll want everything straight before we take Shark for arraignment."

Shark overheard the conversation and said, "Just tell the corp'ral, Shark kicked this big nigger's ass." Shark laughed again, thoroughly enjoying Johnston's fury.

Johnston lunged, but Hanratty stepped between them. "You can't win this one, Johnny."

"Another time," Johnston replied and stomped away to finish his report.

"Yeah. You'll get another lickin', nigger. Bet on it."

CHAPTER 4

"Brewer. Wait up," Beanie Yettle, retired busybody, called as Jake stepped out of his truck in front of the Chat N Chew Coffee Shop. Beanie's unbuckled boots, a hunting cap with the flaps dangling, and a threadbare Army greatcoat from wars past cast a unique portrait. Red-faced and unshaven, he gasped, "Heard ya got problems."

"Yep. Some jobs crept up on me. A good Samaritan would lend a hand."

"Don't care much for jobs, but I'm a great boss fer a man with a few beers on hand. Course, my supervision doesn't come cheap. Too much experience to give my time away."

"I'm married. That's all the supervision I can handle."

"Good Lord, I hear ya. My woman's always got a project."

"Ever get any of them done?" Jake asked, knowing Beanie's reputation.

"So much comes up that I can't get 'em all."

"Be grateful for interruptions, Beanie. They're great energy savers."

"Tell me about the poisonin'," Beanie said.

"Nothing to tell," Jake answered and he didn't break stride; the comment didn't deserve a reply. He heard Beanie's curses as he entered the old-time Parker Hardware, which carried memories of times past. Loyce Bright ran the store as his father had before him; his brother Hardy helped some. The Bright brothers could have been twins, with short white hair, slight builds, and thick coke bottle glasses forever pushed up pug noses. They had the same "haha" laugh that rumbled from deep within. Loyce's laughter was spent laughing with people, Hardy's laughing at them. Both used smokeless tobacco, Loyce dipped snuff, and Hardy always had a chaw straining his cheek. They sold fancy brass spittoons but used individual coffee cans instead.

Folks spoke highly of Loyce Bright, who earned the reputation of being a friendly handyman who could talk customers through most projects. On the other hand, Hardy was nasty and too lazy to do much more than complain about "the work I usta do." Folks talked about him too, but it was seldom positive. Growing up, the brothers acquired descriptive nicknames that stuck; Loyce was OhSo, and Hardy was NotSo; OhSo Bright and NotSo Bright.

OhSo ran a real hardware. Unlike sterile box stores, the Parker hardware smelled and looked like a hardware. Narrow aisles surrounded by shelves that reached the high ceilings, each packed with merchandise. At strategic locations, mechanical pickers stood ready to grab out-of-reach items. There was one or two of everything imaginable, and if the customer couldn't find what was needed, the help usually could, that or a suitable substitute. On the rare occasion when the long-employed counter people couldn't find something, they signaled OhSo Bright. If they ever carried it in stock, he knew where it was. They seldom called NotSo, realizing he would launch into a tirade about poor help and customers that expected him to jump no matter how busy he was, which was usually not very. The elder Bright knew what he was doing when he willed the store to OhSo with the provision that he kept NotSo in his employ. The store was well run and prosperous, and NotSo was guaranteed an income; not a job as such, he did little more than was necessary to look busy.

Everyone who worked in the store was a native. Like most small-town staffs, they knew the county's business, and this day they knew Jake had a problem on the Hill. "What brings you to town, Mister Brewer?" Connie Smith asked with a knowing smile.

"The need for window glass, staples, batteries, and the latest news."

"You are the latest news. What happened?"

"Jeanne was drinking again. Staggered into a window."

"Thanks for sharing that bit of fiction, you big BSer. What happened?"

"You probably know more than I do," Jake said.

"That Coleman boy almost died from your poison. You coulda killed him."

"You sold me the D-Con last fall. You're an accessory."

"C'mon, Jake; I had no part in this."

"No, and that's the point, Connie, neither did we," Jake replied. "If somebody got poisoned, it's because of something they did and not something we caused. You didn't sell D-Con for human consumption, and I didn't buy it to poison people."

"That's true," she agreed, nodding her head.

"This place will be buzzing today. Let people know whoever broke in had a lot of choices, and they made all the wrong ones."

"You know Punk Coleman broke in."

"I thought that way until the investigating officer convinced me we shouldn't speculate on such things. After being chastised for judging others, I changed my sinful ways."

"Right, Jake," Connie replied sarcastically. "What size glass do you need?"

"36 X 48. Or is it 48 X 36?"

"What difference does it make?" Connie asked with a concerned look.

"Not sure there's a difference. I'm not the glass expert."

"Oh, you," Connie said in an exasperated voice, "You haven't changed. Jeanne's a saint. Now, one pane?" she asked as she walked back to the glass rack.

"Better make it three."

"Did Punk . . . uh, did somebody break three windows," Connie asked?

"Just one, but I have a cracked window, and I always break one installing the stuff. Cheaper to throw a pane away than to make another hour round trip to town. Where do you keep your glazing compound?"

"Back with the glazing points. You got a putty knife?" Connie automatically called out her verbal checklist remembering the items people returned to purchase so they could complete jobs.

"Had one but better get another one just to be sure. The intruder took a bunch of tools."

Connie returned with the wrapped glass as NotSo stomped through. Looking Jake a mean face, he said, "Fred Collins told us you poisoned that Coleman boy. You come up here expectin' everybody to kiss your fanny, and when we don't, you take to poisonin' people. We should gate every road comin' into the county and keep you flatlanders outta here. You lazied around in the military until you got yourself a fat pension. Now I'm way overtaxed to carry the likes of you."

Jake fought back the urge to feed NotSo a fist, realizing such action would serve no purpose. Hating outsiders was an unchanging attitude of NotSo and a hundred like him.

"People are mad about what ya done. The DA was there when Fred told us what happened, and Penny said you ain't much of a man and never were. He said he stepped over better men than you on the way to real fights. Said he can't figure why your woman ever —"

Jake snatched NotSo by the shirt and pulled him close, raising him to his tiptoes. "Friend, keep your mouth off my wife. This is your only warning." Letting loose of his shirt, Notso dropped. Jake noted his white, hate-filled face as NotSo climbed to his feet and headed for the door.

Connie heard the tirade and had no desire to become part of it. "Sorry, Jake. Loyce would be fit to be tied if he knew that went on."

Jake shrugged. "He's getting miserable in his old age."

"No, Jake, He's always been a miserable jerk. He's just getting older."

CHAPTER 5

Shark maintained a steady stream of racial epithets, his breath as offensive as his body odor, while Johnston showed anger with dark-eyed glances in the mirror. As the troopers removed him from the vehicle, Shark looked at Johnston and said, "Corp'ral's gonna be upset when he sees ya, Sambo. Yer in big trouble."

They were ushering Shark inside when Corporal Repicci saw Johnston's face. "You get hit by a train?"

"Hell no," Shark interrupted. "City boy attack me an' got his black butt whipped bad."

"You read him his rights?" the corporal asked, ignoring Shark.

"We did, but he held his hands over his ears," Johnston returned.

"He's a liar, Corp'ral. The nigger can't read."

"Johnston read Mr. Coleman his rights, Corporal," Hanratty stated. "Shark's been trouble since we picked him up."

"Damn you, Ratty," Shark said. "Yer in trouble too. Cop brutality."

"Get him back to my office! Open the windows! I'll be in to go over statements."

Johnston started back as directed while Hanratty stopped at the restroom. The door closed behind Hanratty when thumping erupted on the wall, followed by the thud of a heavy object slamming into the floor. Hanratty rushed out to find Johnston kneeling on Shark's back, one hand squeezing his neck, the other wrenching his handcuffed arms up behind his back. Shark screamed obscenities. "What going on?" Hanratty demanded.

"He tried to kick me in the privates," Johnston snarled, his words clipped short in anger.

"Nigger wants ta kill me," Shark said, using his best victim voice.

Corporal Repicci rushed in and witnessed what was happening. "Get off him!" Grabbing Shark, he led him out to the desk officer. "Shoot him if he tries to get away! Hanratty, Johnston, in the back! Now!"

When they were in the booking room, the corporal began. "What should I know before I interview Coleman?"

"I'm through being called a nigger," Johnston replied.

"He'll bait you," the corporal cautioned, "and Squire will take care of him for doing it. Make sure everything's in your reports. Here's something you need to learn. A lot you learned in the academy has marginal application here. You start complaining about discrimination, and the word will get out. Some folks don't have much use for cops, especially city-bred cops. On the other hand, good folks make serving here a pleasure. Your actions determine who sides with you. Capish?"

Johnston nodded angrily. Repicci had Shark brought in and quickly conducted his prisoner interview, tying up loose ends before Shark appeared before the Squire. "I'll call Squire Jacobs to set up a hearing. Sheriff Newhouse too, so the misses can have clothes and a bath ready."

The corporal looked at Johnston and commanded, "Load your prisoner and be careful."

"Right, Corporal," Johnston angrily answered. "He wouldn't stand a chance if I was ready for him."

"Trooper Johnston, there's no instant replay in police work. Boy scouts know enough to be prepared. You'll learn that too if you don't get yourself killed first. Hanratty, stay put! I need a word with you."

An even angrier Johnston ushered Shark out to the waiting Cherokee. When the door closed, the corporal began. "Hanratty, watch Johnston! He doesn't understand life up here and living in Pittsburgh are different. You're his mentor. Understand?"

"Yes, sir, I do."

"Johnston might be tough in a game environment, but he isn't ready for guys like Shark, and for certain, he won't be ready for Squire Jacobs. Prompt him on conducting himself at this hearing."

"Yes, sir," Hanratty agreed, his face flushing as he recalled how the old town justice ate him alive.

Hanratty walked into the parking lot to find the uncooperative prisoner refusing to get in the vehicle, and the frustrated trooper couldn't bend him without force, an alternative he was avoiding. Sizing up the situation, Hanratty threatened, "Shark, remember Squire and the sheriff are your next two stops."

Shark glared at Hanratty. He had dealt with the town justice and the sheriff on several occasions and didn't want either upset. Without argument, he climbed into the vehicle.

Hanratty motioned Johnston away from the vehicle so they could talk. "What was that all about?" Johnston asked Hanratty.

"That's why we need to talk. Squire Jacobs is a tough man. He takes no crap from anyone. He demands 'Yes, your honor' and 'No, your honor' answers."

"How does a hillbilly town justice get off demanding 'Your Honor?' He's no judge,"

"Squire just does things. Don't question them, and we'll get this matter satisfactorily concluded. Okay?"

"Okay, Ratty."

Bristling with anger, Hanratty snapped, "Johnston, Shark, may get away with that, but I don't expect it from you. Understand?"

A shocked look swept across Johnston's face. Hanratty's reaction was out of step with the too soft mental picture he held. "Understood," Johnston apologized in a low voice.

Silence ruled during the five-mile trip to the district justice's office. They entered and logged in as directed by the sign on the door. Squire's hearing room formerly served as a formal parlor. The wallpaper was a floral pattern in colors circa the 1940s; the hardwood floor and ornate cherry trim spoke of earlier affluence. His cherry lectern previously found service as the pulpit at First Baptist Church, where the cherry benches on the opposite wall served as pews. The oak library table located inside the front door contained the sign-in register and a Bible. Three two-by-six foot rectangles on the floor placed in front of the podium had the accused, witnesses, and law officers close to the domineering justice. The law officers' box stood to the left side of the accused. All was in order in the Squire's realm, in order and a step back in time.

Squire entered, a bear of a man with a rough face that looked hewn out of an old hemlock stump, a thatch of hair more black than gray, craggy eyebrows, a thick mustache, and black eyes that ate inside people. Squire's unbuttoned shirt exposed a wad of hair. His deep bass voice echoed like he was talking from the bottom of a well. "What in the world happened to you, trooper?" Squire asked, viewing Johnson's battered face and bloodied uniform.

"Shark sucker-punched —"

The booming voice of the unsympathetic justice cut him short. "Only suckers get sucker punched. You'll learn a lot up here in the mountains, that is, if somebody doesn't beat you to death first. Police Academy trainin' never hurt anybody that wasn't afraid to learn a little something when they got out. Appears your advanced training started today. Comprende?"

Squire looked back at Hanratty. "Corporal Repicci called with a rundown on this case, and I have the charge sheet. Said you were gathering evidence at the Brewer place. Is that Jackson Brewer's place?"

"It was your honor. Jake has the place now," Hanratty replied.

Squire nodded. "I remember Jake. He traveled with Jackson a good bit. Nice kid, maybe a little rough around the edges. Riffraff wouldn't want to fool with Jackson Brewer. He cleaned up Shark's old man and a couple of his uncles. Never looked for trouble. Never ran from any neither. That's enough chit-chat for today. Bring in your prisoner."

Hanratty remembered the look he got in the Brewer bedroom and knew Jake would have sand enough if pushed. He stood quietly while Johnston escorted Shark in front of the town justice, then stood with Hanratty. Squire carefully looked over the prisoner. "You stink, boy. Worse mess I laid eyes on since you were here last time. Hear me?"

"Yes, yer Honor," Shark answered, looking at the floor, his voice manifesting shame.

"Boy, look at me when I'm talking. I can't tell if yer lying when yer gawkin' at the floor."

"Yes, yer honor."

"Your breath would peel paint," Squire boomed, carefully looking the three men over.

Satisfied they knew who was in charge, he proceeded. "I'm gonna ask you men questions, and I expect truthful answers. Damn the soul of anyone who lies to me."

They nodded as the Squire's black; piercing eyes met theirs. "The charge sheet has Mr. Coleman for aggravated assault, obstruction of justice, and resisting arrest. He's also charged with ethnic intimidation for his racial slurs. Trooper Hanratty, let's hear what happened."

"Yes, your honor," Hanratty replied and quickly related what happened on the hill.

When Hanratty finished, Squire looked at Johnston, "Trooper, what can you add to this testimony?"

"Okay, —" Johnston began, but Squire's booming voice cut him short.

"Don't you ever okay me again! Understand?" the squire asked, his voice angry and neck waddle shaking.

"Yes, sir, I —"

"Not yes, sir!"

"Sorry, your Honor," Johnston replied, his face reddening. After collecting himself, the trooper timidly explained Shark's actions.

"Do you have anything truthful to add, Mr. Coleman?" Squire asked, glaring at Shark. "Brewer poisoned Punk. That frosted me off," Shark blurted.

"Hold it, Mister Coleman," the Squire bellowed angrily. "Yer the fault of your brother's demise. Ya don't take care of him. Understand?"

Shark didn't want to acknowledge he understood, and he didn't want to accept blame for Punk's poisoning. Squire quickly tired of hesitation, "I'm not talking for my health. Did you understand what I said?"

"No, yer honor . . . well yes, yer honor —"

"Don't him-haw me. It can't be too difficult to understand a question requiring a yes or no answer. Now, which was it?" Squire roared, sounding mad enough to eat railroad ties, thoroughly intimidating Shark.

Shark knew Squire Jacobs by action and deed, and he didn't want any more of him than he had to have. "I understand, yer honor," Shark quickly answered.

"You better! Now, does anyone have anything more to add to this case?" When no one did, he continued. "Mr. Coleman, how do ya plead to the pending charges?"

"Not guilty yer honor," Shark replied, fearful of what would follow.

"What do ya mean, not guilty?" Squire boomed in Shark's face. "These fine officers wouldn't waste their time bringing you here if you weren't guilty. Yer guilty, and I'm remanding you to the county jail until yer trial. Sheriff Newhouse will be happy to see who's comin' to visit," Squire remarked. "He's cleaning up Sterling County one Coleman bath at a time." Turning to Hanratty, he ordered, "Get Mister Coleman right over there."

With Shark loaded, they drove into Parker, parking in the narrow alley behind the jail where Sheriff Newhouse met them. Getting a prisoner was a mixed blessing. He made a little money off his wife's meals, and he received near new prices from the county for the thrift store clothes he issued prisoners. He also experienced considerable trouble when he had any of the Colemans in jail. The family came visiting, and that was always a zoo parade.

"Okay, Shark, get them stinkin' clothes off an' throw 'em in that trash can," the sheriff ordered as Shark climbed out of the vehicle.

"C'mon, Porky, it's too cold to undress in the snow," Shark pleaded.

"That'll be Sheriff Newhouse to you, boy," the sheriff angrily corrected. "Boy, if yer looking for sympathy, you'll find it in the dictionary between shit and syphilis. Now get hot!"

Shark undressed and slammed his clothes into the trash. Realizing argument would prolong his agony, he turned his back to the others and began scrubbing down in a bucket of soapy water that smelled strongly of Pine-Sol, using the brush and brown soap the sheriff provided. Steam rose from his body as he shivered in the cold.

"Wash everything," the sheriff demanded. "Get that stinkin' butt of yours clean."

When Shark finished scrubbing, he rinsed off in a bucket of clean water, dried with the towel provided, and began dressing in the clothes handed him. The pants were clean but several sizes too large, and since Shark arrived without a belt, the sheriff went into the garage, cut a length of rope, and handed it to Shark. Shark threaded it through the belt loops and tied it in a knot. Under the sheriff's supervision, he dumped the buckets and marched into the jail.

Alone in the vehicle, Johnston turned to Hanratty, "Shark could get frostbite and pneumonia washing up in the cold. And that pine stuff can't be good for his skin."

"Fancy you worrying about Shark Coleman."

"I never dreamed people lived like this. Shark must never have had a bath before today, at least not since he was a baby."

"You can bet he had one the last time he spent time in Sheriff Newhouse's jail."

Johnston was quiet for a bit, and then he added, "I learned more today than any other day in my life, and I learned it all the hard way. Got my first class A whipping ever, upset you, and had a town justice chew me up like I was a little kid."

"Not just any town justice, Squire Jacobs."

CHAPTER 6

Hands clasped behind him, the prisoner shook from apprehension and the cold rain of early winter as he was ushered into the Pennsylvania Parole Board hearing room by a burly guard from his current home, the Camp Hill Penitentiary. Here, this stern-faced parole board would decide his future. Poorly educated, the prisoner experienced difficulty with printed material, but reading people was another matter.

Placards introduced this board, helping him put faces to names. Gary L. Billingsly, Lt. Governor, headed the table. Stern faced Attorney General Peter Morrelli, and angelic Father O'Donnell sat to his left, Marion Herms-Cramer and John Richards to his right. Father O'Donnell was both a Catholic Priest and a criminal psychologist. Herms-Cramer was a wealthy patron of the Republican party sat beside ex-state senator John Richards who had lost the last election. Reading faces, the prisoner immediately realized he was in for a tough go. He heard the parole board had stiffened considerably after the recent release of a twice-convicted murderer who raped and murdered a 15-year-old parochial school student soon after his release. This prisoner's quest for parole faced a monumental hurdle.

Lieutenant Governor Billingsly peered over half-glasses, blond hair swept back on both sides, chocolate roots telling the world it wasn't his natural color. His too pretty looks suggest he might be more appearance than substance.

The prisoner's eyes moved to Morelli, who immediately looked up. Dark eyes caught and held his. His hawk nose and gaunt face gave the appearance he could be more mafia than the state's chief law enforcement officer.

The priest's cherub-like face and receding hairline provided an appearance that clashed with the stubborn set of his mouth. His clothing and cross told what he represented but not who he was. His distrust suggested he would evaluate every action and word, searching for inconsistencies.

Herms-Cramer, despite her sophisticated appearance, would be no pushover. The rocks on her finger and diamond broach spoke of money and power. His glance dropped to full breasts straining her cashmere sweater and suit jacket. Like the wild thing she might be, she felt his gaze and met his eyes. He looked down, and when he thought it was safe, he looked back in her direction. Her eyes were evaluating him, forming opinions. Those eyes spoke of skepticism.

After a brief time, he gave John Richards a once over. He was difficult to read as he sat staring at his prisoner-related material. His thick eyelids appeared set on eating his eyes, and protruding teeth thrust through thin lips gave him a tough guy appearance. This hearing would be no cakewalk.

The prisoner stood humbly waiting to be seated. He squeezed his powerful hands to hide his nervousness, steeling himself for the grueling he knew would come. His rehearsed answers mentally replayed while he waited.

"Lester Coleman," the Lieutenant Governor began, "this board has the awesome responsibility of determining whether or not you're ready for early parole. We must determine if you're ready to become a productive, law-abiding citizen and, if so, which community support efforts such as halfway houses or religious groups we might employ to support your successful return to society. Yours is an unusual case. Most petitions that reach us for consideration for early parole exhibit both a solid personal life before prison and an exemplary track record during incarceration. Your life before prison was anything but that of a model citizen. Can you help us understand how you got to Camp Hill and how you seem to have turned your life around?"

"Yes, sir, I can. I was born poor in the mountains. I quit school in sixth grade and went to work in the woods —"

"In the woods?" Marion Herms-Cramer asked. "What could you possibly do at that age?"

"Loggin' Ma'am. Our family's been loggers for a long time." He couldn't admit he spent most of the time firing his grandfather's still.

"How old were you?"

"Fourteen, maybe fifteen. I was behind some in school and big for my age."

"And the school officials allowed you to quit school?"

"I just quit goin'. Had to. There were fourteen of us to feed. Nobody at school much cared."

"Your first recorded criminal incident was theft," the attorney general stated. "Can you explain that?"

"We didn't have money for chainsaw parts. Unc the Drunk said he knew —"

"Who said what?" Morelli asked in disbelief.

"Unc the Drunk's my uncle. It's the name they give him."

The attorney general shook his head in disbelief, then continued. "The record suggests you stole more than a few parts."

"It was dark. We couldn't find the parts we needed, so we took some saws."

"How many are some?"

"Three, sir," the prisoner replied, staring at the floor.

"You needed three saws for parts?"

"We figgered we could use 'em. Didn't think past that."

"Ah hah. Your record would suggest you looked past a good many things. How about explaining this drug possession charge?"

"We had to make restitution for them saws or go to jail. We was desperate. This guy met with Unc. Said we could make some quick cash handlin' some business for him. The business turned out to be drugs and some stolen stuff the guy needed to unload. We got ourselves caught. Unc had me take all the blame. Figgered the law would go easier on a kid."

"Who was this guy with the drug business?"

"Guess I don't rightly know. Unc took care of that stuff. Can't say that I ever heard who it was." Coleman held his breath. If the authorities discovered the official running the drug business, he might never get out. He was walking a tightrope.

"You had other problems," the attorney general said, enumerating the offenses and the punishments. "Dropped charges include rape, arson, and burglary. You're going to have to help us with this."

"We was gettin' blamed for everything. That's the way it is when yer poor and screw up. Nobody cared nuthin' for us. Maybe you don't know how that feels, but it hurts. Makes you think different." He paused to wipe tears on his sleeve, nervously licked his lips, then continued. "It's hard to crawl out of a hole like that. Family wantin' revenge on everybody for the troubles you got, everybody else wantin' a piece of yer tail 'cause yer the way you are, an' the laws just waitin' to catch you. Everything that happened got blamed on us."

"Did you or did you not do them?" the attorney general asked, his black eyes searching the prisoner's soul.

Coleman paused a bit to get his practiced answers straight. "I never raped that woman. She wanted me, but I never took her 'cause she was my brother's woman. She said I did it jus' ta get even. It's kinda like Joseph and Potiphar's woman in the Bible. The other stuff was about an ol' man who got his house burned up with him in it. Unc said his wood stove prob'ly caught the place on fire an' they blamed us jus' to get the case closed. That's why they dropped charges when they couldn't pin nuthin' on us."

"The record shows the old man in question was once the sheriff of Sterling County, it was July and no need for a wood stove when the place burned, and you might have had cause to take action against him."

"Oh no, Mister Morrelli, ain't nothin' like that. Him an' my grandaddy was good friends. My uncle and him were deacons in a church." Coleman was in a sweat. Things weren't going the way he had planned, not at all. "We might a done some dumb stuff but nothin' like that. No, sir."

"This begs many questions," the attorney general suggested, searching Coleman's face for signs. When he didn't find any, he changed directions. "How about the charges that landed you in Camp Hill?"

"Yes, sir, I did screw up there. Them cops stopped me for a charge that didn't stick. But I was so sick a bein' blamed for everything when that cop attacked me, I punched him. I had a joint on me, so they got permission to search my truck. Unc borrowed my truck the day before I got stopped, an' they found his stash in there. But it worked out fer the best. The good Lord must a had plans ta get me straight, an' I ended up at Camp Hill.

You can hardly argue about what happened since then," Coleman ended, endeavoring to shift the conversation to something positive.

"The Lord is responsible for your being in Camp Hill?" Father O'Connell asked, scratching his balding head in contemplation.

"Seems you gotta hit bottom before you get saved. I got mixed up with some Christians and saw I was headed way wrong. It's the first time anyone ever talked to me about the Lord. I became a born-agin believer. It made me see things we was blamin' on others was mostly our doin's gone wrong. Bein' a man of God, maybe you can see how this happened. I don't hold no grudge on nobody now. Went to work to fix my life. I got my GED and been workin' on an associate degree in social work with some police science stuff throwed in."

"Could there be alternative motivation for police science subjects?" Richards asked. "Your college record shows one of the courses concerned conducting investigations and handling evidence. A criminal might want to know about such things."

"Oh no, sir. I just thought them subjects might help me with my Bible studies."

"Really?" Marion Herms-Cramer retorted. After a brief wait for an answer from Coleman and receiving none, she continued. "The warden's recommendation states that you're now a protestant lay leader. Can you tell us about that?" Herms-Cramer asked, turning her head slightly so the light caught the diamond stud in her ear.

"I changed when the Lord got holda me. He led me to a Bible study course from the Moody Bible Institute. I signed up for stuff from Reverend Stanley an' Billy Graham too. Good stuff that helps you get yer head straight. Then the Lord saw fit to use me to convert others. I jus' caught fire for the Lord."

"Many prisoners seem to find the Lord while they're incarcerated but lose Him soon after reentry into the world," Father O'Connell skeptically reminded the prisoner.

"Maybe they wasn't saved."

"And how can we be sure you are?"

The prisoner paused, quietly searching for an answer that suited his cause. Licking his lips, he answered, "Guess you gotta trust me some on it. Only the good Lord knows for sure. You know my track record since I got here, not just my work for the Lord but my education, teachin' other prisoners to read and all, and my work in the prison laundry. I'm in charge there now."

"What would you do if you were paroled?" Richards asked.

"It'll hurt to leave this work behind, but I got work for the Lord at home too. My family needs me. I can see my blessin's and want to serve others. That's what I'm livin' for now. Most of my family can barely read and write. One's a full retard. He can't even talk. They need my help real bad."

"The warden speaks of that in his recommendation, but is this a temporary change until you're released?" the lieutenant governor asked. "It's easy for us to be fooled by well-intentioned or disingenuous prisoners who build positive prison records when they have nothing else to do with their time. The sad truth is, sterling records aren't always proof of a person's rehabilitation."

Reading the skepticism on the faces of the board members, Lester searched for suitable answers. "I understand what yer sayin'. You folks gotta be in a pickle after that parolee just murdered that poor little girl. It made me think I might be wastin' time comin' here today. But I prayed on it, and if it's the Lord's will, I'll get me another chance. If it ain't, I'll continue His work at Camp Hill. The Lord knows where He needs me most."

"Are you saying parole isn't that important to you?" the attorney general asked.

"No sir, but ya gotta know God is working in my life, an' He has a perfect plan prepared for me. His Bible says so. A lady that wrote one of the pieces we read in my college sociology course is doin' a study on me and my family now. She's lookin' at what caused me to be here, an' what I did to change myself. She might be the first person who ever cared about me. She thinks I could have a career in social work because with my past life, I can understand what others are goin' through. I know I did some bad stuff, but I got that behind me."

As the questions slacked, the lieutenant governor reviewed what they had learned. Then he asked the board, "Does anybody have any last questions for the prisoner?" When they didn't, he continued. "Mister Coleman, Governor Burger will have the final say on your parole efforts based on our report to him. If you have nothing else to say, we'll adjourn."

Coleman had things he wished he had said, but more than anything, he wanted the meeting closed before anyone asked him additional questions on the drug business. If he gave up The Man, he realized a hit was likely. "No sir, I ain't got nothin' to say except thank you all for your time an' listenin' to me. I surely appreciate it."

CHAPTER 7

"Wells, I understand what you said."

"I didn't think you heard me." Wells was upset. Neck veins stood out, and his face stormed.

"Those changes eliminate our team's bonuses and profit sharing. You can't do that."

"Who do you work for, Jake?" Wellington "Wells" Reeves paused, blue eyes glaring, thinking, running his hands back through his wavy, gray hair. Red pushed through his tanned face, a mixture of anger and embarrassment. The Christian ethics he professed and the ornately framed painting of Jesus Christ hanging behind him stood in sharp contrast to this plan. A conglomerate purchased the businesses he nurtured for a lifetime, and the final sale price was contingent on first-year profits. Wells took off his glasses, laid them on the ornate cherry desk, and leaned back, sighing heavily. "Come on, Jake, look at this from my perspective. Environmental Solutions Inc. has to make your business plan's profit and growth targets, or I'll lose my shirt."

"Rob's business plan," Jake corrected. "I told you, and anybody who would listen, Rob's revised plan for 1994 is a cross between wishful thinking and fantasy land. His plan for 95 is worse."

"Yes, you said that, and I saw it as a defeatist attitude. Impossibility thinkers never achieve much."

"I see real possibilities, but this plan isn't one of them. We promised performance bonuses and profit sharing if our people made this year's plan. It's unethical and may be illegal to change that plan now. Our team worked hard to create these results.

"For years before you arrived, there was no profit in ESI, but I kept plugging on. I should have closed the doors, as Rob suggested."

"That's plowed ground. Reporting to Rob is another matter. No one trusts the man. When they discover we'll be reporting to him instead of you —"

"They aren't going to discover it. You're going to tell them, Jake, tomorrow morning at the management meeting and then again at an employee meeting in the afternoon, close to quitting time to minimize impact on production. I expect the announcements to be plan supportive."

"Should I also tell them about the work we're writing off as paper losses this year so it can be collected as profit next fiscal year or the retroactive reassessment of costs between the companies that will return next year? How about —"

"Just tell them about the realignment. Revised profit projections come later. Skip any mention of bonuses or profit-sharing."

Wells stood up before Jake could comment, signifying the meeting was over. "I hope I can trust you, Jake? And I don't want this matter discussed before the meeting."

"Can this be revisited in the morning after I've had time to analyze this plan?"

"The decision's been made. Invest your time preparing your presentation."

The following morning the ESI management team intently listened as Jake walked them through the organizational realignment, telling them it eliminated waste, which made the organization more competitive. The team was with him until he informed them Wells had them reporting to Priest in his promotion to the executive VP position. Robert I. Priest, Rip for short, was a crafty intimidator whose outward appearance ran from the suave charmer with lofty ideals to the clever bully who ran roughshod over those who stood in his way. His real personality was closer to the latter, and other than Wells, few saw much they liked in RIP. Many said you could tell when he was lying; his mouth moved.

"What happens to you, Jake?" Hollis LeFever, engineering manager, asked. "Rob fires anyone who doesn't see things his way, and no one with a conscience could."

"Anything's possible."

"Yes, and then what happens to us?" Hollis asked.

"Rob designs everything to set people up to do his bidding or take a fall."

"Jake, he's not trustworthy," Pete Miglicio, the Service and Installation Manager added. "Both of his nicknames fit. If he isn't Robbing you, he's Ripping you off."

Jake held up his hand, stopping comments. "We're here to discuss reorganization. Let's keep to that purpose."

Although it proved difficult to maintain focus, they worked through each planning phase with carefully controlled objections. Only when it came to Rob was their outright dissension. "Rob has over-promised Wells, and when his promises fail, he'll feed us to the wolves," Dexter, the sales manager suggested.

"Yes, but he'll cook the books to make it look like what he promised is happening," Caye added.

"No, Caye, he won't; he'll make you do it," Dexter contradicted. "When things go wrong, he'll plead ignorance and suggest you should know better since you're a CPA. Then he'll dismiss you for the problems you caused."

"I hate that ass," Caye said. "I can tell you why —"

"You obviously have strong feelings, Caye," Jake interrupted, hiding the aggravation he felt.

She glanced at Jake, scarlet showing through her pale complexion. Caye seldom spoke out against others or used coarse language. Tears flowed as she explained, "Rob transferred me to ESI to take Dexter's place when I was eight months pregnant. I hardly knew how to sign on to the computer system when my pregnancy leave began. Rob told people he shafted two birds with one stone, screwed up ESI accounting, and screwed me out of a promotion."

"As far as design and estimating goes, this could be perfect," Kevin Mitchell, the department manager said. "We could take on bigger projects and have the resources to back us up. We'd be tough to beat except for one thing; Rob lies when the truth suits better. Wells can't see through him, but his wife can. As CEO, Marie fired Rob several times. Each time Wells begged him back on the team. Marie said Rob is a compulsive, world-class liar, and if they ever have lying contests at the Olympic games, Rob'd win the gold medal."

"Mark today as the beginning of ESI's downfall," Miglicio injected.

Jake understood their frustration, but he knew it didn't change the situation; they would soon report to Rob. With nothing left to discuss, Jake dismissed the group. Bob Morrell, technical director, and Dick Wilson, manufacturing manager, remained behind as Jake gathered his papers. Their dark looks said they were disturbed.

"Thanks for informing us before the meeting, Jake," Bob said. "Shouldn't we have had an input?"

"I didn't."

"No?" Dick questioned.

"I was informed last night after everybody departed."

"You could have called."

"Wells told me not to discuss it until the meeting."

"What's so secret?"

"Can't say."

"Hope you know what this means."

That evening, flickering firelight caught Jake's long face; an open Bible lay on his lap. Old Gus sat on one side and Jeanne the other. Holding hands, they watched the fire dance.

"You're quiet. Jake. Is there a problem at work?"

"Might as well float my resume."

"What caused the change?" Jeanne asked, kissing him lightly on the cheek.

"Rob convinced Wells to cook our books by shoving money earned this year into the next fiscal year. They wrote off debt that we'll collect in the new year and other stuff that screws our people. Our bottom line suddenly looks anemic, but it will make Mr. Rising Star look great next year."

"That's not right," Jeanne said, her frustration evident.

"No, but that's the way it is. Rob made big promises for this corporate sale, and he's setting up the books so he can deliver."

"Look for another job Jake."

"What about the bills?"

"What would you do if you could do anything you wanted?"

"Write."

"Well, Mr. Brewer, let me get you pen and paper."

Jake wondered if he could write successfully or if it would be his Waterloo like it was for so many? "I've tried. My mind movies elude capture on paper."

"Try something humorous, maybe a story about the hill gang or the class of '59'".

"I could waste years writing something that might not even interest me."

"Like you tell our kids, you never earn a dream until you begin working toward it. Trey suggested a book of 'Letters From Daddy,' including your letters signed Cuddles when he was in Somalia. He said they were a big hit with lonely warriors."

Jake shook his head. "I invest all my energy in a job that might not matter to anyone but me. Between that frustration and the Hill Place, I don't feel creative."

"You worked around the clock as a Marine, completed college degrees, found time to serve our church, coached kid sports, and had plenty of energy left over for our marriage. You seem so easily angered lately, and you're tired to the bone. Your up all night prowling around or down in your man cave working out. It's getting worse, Jake. I'm worried about you. Us."

How could he tell her about the endless nightmares that were getting worse? He was seeing things during the day too. People were moving behind cars. In the woods at Hill Place. Am I going nuts? He wondered. The war at work wasn't helping. After a morgue-like silence, he answered without looking away from the fire, "Being a Marine is a way of life. Your entire purpose is preparing men to fight and perhaps die for this great nation." After a pause, he added, "I never realized the awesome responsibility inherent in leadership until I invested the lives of some fine young men in a war that didn't matter to anyone but us. Their names ended up on that damned black wall. Maybe the difference is purpose. Service to country is a professional calling beyond the business world's drive for money and power."

"Writing could help you regain purpose, Jake. It might calm you before we both go over the edge. I'm scared, Jake. I love you so."

"If God has a plan for me, I wish he'd favor me with a sign."

"Your sign might come with writing. Remember those wild certificates you used to write, Letters of Condemnation, things like that. You can put out a lot of BS in a hurry. The kids love it, and everybody enjoys reading it."

"What publisher is willing to pay for junk that makes kids laugh?" Jake ridiculed.

"Honey, give it a try. Practice what you preach."

"Yes, Dear. Mother knows best," Jake scoffed.

"Make fun if you want, but remember, you say if you don't do something because you're afraid to fail, you've already failed."

CHAPTER 8

"What next, Lord?" Jake asked aloud as he drove to work the Monday before Christmas. Thoughts as cold and forbidding as this gray December day rampaged through his mind. Today they would learn what the reorganization plan consisted of, and he knew with Rob Priest being a part of it, he wouldn't like it. The morning dragged while he busied himself on projects requiring minimal concentration. At the appointed hour, Jake, Dick, and Bob anxiously waited in the board room making small talk. Dick was a retired Army Special Forces officer who pulled no punches. His athletic body, jutting jaw, and bushy eyebrows cast a no-nonsense picture that fit. The staccato beat he drummed on the massive table interrupted Bob's artistic doodling. Leaning over, Dick quietly asked Jake, "How close are the end times?"

Jake smiled. Their adverse relationships with Rob and their concepts of moral business practices would make them expendable. Bob was an engineering genius whose future was reasonably secure. Give him a contamination problem, and he would design a cleanup system to fix it. His many patents and designs were well known for simplicity and reliability.

When Jake didn't answer, Dick added, "I typed my resignation letter."

"I hate to give up. We have so much going for us."

"We aren't quitting. It's being jerked away by a BSing liar."

"Hope you two aren't bailing out," Bob said, but it was more like a question.

Within minutes the door to Wells' private office opened, and Wells entered, followed by Priest and Wells' secretary, Claudia. Rob sat beside

Wells at the head of the large cherry board room table. Hunter Ward, Wells' executive VP, joined them and sat opposite Rob. Wells apologized for being late, "Sorry we're tardy. I became engrossed with some key elements of Rob's realignment plan. I must say it's exciting."

Wells paused, looking at each attendee, searching their facial expressions. He knew this group was apprehensive. The discussion went well until Wells asked Hunter if he saw any drawbacks.

"Maybe a question. Who heads the new ESI?" Hunter asked.

"Do you sense problems, Hunter?" Wells prodded.

"Big problems if Jake isn't there. I see ESI as the most versatile group in our business family. They're profitable after years of losses before Jake took over. I'd hate to break up this winning team. Rob addressed the business backlog for his SAM group, but my question is —"

"That backlog is real, Hunter," Rob interrupted.

"It's not the backlog's size but its profitability that bothers me," Hunter said. "You underbid competitors in new fields who have considerable experience in those areas. As a first-time contractor, there's a distinct possibility you'll run into unforeseen problems."

"Such as?" Rob demanded, interrupting Hunter again.

"Substantial rock at Stony Brook that would escalate costs by millions. The adjoining housing development hit limestone problems. Engineering confirmed that before you finalized the bid. Then there are new construction equipment costs, additional costs for pumps if —"

"The profit's there," Rob snapped.

"Rob, I'll listen to you, but I desire to answer Wells' question without interruption." Hatred flashed on Rob's face. He disliked Hunter, and he hated challenges on anything, especially in front of Wells.

"Let's cool it," Wells injected. "Please continue, Hunter."

"I have concerns with the bids in these new fields and combining the groups. Until you're established in any field, there are costly lessons to be learned. What happens to ESI if Rob's current groups fall flat on their profit projections? I believe Jake, Dick, and Bob are key to continuing progress in ESI. Jake and Dick have had serious confrontations with Rob while he served as our Contract Administrator. Rob screwed ESI out of money that cut their bonus and retirement funds, and we allowed it to happen. Personnel changes will further impact performance with this proposed alignment?"

Wells turned to Priest, "What about those concerns?"

Rob snapped out angrily, "I have two things to say. One, the profit is in our projects. And two, there will be no personnel problems if things are structured my way. I have nothing more to say."

"That's it, Rob?" Wells asked.

"For now, yes," Rob answered angrily.

"How about you, ESI guys?" Wells asked.

"I believe I speak for all of us," Jake began. "We believe reorganization can work, but we are adamantly opposed to financial and business plan changes. Our people earned bonuses and profit sharing. They should receive both. Then there's —"

Wells stopped him, "Rob's plan precludes those options. Claudia, please pass out Rob's package."

While Claudia passed out the plan, Wells continued. "As you know, I've promoted Rob to senior vice president. He'll head ESI and his current group as one company. Jake will report to Rob instead of directly to me. The ESI chain of command remains the same. Are there questions?"

"Comments," Hunter volunteered as he looked over the organization chart. "The only change I see is Rob adds a costly management layer to ESI. How does that improve anything?"

"I know it upsets you, Hunter, but I'll make ESI a real profit engine," Rob snapped.

Wells sensed what was developing and stopped Hunter from a rebuttal by holding up his hand.

"Rob," Wells began, "that wasn't called for. It reflects why there are personnel concerns." Then flashing his eyes around the table, Wells continued, "Rob promised to deliver nine percent net profit from ESI next year, and I believe he'll do it. Do you have questions or concerns, Jake?"

"I don't see this as a workable plan, Wells. We already have the best pricing possible from our suppliers. We are nearing a seven percent profit margin, which our benchmarking efforts say is tops in our industry. Nine percent profit is not —"

"Didn't I tell you, Mr. Reeves? ESI has a negative attitude from the top down," Rob interrupted. "Attitude changes are required to make my plan work. I can assure you that will happen if I have to hire a new management team."

"It's not an attitudinal problem, Rob," Dick challenged, "it's reality. I fail to see how you can make such promises without knowing —"

"Just one more example, Mr. Reeves," Rob countered. "You may as well add your negatives, Bob. It's your last opportunity."

"Wells, in the last few minutes, Rob has acted out my concerns," Hunter interjected. "He knows little about ESI other than he viewed them as someone to take advantage of, and we allowed him to do it. Rob has no manufacturing experience, and his past relationship with the ESI team is questionable at best."

"I hear your concerns, Hunter, and I'll keep them in mind as I monitor ESI progress. However, I'm confident this plan can work. If there are no further questions, let's adjourn."

The following morning, Rob marched into the conference room 48 minutes late for the meeting he called and arrogantly strutted to the front, casting the image of a Prussian general. His turned-down mouth evidenced extreme unhappiness. Pausing to look over the assembled information, he sarcastically snapped, "At least you didn't need to be kick-started today. That's an improvement."

Without comment, Jake flipped back to the first chart and waited while Rob read through it. The teams' collective looks announced the spirit of cooperation that flowed before Rob's arrival was now a dead commodity, killed by his opening statement.

"Look," Rob snorted. "I promised Mr. Reeves a profitable first period. You're 600 K short."

"We'll pick up $125,000 with in-month rentals, emergency repairs, parts sales, and —"

"Get it through your heads; we will make this period," Rob said. "Any questions?" After a pause, he began, "Add GE to that list for 280 K and add another 100 K to in-month sales."

"GE?" Dexter questioned. "I haven't received that order."

"It's part of a system job," Rob snarled. "Put it on the list."

"Wells issued strict guidelines about putting jobs on the certain list until we have a signed customer order and credit checks clear," Dexter informed him.

"I said list it!" Rob demanded, "and enter it into the computer with a customer order number. I want it to show up on reports."

"It isn't that simple, Rob," Dick said. "The sales report is balanced against the in-process inventory by job number so that ordered parts —"

Rob cut him short. "When I say I want something done, find a way to do it. Anyone who can't keep up with this new Environmental Solutions Inc. high gear machine can find a work address where mediocrity is acceptable. Now add vertical turbine pumps with variable frequency drives to our product lines. We'll be bidding on more than environmental cleanup stuff."

Bob questioned these products. "There may be sales in water and wastewater systems, but is there the 9% profit you promised ISC or even the 6% they demand? Competition —"

"Mr. Technical Director," Rob said, "you're in charge of making this happen at the required profit. No excuses! Now, let's discuss cost-cutting. I expect cuts in vendor pricing with improved multipliers and discount rates. Understand?"

"We already have the best pricing possible on every equipment line we use," Bob replied.

"You guys aren't getting the picture," Rob roared. "I expect improvements." Rob turned to Jake. "Here are additional ways we'll save money. I want everyone earning more than twenty-five thousand a year converted to salary. You're good at writing job descriptions. Start with Hardy Mitchell. Salary him and put him on the estimating team. Any questions?"

"There are people in critical billets who won't work overtime without compensation. The chief estimator is one of them."

"Mr. Brewer," Rob retorted, "Your assignment is to write job descriptions the wage and hour people are thrilled with. If anyone, including the chief estimator, doesn't want to be salaried, they can find a workplace where they dictate policy. And, I want an engineer cut from payroll before I meet with Mr. Reeves on Thursday - anybody but Hollis."

Jake shook his head. "Losing any of the engineers will leave a hole that cuts us out of a major market segment. And who'll estimate the big construction jobs if the chief estimator leaves."

"Find a way to make it work. That's why we pay you the big bucks."

"Can we talk after the meeting?" Jake requested, hiding his anger.

"We've talked enough. It's time for action. Meetings over!"

Dick followed Jake to his office. "The man's a perfect ass," Dick uttered vehemently, "well maybe not perfect, but he's close. What engineer do you intend to fire, Jake? I can't afford to lose anyone with the workload we have."

"If Rob wants someone fired, he can fire them. We've already advertised for an additional electrical engineer just for the work in house."

"You could lose your job," Dick said in a counseling voice, a smile easing over his face.

"Such is life. One way or another, I'll be on the street before summer's over. I won't write phony job descriptions. Rob salaries people, then forces them to work longer hours without overtime pay. They end up making less money for more work. He won't do that through me. I'll make a tin bill and pick dung with chickens first."

Midmorning Wednesday, Rob breezed into Jake's office carrying a handful of papers, a sly smile pasted on his face. "I roughed out your presentation for tomorrow's team meeting with Mr. Reeves. Personalize this plan without changing the content. It's best if you make this presentation. Mr. Reeves trusts your forecasts."

Rob departed, leaving Jake to read the document. There had been no discussion about changes that would be impossible to accomplish given their manufacturing capacity. Jake made a list of questionable elements and called Rob. "We should rethink some elements of this plan. The plant—"

Rob cut in, "Your orders are to personalize it but leave the content the same. That seems plain enough. Changes were necessary to make this plan acceptable to Devron Power. You better understand what I'm telling you," Rob finished, his voice growing nasty.

"Your changes make the plan sound acceptable, but that doesn't make them achievable. Our suppliers can't deliver custom material for these projects in time to meet ship dates, not even if they had the order today. I made most of the calls to —"

Rob interrupted again before Jake could explain why shipments couldn't be moved up. "I don't care who made what calls. Call them back and tell them to move the order up, or you'll get the junk elsewhere. It's past time to take charge of this business."

Anger flooded over Jake. "We don't have the luxury of selecting vendors," Jake said in a controlled voice, clutching his fists until his nails dug into his skin. "Most contracts specify the equipment brands to be used and don't permit substitutes. And the delivery time listed on the order report was the expedited time. We had to fight to get that."

"Look, Mister General Manager," Rob snarled, "I waited ten years for this opportunity, and your failures aren't going to take it from me."

The dead phone told Jake he was in a quandary. He could follow Rob's orders and personalize the plan, presenting it as if it were his own, and take the grief when the inevitable happened, or he could disobey and change the plan to something achievable. Or were these his only options, he wondered? Wells tended to question loose ends, and incomplete information begged questions. He wouldn't lie to Wells.

Jake closed his office door, bowed his head, and prayed, "Lord, I know you hold the answers, but I'm having problems seeing them. Can you let me in on your plan?" Then he began work in earnest.

Jake answered his phone just after three that afternoon and heard the caller growl, "Dick here. I read your presentation. This rag won't pass the Hee Haw test."

"Rob's plan, not mine."

"It has your name on it," Dick said, "and it says 'Developed by the ESI management team.' For sure, the Wilson part of the team had no role in this."

"Dick, let's go over my copy of the plan. We'll meet here in a half-hour."

"I'll be there," Dick snapped angrily and hung up.

Jake realized why any team member would be hostile to Rob's plan; it was out in fantasy land.

If approved, it would become their responsibility to bring it to fruition.

Dick arrived before the given time and talked angrily from the time he entered Jake's office. When he stopped, Jake asked, "We've worked together for years. What part of this plan do you think is mine?"

Dick paused. "You can't present this crap. It's impossible, and when it fails, you're history."

Jake nodded agreement, then lowering his eyebrows, he said, "Just ask questions when you disagree. That should prompt others to do likewise."

"If you aren't floating resumes, you should be. You can't work with Rob, and neither can I. If we ordered a truckload of worthless idiots and only Rob fell out when the delivery driver opened the trailer door, you couldn't feel short-changed."

The ESI management team entered the boardroom a few minutes later and took seats. Jake bowed his head in silent prayer. *Oh Lord, help me walk an honest, ethical line between business success and taking care of our people. I need Your guidance to steer this meeting to an acceptable conclusion. I thank You for —"*

"Good morning," Wells cheerily greeted, walking into the conference room with his team. "I've read your revised 1994 business plan, and I must say it's aggressive, maybe a little too ambitious, but we can decide on that after your presentation."

Rob introduced the plan as the management team's, accepting no personal responsibility, and Jake began. When he completed the first section on period sales, Wells questioned it. "This would be the best first quarter we've ever had, Jake. Are all of these firm jobs?"

Jake was hoping someone would ask that question, and Wells was the perfect candidate. "All except the GE job, and we may have projected in-month sales too high."

"Why then is GE listed?" Wells questioned, anger evident in his voice. "You know the rules, signed contract, and completed credit checks before listing it. There are no exceptions. And how high might the in-month sales projections be?"

Rob jumped into the conversation, hoping to ward off further questions. "Mr. Reeves, this GE job's in the bag. All we have to do is process a job order."

"I don't recall a GE order on the job report, Rob," Hunter said.

The comments upset Rob. He struggled to keep the edge off of his voice. "We're expecting a signed contract this morning. GE legal had to fix a couple of things."

"Rob," Wells began, "I can let GE go this time, but I want signed contracts and credit checks completed before listing contracts. We require down payments from all customers except those on the shortlist I worked out with Jake. And I want accurate in-month sales projections. Understood?"

"Maybe we're premature, Mr. Reeves, but we must make the right impression with Devron Power. We have other projects we can move in if there are any glitches."

Hunter took exception. "Your reports show there isn't time to get the materials to move up any project regardless of your team's efforts. What am I missing?"

Rob was angry. Hunter was correct, but he couldn't let the question go unanswered. "Our team believes we have the business to make this period. I'm not prepared to spend a lot of time on individual orders, but we can do that after the meeting."

"Hunter, if ESI says they have the business, I must believe it's there," Wells said. "Jake's provided pleasant surprises in the past."

"I agree with your assessment of the past, Wells," Hunter said, "but the ESI team wouldn't put jobs on the report when you disapprove. They don't work that way. Let's ask Jake to assure us this workload is real. He's the one who'll be responsible for making the bottom line, not Rob."

"Hunter," Wells snapped back, "Rob says it will be business this period, and Rob speaks for ESI. I must assume the work is there. Why would it be on the report if it wasn't a sure thing? Jake?"

Jake hesitated, carefully choosing his words for effect. "GE is Rob's project, but we're eager to get details."

"I'm sure he has it under control," Wells said, but his tone signified doubt. Rob nodded, smiling in return. "Thank you."

Jake worked to the last section titled "Personnel." He began by saying time constraints prevented discussion of this area before the meeting, and he held reservations in several areas. Upon completion, Rob said, "That section is cut and dried. Are there any questions on the overall plan?"

"Not so fast, Rob," Wells said. "I see more loose ends in this section than in the total rest of the plan. You've moved several people into new positions. Are those positions properly defined and the people trained? If not, how long will it take, and at what cost? I don't want any HR problems." Rob attempted to interrupt Wells, but Wells held up his hand, "I question who will complete the work done in these old positions. And you state moving Pete Miglicio from service to a new purchasing czar position will generate millions of dollars in vendor savings. I've been under the impression that ESI already has the best pricing possible. How can that level of savings be achieved?"

"It's there! Trust us." Rob emphatically assured Wells. "We're combining jobs, eliminating underutilized personnel, and tightening operations. And we're working on pricing improvements that will generate sales increases. We're on a roll."

"Rob," Wells said with concern, "I have to trust you because I can't see it on paper. This plan seems overstated, and it doesn't have to be. ESI was already on track. You better hold up on the layoffs until you see how you handle the heavier production load. We can't chance problems with sales increasing the way you report them." Turning to Jake, Wells asked, "Is the management team united behind this plan?"

Jake reflected on the question before answering. The plan was all but impossible for the first period, but it might be possible over the year. If he didn't stand behind the plan, the rest of the team wouldn't either, which spelled disaster. "This plan's ambitious, but it has to be to meet the promises made to Devron Power. We're team players. We'll do our best."

The hedging wasn't lost on Wells. "I suppose that's a 'we're behind the plan' statement, but you were considerably more positive on previous plans. Why?"

"There are many unknowns and good intentions in this plan, but it might succeed."

"Good intentions, Jake? I'm concerned. Hunter provided insight on pitfalls that we must carefully watch. And Rob," Wells continued, shifting his focus, "I expect you to come to me immediately if you see problems. No flim-flam stuff."

Rob nodded understanding without answering, closing further discussion, and the meeting adjourned. He flagged Jake just outside the board room in a threatening manner. "We need to talk." At his office, he slammed the door behind him and pointed to a chair for Jake. Glaring at Jake, he began, "I'll make the Devron Power presentation, and I'll do it without ESI personnel present." Then with a lowered, threatening voice, he added, "You better make this plan work Brewer. Heads will roll if you stumble. Understood?"

"I believe everyone knows where you're coming from."

"What's that supposed to mean?" Rob angrily demanded, slamming his fist on the desk.

Jake hesitated, wondering why he should answer. "Wells called it correctly when he said flim-flam. This smoke and mirror stuff might be possible with some miracles, but it's not probable."

It was silent briefly, then Rob snapped, "You have anything else to say?"

Rob expected Jake to snap back, but instead, he quietly answered, "My friend, I'm a good Marine. I understand orders." Their eyes locked when Jake said, "my friend." The growing hate was evident. Jake had plenty to say but saw little use in saying it. It would only serve to increase the bad blood that was building. He walked out.

Dexter met Jake in the hallway and followed him into his office. "Man Jake, I don't know how you kept your cool. 'This is a good plan, Mr. Reeves. You'll see.'" Dexter mocked Rob. "That ass kisser makes baloney sound like prime rib. He continually lies to Wells, and Wells can't see it. When things go wrong, it's never Rob's fault. How could Mister Perfect possibly make a mistake?"

"You through?" Jake asked in a warning manner. When a shocked Dexter nodded, Jake added, "Ease up on the boss, Dexter. He has faults, but we have ours too. Let's give him our full support, and then if we fail, we'll deal with that. And another thing," Jake added angrily, "if you had something to say about the plan or Rob, the meeting was the place to say it, not here. It's time to carry out our orders. Understood?"

Dexter stared quietly at Jake, his face red, his mind searching for correct words. "Maybe I was out of line, but I have concerns," Dexter said, his voice less harsh.

"Concern is expected, but so is performance. That's how we earn our paychecks."

CHAPTER 9

"Today's yer big day, Lester. You'll be home for Christmas."

"There's gonna be a big payoff for my slammer time before this week's out."

"Ya got a job lined up?"

"The business owes me, Jesse. Gonna have me a new Dodge 4X4 come next week."

"Gotta cost fifteen grand."

"Thirty."

"Man, how ya gonna make payments on something like that."

"I'm not. I earned it by keeping my mouth shut and serving time. Mr. Big'll be helping me for a long time. Lot of people are in for surprises. I'm gonna take back land that's rightfully mine. Folks just hafta find out what it's gonna cost 'em to keep it."

"Yer talking crazy, Lester. Did ya pray on it?"

"Don't need that crutch no more, Jesse."

"Look, I been yer guy. I listened to everything you told me since I been yer bunkie. Yer funnin' me, Lester. Say ya are."

"I'm serious as a heart attack."

"Gettin' out has gotten to ya. C'mon, ya better pack yer stuff. I'll help."

"Got everything packed I'm takin'. What's left is yers."

"Ya worked hard fer this stuff, man. Ya can't leave yer Moody Bible School certificates behind. They could come in real handy fer a con lookin' fer work. You'll use that Holman study Bible the Prison Fellowship gave ya a lot."

"That religious crap got all the use it's ever gonna get from me. It got me outta here early."

"What are ya sayin', big guy?"

"They bought four years off my time when I had nuthin' else ta do. Got me outta some lousy jobs too."

"Yer a saved man now. Tell me ya are."

"Until I hit the street. Then I'm Big Link an' I got work to do. Gonna be different. I'm a lot smarter now, an' some folks are gonna pay big time. They don't even know it's comin'."

"C'mon, Lester. Ya been my rock. Got me readin' an writin'. Saved too. Ya tol' me you'd get me a job and take care of me when I got out, didn't ya Lester?"

"Man can say some funny things when he wants something."

"Ya said ya cared for me. Ya can't be saying this ain't been for real. I trusted ya."

"Guess that's why they call us cons, Jesse."

CHAPTER 10

The Brewer kids opened presents and departed for the evening, leaving Jake to rehash the Christmas Eve message, "The Muddy Road to Christmas." Mary, a pregnant, unmarried teenager, traveled ninety miles over muddy roads on the back of a donkey to register for a Roman census. Joseph carried a troubled mind, his fiance was ready to give birth, and he wasn't the father, yet he held the responsibility for getting her to Bethlehem. The ten-day trip in winter held many dangers. There was no room at the inn; the baby would be born in a cave. I identify with you, Joseph, Jake thought; there seems to be no room in the inn for me either. Jake muttered, "Oh Lord, help me see your plan 'cause I can't see it for myself."

He stood looking at "The Wall" painting by Lee Tater that replaced the tranquil lake and cabin scene Jeanne painted years before. "The Wall" was a Christmas gift from their kids who insisted that it hold this prominent place. They couldn't know the effort he took to pigeonhole Vietnam memories. Jake clamped his eyes shut, feeling the pain of the lonely man leaning on that stark, granite wall, touching the spirit warriors reaching out to him. His mind placed many of his men there. He fought their battles and survived, heavy with scars but alive. They made it to the wall, their deaths just so much waste. Their memories clanged through his mind like a ringing chapel bell. It was his first tour in Nam, he, a fresh-caught sergeant, when he invested their lives in the meaningless war. Haggerty hurt the most. They were blood brothers, Haggerty's two little boys were like his own, and Haggerty bought the farm.

Man, and I lost my wife, Jake remembered. The letters quit coming until it became an embarrassment to attend mail call. Oh Lord, I prayed I wouldn't lose the love of my life. Her love slid away, and the best part of my life died with it. I prayed harder, and life got tougher. I trusted you, Lord, and when I needed You most, You weren't there. My life became a constant kick in the privates. Combat was my vent. My friends died, and my bitterness increased. How could a righteous God let such hell as that war exist?

"Where have you been all night?" Jeanne asked, slipping up behind him and putting her arms around him.

"With you." Jake steeled himself for what was to come. Jeanne was going to pry, and he couldn't let her."

"Not tonight, Jake," Jeanne said when he didn't turn around. "You were lost during the sermon and didn't give the kids the usual sergeant major directions when they went out."

Jake turned to hold her hands, quietly trying to make sense of the overpowering melancholy eating him. Jeanne was his pot of gold written into the love file of his mind. Sometimes a bitter whisper from the past popped out, one from the forbidden times, and he hurriedly reburied it. It was better when he selected beautiful times when their love bloomed. The time they sat in the field, and he tickled her toes with a daisy. They had been swimming at the mouth of Cold Springs Gorge. It was the day he first realized he loved her and would for all his life. He didn't know how to tell her yet, but that would come. It —.

"Jake, what do you really want in this life?" Jeanne asked, struggling to find where he was.

"You and peace."

"Peace?"

"Yeah. Life without —. Maybe I don't know what peace is."

"Is it the picture the kids gave you?"

"Maybe the sermon hit home," Jake said, refusing to acknowledge the mind movies racing by.

"Maybe it reminded me of our mess on the hill, that and the situation at work," Jake lied.

Jeanne hugged him tightly. They kissed tenderly, a healing kiss. "Honey, start your writing career."

"There are a lot of hungry would-be authors out there."

"I don't want to hear that. You've already had four books published."

"Not fiction. I get hung up on ideas for a novel. I know what I want to say but can't."

"Maybe you're starting with the wrong novel. Try something lighter."

"We've been through this before. The bills don't go away when the paychecks stop."

"You preach to others to do what they want with their lives - that you always have. Don't become a hypocrite. Did you forget the recent sermon from the parable of the talents?"

"When I saw you feverishly taking notes, I knew there'd be a repeat."

"On the way out of church, you used your 'Pastor, that sermon went from preaching to meddling' line because that sermon slapped your face."

"I don't have time to write with all that is happening," Jake protested.

"You made time in the past," Jeanne reminded him, emphasizing the "made."

"Our kids complain you haven't been writing them. They love your wacky letters. You could polish copies of past letters and get them published. Many have told you they'd sell. People need to laugh."

"I don't know."

"No, Jake, and you won't know until you try," Jeanne said. "Besides, this job isn't good for you. You work sixty hours a week, can't sleep, and your anger waits to pounce. Between your job and the mess at Hill Place, you forgot how to laugh. I want my man back. You have a dozen novels running around in your head. Let them out."

"Maybe, I will."

"No maybes, Jake."

"Who died and left you boss?" Jake asked with a grin.

"I hate to mention the source of my power, but I'm getting sleepy," Jeanne said mischievously.

She hugged Jake tightly. They kissed gently, then more passionately.

Jake held her, kissing her lips and neck. "Jeanne, I love you so," he whispered. "No one else could love you like I do. Oh, Honey, you're so beautiful," Jake whispered hoarsely, breathing deeply as he talked. "I'm crazy about you."

Holding him away and smiling, she whispered in a husky voice, "Quit talking, big boy. There'll be time for speeches later."

*   *   *

Christmas Eve in the Pandemonium Bar exhibited a different slice of life. A drunk man in shabby clothes sat at a table in the shadows, head in hands as if he waited for the gallows. At another table, a heavily made-up, portly woman in a red and green Christmas sweater and a skinny, ill-kept man with a greasy ponytail held hands whispering. At the bar, a well-dressed woman struggled to get what must be her drunken husband to come home. At the other end of the bar, a trio of drunks struggled with the words to the second verse of Silent Night while four men shot pool well past the time of night when skill was involved. A large muscular man with tattooed arms eased up to the bar and ordered a beer pitcher refill with peppermint schnapps shooters around.

"Damn, Link, where are you getting all the jack?"

"Ivory, ya writin' a book or servin' drinks?"

"Link, I thought —"

"There's yer basic problem; you were thinkin'. Too many people been thinkin' while I was gone. They're gonna pay."

CHAPTER 11

The gray winter sky hung like an old Navy blanket as dusk settled around Hill Place with Jake, Jeanne, and their son Trey sat eating an early supper. Outside, the blustery wind swirled snow streams building a drift around the truck. This storm marked Jake's brother-in-law Mac's arrival. Like his mostly Scottish father, Mac was a friendly man with dark, flashing eyes and a wide smile. His leather-hued skin spoke of his Italian mother and years weathering outside as a logger. Mac usually knew what was happening and was always eager to share the news. He was talking in high gear when he entered the dining room. "Coleman's army's back to full force." Spotting Trey, he added, "Well, I'll be. Trey. Didn't know you were home. Good to see you. Them Seabees treating' ya OK?"

"Good as can be expected."

"What's with the Coleman's?" Jeanne questioned as she set a place for Mac and began passing food.

"Shark got out of jail yesterday, and the hospital put Punk out last night. They officially discharged him last week, but the Colemans wouldn't go get him. Fred Collins hauled old lady Magelli to the hospital this mornin' with her annual Christmas heart attack, an' they sent Punk home with him."

"Being home could be a mixed blessing for Punk," Jake suggested.

"An' bad news for you," Mac countered. "Link's threatenin' retaliation for poisonin' Punk and gettin' Shark locked up. Fred said they let him out early 'cause of prison overcrowdin' an' cause he's been a model prisoner," Mac said, forking in ham and potatoes. "Link's says he's upset with the way folks been treatin' his family."

After chewing briefly, Mac continued, "Fred said takin' Punk to the hospital was the longest 37-mile trip he ever had. Punk stunk so bad they were sick before they hit the hard road. If you ever had the pleasure of being close to Punk, ya know the odor would knock down a turkey vulture. Punk had messed pants with running sores from his waist to —"

"MAC!" Jake roared, "We're eating."

"Sorry. The rest of the story ain't bad guys," Mac stated, searching for approval to finish. "You may as well give it to us," Jeanne authorized, noting Mac was bursting to get it out.

"They pumped a bunch of poison outta him. Cut two toes off a frostbit foot, but figger the rest will heal. The doctor said the rash he got messing himself was worse than the frostbite. Took 'em an' hour to get him clean enough to operate. Punk came to hollerin' 'Help Me' and 'Chickerdee.' They thought he was delirious from poison. Didn't know that was most of what he says. Then Fred wondered if ya poisoned Punk to keep him from breakin' in again."

"Where'd he get that idea?"

"Everybody's talkin' it. Link's swearin' ta get even."

"How can they transfer the results of a problem they created into the need for revenge on their victims?" Jeanne asked, her face twisted in an angry scowl.

"They jus' do an' don't forget; they retaliate," Mac said.

"Anybody hear him besides Collins?" Jake asked.

"The cops an' EMTs when they brought Punk home. Hanratty cautioned 'em about retaliation, but ya know, cautions spur on them goofballs. I'd be ready."

"You recommend filling sandbags?" Jake asked angrily.

"Glad I ain't in your shoes, that's all I'm sayin'. I can see this place in a pile of ashes after all your work. Hope your fire insurance is paid up," Mac said with some finality. "If it was me, I'd take anything I wanted outta here."

"One thing about you, Uncle Mac, you're a real positive thinker," Trey said.

"I call 'em the way they are. Everyone knows the Colemans burned the church and prob'ly your grandad's place too, truth be known."

"Let's change the subject. How's the weather over on your end of the table?" Jake asked.

"Oh man, ya shouldn't ask. Weather guessers call for a couple more feet of snow with heavy winds. You could be diggin' out in June."

"You haven't been here fifteen minutes, and you have the place burned down and us snowed in until June."

"I'm not cookin' up problems. I'm relayin' news. There's a difference."

"Is there? Job said, 'That which I greatly feared has come upon me.' I'm going to try to look at things in a little more positive light."

"Be positive all ya want, but keep them fire extinguishers handy."

With supper over and the weather approaching blizzard-like conditions, Mac departed, leaving the Brewers discussing the seriousness of the latest Coleman threats. The conversation abruptly ceased when Gus growled, hackles raised. A stomping noise on the front porch marked Mac's return. "Got my truck stuck," Mac angrily retorted as he stomped in. "Backed back."

"Never get a Chevy out of here tonight, but you can borrow my Ford," Jake teased.

"How are you going to let Sis know?" Jeanne asked.

"She said if I wasn't home by eight, she'd know I was stuck up here. You need to get a phone."

The storm gathered intensity, and gale-force winds drove sledgehammer blows, pounding the old log home. Hill Place creaked in protest as huge drifts built. Inside, the occupants talked in hushed tones. A furious blast of air shook the place. Lights flickered a couple of times, went out, tried to come back on, flickered again, and went out for good. Jake lit one of the kerosene lamps, then curious, he checked the thermometer with a flashlight. It read fifteen degrees above zero, and the snow continued to fall. At some point, a piece of window trim tore loose and slapped back and forth, creating a rhythmic wham, wham. A tremendous wind blast rocked the house.

With it came the crashing roar of something being twisted and smashed. The occupants, worried now, questioned the source of the noise. "Coulda been the barn going down," Mac murmured.

After what seemed like an eternity, the wind slacked some, and Jake and Jeanne turned in for the night, leaving Mac and Trey talking by the woodstove. Sleep came quickly for the Brewers and lasted until Jake got up to fix the woodstove fires.

The sun slid up over the horizon a few hours later, painting the eastern sky a light pink. Wind whipped snow sculptured a virgin land removing all traces of man's passing. The lane became part of a smooth white sea with three trucks partially buried in the snow. The old chestnut log barn stood proudly in the morning light, a witness to its toughness. Beyond it lay a twisted mass of wind-downed trees. The house, partially buried by the drifted snow, remained without power.

Dressed for cold and wearing snowshoes, Jake and Mac made their way around the house, checking for storm damage. "Man Brewer, can you believe these drifts?"

"Haven't had a storm like this since 57. We didn't go to school for a week. We broke a trail out to the barn and took care of the stock. It took the rest of the day to shovel out the outhouse and get a path down to the spring. Wind piled snow ten feet deep just past the lilac bush and kept drifting our paths closed."

They spent the day opening paths to the spring and woodpile. As a busy day ended, Dean plowed out Brewer's road. This came with a Vance family invitation to supper. Now Jake leaned on his ax handle, watching Mac lug the old toboggan back for the last load of cookstove wood. Smoke curled skyward from the chimneys into the reddening evening sky as the temperature dropped steadily.

"Gettin' colder than a well digger's fanny."

"Guess that's chilly, Mac."

"Chilly enough," Mac agreed as they watched Trey struggle up from the spring with two buckets of water. "Better have lots, Trey. Misty's gonna need to use the bathroom. She ain't much for squattin' in the woods, 'specially in all this snow." Mac smiled broadly. "You shoulda been there, Trey, when the Vance family held the picnic for Dean to introduce Misty. She refused to use the outhouse, an' the hill folks never forgot that day. 'Oh, Dean, I couldn't use that thing, not with the flies and smell. It's such a barbaric place,'" Mac mocked in a falsetto voice. He continued in a deeper voice with lines delivered by Dean's father. "'Good lord girl, you ain't holdin' a tea party. Yer going in there to relieve yourself. Don't worry about our outhouse flies. We got lots an' if they can't handle yer vapors, we'll grow us a crop that can. They ain't that hard to raise.'"

Mac and Trey laughed heartily while Jake offered a polite chuckle. He remembered Misty's encounter with Dean's father. Crying, she ran for Dean's car and wouldn't talk to him or return to the picnic. How they got from that scene to the altar was often debated. Why they did was a bigger question.

"Did that really happen?" Trey asked.

"Uncle Mac wouldn't lie."

"Right Dad."

Inside, Hill Place was toasty with both wood stoves running. Jeanne had kerosene lamps lit. A bayberry candle and a small light burned in the bathroom, with several more lamps ready for use on a stand in the kitchen. With chores finished, the men sat around the table sipping coffee and snacking on fresh-baked bread while Jeanne finished the meal. Trey tapped his fingers on the table as he watched for lights coming in the lane. Finally, he announced on his way out to greet them, "The Vance's are here."

"Welcome all," Trey announced as the Vance family climbed out of the truck.

Dean looked at Sherrie, "See, I told you Trey was falling all over himself to see you."

"Dad! We're just friends."

"He's a sailor, and you've heard your uncles talk about their wild Navy times."

"Can we change the subject?" Sherrie asked, her face turning red. She smiled at Trey, "Don't worry, I don't plan to elope tonight."

"I've been getting ribbed all day. These old guys all think alike. They'd like to be young again."

"How have you been, Trey?" Misty asked in a too-sweet voice that suggested she didn't care. Sensing her feelings, Trey answered, "Fine, Mrs. Vance. Let's go in."

"Great idea, "Misty agreed. "I've been cold all day."

"You'll soon be sweating," Trey assured her. "Mom has both stoves glowing."

"Perspiring, Trey," Misty corrected in a disdainful voice. "Ladies perspire."

"Whatever," Trey murmured.

After the initial pleasantries, Jeanne took beverage orders, and Jake went into the kitchen to pour them while Trey collected coats. Following Jeanne to the kitchen, Misty complained. "The power could be off for days. Might as well be living in caves. This isn't a weekend retreat for us; we live here. You have a real home elsewhere."

"This is our real home."

"A part-time house by choice," Misty groused. While Jeanne bit her tongue, Misty continued. "I'm stuck. Our place is so cold without electricity. It's so like poor white trash."

Tiring of the topic, Jeanne announced, "If anyone needs to freshen up, the bathroom's available. The commode is useable, and there's water on the stand."

Relief flooded over Misty. Since morning, she held the need but couldn't force herself to seek relief in the woods. "May I be excused?" Misty requested and disappeared into the bathroom with her drink. Later, she emerged with an empty glass and found everyone ready to eat. Seeing people were waiting, Misty said, "Oh my, I guess I overdid it."

Holding hands around the table, Jake asked the blessing, thanking the Lord for friends and friendship, a warm home, and the great food they were about to eat. With a hearty chorus of "Amens," everyone was seated and began passing the bowls of steaming food. Hearty appetites abounded; the clink of utensils suggested they were being satisfied. "Great food Jeanne," Jake said, looking at the woman he loved, feeling warmed through as their eyes met.

"The meat tastes like elk. You guys jacklight one?" Dean asked.

"Nah," Jake said. "It's western meat, elk, and mule deer. Mac got 'em out west."

"Man, Jeanne, the way you cook, I should have filled your freezer," Mac said.

"Brings a truckload next trip," Jake said, "with a couple of bottles of expensive wine to wash it down and maybe a little ice cream."

"Just bring ice cream, Mac," Jeanne said. "Jake's latest weird flavor is Zagnut Royale. Add that to Strawberry Flip, Crunchberry, and Plank Road. We ate all but the Coffee Mocha, and Gus, the ice creamaholic, didn't even like that. I made him eat it as punishment for barking at the mailman."

"Do you really buy such weird flavors?" Sherrie wondered.

"Hold it, young lady," Jake scolded. "You're not a family member yet, and you're already calling me weird. You two tie the knot before you climb on me."

Immediate embarrassment resulted. Jeanne stepped to the rescue, "Ease up, Brewer."

"We should know if this young lady has designs on our son."

"Dad, you're impossible," Trey said, anger bristling in his voice.

"Your dad's on to something." Sherrie winked. "I like sailor suits."

"Uniforms," Trey corrected without thinking.

"OK, uniforms. It goes with your tattoo. I like that too."

"Geez, Sherrie, you sound like my Dad."

"Mine too," Sherrie said, smiling at him.

"Sherrie, you're irrepressible."

"Lighten up, Jason. A smile won't crack your makeup," Sherrie answered lightly.

"Jason Michael! Sherry Linne! We're eating!" Misty admonished.

Mac hated to see the makings of a good argument die. "What's a little squabble?"

"I was raised to believe arguing during a meal was the sign of poor breeding."

"Breedin' at the table could be a problem," Mac acknowledged. "I've never known—"

"OK, Mac," Jeanne warned, "We're getting a little out in left field."

"Sorry. Thought you might have a sense of humor. Look who ya married."

That comment brought a chuckle that lightened things.

"Anybody for a refill," Jake asked, picking up the water pitcher. Draining it, he refilled it from a water bucket and passed it around. Misty politely poured a little into her glass and then passed it on. Without drinking, she set the glass on the table. Jake received the near-empty pitcher back, refilled it, and sat back down.

"Great meal Jeanne," Mac said, talking around his food as he started the meat platter around again. "Seconds anyone?" he asked, giving the plate to Dean. Dean took meat and passed the platter to Misty.

"I'll pass, thank you," Misty said politely, her face taking on a red glow. "I'm not into eating wild animals."

"You're married to a Vance an' don't eat venison?" Mac asked, puzzling over her comment. "That's all they useta eat; them an' a lot more of us."

"We don't eat venison, nor do we drink water out of buckets like cattle," she said, only to have the comment slap her when it became instantly quiet.

Dean's face burned crimson, and Sherrie looked uncomfortable. Trey looked his father a "Please don't say anything" glance. Mac couldn't pass up the opportunity. "Good lord lady, how do you haul in your drinkin' water when there ain't power to run the pump?" Mac asked, looking confused. "An' that meat's as good as eatin' gets. God didn't put elk and deer on this earth to die of starvation or old age. He put animals under man's dominion so we could eat 'em."

Mac was half kidding and half educating, but Misty, not knowing him well, couldn't tell. Embarrassment flooded over her, softening her voice to a whisper, "I don't condemn you for what you eat, but isn't it all right to be different? And we have water at home. I bought two gallons at the Handee Mart for emergencies."

"Good lord, two gallons wouldn't keep this place in coffee for a day, and I'm not sure what's wrong with drinkin' from a water bucket," Mac pushed.

"It's so very primitive. Refined people drink from glasses," Misty responded, clearly upset that Mac couldn't understand.

"We aren't drinking out of buckets; we're drinking out of glasses, but we drank out of water buckets at grade school, Misty," Dean said, his face a signboard of embarrassment. "We took turns carrying the water from the spring."

"Yeah, everyone shared a dipper except little Jimmy Michaels," Mac said. "His citified mother said it wasn't clean. She sent Jimmy to school with his little tin cup hooked on his belt. Boy, did we torment that bird."

Jake was never proud of harassing Jimmy, and he closed the subject. "Those were fun times, but we live differently now."

CHAPTER 12

With the meal over, Trey and Sherry quietly disappeared upstairs. Their legs touched as they sat together during dinner, and both found it enjoyable. Trey often wondered if there might be an opportunity for something more than friendship, and although he desperately wanted that, he never got around to finding out.

Much to his chagrin, Jason followed them to the lookout, a cozy nook at the top of the stairs. A small table surrounded by armchairs faced large windows that looked over the surrounding mountain ridges and the deep valley below, a spectacular view during the day and fuel for romance on starry nights. If it could talk, the lookout could delight the romantic or the gossip.

An antique kerosene lamp cast flickering shadows. The trio made small talk until Jason placed his finger to his lips, motioning for the others to be quiet. The floor vent behind them led to the kitchen below so that when opened, heat from the wood-burning cookstove flowed upstairs. The conversation drifted up as the men worked through the supper dishes, a long-held custom at Hill Place.

Jeanne sat chatting with Misty in the dimly lit front room, enjoying the heat from the wood burner. Misty's Jack Daniels had unhinged her tongue with a growing slurring of words. "I 'spose you think I'm a wretched person after the things I said during dinner," Misty said. "I was raised so differently. Daddy came up here gunning a few times, but we never ate wild things."

"Venison may not be for everyone, but no meat could be purer. We raised chickens and saw what they eat."

"I guess. I also detest drinking out of these springs with dirt bottoms. How hygienic can that be? And buckets seem to be such an unsanitary way to store water. I'm so thankful you had bottled water for coffee."

Jeanne half-listened as Misty talked. She dipped the bottled water from the bucket to keep it cold in the refrigerator while the power was still on, and they never used the water buckets for anything but drinking water. Wonder where she'll find water that doesn't have its origin in something dirt bottomed, Jeanne reasoned, fighting back a smile. Reservoirs and wells are dirt bottomed too.

"Living out here grows worse with time," Misty said, pausing to work on her drink. "There's nothing to do, nothing as in zero. I invest considerable time with my workout equipment to maintain my figure, but it's disappointing when no one notices. I had a satellite dish installed, and that became another depressant. Every channel carries an endless parade of beautiful people living in luxury homes while I sit stuck in this wasteland," Misty said in a voice begging for agreement.

"You have a beautiful home and a fine family," Jeanne said, endeavoring to steer her toward a different topic. Me, myself, and I were wearing thin.

"Boring. I'm thinking of doing a few cruises and maybe a few crew members too." After a giggle and a sip of her drink, she continued. "Daddy named me Misty on a cruise. I was wearing a green negligee that he bought me. He said I was much too foxy to be Paige Renee, so I became Misty."

Where's this conversation headed? Jeanne wondered. "Our dream is living here with a quieter life."

"Here? When I escape, I'll never look back. Daddy said I was nuts for marrying Dean. I see his point ever more clearly as the years wear on." Jeanne did not answer, and Misty rambled on, ever bolder, as the drinks grabbed hold. "You know what I'd like to do; I'd like to stroll down one of those nude beaches turning heads. That would light my fire. You've had those fantasies?"

"Heavens, no."

"Don't be modest. You have a nice shape for your age. Another man could add a little excitement to your life."

"No, Misty, one couldn't. I know how much Jake means to me. I could never —" Jeanne stopped allowing the matter to drop.

Misty was reflecting on that comment when Jason stomped down the stairs. "Did you abandon your sister to that sailor?" Misty asked in her disparaging manner.

"Those squares are harmless, Mother. From the laughing we heard, the action's in the kitchen. They have a male bonding thing going. I'm off to bond."

The men in the kitchen were reminiscing about country school. "Hey guys, do you remember how —"

"Hi, Jason," Dean loudly interrupted, cutting off the conversation in the kitchen. "They bore you out upstairs?"

"Heard you guys laughing about school in the old days and wanted to join you."

Catching on to what was happening, Mac asked, "Remember Allison. He had that thing going with Wentz, the high school principal."

"I remember," Dean agreed. "No one much liked old Wentzie. We decided we'd make everyone in town aware of Mr. Richard Wentz and his womanizing after he knocked up Busty Newhouse, and they blamed it on her boyfriend."

"Yeah. That Halloween, we pulled one of the best tricks ever," Mac excitedly agreed. "Soaped every window in the high school where we announced Wentzie's antics to the world."

"Journalistic excellence at its best," Dean agreed. "They still talk about us at school; the older teachers say our class was the worst ever to graduate Parker High School."

"It was a hoot when Scoops Trimmer read the Wentz messages on the school windows and printed them in his newspaper," Jake remembered. "That cooked Wentzie's goose for him. He started suffering some well-earned grief. Maybe what we did to Wentz serves as an example of handling the Coleman problem."

"Great idea," Mac said. "We'll soap Coleman's names on the high school windows. That'll fix 'em."

"C'mon Mac," Jake replied, "I meant we should communicate what's happening here. Maybe someone would do something about the problem. The town ran Wentzie off when his actions became known."

"Times have changed," Dean said. "The Scandalizer prints very little about local problems."

"Why not?" Jake asked angrily.

"The town fathers wouldn't like the impact it might have on tourists," Dean said. "The Scandalizer might lose advertising revenue if they print local problems and the town fathers get upset. We need to take care of problems ourselves. You ready to help, Jake?" Dean asked.

"Need to know more about it."

"Better think on it before it's too late," Dean declared, upset once more with Jake's resistance. "Ready, Jason? It's getting late."

"I was ready to leave before I got here," Jason replied pretentiously, much like his mother.

Traveling home, Sherry broke the silence with thoughts about the evening. "I had a great time. The Brewers are so easy to be with."

"I've had more exciting evenings swatting mosquitoes," Misty began with a noticeable whiskey slur. "I found everything to be rather hillbillyish. Jeanne's nice, but she's so common."

"If Mrs. Brewer's common, maybe more of us should be common," Sherrie injected.

"You might enjoy these rednecks Sherry Vance," Misty barked. "I'm sick of living like Neanderthal woman."

"Mrs. Brewer worked hard to make our evening a pleasant one," Sherry said, annoyed at the comments. "She shared her warm home and a great meal. We could have been home freezing over a can of soup warmed on the barbeque. I doubt if she's back there running us down."

"You promote the Brewers because you're stuck on Trey," Jason griped. "You can't see —"

"Hold it, Jason!" Dean demanded. "You're an embarrassment. I should have beaten your fanny a long time ago, and if you keep running your big mouth, it might happen tonight."

"You touch my boy, and I'll have you arrested, Dean Vance," Misty shrieked. "And Sherry, that Brewer boy's just a laborer in the Navy. Don't get tangled up with someone like —"

"— like your father, that's what she's trying to tell you, Sherry," Dean finished angrily. "Can't we just let this ride until we get home? Then we'll write down all the things we dislike about the Brewers, how we hate the meal they shared with us, their common thoughts, and all the other nasty, unappreciative things we can think up. We'll send them the list in a thank you card. We'll publish it in the Scandalizer, so the world knows how the Vance family treats good Samaritans."

"Dean Vance, Daddy's right. You're a miserable jackass," Misty said.

"Right on, Misty, and a fool too. You forgot to mention your old man thinks I'm a fool."

Back at the Brewers, things were far more friendly. With the dishes done, they were retiring for the night. When Jake arrived, he found Jeanne sitting on the bed with her head in her hands. "Is something wrong, Honey?" he asked with concern.

"Nope," Jeanne said without looking up. "Just waiting for some love monkey to warm up the bed. Even flannel sheets are cold when you first crawl in."

"You know what you remind me of, sitting there like that?" Jake asked quietly. "You were sitting that same way on our wedding night. You had on that peach negligee. I asked you if something was wrong. Remember what you said?"

"I was so scared."

"You said, 'Jake, you're going to be so disappointed.' I couldn't decide what you were talking about, so I sat beside you and put my arms around you. You whispered, 'I don't have big breasts like all you guys want.'"

"Yes, and you started laughing, Brewer. I thought you were laughing at me, and I got mad."

"I told you your breasts were plenty big enough to suit me. I married you for you."

"I needed to hear that. I was so unsure of everything."

"I've never been disappointed, not for a second. You were beautiful then, and you just keep growing prettier. Better yet, you're nice to everyone." He tenderly kissed her neck and took her face in his hands; they kissed passionately, leading to real love.

The night passed peacefully, and a new day rode in lamb-like, the weather calm and clear. Striding along on skis in the early morning with his breath creating puffs of white fog crystals in the sub-zero air, Trey carried a thermos of coffee for the Vance family. After a sleepless night filled with romantic notions and an early morning talk with his father about the Vance Family, he was on his way to visit Sherry. Stepping out of cross-country skis on the Vance porch, he knocked lightly, hoping that someone would be up and that someone would be Sherry. Instead, Misty came to the door, wearing an emerald green silk robe, her glistening blond hair neatly brushed, the light scent of her perfume reaching out with a sensual message. She smiled, holding the door open. "Well, what do we have here?"

"Thought you folks could use some hot coffee," Trey said.

"That's sweet, Trey," Misty cooed. He handed her the coffee, stopped just inside the door, and slipped out of his boots. Their eyes met as he straightened, and she gave him a come-on smile. She stepped forward and kissed him.

"Thanks for thinking of us," she said, smiling.

The slight odor of kerosene space heaters struck Trey as he entered. Misty pulled out a chair for him; the movement opened her robe showing cleavage. The rising tide of desire pushed red across his face. Pulse quickening, he looked away.

"Whoops," Misty said, smiling seductively.

Their eyes met, and Misty winked coyly, stoking the fires that inhabit young men.

Dean emerged, flashlight in hand. "Morning, Trey." Looking closer, he added, "Something sure has your face red this morning."

"It's cold out," Trey murmured, the heat of embarrassment replacing erotic thoughts.

"Trey brought coffee," Misty said as she poured three cups of coffee. She carried two of them to the table and then sat on a stool at the counter behind Dean.

"My brother Howard radioed us," Dean said around sips on his coffee. "Dozers opened the road to his place about five this morning. Power will be out for several days. They're bringing in crews from other parts of the state to help restore service. The governor declared our five-county area a state of emergency. It might be the last call we get. Battery's running low."

"Trey must bring us coffee every morning until they restore power," Misty said, attracting Trey's attention when she recrossed her legs.

"... don't you agree, Trey?" Engrossed in Misty's performance, Trey caught the end of Dean's question, but he didn't know what he was supposed to be agreeing with.

"Beg your pardon?"

"Just wondering. Parents aren't much of a reason for a young sailor to bring coffee way up here. Wouldn't you agree?" Dean kidded.

Trey fought to focus on what Dean was saying, but he couldn't resist snatching glances at Misty, who smiled whenever their eyes met. "Not much to do, snowbound the way we are."

"Oh, I see. If you could get out of here, you wouldn't bother with us?" Dean asked. "That's not it at all," Trey sputtered.

The sound of a door closing prompted Trey to look across the kitchen. "This is a pleasant surprise, Mr. Brewer," Sherry said with a broad smile as she seated herself at the table. Although her eyes were still puffy, Sherry presented an innocently sweet image entirely different from her mother's beauty.

"You college girls sleep late," Trey returned in the way of a greeting.

"Poor Trey's bored to tears with us old people," Misty said, catching Trey's eye and winking.

"I wouldn't say that," Trey mumbled, trying to get his mind on other things. "You doing anything special today, Sherry?"

"I might lay out and catch some rays this morning and then swim at the gorge later. How about you, Trey?"

Trey grinned, realizing he had fumbled clumsily. "Thought we might try out cross country skis."

Before Sherry could answer, Dean spoke up, "Sounds like fun. I'll go."

"I don't think you're what Trey had in mind, Dad."

"No?" Dean questioned innocently.

"Dad!" Sherry said, her annoyance evident.

"Just being friendly."

"Sure, Dad," Sherry said, looking back to Trey. "Let's meet in an hour or so."

"Eat breakfast with us," Trey urged.

Before Sherry could answer, Dean asked, "How about us? We'd enjoy breakfast too."

"Dad, quit picking!" Turning to Trey, Sherry asked, "Are you sure your parents won't mind."

"You know, Mom. She'll have enough food for a small army."

"We won't be coming," Misty said with ice in her voice. "Meals two days in a row is a bit much."

Sherry decided to take Trey up on the breakfast offer and excused herself to dress. She returned in Levis and a powder blue ski sweater that picked up the color of her eyes. She's a beautiful young lady, Trey thought as they stepped into their skis and departed. When they were out of view of the house, Sherry took his hand. "Are you someplace else, Mister Brewer?" Trey took her other hand. Looking into her eyes, a natural bond pulled them together. They kissed tenderly, smiled at each other, and continued on their way.

Later in the morning, with breakfast over, Trey and Sherry tracked out along the desolate ridge road on skis, taking their time for it was a beautiful day. The old wagon road hung on the mountain's sheer face, hand-carved there by the earliest settlers seeking the most direct route to the Allison Family logging camp where Hill Place now stood. The bright blue sky met the newly fallen snow, chasing sun jewels dancing across the landscape.

The day sped quickly by, with Trey and Sherry growing ever closer as they skied together, ate at the Brewers together, and then headed home to the Vances. "Trey," Sherry began, "I don't want you to leave. I knew we had something going together for some time, but now it's real. I love you."

"I love you too, Honey, but I don't have a choice. I did come to a decision in the past few days. When my hitch is up, I'm getting out of the military if you're still interested in a life together."

"Trey Brewer, you know I want a forever relationship. I've never been with anyone that made me feel like I feel just holding your hand. When we kiss, I'm on a different planet. I love you. I can't let you leave when your parents go home. Would you stay at our place a few more days if my parents are OK with that?"

"I'd love to, Sherry. It hurts to think about leaving you now."

"Plan on staying or me going with you. That's how I plan to sell it to my parents."

"It'll be a long night for me until I find out if your parents buy your plan."

*   *   *

"... the Northeast remains paralyzed by the blizzard of '94, now characterized as the storm of the century. The Allegheny Mountains remain isolated. Gale force winds build mountainous drifts that strand hundreds in outlying sections of the big woods country. Heavy equipment works around the clock to open roads. Crews struggle under harsh conditions in remote areas to restore power. It appears as if this —."

"What the —?" Jake mumbled as he searched for the volume control on the radio and killed it. The light on his nightstand was on, and as he checked the time, it hit him - power was restored. Lights burned throughout the house, the aftereffect of people accustomed to power absent-mindedly turning things on, forgetting they had no electricity, and neglecting to turn them off when nothing happened. Jake traveled around the house, turning off lights, added wood to the fires, and returned to bed.

He snuggled against Jeanne raising an immediate protest; he was cold. He waited a bit, kissed her neck, and when that proved acceptable, he kissed her again. Jeanne reminded him the bedroom door was ajar, and he slid out of bed to close it. Returning to bed, he stumbled over Gus, who growled viscously. "It's okay, boy," Jake whispered, scratching his ears, then sat where he thought the bed was and missed, crashing like a bomb.

"You can say it's okay, Brewer; nobody jumped on you," Jeanne whispered.

Later after a loving interlude, dawn was breaking when Jake let Gus out, fixed the fires, and made coffee. Joining him, Jeanne asked about the weather. "Three below, but it doesn't seem that cold now that the wind stopped." Jake poured two cups of coffee and took one to Jeanne. "A storm can be good for us, Honey. It shows us we can get along without all the niceties."

"Guess that's why you perked coffee on the woodstove."

CHAPTER 13

The day drug on while Sherry waited for her parents' decision on Trey staying over for a few days. She was surprised and thrilled when she received parental permission for Trey to remain after the Brewers returned home. With the decision rendered, Dean asked Misty to go to the Brewers while he took Sherry back for the evening. When she declined, Sherry and her father departed together. En route, Dean felt Sherry looking at him and searched her face in the instrument panel light, wondering what was on her mind. She finally asked, "Dad, what do you see in my Mother?" Sherry asked, shaking her head.

After a brief pause to gather his thoughts, Dean responded. "She's a beautiful woman."

"Yes, but what do you have in common? Surely mother's ongoing caustic comments must hurt."

Dean found himself embarrassed by his daughter's questions. Memories flooded back. There is so much Sherry can never know. I was an Army vet several years older than the blond, buxom, and passionately hot teenager who is now her mother? We met at college, and her mother made the first moves in our relationship. After a few dates, she would have my zipper down as soon as we had the doors closed in her new red Pontiac convertible. Her purse always held a 35-mm film canister of Vaseline, and she couldn't wait to use it. Our time together was a constant string of promiscuous events, with most of our activities staged so we could be alone to make love. I moved into her apartment during my last year of undergraduate work. That allowed me to complete grad school while Misty finished college. Our grades suffered because of her insatiable desire for sex. Man, has that changed over the years. Maybe she has someone else. Dean couldn't let himself think beyond that point.

"Dad, you didn't answer me," Sherry said, breaking the silence.

"We enjoyed each other," Dean answered, searching for words that wouldn't betray secrets. "During the summer, we went to your grandparent's place in the Poconos - swam and boated, things like that. What do kids do now?" Dean asked, trying to shed the spotlight.

"Depends on who the kids are," Sherry answered. "I like the simple, just being together kinds of things the Brewers enjoy. Outdoor games. Horseshoes. Picnics. I never liked the Poconos. Mother's parents continually brag about how much they have or who their important friends are. Jason thrives on that crap, but it sickens me."

Dean felt much the same way, but he couldn't allow Sherry to know that. "Don't be too hard on your mother or grandparents. We all enjoy different ways to live our lives. With all our differences, I love your mother."

"Good luck," Sherry muttered.

At the Brewers, the topic quickly zeroed in on the hill situation. "Crow stopped us when we returned from town this afternoon," Dean began as he took a sip from the glass of wine Jake handed him. "Came running out with his coat buttoned one hole off. He stopped at Sherry's side and darned if my daughter didn't roll the window up on him."

"His coat sleeves were slick where he wiped his nose," Sherry said, obviously reliving the situation. "His teeth look like rotten vegetable salad, and his breath would gag a sewer rat. When he talks, he sprays spit. If you talk with Crow, give yourself some distance. And always remember, the Laceys are two of the world's nosiest people," Sherry added.

"Amen," Jake agreed. You know, we may be missing something with the Laceys. They tend to know most of what is happening in the county. We should use them to help us with this Coleman thing."

Dean wagged his finger, "Only raw force will stop the Colemans."

* * *

Jake sat enjoying a cup of coffee and the morning paper when Trey arrived home from the mountains two days early. "You got up with the roosters."

"Before them."

"Problems?"

"Nothing I care to talk about."

Jake sensed his son's hurt. Being a private person, he could understand Trey's pain without prying. "I won't stick my nose in your business, but I'll pray for you."

"Prayer can't undo what's already done."

"Prayer always helps Trey," Jake said softly, not wanting to seem argumentative. "Nothing is too tough for the Lord."

"Chirp" "Chirp," the phone summoned, startling them. "Good morning," Jake answered, trying to sound cheerful.

"Mr. Brewer, this is Sherry. I'm worried. Trey was gone when I got up," Sherry said with obvious concern. "Is he there?"

"Would you like to speak with him?"

"Please," Sherry replied, her voice wavering.

Trey was shaking his head, holding his hands out in front of him in a "no-deal" kind of way. Jake knew his son was hurting. He also knew you can't walk away from problems and have them fix themselves.

"Trey, you owe it to her," Jake replied with his hand cupped over the receiver. "She's concerned. Maybe the Lord's already at work."

"Maybe He isn't because I haven't been praying," Trey challenged.

"I have," Jake said quietly and departed to allow privacy.

Jeanne was dressing when Jake walked into the bedroom. "Something wrong?" she asked, sensing her husband was deep in thought.

"Trey's home early. Haven't figured out why but I'm not alone. Sherry can't either."

The detective in Jeanne went to work, and she began developing theories. "Maybe things were getting too serious, and Trey decided to bail out. You ran off to the Marines."

"Yeah, you chased me until I caught you, and your life's been a mess ever since. I bet you kick yourself in the fanny every time you think of all I got you into. I'm going to start checking you for bruises. You had the opportunity to marry a nice guy. Remember, Mac had the hots for you."

"Watch it, Buster!" Jeanne snapped back.

After a moment's reflection, Jake replied, "I'm concerned, and Trey won't talk."

"Wonder where he gets that, Mr. Keep everything to yourself, Brewer?"

Jake waited until he heard Trey in the bathroom and returned to the kitchen to refill his coffee. Soon the three of them were in the kitchen, Jeanne preparing breakfast with Jake and Trey sitting at the table. Trey busied himself with the sports section of the morning paper, but his troubles consumed him.

Finally breaking the silence, Jeanne asked, "How's Sherry this morning?"

"Fine."

Jeanne was curious, and as was her habit, she quickly fired several questions at Trey without giving him time to think through them. "Is it something to do with the Navy, Trey? Is there something we —?"

"Hold it, Mom!" Trey said, an intenseness in his voice that said I need time to work this out. "And no, I'm not in trouble with the Navy."

"Trey, I worry you'll throw away a beautiful life over something that's not worth a second glance. Sherry is a special young lady."

"Can we just give it a rest?"

CHAPTER 14

Jake searched each person's eyes, stopping at Dexter Ritchey. "We're starting the third week of the period, and we still need $600K in sales. We can make this period with a little luck. Did you get the GE contract and down payment?"

"Rob's words were 'you're going to have to trust me on this one.' I plan to do that."

"And risk missing the first period?"

"We'll make it up in the second period. We're already a million over without Rob's help."

"That won't work for me."

"Why not?" Dexter asked sarcastically. "Rob accepted responsibility for the month when he forced GE on the job list. I'm not —"

"Hold it, Dexter!" Jake commanded, his anger apparent. "You're the one who insisted Rob would screw things up and pass down the blame. I'm next in line, and I plan to fight this thing down to the last minute."

"Good luck. We're doomed without GE."

"Never served in combat, did you, Dexter?" Dick Wilson asked.

"What's that have to do with anything?"

"If your butt was on the line, you might learn to fight," Dick said. "Maybe not. Some folks are all talk."

"We're getting off track," Jake said, holding his hands in a "Stop" signal. "Dexter, I want you to call our Miami, Houston, and San Diego offices. They all have near-term projects working. Personally go over every job possibility and put pressure on those guys to produce sales, especially standard product sales."

"If they had anything, we'd have it."

"They may be holding something over until next month for the additional bonus value for sales above goal. I looked over their 'in work' projects. They have possibilities."

"It's a wasted effort, and I have other —"

"Dexter, start calling! Ensure everyone knows I expect support."

Dexter stomped off, leaving the team working on the problem. After checking the status of every project and all potential sales, they settled on Blackburn Manufacturing, a company anxiously searching for someone who could meet a close-in deadline.

"Why can't we meet Blackburn's date?" Jake asked. "We should have most of the required equipment in that GE stuff, and that order isn't coming in this month. Franklin Tank had an oil/water separator they were trying to unload. That leaves two smaller tanks to worry about."

"Franklin's separator costs too much, and it's too big to fit into the building," Bob said.

"Maybe we can stack equipment. A bigger system would increase capacity and clean up their problem in less time. The cost might be a wash. Let's call Blackburns," Jake said.

"Why bother? Their project manager is Blackburn's daughter. She won't listen to anything," Bob said.

"Seymore Blackburn's tough, but he's a shrewd business person. His daughter might be too.

What can we offer them if they make the changes?"

"Additional costs for a bigger system," Bob said.

"Let's get Metzger up here," Jake said as he picked up the phone and punched in her extension. "Janet, you got a minute." After a pause, he said, "Good. Bring your calculator."

Janet walked in and took a seat opposite Jake. "You rang?" she asked lightly.

Jake quickly explained the situation. In minutes, they had her agreement that a bigger system was a viable option. "Do you know Sheila Blackburn?" Jake asked Janet.

"She's a libber. Everywhere I used "erection" in a proposal, she scratched out 'erection' and replaced it with 'construction.' Other than that, she's a pro."

"I better call Franklin Tank before we call her," Jake said. "They owe us a favor."

Jake dialed Franklin was connected with Budd Owens, the vice president. "Budd, I'm in a jam. Do you have that separator you tried to pawn off on us last fall?" Jake asked.

"It needs to be cleaned and repainted. It sat outside all winter."

"Can you let it go for the price of the one you quoted last week?

"Pheeww," Budd exhaled while he thought through the proposition. "I can't, Jake. I need another four grand. Maybe we can deal a bit."

Armed with that information, Janet recalculated the figures while the rest of the team prepared a sales strategy. Jake was soon on the speakerphone with Sheila Blackburn discussing the proposed system and its benefits. "What will it cost me to enjoy all of these benefits? Should I sit down?"

"I don't think that's necessary, Sheila. We can erect a —"

"Construct is the word I think you're looking for," Sheila injected.

As Janet mouthed, "I told you so," Jake picked up where he left off, careful to use the word "construct." When he completed, he endeavored to close the sale. "Do we have a deal?"

"Can you get it installed by the twenty-seventh?"

"Can we work that weekend if we need it?" Jake asked.

"Will the overtime cost you or me?" Sheila asked.

"You drive a hard bargain. We'll split overtime costs if we need it," Jake said.

"Get me the proposal this afternoon. I need drawings too."

Jake looked at Janet, and she nodded, "Sheila?" Janet asked, "Can we get the proposal to you today and the drawings by Wednesday. Our CAD shop is backed up and on overtime now? We'll include a sketch with the proposal."

"I can live with that," Sheila agreed.

"Sheila, this is Dick Wilson, manufacturing manager. Can you sign the proposal and get it back to us overnight? I need a signed proposal to get this thing in production."

"I'll look the proposal over tonight, and if everything is as it sounds, you'll have the signed order tomorrow."

Dick shrugged and smiled, "I tried."

When they hung up, Jake tied up loose ends. "We won't schedule the job until we get the signed order. We don't need another GE. Bob, call Budd and tell him we need that separator in Springfield next Monday. We don't want to work the weekend to complete the installation. Be a hero; tell him how hard you worked to get him his money. Janet, when you work up the proposal, try to keep it a bit under the price we quoted. You can bet Sheila will see you as her number one problem solver. She needs to get that system in as bad as we need the sale. The best part of it is we have the money in the project if we need to work the weekend but let's work, so we don't. We can use the additional profit."

Jake was departing for the weekend later that afternoon when Rob walked in. "We need to discuss your sales and production," he said, pulling a chair up to Jake's desk. His tone indicated it wouldn't be a short meeting or a pleasant one. "You're behind the power curve to make this month's sales goal, and production is lagging."

"Production isn't lagging, Rob. We're ahead of our production dollar per hour targets."

Rob pounded his fist on Jake's desk. "It sure doesn't show on sales or shipping reports."

"Trucks couldn't get in last week because of the snow, and those shipments —"

"I expect better. Do you understand?" The veins stood out on Rob's neck.

"Engineers and salesmen are working weekends —"

Rob cut Jake off, banging his fist on the desk. "I won't accept failure."

"Whoa!" Jake snapped. "We're short because your GE job hasn't come in. That's costing us both vendor friendship and inventory costs."

"You put GE on the list, or it wouldn't be in your sales projections," Rob snarled, refusing to accept responsibility for the problem. "Now round up those loafers and get hot."

Satisfied that everybody was doing all that could be done, Jake let Rob storm out. He purposely neglected to inform Rob about the Blackburn project, and when his phone buzzed, he ignored it, picked up his coat and briefcase, and departed for the day. Someone yelled from the doorway as he climbed into his truck. Fighting the temptation to look back, he started his engine and swung into the exit lane. A glimpse of Rob shaking his fist made Jake forget his headache as he headed for the interstate.

That only lasted until he considered the frailty of his position. Defeat hovered about as he wondered what else could go wrong. "Oh Lord, I see the end in sight. So can the team. What have we done to deserve this?"

Six hours later, the Brewers arrived on the hill tired from a problematic trip in blowing snow. Fresh tire tracks led in and out of their place, indicating something was wrong. Jake's heart beat faster as he considered who would be traveling at this time of night. Would Mac be right and the Hill Place be burned? When he backed in front of the house, he pulled his Colt revolver out with his flashlight in hand. He found the front door standing open, forced by something heavy. Inside, furniture lay tipped over, and someone threw the contents of the dining room buffet around the floor and cleared the top of the coffee maker and toaster. Pans, broken dishes, and silverware littered the kitchen floor. Furious, Jake kicked an iron skillet, cursing softly from the pain of impact.

Further devastation awaited upstairs. Dressers lay face down on their contents. Mattresses flipped off of their beds compounded the mess. A strong petroleum odor drew Jake into the middle bedroom. A red Chimfex tube designed to suppress chimney fires, most likely mistaken for a fusee, had been lit and tossed on the kerosene-soaked mattresses where it vented fire retardant. An empty matchbook from the Pandemonium Bar lay discarded on top of the mess, a symbol that said the lack of matches saved the place. Luck had been with them this time.

Choking, Jake opened the window and returned to the truck.

Dammit!" Jeanne screamed, smashing the dash with her fists when she learned of the problem. "Let's torch Coleman's place ourselves. At least I'd feel better about cleaning up another mess."

"And the cops will get us. Like football, the guy who returns the blows gets the penalty."

"What is it you're so fond of saying, 'The Good Lord takes care of them that take care of themselves?' Isn't that it? I'm out of patience with cops. I want to kill somebody. What are you afraid of, Jake?"

He softly answered, "I know what I can be. You wouldn't like me if you knew."

"I sure don't like things the way they are," Jeanne shouted angrily.

Jake quietly climbed in, backed the truck around, and headed for the Lacey's. They never seemed to sleep. Might miss something. A light peering through the softly falling snow suggested he was right. Getting grilled by the Buzzard and Crow is better than driving into Parker, Jake thought as he pulled into their driveway.

Blowing snow greeted Jake as he stepped out of his truck. The front door opened before Jake could get to the porch. "Come in," the Crow said eagerly. "What brings ya out this time of night?"

"Can I use your phone?"

"Calling the cops?" Crow asked, excitement rising in his voice. "They ain't doin' ya much good, are they?" he asked, a silly grin gracing his face. Sensing Jake's silent rage, Crow quit pressing. "Phone's on the table."

The Crow stood perched like his feathered namesakes, anxiously waiting to gather information. If Jake called from the Lacey's, Crow would hear the conversation. He pulled out his wallet, but Crow spoke before he found the number. "Let me get it. I know the number by heart, but I gotta punch it in myself. It's the way my mind works."

Jake provided the necessary information to the duty trooper and hung up. "Anyone other than Vances come in here tonight?" Jake asked, studying Crow's face.

"Not that I saw."

He was lying; it was in his eyes and his voice. "Joe, I'm in no mood to fool."

The threat settled on Crow's shoulders, telling him he was in trouble if he didn't cooperate.

Worried, his face white, Crow wiped a dirty handkerchief across the sweat collecting on his brow. "We can't get mixed up in this mess. Me'n Beatrice gotta live here."

Crow paused until the silence overwhelmed him. "You can see my problem, can't ya?" Crow pleaded, fearful of what might happen if he didn't talk and frightened that the wrong people would find out if he did. Jake stood waiting, his eyes narrowed. Crow couldn't find the strength to hold out any longer, "Jake, ya can't tell a soul, ya gotta promise."

Jake stepped closer, graying eyes boring in. Crow talked, told of seeing the Dodge truck drive slowly in just after dark, looked to be Swifty's, and after a bit, it came tearing out again. Crow tried to step back; an ashen look plastered his face. He bumped into the chair he had pulled out when he dialed the phone and fell into it. "Good god Jake, they'll torch my place if they find out I talked. Ya know they will. They torched the church and yer Grandaddy's place too."

Rage boiled up within Jake. His grandfather, his friend, the man who taught him the Bible, was murdered and burned beyond recognition in that arson fire. At his age, the old man couldn't protect himself. The coroner reported someone shot and severely beat him before the fire. Jake was serving in Vietnam at the time. The letter from his sister waited when he got off patrol.

"They'll kill me if they find out you was here," Crow said in a fearful voice. His chin quivered. "Good god, Jake, don't tell anyone I talked. Please, man."

"This'll be your secret to tell."

"Is someone down there, Joseph?" a sleepy voice called from the stairway. "I seen lights."

"We'll talk later," the Crow answered. Catching himself, he turned, seeking Jake's permission.

"Joe, if anyone finds out, it's because you talked, you or maybe Bea."

Jake completed the call and returned to the truck where Jeanne sat looking out her window. "Sorry it took so long, Jeanne. Sorry I talked rough to you too."

"I'm the one that should be apologizing, Jake, but I'm not going to. I'm upset. I could kill somebody."

"Please don't say that," Jake softly urged, knowing that she might be capable of the act. "Once you cross that line, your life changes forever."

"Somebody better do something soon, Jake Brewer!"

The Brewers headed back to Hill Place, waiting in silence until vehicle lights came around the bend in the road and pulled up alongside Jeanne's truck window. "This the Brewer Place?"

"It is," Jeanne answered angrily.

The trooper stepped out of his vehicle, engine running, lights on, and pulled on his coat. Jake stepped out to join him. "Corporal Poskevich," the trooper replied, shaking his hand.

"Jake Brewer," Jake returned, shaking his hand.

"Jake Brewer. Have we met? Name Sounds familiar."

"Not that I know of. You new here?"

"Be three weeks Wednesday. The dispatcher said someone broke in?" the trooper questioned, getting right to business. "Can we look at your problem?"

Jake quickly sized the man in the headlights, a stocky man with close-cropped hair showing gray at the temples and a professional air about him. Jake took the corporal through the home, showing him the problems as they went from room to room with the trooper jotting down notes in a memo book. He noted the calendar from the Parker Hardware in the kitchen and wrote something in his book. He occasionally shook his head as he took notes. In the master bedroom, he noted the pictures of a medal ceremony, Jake's retirement with his family surrounded by other Marines and a few civilians, and a wedding photo, taking notes without comment.

At the door to the small bedroom, the trooper sniffed heavily, "What's that smell? You can taste it."

"A kerosene sawdust fire starter mixed with zinc oxide from a fire retardant. It was mistaken for a fusee."

"Who did this?" The trooper asked, studying Jake's face.

This approach surprised Jake. Jake studied the corporal, realizing he was nearing mandatory retirement age, long past the age most troopers transferred into a place like Sterling County. His dark eyes were steady, looking directly into Jake's, and he seemed self-assured. "Ideas but no proof that would stand up in court."

Corporal Poskevich returned the intense face reading. "Mr. Brewer, give me what you know, then what you believe but can't prove. I'll try to sort out the difference. I heard the people at the end of the road know most of what's happening and can't wait to tell anyone who will listen. I'll stop and talk with them on the way out. What else should I know?"

Jake smiled wryly. Here was a man who sifted information, mixed in some hunches, and came up with an investigation that led somewhere. Understanding this, Jake provided background information on recent problems and the information he retrieved from the Crow. He also told him about Link's early release from prison, his threats, and what that could mean. "And I have a wife who is mad enough to spit nails."

"Understood," Poskevich replied. From what I've gathered, she has reason to be upset."

They talked as they returned to the front room, where the trooper noted the large logs that made up the outside wall. "Looks like someone built your place with hand-hewn logs."

"They did. My dad cut and barked them by hand. Mostly put them up by himself too."

"That would be Jackson Brewer of Brewer Logging. Already heard about him. Sounds like a real man."

"He is. Decorated Marine from the "Big War" as he calls it."

"Seems like he's earned a larger-than-life reputation."

Jake smiled, thinking this trooper probably had never uttered truer words.

"Got some nice pictures here. I love the Ned Smiths and the one of the elk. Like the cabin and lake painting over the fireplace too. Local artists?"

A man who lives just over the hill painted the elk picture. Jeanne painted the one over the mantle."

The trooper stopped when he came to an old log cabin photograph with an elderly man sitting in a chair on the porch and a young man sitting half turned on the porch railing. "Someone you know," he asked as he looked at the picture.

"That's my grandparents' place before it burned. My granddad is sitting in the chair smoking his pipe. That's me sitting on the railing. I was in high school."

"That the place that burned?"

"It was."

"I heard it's an unsolved murder and arson."

"It is," Jake agreed, wondering how this man had gathered so much information in such a short time.

"Anything else I should see?" the trooper asked as he looked up from his notes.

"Let's look outside," Jake suggested. When they were where they could see, Jake shined the light on the human tracks, "See anything strange?"

"They walk duck-footed," the trooper answered.

"Many in the family walk that way, some worse than others. Notice these tire tracks. They're nearly new tires with an aggressive off-road tread."

The trooper nodded, then stepped into the headlights and wrote some notes. "You staying here tonight?" the trooper asked, looking up from the headlights, his broad face and thick neck giving him the look of a determined bulldog.

"Plan to. No other place I'd feel welcome."

"I'll get fingerprints and some pictures before you begin cleaning up."

The trooper snapped photographs inside and outside before he began searching for fingerprints. Jake built a fire in the stove, and while it was coming to life, he carried water from the spring. The trooper finished his work and prepared to depart. "Look, if you think of anything else, call the barracks, and if I'm not there, tell the desk officer that you want to talk with me. Don't give them the information." They shook hands, and Poskevich departed, leaving Jake wondering why he shouldn't give information to others.

Jeanne came in with the trooper's departure. With the fire going, they heated water for the dishes and unpacked the cooler and groceries. They worked on, bone-weary, and at 2:30, their energy long drained, they collapsed in bed.

Poskevich arrived early the following morning while the Brewers drank coffee, and Jake invited him in for coffee and donuts. "Don't mind if I do," Poskevich agreed. "Us cops have a thing for donuts. I already had my daily quota at the Chat N Chew, but these look good."

Half grinning, Jake remarked, "You're up and about early this morning."

"Up late," Poskevich corrected him. "Haven't been to bed. I figured you'd have questions, so I dug up some answers." The trooper pulled his memo book from his shirt pocket, licked his thumb, and leafed back through a few pages, then stopped and read the page. "I discovered they have mean dogs over at Colemans. Also found the tread we saw on your road matched the tread on two Dodge trucks, one red and one black. The red truck belongs to Rusty Coleman, who worked on a State snowplow until after eight last night. The black truck belongs to Swifty. He just got out of the hospital. Shark was at the sawmill until a few minutes past four when Gore and Punk got off work. Swifty picked them up. Made Punk ride in the back."

You mean Mousey, not Punk," Jake interrupted, "Punk's too retarded to work."

"I mean Punk. Mouse left by himself in his old Chevy. Punk's worked at the sawmill since they discharged him from the hospital. Folks at the hospital cleaned him up. Hanratty strong-armed a church member who happens to be a mill co-owner, and he gave Punk a job. Hanratty hopes work will keep him out of here."

"What in the world could he do in a sawmill?" Jake asked in disbelief.

"They heat the mill and lumber kilns with the slab waste off the logs. Punk feeds the fire. They say he keeps at it."

"Well, I'll be," Jake returned without saying more.

"Talked to Hanratty before I came back. These Colemans stepped right out of a hillbilly novel. Course the crap they're pulling is becoming Main Street America stuff whether we want to admit it."

Jeanne angrily shook her head. "We've taken about all the Main Street America stuff we can handle."

"I've been praying for answers but haven't got any so far," Jake added.

"You think that praying stuff ever works?" Poskevich asked sarcastically, looking from Jake to Jeanne and back. 'If there's a god, I haven't found him."

"It works for us," Jake replied with conviction. "We strongly believe in God."

"Believe what you want, but what's it getting you?"

"It got you here. Your actions make me think things are looking up for us."

CHAPTER 15

Rob arrived for the emergency management meeting in a foul mood. After slamming his papers on the table, he turned with hands-on-hips, raring to deal an A-1 fanny fire. Surprise slid over his face as he eyed the new sales listed on the Write-Board. With most businesses closed for the weekend, he wrongfully believed the ESI team would have no new sales. Rob's disbelief followed Dexter's report of stock equipment sales and the two pieces of equipment sold by the service team for a West Virginia emergency job.

"We sold a rental tower," the rental manager announced. "They're getting the system they need, and we're selling equipment we may never rent again. It's paid for itself many times over, so it's all profit."

"How'd you get the sale?" Rob asked.

"Jake picked it up."

Fresh off the quick road trip he was assigned, Dexter asked about the GE contract. "GE is still the key to making our goal. How's that coming?"

"There's a glitch," Rob snapped. "But remember this, I expect goal made with or without GE!"

The phone buzzed, and Dick Wilson answered. "Yes, Wells, he's here." He handed Rob the phone.

"Good morning Mister Reeves. What can I do for you?" Rob cheerfully answered. Then after a pause, he replied, "I'll be right over with some great news." After hanging up and with the growl returned to his voice, he said, "Get hot. You still have considerable ground to cover."

As the door clicked closed behind Rob, Dexter mocked him. "Good morning Mr. Reeves; this is Rob, your superstar. I have great news about my superb accomplishments. May I come right over and kiss up —"

"Better pray the place isn't bugged," Bob Morrell suggested.

"He promised GE, falls on his sword, blames it on us, and takes credit for what we do to bail him out," Dexter said. "What an ass."

"Okay, Dexter," Jake spoke sharply. "Stop!"

"Jake, I called GE last night. No one promised Rob a contract."

"You sure?" Jake asked in a measured voice.

"Positive," Dexter answered in a pleasure-filled voice. "This won't bode well for Mister Priest, now will it? First, he moves it out a period at a time, and then —"

"Stop!" Jake stopped him once more. "We'll play the hand dealt. Winners win because they play their cards while losers whine."

The week passed quickly, and late Friday evening, the last day of the first business cycle, Rob paraded in as Jake worked on end-of-period reports. "Brewer, you had to try me on for size, didn't you? You and your incompetents are replaceable. Any more failure, and I'll be throwing people out in the street." When Jake didn't answer, Rob demanded, "Well, Brewer, don't you have anything to say?"

"What's to say?" Jake asked.

"You have nothing to say?" Rob barked. "You ensured Mr. Reeves you'd make the period, and he presented the information to Devron Power. There'll be hell to pay now."

"You told Wells you made the period when the Blackburn deal closed," Jake corrected. "You had to know GE wasn't coming in. Dexter did. He called them."

"Forget GE," Rob growled. "You're responsible for goal, but that could change. You're walking on thin ice."

A cold smile broke over Jake's face. Pulling a business card from his desk drawer, he scribbled a few words on the back, signed it, and handed it to Rob. "What's this?"

"What's it say?"

"I quit."

"That would be my resignation."

"I might remind you your annual performance evaluation isn't complete, and you'll need another job."

"The only way you can hurt me with an evaluation is to roll it into a sharp point and poke me in the eye. You wouldn't want to try that."

"Brewer, don't come back here begging for —"

"Rob, I'll never work with you or around you again. Now get your fat fanny out of here so I can pack my boxes!"

Jake fought through anger as he packed personal items. The drive home provided time to reflect on his sudden career change. He was worried. He needed a job. "Maybe Jeanne's right; maybe it's time to start writing," he said aloud.

As he thought through his situation, everything had roared around the bend of no return. "Lord, You know how badly I need Your help. I couldn't carry out the plan for our people, not and call myself a man. Please help me tell Jeanne."

He wasn't home long when the phone chirped. "Jake, Wells here. Rob said you resigned. Why?"

"I shave every morning and see a Christian man of his word. I'm not up to cheating people out of earned bonuses or rewriting job descriptions that shaft them out of overtime."

"It'll smooth out when we get by this initial month or two. You'll see. I need your support now more than ever before. You owe me that much."

"No, Wells, I don't owe you or anybody help with what's planned."

"Jake, I want you here. Think it over."

"Wells, the thinking part is behind me. You had to know I wouldn't be a part of this charade. It took me a few weeks to find it out for myself."

A wet blanket of doom descended with the click ending the phone call. Despondent and heavy-hearted, Jake knelt to pray. "Dear Lord, please help me. I'm fearful about all that's happening. Oh Lord, you have a perfect plan for me, but I can't see what it is. Where's my sign? Please don't leave me alone. Not now."

CHAPTER 16

Spring was winging in as Jake busied himself submitting resumes and attending offered interviews. Nothing followed in the way of a job that fit, and he grew edgier each passing day. There was no resolution to the latest incident at Hill Place which added to his frustration. This night Jake and Jeanne discussed a writing campaign, and Jake began work on letters to various officials informing them of the county situation.

"Send a letter to Don Maynard, Executive Director of the Parker Chamber of Commerce? His recent article in the paper inviting people to retire in Sterling County asked, 'Are you tired of crime and vandalism? Why not retire in peaceful Sterling County with its majestic mountains, beautiful streams, and serene forests, a paradise where you can live the life of your dreams.' That phony should live on the hill."

"He needs a letter," Jake agreed. Each letter detailed problems and the numerous investigations that resulted in nothing to date. He knew the letters weren't much, but they were a start that might spur action. After printing the letters, he faxed the letter requested by the Parker State Police stating the Colemans must not trespass on Brewer property.

The trip north that night was a tense one with little conversation. Jeanne was nervous with much of her dismay directed at Jake for refusing to take more decisive action. Passing the Vance home on the road into Hill Place, they viewed Misty's Park Avenue loaded with suitcases, hanging clothes, and boxes. "Oh Lord," Jake prayed to himself, "let me be helpful and not a hindrance."

"Need a hand?" Jake asked as he stepped out.

Dean paused, head down, "It's not much of a secret that Misty and I have problems, but God knows I didn't see this coming. I'm hoping her departure is temporary."

"Let us know if there's anything we can do to help."

Late that afternoon, Poskevich arrived to update Jake. "The fingerprints are back. None of the Coleman's showed up. Probably wore gloves."

"Don't tell Jeanne! She's already upset."

"Jake, I won't tell Jeanne anything, but I'm concerned about you. Sergeant Major Brewer, as they say in the Corps, it's a small world. You aren't exactly the Mister Rogers type. I was a Marine private when they took the picture of General Grant Johnson presenting Gunny Sergeant Brewer with a Navy Cross, Bronze Star, and two purple hearts for two separate actions. After the ceremony, our sergeant major said, 'Gunny Sergeant Brewer is one helluva marine.'"

Jake held up his hand to stop. "I remember that day, and I didn't feel like a hero. I was afraid I might be up for a medical discharge. Wondered why Jeanne would hang in with a cripple struggling along with two canes."

"That was your second Vietnam tour cut short with major wounds. Our sergeant major said you had NVA piled up like firewood after being wounded twice."

"Am I under investigation?"

"Not hardly. You can never know too much about the people involved in your cases. Sergeant Major Mitchell said Brewer had a hunter's eye, a killer's instincts, and fought like a Viking. Somewhere along the way, Brewer earned the nickname 'The Death Wind'"

"Ambrose Mitchell talks too much."

"Sergeant Major Mitchell thinks highly of you, Jake. He told me I'd better get this mess settled before you take matters into your own hands. Mitchell said if he wanted to describe a dangerous person, he'd picture Jake Brewer when he was upset. He also said Jake Brewer would get in my knickers. Said I'd know when it happened." A smile broke over the trooper's face, easing the tension.

Jake stood arms crossed, but his anger was draining. "Who else has this information?"

"Only the sources that provided it.

Pulling out his little green notebook, Poskevich leafed through his notes. "Spent some time at the Parker Hardware. I talked to Connie Smith and Loyce Bright, the owner. I met his brother Hardy too. They could be twins."

"That's the Bright brothers, OhSo and NotSo."

"Come again?" the trooper questioned.

"OhSo Bright and NotSo Bright."

"Loyce has to be OhSo, and that figures with what folks told me. Loyce followed me out of the store where we could talk. A couple of his lodge buddies are community leaders and believe this problem is bigger than you or the Colemans, and it might involve the DA and one of my cop brothers. He holds sympathy for the Coleman Clan's sad state and anger about their conduct. Said they do pay their bills."

"Corporal Poskevich, I was friends with a couple of Colemans before joining the Marines. Chance was as fine a friend as a man could have. He joined the Navy and never came home. They found his brother hung at the rock quarry. That family hasn't had it easy."

"Look, you can call me Glen or Poskie," the trooper said. "The Colemans may not have it easy, but they earn most of what they get from what I gather. The boys that hang out at the Chew seem to side with the Colemans because they're natives. I wanted to ask them what they thought you were, but you can't fight people you're pumping for information. The DA came in this morning. First time I met him. Pennington is not on your side. He mentioned the Colemans believe your family and the Vances stole a bunch of land from their grandfather, and Link's bragging before this is over, you'll be glad to give it back. I'll fill that picture in as I go."

"That stealing land is a bunch of crap, but I give you credit. You learned more in a few days than other investigations have turned up to date."

"Jake, I worked a lot of years as a detective. Your Parker Hardware Calendar got me started on leads that provided important info. The Chew sells donuts and has more than a few retired customers who need someone willing to listen to their time-worn stories. I fit that bill. That empty Pandemonium match pack has already provided leads, and it will be a gold mine when I have time to stop in without my uniform. That Pizza Palace menu on your fridge said you know someone there. The owner said you were close friends. The sheriff speaks highly of you and Jeanne. Should I go on?

"Look, our life has become a walk in darkness. Every time we think we see the light, it turns out to be a lightning bolt that knocks us flat. It's maddening. I'm ready to —"

"Careful, Jake, threats come back to haunt you. "For sure, I'd keep talk of retaliation to myself."

"Corporal, there are more problems here than meet the eye. Link's after us, but somebody sicced the Colemans on us. Somebody is making money off of them, and talk says big-time drugs are involved."

"Jake, we're thinking alike. I'll get to the bottom of this, but it will take time."

"What are we supposed to do in the meantime?"

"Gate your road with a steel gate that locks as soon as possible. That cable hanging on a tree with the no trespassing sign is useless. Get motion lights and cameras on the house. It would help if you considered installing a telephone and an alarm system that will ring into our barracks. For sure, I'd get Jeanne a handgun and teach her how to use it."

"That's a lot to consider. I'm unemployed."

"Jake, there's a lot at stake. I heard Adelphia is running free TV cables here on the hill and will soon hook phones to them."

Later that afternoon, Jake ran through his situation on his trip to town. Poskevich's recommendations made sense, but they required money, and with no job, Jake didn't have much to spare. What next, he wondered. After picking up groceries, Jake swung into Dixon's Guns and Fun Store to look at handguns. Money or not, Jeanne needed one.

After serving a hitch in the Navy, Barry Dixon returned home to the mountains he loved, married, and had a houseful of kids. An avid outdoorsman, Barry began the store part-time to support his hunting and fishing habits, and as the business grew, he migrated into running it full time.

"Afternoon, Jake; what brings you to town?"

"Thought I'd look at handguns."

"Fred Collins said you had problems. Plannin' on going to war?"

"Buying Jeanne a Mothers Day present."

"Could be the same thing. Hoped you were smarter than that," Barry chuckled, devilment in his eye. "No way I'd give my wife a gun. She'd stick it in my kisser every time I screwed off."

"There's your answer Barry," Jake grinned. "It's time to quit screwing off." Pointing at a small pistol in the case, Jake asked, "What's that, and what's it worth?"

"It's a Colt Government .380, worth about four hundred and sixty bucks."

"Pretty steep, Barry."

"Maybe I can give you some off," Barry said as he took the gun out. "I'll see what I got in it." He locked the slide back and handed it to Jake, grip first. "It's a scaled-down version of the 1911Army Colt 45. The only difference is this 'uns smaller and doesn't use the grip safety. It weighs less than a pound and a half. What else can I tell you?"

Jake hefted the gun, checked the chamber to ensure it was empty, and then pointed it at a deer mount on the wall. "Holds nice. Does it shoot?"

"Goes bang every time you pull the trigger."

"Right on, Smarty," Jake said, shaking his head. "Is it accurate?"

"Accurate enough for government work. Maybe that's why they call it the Government Model," Barry replied as he checked a notebook to see what he paid for the gun. "Hmmm. For you, I can let it go for four and a quarter. I'll throw in a box of shells to boot. Won't have money to buy baby shoes, but then barefoot keeps her home."

"I'll take it with me," Jake said.

"Law says you wait three days. That's soon enough to put your life in jeopardy."

"I hear you," Jake conceded as Barry began filling out the paperwork. "Those arrows are different," Jake remarked, pointing at a box behind the counter.

"They're special made. Swifty buys two dozen at a time. I only sell the Penn State blue and white ones to Colemans. Heaviest shafts made, special ordered at thirty-three-inch lengths. They all got ape arms. Hope Swifty buys them before his money runs out," Barry remarked.

"Works at the mill, don't he?" Jake asked, "Even Punk's down there."

"Did. Klinestiver fired them all an' sicced cops on them," Barry said, looking up from his paperwork. "Colemans found out they were gonna let Punk go for the summer. They don't fire boilers full time when it's hot, and he can't do much else. The other Colemans took exception because they spend Punk's check. Some of them loaded up at the Pandemonium. Wrecked one of the big forklifts at the mill, smashed windows, and poked holes in some truck radiators."

"Hope you get your money."

"Sooner or later. Hey, I was up yer way this morning listenin' for gobblers in the head end of the Cold Springs Gorge. I watched a cop drive in about daylight. Was it Ratty?"

"New guy. Poskevich," Jake answered.

"He's been in. Bought some topographical maps. Tough-looking bugger."

"I'd want him on my side."

The week passed quickly with Jake waiting to pick up Jeanne's new .380 on Saturday morning. When it was his turn, Barry placed the pistol on the counter. "Could a sold your gun half a dozen times this morning."

"Jeanne's gun," Jake corrected, paid Barry, and headed for the sheriff's office for a permit. In the truck, Jeanne carefully looked it over. "Thanks, Jake," she smiled, "I love you."

"You're welcome. The shells are on the dresser."

Jake took a deep breath and inhaled the familiar smells from childhood as he walked into the old courthouse. His grandfather had served two terms as sheriff here, and the building held memories. High ceilings and ornate woodwork had survived well over the years; the floor glistened. The person who maintains this building exhibits a lot of love for it; Jake thought as they walked to the sheriff's office, their heels clicking on the old oak floors.

"Morning, Sheriff," Jake greeted. "Been a while."

"Since you got your last pistol permit," Porky replied. "Good to see ya."

"Be careful. A guy who would lie about that might lie about other things too."

"C'mon, Brewer," Porky protested. "It's good to see you. Barry said you'd be by with the little woman. Way things are headed, everybody should be armed, maybe with bazookas."

"That bad?" Jake asked.

"Received your letter, and you seem to think so. I plan to use the letter to put pressure on some folks. We have problems with the DA. His priorities are reelection, chasing skirts, and maybe something else. And that's the nice things I have to say about Mr. DA. Criminals get off time and again with small fines or time served. Looking at Jeanne, he asked, "Marie ain't it, your middle name, I mean?"

Jeanne nodded.

"Need a picture for your ID," the sheriff said, picking up his Polaroid. "Step right up to that line. Look here - now smile. Hold it." After the flash, he added, "I need three professional type people's names and phone numbers to verify you're okay to carry a firearm. I'll get police checks out today. Try to have the permit for you in a week."

"I'll be waiting," Jeanne agreed and provided the necessary information.

"That'll be ten bucks, Jake," Porky said. "It's a special rate for you."

"Everybody else getting permits for five?" Jake queried.

"Sounds about right," Porky grinned. "Get a little more from flatlanders. We can smell big bucks on you guys."

"Porky, if I had your money, I'd pile what little bit I have in your ashtray and burn it. Would hardly see the flame."

"Get your pant legs up," Porky said, hiking his. "It's too late to save your shoes."

CHAPTER 17

Dust boiling up behind his truck added to the ugly mantle on the trees lining the road, a picture not unlike Jake's mood. He considered the reception he'd receive. Hearing the vehicle, Dean peeked through the curtains before walking out. He looked rough but called out in a voice absent of the raw nerves apparent a week earlier. "Got time for coffee?"

"I do. How's it going?"

"So glad you asked," Dean answered sarcastically. Thinking better of his tone, he began again. "Had a rough time taking Misty to her parents. She didn't mention divorce, but it's coming. Her old man has been agitating for this for a long time, but he isn't the only problem; there are signs of another man. She talked about you a lot after the storm, and I thought there might be something. I checked our long-distance phone bills."

"She didn't call, and I didn't either. No reason to."

"Affairs of the mind are difficult, but it's maddening when the heart is involved."

"It is," Jake agreed.

The conversation stalled, and Jake excused himself to dig gate post holes. "I'm expecting a call from Sherrie; then I'll be over."

"Better bring gloves. It's solid rock."

"Won't need gloves. I can hand tools and keep you company without hurting myself."

"As Jeanne would say, right, Buster," Jake said as he stood up to depart. "And speaking of Jeanne, she said to invite you down for supper and don't accept any excuses."

"Can't make any promises with my active social calendar." Dean smiled, a first for the day.

Dean followed Jake outside, talking as they walked. Jake had the door open and one foot in his truck when a piercing scream rode up through the trees. "Heeeeeellllppp!" Jake knew Jeanne's cry. Panic seized him. "Call the cops!" Jake yelled, jumping into his truck.

Stones rattled against the fenders as he gunned the truck out across the hill. His heart pounded as he slid sideways around the sharp curve at the top of the mountain and headed down the steep grade. Jake drove out of the woods and slid the truck into the field, cutting the trip in half. His heart hammered in his ears. Clearing the top corner of the field, he could see where Rusty Coleman leaned against the fender of his new truck sitting in front of the garage. Jake aimed dead on and floored it, grabbing the magnum from under the seat.

Alerted by vehicle noise, Rusty stood watching out along the lane until he saw Jake speeding directly at him from the field above. Hysteria followed. Jumping into his truck, he laid on the horn with one hand and hit the starter with the other.

Soon after Jake departed, Jeanne had layer cakes baking and frosting working. A noise beckoned her when she switched off her electric mixer. Curious, she hurried to the living room, arriving just in time to see a giant hand push through the screen to unlock the door. "Heeeeeellllppp." Screaming, she ran for her gun. Link lunged and grabbed her as she passed. She sank teeth into his hand, clamping down with all her strength, drawing blood.

"You little whore, look what ya did," Link howled angrily. Blood ran off of his hand.

Instantly furious, he hurled Jeanne backward onto the sofa. She instinctively threw up her feet. One foot slammed into Link's face; the other caught his throat. Jeanne kicked forward with all her strength. Link slammed against the stone fireplace and cut his head.

Jeanne screamed and ran for her pistol. Link lunged like a big cat. Snagging her ankle, he pulled her to the floor. He jerked her to him, his prison-built muscles easily overpowering this woman half his size. Jeanne rolled over and kicked, hitting Link a glancing blow in the privates. He grunted, bent forward, gathered his senses, then struck savagely.

Straddling her legs, he fended off her blows with one hand and shredded her blouse with the other. Mustering strength, Jeanne dug her nails into his face and pulled forward with all the power left in her. Blood ran from deep gashes across Link's cheeks. Link backhanded her, snapping her head against the floor. Her lights went out.

"Fight now, ya little whore," Link grunted, wiping blood from his face. He tore Jeanne's zipper down and attempted to jerk off her Levis. When he couldn't, he grabbed them by the crotch seam, and straining, tore them apart. He discarded them, tore off her underwear, and forced her legs apart. Grunting from exertion, Link snarled, "You'll pay now. Yer gonna get it good."

"BeeeeeeeeeP" A horn blared, and Rusty's engine started. Puzzled, Link looked out the window in time to witness Jake's truck slamming to a stop against Rusty's. Jake jumped out, firing a shot in Rusty's direction. For a split second, he thought about taking Jake on, gun and all, but decided against it. He bolted for the back door, struggling to get his pants up as he ran.

Jake dove through a window, landing on the sun porch. Glass flew, and he scrambled into the front room. Jeanne lay crumpled on the floor, bleeding. Kneeling beside her, he felt her throat for a pulse, "Oh God, please help her." Her pulse was strong, and he gently laid her on the sofa.

With a metal against metal screech, tires spinning, Rusty pushed Jake's truck backward. He spun past Jake's truck and slid to a stop at the back porch where Shark stood as the lookout. Link crashed through the screen door, and both Colemans scrambled into the truck. Rusty gassed the truck, trying to turn back up through the yard. The powerful engine spun the truck sideways out of control and into a clothes pole. The crossbar severed from the post. Lines to the second pole jerked taunt and drug the hooks back through the hood. The Ram careened down the steep bank through Jeanne's flower garden, smashing through the split rail fence at the bottom. Fencing flew. Out of control, they jumped over the bank into the lower field, bouncing the truck high into the air. Landing on the second bounce, the truck slid sideways, hitting the old stone fence, and almost rolled over.

Link grabbed the wheel, stomping Rusty's accelerator foot to the floor. The surge of raw power spun the truck, and it careened sideways, throwing sod clumps. Gaining traction, they tore across the field toward the Vance

Homestead. Rusty screamed as they slid to a stop in front of the steel gate across the Vance road. "How are we gonna get outta here, Link?"

"Turn around. We'll go up the old road by Brewers."

"Brewer'll kill us," Shark protested. "You ain't foolin' with some woman now."

"Turn this friggin' truck around."

Link spun the wheel to the left and jammed the accelerator, spinning the truck around. They shot down the ditch headed toward the old dug road at Brewers. "Drive!" he commanded Rusty.

"We should leave the truck and run for it," Shark muttered.

"Not when I can ride," Link snapped.

Link held the accelerator to the floor. Rusty fought for control as the truck shot forward.

Shark slid down in the seat, his eyes big. Never before had he known such fear.

In Hill Place, fury raged through Jake. Jeanne's eye was rapidly swelling; blood ran from her nose and the corner of her mouth. Jake picked a blanket off the sofa back and gently covered her nude body.

"EEEEEEIII!" Jeanne screamed as she saw the form leaning over her. "It's okay, Jeanne," Jake said softly, touching her gently. "They're gone." In a worried voice, she asked with pleading eyes, "Did he get me, Jake?"

"No, Honey, I got here in time." His focus returned to Link. He raced up steps two at a time to the bedroom and scooped the M-1 carbine from the hideaway holder inside his bed frame. He released the slide. The bolt slammed home a round with a deadly "Kerthunk" as he raced for the deck. Rusty's truck sped into view. Steadying the rifle, Jake squeezed off a shot that blew out the front tire on the driver's side. The truck careened out of control and nearly rolled, sliding sideways down through the field. Dirt flew. The back end slid around in front. The rim on the flattened tire dug in. The truck rolled cab away from Jake. Glass flew as the force crushed windows. The truck slid to rest on its side, drivers' side down.

Inside, men scrambled wildly to separate themselves. Shark got loose and climbed out the window, crouching behind the truck expecting more shots. Pain pounded his forehead, and he put his hand up to inspect. Blood oozed around his fingers. He clutched the wound to stem blood flow with one hand while he pulled a filthy red handkerchief from his back pocket.

He rolled the cloth round on his leg, then slid part of it under the hand holding the wound. Grabbing both ends of the dirty rag, he tied it.

"Help me outta here!" Link growled from inside.

Link was a load. Brutishly big and muscular, he couldn't crawl out the window. With Shark's help, he managed to get the door open and climbed free. Link sat on the ground behind the truck and caught his breath. Noticing Shark's handkerchief, Link laughed. "Ya look like a friggin' pirate."

"We gotta get out of here," Shark begged, but he was too scared to move.

"Get Rusty first," Link snarled, motioning toward Rusty.

Shark sat frozen in fear. Noting the problem, Link reached in with one powerful arm feeling for his brother; the other arm braced against the side of the truck. Finding him, Link dragged Rusty free of the vehicle and dumped him on the ground. Dazed, Rusty would have to be carried out or abandoned. Leaving him would ruin the stolen truck story. Shark wasn't strong enough to carry him far, which left Link.

"Run for it!" Link commanded Shark and shoved him out from behind the truck. Fearful, Shark streaked for the woods. When no shots followed, Link shouldered Rusty and ran for the tree line.

They struggled through the woods until Link winded and dropped Rusty, slumping down beside him to catch his breath. Rusty complained, "My truck's ruined, and my ankles busted."

"Shut up!" Link said. "We're headed home. Gotta be there when the cops come."

Jake followed the men racing for the woods in the carbine's sights, resisting the powerful temptation to end their lives. Satisfied they wouldn't be back, he slipped the gun safety on and returned to help Jeanne. Now dressed, she was coming down the steps carrying her new Colt with tears running down her cheeks. Old Gus followed. "You okay, Honey?" Jake asked.

"No, I'm not alright," Jeanne said through clenched teeth. "And if I would have had this gun, that ass wouldn't be either."

Jake helped her in the truck without comment and put Gus in with her. "Lock the doors. Head for Dean's if they come back," Jake directed. "Run over them if they get in your way."

"Where are you going?"

Jake trotted off without answering, his father's words running through his mind. "When you know there's gonna be a fight, and you can't walk away, get the first licks in and make them good ones." Maybe he shouldn't have let them get away. They'd be back with a vengeance.

The new Dodge looked strangely different, laying on its side with the door pointing skyward as if saying, "I surrender." Peering inside, Jake saw a shotgun and a box of arrows lying where they had fallen when the truck rolled to a stop. He laid his carbine on the ground and retrieved the shotgun and arrows, throwing the arrows on the ground beside the carbine. He walked around the truck and stabbed holes in the bottom of one of the fuel tanks with his pocket knife, and holding the shotgun at arm's length, he turned his head away and fired into the gushing gas.

BAWHOOM! The ensuing explosion flattened him.

He tossed the shotgun into the truck cab, shielding his face from the intense heat. He emptied the arrow box and threw the box into the fire, then grabbed the carbine and arrows. Running to the house, he paused at the drain pipe for the back gutters and pushed the arrows in out of sight. Breathing raggedly, Jake rushed inside, peeled off his smoke-blackened shirt, and wet a washcloth to clean soot from his face and hair. He eased into a ball cap and a flannel shirt to hide singed hair and burns, grabbed the carbine, and hurried for the front door. Jeanne unlocked the door, and he slipped in behind the wheel.

"What was that explosion?"

"Truck." That was enough information, Jake thought, noting how badly Link beat her. "I'm sorry, Jeanne."

"This isn't over," she snapped, intense anger evident in her strained voice. "Link Coleman might get away with beating some people, but he won't get away with beating me."

Dean was getting in his truck as they drove in. "Everything all right," Dean asked as Jake got out. Looking into the truck, he knew better. Turning to Jake, he said, "Sherrie called just as you left. I told her there was an emergency. Then the cop's phone was busy. Took forever to get through."

An explosion ripped across the hills.

"What was that?" Dean excitedly questioned, pointing at the billowing smoke.

"Hard to tell," Jake replied, thinking it was probably the second gas tank.

"What happened?"

Jake provided a partial explanation as they watched the smoke. Sirens coming closer howled along the mountain tops. Accompanied by an occasional explosion, smoke rose, carrying the acrid smell of burning rubber, fuel, and plastic mixed with paint. Jeanne sat in the truck, anger etched on her face.

Sirens blared ever louder, accompanied by vehicle noise. A fire truck rolled in, followed by a police cruiser, their dust cloud swarming over them.

"The fire tower reported heavy smoke in here somewhere," the driver said, "an' that cop is looking for a problem." Without turning, Jake pointed his thumb over his shoulder in the fire's direction. "Damn," the driver said excitedly as he saw thick, black smoke swirling up over the trees. "How do we get down there?"

"Right down that road," Jake pointed. The driver acknowledged understanding, quickly shifted into reverse, and backed into the police cruiser with a resounding crunch. Without stopping, he roared off toward the fire.

The trooper stood listening to Jake's directions and held his hands over his face when the fire truck backed into his squad car. "Is that where the problem is?" the young officer asked nervously.

"Was," Jake corrected him. "It's over now."

"It doesn't look over," the trooper answered, pointing at the smoke. "I smell trouble."

"That's smoke you smell," Jake returned, showing his frustration. "My wife had the trouble. You might want to ask her what happened, officer."

The officer rushed around to the passenger side of the pickup, where he noticed Jeanne's severe beating. "You okay, ma'am," he asked innocently.

Feeling mean, Jeanne answered. "If you mean am I still breathing, yes, I'm still breathing. And, yes, I'm mad, and Link Coleman will pay for what he did to me. Keep your shoes shined, young man; Link Coleman may need pallbearers."

"Ma'am, you can't take the law into your own hands. This is a job for —"

"Better stick to ticketing speeders and siren blowing, things you can handle. You're out of your league when it comes to bad guys."

Jake was uncomfortable. This wasn't Jeanne's nature, but then she wasn't used to being manhandled, Jake thought as he drove off toward Hill Place.

Jeanne squeezed his arm. "I love you, Jake," she said softly. "And before you say anything about my being nasty to that cop, I took the cue from you."

"Me?" Jake questioned.

"Ya, you. I heard the BS you gave him and followed suit."

"Be careful, Jeanne."

"Careful? Torching their truck isn't exactly being careful."

"What?" Jake questioned innocently.

"Hey Buster, I may be slow, but I'm not stupid," Jeanne said. "I heard the explosion and smelled smoke on you. You torched their truck."

Jake allowed the comment to slide past without comment as they entered the drive. "Oh my god, Jake, the house is on fire!" Jeanne screamed, pointing to the smoke billowing out the kitchen window.

Jake slid the truck to a stop and ran for the house. Jeanne followed. Smoke poured out of the kitchen door as they entered the heavy, near opaque air. The origin of the problem struck Jeanne. "My cake!" In the limited light, she grabbed potholders, opened the oven, and threw the smoking mess out into the yard. "That's why I didn't hear him enter," Jeanne said.

"Because your cake was on fire?" the puzzled trooper asked.

"No, dammit, because I was making icing. Coleman's alive because of a noisy mixer."

The officer shrugged, not knowing what to say. Jeanne pointed at the cake, "Well, buddy, it might not be my best job, but there's your birthday cake."

"My cake?" Jake questioned in surprise.

"Today's your birthday. You always say you liked spur-of-the-moment things; they work out better. This is your kind of shindig."

Jake shook his head, "I must admit this is a surprise."

CHAPTER 18

Dean arrived with Hanratty closely behind. The trooper met them as they got out of their vehicles, hand gesturing and nodding. "What happened?" Hanratty asked.

Jake looked carefully into Hanratty's eyes as he provided attack highlights. "Where are the perpetrators now?" Hanratty asked, holding his tablet ready to write.

"Last I saw, they drove their truck down over the bank and parked in front of our place," Jake answered. "You can see it from the deck."

"Let's have a look," Hanratty said as he walked toward the deck. Jake fell in beside him, watching closely to witness Hanratty's expression.

"Good lord," Hanratty implored when he spotted the truck. "What happened?"

"Must have caught fire," Jake replied, fighting to paste innocence on his face.

Dean added what he heard. "After I called you guys, the Brewers arrived. Explosions began going off sporadically - then a loud boom. Black smoke boiled up out of here, followed by more explosions. Then we heard sirens and the fire truck and cruiser came rolling in."

"What time was that?" Hanratty questioned without looking up from his writing.

"Not sure," Dean answered.

"Who called the fire truck?" Hanratty asked.

"Must have been the fire tower."

"What caused the truck fire?"

"Maybe the Colemans torched it for an alibi."

"Come on, Dean," Hanratty said condescendingly. "Nobody would torch a new truck for an alibi. What do you take them for?"

"Fools, rapists, thugs, liars, thieves —"

"OK," Hanratty said. "I asked for that."

Hanratty turned to Jake. "What can you tell me about the fire?"

"Dean said it all."

"You smell like smoke Jake," Hanratty said suspiciously.

"We had a bad cake fire," Jake replied innocently.

"Cake fire?"

"Yeah. My birthday cake burned when Jeanne had to run from the rapist Dean mentioned. Want to see it?"

"Let's look at that truck," Hanratty answered curtly, ignoring the cake fire.

Hanratty approached a fireman and asked who was in charge. The driver pointed to a tall man standing beside the truck, taking off his coat, his face blackened by smoke. "Smitty's in charge, Ratty," and turned to place his fire gear on the truck.

Hanratty rankled; he detested that name. "What do you make of this Smitty?"

"An expensive rig's destroyed, and the fire didn't do it all."

"Why do you say that?" Hanratty questioned.

"The hoods been ripped back like a big claw grabbed it," Smitty replied.

"I'd guess that happened when they mowed down our clothes' pole," Jake suggested.

"Ratty, I'd look it over. Your inquiring mind might come up with something new for a change."

Hanratty disliked Smitty's tone and answer, but he walked around the truck, describing details in his notes. Returning to the firemen, he asked if they had any other information.

"Yeah, Ratty, I do," Smitty volunteered brusquely. "It's time them Colemans got what's coming to them. Take care of them idiots, and let the good Samaritans alone."

Hanratty ignored the comment. "Thanks for your cooperation."

"We're tickled to help Ratty," Smitty returned sarcastically. Hanratty wasn't forgiven. Not long after he arrived at the troop, Hanratty arrested a volunteer fireman for drinking and driving after returning from fighting a fire and having a few beers at the fire hall.

The sound of a third police vehicle alerted the group. "Just came from the Colemans," Johnston, the newly arrived trooper, informed them. "They reported Rusty's pickup stolen. It's a beauty too."

"Was a beauty," Hanratty corrected, pointing at the burned hulk.

"Wow! What happened?" Johnston asked.

"Looks like Rusty drove Link and another brother in here. How did Rusty look?"

"Rusty's bunged up and limping, and Shark has a head wound."

Hanratty made a few notes in his book. "Did they seem worried?"

"Rusty was. Shark was his belligerent self."

"Was Link around?" Hanratty asked.

"Shark said he went fishing last night. Won't be back for a few days."

Jake felt heat rising through his face. "While you're gathering facts, here's one for you. The guys in that truck tried to rape my wife. Ask her if she might be able to identify them."

"Can we talk to her now?" Hanratty asked, struggling to maintain a calm voice.

"If she'll talk to you," Jake said. As they entered the house, Jake called Jeanne. "Officer Hanratty has questions for you."

"Let's sit on the deck. The house is full of smoke."

Hanratty shook his head in disbelief when Jeanne sat down. Someone had beaten her badly. Gathering his thoughts, he asked for details.

"I can tell you what happened until I was knocked unconscious," Jeanne responded coldly.

She described the assault and then added, "Write this down, officer. Link Coleman attacked Jeanne Brewer on this day, and Link Coleman will pay dearly."

"I can't say who did this until I can prove it."

"Just write it down," Jeanne snapped, cutting him off. "I have something else for your investigation." With that, Jeanne retrieved an envelope from the bathroom. "Here's some meat from Link's face," Jeanne said, her anger ringing.

"Where'd you get that?" Hanratty asked quietly.

"Under my fingernails. I dug it out of Link's face when he was pounding me."

"I'm not sure how good it will be for evidence, but —"

"Officer, I'm not an evidence expert, but if I give you skin that I say I dug out of Link Coleman's face, and you find Link Coleman, and he has skin dug out of his face, and this skin proves to be his, wouldn't you say there may be some connection between the two incidents?"

"How'd the intruder get in?" Hanratty asked, eagerly changing directions.

"Why don't you take a look?"

The screen held an extended cut just outside the latch area. Hanratty mentally measured the length of the gash and noted the screen had been pulled outward, most likely by someone pulling his hand back. Surveying the broken windows and glass lying around on the sun porch, Hanratty asked about it.

"I came home in a hurry," Jake answered.

Hanratty looked Jake's shirt over for glass and noted his hand burns. "Where did the assault occur?" Hanratty asked, looking at Jeanne now.

"In the living room," she said, pointing at her jeans. She described the rest of the scene as it replayed through her mind. She added, "I want him tested for AIDS too."

"I can't promise that, Jeanne," Hanratty said softly. "I can understand —"

"Suppose I shoot the bastard and take samples for testing. Would that suit better?" Jeanne asked with bitterness boiling over in her voice.

"It's best to exercise patience."

"Screw patience; I want to kill someone," Jeanne raged.

The officer looked away. Picking up Jeanne's torn jeans with his pen, he looked them over, noting what he saw. "May I take these with me?"

"I'll get a bag," Jeanne procured a garbage bag, and Hanratty dropped them in. Spotting the underwear and shredded blouse, he put those in without asking.

Hanratty hesitated before broaching the last area. "Jeanne, I'd like to ask you a few personal questions. You don't have to answer them, but the defense will ask them in court. Do you mind?"

"No."

"Did you allow him into your home?"

"Are you nuts?" Jeanne asked. "You saw the screen."

Hanratty wrote down the comments. "Did either of you give the Colemans permission to be on your property after the 'No Trespass' order?"

The Brewers simultaneously shook their heads. Hanratty paused briefly, mentally framing the next question. Jeanne grew uneasy. "Have you ever given the intruder reason to believe you were interested in him, or have you had past relations with this person?" This was a touchy question, and Hanratty wished Jeanne were alone when he asked it. Her voice told him it didn't matter who was present; the answer would have been the same.

"Officer, I'm not sure what you think I am. I never led any man on, and I damned sure never had any relation with Link Coleman. Now leave my home."

"Mrs. Brewer, please don't —

"My friend," Jake interrupted, warning in his voice, "My wife asked you to leave. You better go." He handed the plastic sack with the clothes to the officer, pointing to the door.

Hanratty took the clothes and paused to apologize. "I appreciate your disgust, but I had to ask that question after recent events. Thank you for your cooperation."

When Hanratty departed, Jeanne collapsed, sobbing into Jake's arms. "Oh, Jake, I'm so scared."

Jake held her close. This unfamiliar Jeanne usually took everything dished her way, but not today. Link gave her a load beyond her ability to carry. "Jeanne, this will not go unpunished."

Later that afternoon, Trooper Elvis Presley Johnston reached for the Squire's doorbell, hesitated, and pushed it with trepidation. After a bit, he nervously rang it again. From inside, a voice boomed, "Hold your horses. I'm comin'."

Johnston made a face and stepped away from the bell as if it were radioactive. Footsteps stomped toward him. The door slammed open against the wall, and the justice busted through. "Yer in a powerful hurry," the Squire angrily remarked. "This the Coleman problem, Officer?"

"Yes, your honor," Johnston confirmed. "We have Rusty and Shark for felony assault and attempted rape. We're still hunting Link. He beat her unconscious, but she got in some licks too."

"Did he get in her pants?"

"He didn't rape her if that's what you mean. He —"

"That's what I meant. Did he rape her, and you say 'No.' Is that it?"

"Yes, your honor," Johnston agreed. "Link tore off her clothes, but Jake got home before he could finish."

"Wonder Brewer didn't kill him. His old man would," the Squire said, seemingly unable to comprehend why a man wouldn't kill someone who tried to rape his wife. "What'd Brewer do?"

"Somebody torched Coleman's truck."

"Wouldn't spend a lot of time investigating no truck fire. Go on!"

Johnston explained what was known to that point, licked his thumb, and went through his notes to make sure he covered everything. At the Squire's order, he departed to retrieve the Coleman brothers. Squire saw Rusty struggling to walk with a crutch and the blood-encrusted rag around Shark's head as they entered. "What's that boy?"

"It's a nose rag, yer honor. I cut my head," Shark answered meekly as they stepped into the square in front of Squire's podium.

"Did you have yer rights read to ya, and did ya understand them?"

"Yes, yer honor." Both Colemans replied in unison.

"Do ya want an attorney present?"

"No, yer honor," came the simultaneous reply.

Satisfied that they had taken all the proper steps, the Squire continued. "OK, Mr. Coleman, supposin' you tell me how you hurt yer head."

"Had an accident."

"At the Brewer place?"

"No yer honor, I was workin' an' —"

"Don't lie to me!" Squire bellowed and stepped closer.

Shark's fear of Squire showed in his eyes, but he was equally afraid Link might kill him. He looked at the floor. "I was limbin' trees, an' one flew back an' about tore my head off. That's —"

"— a lie, and you know it, boy. Look at me when you talk to me," the furious justice roared. Shark had a dilemma. He could tell the truth, and Link would get him, or he could lie, and the Squire would tear him up;

those were his choices. He stuck to his story; his growing hatred of the Brewers made the difference. "I had me an' accident," Shark answered.

"Boy, do you know how to handle the truth?"

"I don't know," Shark replied in a barely audible voice.

"What do ya mean, ya don't know?" Squire howled angrily.

"I'm not sure, yer honor," Shark replied, looking away.

"Damn yer soul, do ya have anything to say of a truthful nature?"

"No, yer honor," Shark mumbled softly.

"Anybody else have anything to add to these proceedings?" Squire asked as he looked to Johnston, then Shark, and finally to Rusty.

"No yer honor," came the unanimous reply.

"I'm remandin' you over for trial. Put him in your car!" the Squire ordered, pointing at Shark. When the officer departed carrying out his order, the Squire began again in a low voice.

"Rusty, this ain't like you. Why'd you go down to the Brewers?"

"Link shoved a gun in my face, yer honor," Rusty said quietly. "He said no flatlander's gonna tell us Colemans where we can go or what we can do. Them Brewers and Vances stole our land. Link's ready to go back ta jail to purtect our rights."

"Yer ol' man made the same claim at the Commercial Hotel. Jackson Brewer drove home and got the deed and a sales letter. Your great-granddaddy thanked them for buying it so he didn't lose it to taxes. You have no right to another man's property, and the law told you to stay outta there. What were you gonna do?"

"Can't say."

"Rusty, tell me! It might keep you out of the pen."

Rusty paused a bit, fidgeting and sweating, then began in a hoarse whisper. "Link was gonna beat Brewer's ass an' screw his woman 'cause they got that trespass thing on us. He said that the 'no trespass' order violates our rights. He's tired of everybody pickin' on us."

"Rusty, ya gotta know better than that," the Squire said, maintaining a low, calm voice. "Folks may pick on you some, but you deserve most of the problems that come yer family's way. You know that, don't you?"

"Yes, yer honor."

"Them Brewers might not be the people to fool with. Old Jackson Brewer's one tough man and the boy's grandfather had plenty of sand too," the Squire warned.

"I never wanted to go down there," Rusty replied, his voice choking, "specially not after drivin' that old Chevy 'til I had cash money for my new truck."

Squire nodded understanding, "Boy yer both an accessory and a victim. We gotta jail you. It's legally correct, an' if we don't, Link's gonna wonder why."

Johnston arrived just as Rusty appeared as if he had something else to say. "What is it, boy?

Speak up!" Squire ordered.

"I'll lose my state job if I go to jail, yer honor. Hank Calloway won't put up with missin' work. I won't have nothin' left," Rusty said passively.

"I'll call Hank myself," the Squire volunteered. "Maybe I can work something out."

"Thank you, yer honor."

"Anything else?" Squire asked, looking from one person to another.

"With your permission, your honor, I should get this man to a doctor before turning him over to the sheriff," Johnston said. "Should get Shark stitches too."

"Shark can get himself stitched in jail," Squire boomed. "Drop Mr. Shark off at jail and then get Rusty over to the medical center."

CHAPTER 19

The morning sun bore down through the cloudless sky this Saturday morning. Stifling heat brought sweat that rapidly soaked Jake as he dug holes for steel gate posts. It was slow going in the rock, breaking the shale with the heavy bar he now leaned on. A blister formed under his wedding band, and he worked it off, placing it on a nearby stump with his watch. Old Gus trotted toward him, kicking up clouds as his feet struck the dusty road. Jake wiped the sweat off his face and stepped over to his truck for a drink, pouring cold spring water for him and his dog friend.

Gus drank thirstily and then laid under the truck. Jake returned to his digging and striking harder rock; he began busting it with a twelve-pound sledge and rock bar. He found satisfaction in this work, feeling his muscles strain as he pulverized his way down to the desired depth.

Mid-morning, he cleaned the hole and measured for depth. Good, he thought to himself, a little more than I needed. Satisfied, he carried his tools to the other side of the road and measured for the second hole.

Time was closing in on the noon hour when the muffled roar of an engine roared closer on the abandoned road. Engine noise echoed through the mountain tops. Shark rolled up on a four-wheeler, geared down, and spun a circle in the road, scattering dogs that howled angrily, raising the hair on Jake's neck.

"Morning, Shark," Jake greeted flatly. Tormented into killing machines, the dogs inched forward, lips bared from flashing white teeth, hackles bristling. Jake's heart pounded. Five killers sensed his fear and closed. Shark made no effort to restrain them.

"Scared Brewer, you truck burnin' bastard?" Shark asked with a mean smile that showed yellow teeth. Before Jake could answer, Shark yelled, "Sic 'em!"

Jake dove into the back of his truck. Two dogs followed. Jake kicked, catching one dog in the face, booting him out of the truck. The remaining dog ripped his extended leg, tearing deeply into the muscle. Lashing out with the other leg, Jake hit her on the side of the face with his work boot.

The frenzied dog tore at Jake, ripping his legs, snarling savagely, blood dripping from its mouth. Jake kept kicking, booting the dog out of the truck. He jerked the tailgate up behind him and pulled the cap door down.

Shark stood on the four-wheeler, laughing uproariously, pointing under his truck. Gus. Those dogs have Gus, Jake thought. A sick feeling grabbed him. He threw the cap door up to climb out. It was too late. Two dogs stretched Gus between them while others tore at him, shredding the Cairn terrier.

Gunning the engine, Shark whistled shrilly. "Phwweett!" The dogs turned their attention to him, wary that Shark might attack. "Better quit screwin' with us, Brewer," Shark yelled above the noise and roared off.

As the sound of his attackers faded in the distance, Jake checked his legs. Blood flowed out of ugly tears. He slipped his T-shirt over his head, tore it in half, and tied pieces over the worst of the wounds. He tied his handkerchief over another hole, then gingerly climbed out of the truck, his legs throbbing painfully, as he limped over to his mutilated friend. Tears streaked Jake's dirty face as he surveyed the body. Kneeling in the dusty road, he carefully lifted old Gus into the back of the truck. Feeling ugly, Jake thought about his little friend with a big heart. The old dog had no chance; his fight was over before Jake got free. Vengeful thoughts raged through him. "Lord, I've turned enough cheeks. They're gonna pay."

Jeanne met him as he struggled from the truck at home. "Good lord Jake, what happened? Where's Gus?"

"Dead," Jake said, fighting pain. "Shark's dogs."

"You need a doctor, Jake?"

"Can you get that wooden box in the back of the garage and a couple big garbage bags?"

"Can't this wait?" Jeanne asked as she surveyed his lacerated legs and blood-soaked rags.

"No," Jake answered as he carried his friend down to the little grove of maples where Gus often laid in the shade watching for woodchucks. Jake returned for tools and began digging. He worked steadily without talking, legs aching from his wounds and his heart grieving from their loss.

Jeanne arrived with burial items, including Gus's bed to line the box, and she gently straightened his fur while Jake continued to dig. The ground was absent of rock on the side hill, and the grave was soon ready. Together they slipped Gus into doubled plastic garbage bags to contain his smell from bears and coyotes. They eased the body into the box, closed the top, and gently lowered it into the grave.

Standing hand in hand, Jake broke the silence. "Lord, I don't know how this all works, but we'd sure like to see this guy again in the hereafter. He's been a faithful friend. Thanks so much for letting us share his life."

His eyes misting, Jake began shoveling dirt into the hole. Task completed, the Brewers struggled up the hill. Jake sat on the back steps while Jeanne retrieved hot water, soap, and a first aid kit. "Better leave those rags tied in place until we get to the medical center. It's bad under there."

Not listening, Jeanne cut away the shredded pant leg at the thigh and went to work. She washed and dried his legs carefully to minimize pain, then bandaged them. They were ready for the trip to Parker when the four-wheeler and dog pack sounds became audible and grew louder.

"He's coming back." Jake walked to the truck and grabbed his .357 magnum and a box of cartridges. Flipping the cylinder out, he shoved the sixth shell in the empty chamber and stuffed additional cartridges in his pocket.

"Where are you going, Jake?" Jeanne asked, her voice worried.

"Get in the house. Lock the door. The carbines ready. Kill him if he tries to get in."

"Jake, please!" Jeanne pleaded as he headed across the field.

Jake didn't acknowledge her. Dog noises and engine sounds roared closer. A killing rage pushed Jake. He was within fifty yards of the gatepost holes when Shark slid around the corner and sped off down the steep mountain road toward Hill Place. Howling dogs followed closely behind. At the top, Jake grabbed the steel gate cable and fastened it around a tree. He jerked off the "Private Road" sign with the orange markers that warned riders of the cable's presence and laid it face down slightly uphill from the cable, retrieved his watch and ring, and headed home. Shark's engine screamed at high RPMs. Entering the field, Jake watched Shark spinning donuts around the yard with the dogs wildly following him.

Engrossed in destruction, Shark didn't see Jake emerge from the woods and drop to the ground; his pistol steadied with both hands. Thumbing the hammer back, he aimed carefully. Kawham! The big revolver jumped, and he cocked it again.

The first round ripped past Shark's head, and he glimpsed Jake. Bending low over the machine, he gunned it toward the tree-lined road. Jake followed him in his sights. Kawham. The bullet came close as Shark raced for the trees. The gun bucked against Jake's hand a third time, then a fourth. Shark roared away, engine wailing. The engine suddenly went quiet. Jake imagined a thud and headed toward the house.

"We'd better get to town before something else happens," Jeanne said as she looked at Jake. Disheveled hair and the missing pant leg revealed blood-soaked bandages that brought home the severity of the moment.

Without answering, Jake crawled in on the passenger seat and removed the spent cartridges, replacing them with fresh rounds from his pocket. Weakly, he slumped against the headrest, wondering how Jeanne would react when she saw Shark. Closing his eyes, he contemplated the implications of his actions. He held no remorse. The deed was earned and consummated. It's ironic, he thought, Shark and Gus met the same fate on the same day; one deserved it, the other didn't. Silently he prayed. Lord, I hope you understand. Shark needed to die.

Jeanne was headed toward Parker when she heard the vehicle. "Nuts," she muttered as Poskevich's new maroon Explorer came into view. She was in no mood for guests. Remembering they had promised to help with the gate, Jeanne shook her head. "They'll have to understand we can't chitchat," Jeanne said as they hurried toward the truck.

Glen arrived on Jeanne's side, "We're leaving for the doctor's."

"There's been a terrible accident on your hill?" Looking in the truck, Glen asked, "What happened?" in a way that suggested his policeman's mind was considering a connection between the accident on the hill and Jake's problem.

"Shark's dogs tore up Jake. Killed Gus too."

"Oh my god," Sue exclaimed. "You poor thing."

"Do you have anything to cover a body?" Glen asked, his face a sick color.

"Couple blue tarps in the garage," Jake answered.

Glen grabbed a tarp and disappeared into the woods while a horrified Sue tried to explain. "Someone was killed on a four-wheeler. Tore off his head. It's gross beyond description."

The Brewers departed for town where prompted by Glen's call; a stern-faced nurse met them in the parking lot. Jake wrapped the towel around himself as he crawled out, protesting that he didn't require a wheelchair. The nurse insisted he sit, and once strapped in, she wheeled him through a side door where she stripped off the towel. "Oh my!" she exclaimed. "You should be in a hospital."

Since there was none in Sterling County, the nurse went to work, noting both legs showed signs of the attack. Standing, she took a closer look at Jeanne, and with a puzzled look, she asked, "Weren't you here recently?" When Jeanne nodded, the nurse continued. "Had your face banged up. You looked terrible. Yes, your eye's still discolored. That Coleman tried to ... ah ..."

"I was here," Jeanne agreed, her face red.

A lean-faced physician's assistant arrived and began asking perfunctory questions. "Allergic to anything?"

"Not that I know of," Jake stated.

"Good," the P.A. answered and gave the nurse a shot order. He returned to Jake and outlined the procedure they would follow. "I'm going to give you shots for pain and infection prevention. Your legs look like the boys that come in with chainsaw cuts. They take a while to sew up. If the shots wear off, let me know, and we'll fix it for you."

Jake winced as the P.A. injected his throbbing legs. "It'll be a few minutes before this takes effect. To the nurse, he added, "You can shave his legs while I'm getting ready." The nurse, efficient from years of practice, soon finished her task. The P.A. returned and sat on a stool beside Jake. "Forgot to introduce myself. The name's Kilgore. Folks call me Doc."

"Feel that?" the P.A. questioned as he snapped Jake's leg with his finger in a few places. When Jake shook his head, he said "Good" and began stitching the leg. The nurse threaded another needle while Doc worked steadily, pushing the needle down through flesh, pulling it tight, tying off, cutting it, completing suture after suture, occasionally stopping to cut off a little ragged meat before continuing. When he stopped for a new needle, he remarked, "This isn't the first time someone worked you over with a needle."

Jake nodded.

"Vietnam?"

When Jake nodded again, Doc added, "Got my start and a lot of practice there. Medic. 101st Airborne."

Doc finally finished Jake's bad leg, arched his back against the stiffness setting in, and without turning, he said, "I'm going to sew up the other leg too. I get paid by the stitch, so I take as many as possible."

Jake laughed. Here's a guy I can like, he thought. Doc finished the second leg, and after inspecting his work, he bandaged both legs. "I'm giving you a prescription for pain pills. Don't be a tough guy - get this thing filled," he ordered. "You'll need it when the shots wear off. Get yourself some large trash bags with drawstrings. Pull them over your leg bandages before you shower."

After picking up the prescription and bags, they headed back to Hill Place. The body and the four-wheeler were gone when they arrived home, but a police cruiser waited. Poskevich and Johnston met them, their somber looks evidence of the gruesome task they had shared.

"Could we ask you a few questions so Johnny can finish his report?" Glen asked.

"Not much to tell. I was digging gate holes when Shark came by with his dogs. Sicced them on me and old Gus. I jumped in the back of the truck, and two dogs followed me. The others dragged Gus out from under the truck and tore him to pieces."

"What was Shark doing while this was happening?"

"Sitting on his four-wheeler yelling 'sic 'em' and laughing."

"What happened then?" Johnston asked, shaking his head in disgust.

"I got the dogs kicked out of the truck, but it was too late for Gus. He was dead. Those dogs tore him to shreds. Shark rode off laughing. I picked up Gus, and we buried him."

"Did you put the cable up when you took your dog in?" Johnston asked.

"No," Jake answered, wondering what he suspected.

"The cable killed Shark. How do you explain that?" Johnston asked.

"I took my ring and watch off while I was working. I remembered them while Jeanne was cleaning up my legs. I walked up to get them. Put the cable up then. He must have already been on his way down in here. You can see he spent a lot of time tearing up the yard."

"Hmm, and you didn't hear him," Johnston remarked, eyeing Jake in a questioning way. "That stuff must have been awful important to have you walk up there on those legs."

"Important enough, my friend," Jake answered, his voice taking on an ominous edge. "So was the dog we lost." That voice jerked the officers' attention to him. There was something about Jake Brewer. Maybe his deadly eyes provided an unfeigned warning, or his baritone voice took on a huskiness that stood neck hairs on end. For sure, when the sergeant major was angry, everyone knew.

"How'd Shark get out of jail?" Jake demanded.

"Old man Coleman put up a section of land to cover bail," Poskie said as he studied Jake for a reaction. "Shark would have been better off in jail. He was barely recognizable as a human being. Beheaded with one arm gnawed about off. Dogs tore chunks of flesh off him."

Johnston asked Jake if he would visit the scene, and they rode up in the trooper's vehicle.

Jake was suddenly worried. What did they know? How much trouble was he in? "Did you have a warning device hanging from the cable?" Johnston asked Jake.

"The No Trespassing sign and orange streamers were lying in the road uphill from the cable," Glen answered for Jake. "I laid them off to the side when I drove in."

"Shark must have knocked them off when he crashed through the cable. How do you hook it up?" Johnston asked as he walked over to the cable.

"Stretch it around that tree," Jake said, pointing at the tree on the opposite bank. "Now hook it back over itself."

Johnston hooked the cable and went back for the sign. "The sign hung here?" he questioned. "It did." Jake agreed.

"Hmmm. No blood on the sign but plenty on the cable."

"Maybe the four-wheeler knocked the sign off before Shark hit it."

"Could be," Johnston agreed. "Where was the sign laying, Glen?" Johnson asked.

"Uphill from the cable, maybe here," Glen replied, scratching a mark in the dirt. "Probably flew there when the cable stretched taunt."

Johnston looked around in the dust to see if he could find other clues, but dogs and men so tracked it up there was little hope of that. Satisfied there was no more to learn at the site, Johnston moved the cable off the road and laid the sign beside it. Together they walked back to the vehicle. "Something doesn't fit," Johnston said, "but as they say, the truth will out."

CHAPTER 20

The Brewers suffered through a tense dinner at Trawler John's. Terse conversation began with a discussion of Trooper Johnston's call clarifying aspects of Shark's demise. It moved to the ongoing investigations, grew more heated, and dropped into a bottomless pit of silence. Preoccupied with the trooper's questions, Jake worried. How much did the trooper know, and could he prove it?

The ride home was more of the same. Fearful thoughts battled Jake. Alighting from the truck, he forgot his stitched legs, and the jarring contact with the concrete garage floor took his breath away. After retrieving the mail, he sat in the kitchen sorting through the stack. In addition to the weekly Scandalizer, as the natives called the Sentinel, the Parker weekly paper, there were letters from the State Police Commissioner's office and the Parker Chamber of Commerce, plus a notice that the carrier had attempted to deliver a certified letter. "People are receiving our letters," Jake remarked as he handed the newspaper to Jeanne. Opening the letters, he learned the State Police Commissioner had assigned the Commanding Officer of Troop F, Montoursville, to complete investigations of the problems in Parker.

The second letter from Don Maynard of the Chamber of Commerce in Parker was upsetting. After reading it, Jake read highlights to Jeanne. "We know the Colemans play rough at times, but there can be extenuating circumstances." "We discussed your problem at our monthly meeting. Everyone agrees something should be done, but we don't know what it might be."

Jake fought back an urge to crumple the paper and throw it in the trash. This letter made it painfully clear that the Chamber wasn't interested in helping them. At least the state police were reviewing the Coleman investigations.

"You won't like the Sentinel's take on Shark any better," Jeanne said, looking up from the paper. "Ms. Allison Carver reports Shark's murder saying half-crazed dogs partially ate him. She neglected to mention they are Shark's dogs, and they killed Gus and tore you up. Shark's obituary makes him sound like one of Sterling County's upstanding. And if you're interested, you can make memorial contributions to First Baptist Church in Parker. Am I going crazy or what?"

"I'll call Mac and see what he's heard."

Mac answered the phone, and it was apparent his supper was interrupted when he talked with his mouth full. "Get yer weekly Scandalizer?"

"I did."

"Bet yer hot."

"Sounds like they got their facts from Link," Jake said, anger riding his voice.

"Write a rebuttal."

"Ya, right. What would that look like after they edited it?"

"People gotta know what's happenin'.

"Anything else, Mac?" Jake questioned, desperately seeking answers to the questions that haunted him.

"Bob Denton got killed Sunday morning. They figure he was run off the road by the drugged-up kids that wrecked further down the road."

"Bob was a good man."

"That ain't all. They let Link out on bail today."

"You kidding me?"

"Some lawyer from Pittsburgh got him reduced bail. Guess the only way we'll get rid of the Coleman problem is to hang 'em all on cables."

"Stop! That crap could get around, and people will believe it happened."

"It's already around. I heard it at Dixon's. Ever'body thought it was funny."

"I don't. People will tell this stuff as a joke, and it'll become gospel."

"Yes, and ya know how gossip flies around this county. This could become another big problem for you."

Late that evening, Jake sat on the edge of the tub snipping stitches and placing them on the growing pile. His legs reflected a mauling by a grizzly, but the sutures evidenced an artist's work.

Standing under the pulsating shower, his mind wandered to the certified letter that awaited him, and a panic blanket dropped. He beat it back with a short prayer, satisfied that there was no concrete evidence of his misdeed. The Link thing puzzled him. Why would a lawyer from Pittsburgh be handling the case, and with the seriousness of charges, why would bail be considered when he violated the conditions of parole? Why wouldn't the DA strenuously object? Even more, how was the DA hooked to the Colemans? Nothing fit.

On Saturday morning, Jeanne met Jake at the door when he returned with the certified letter. "You won't believe this!" Jeanne exclaimed angrily. "I answered the phone, and this voice said, "Hey bitch, you better drop charges if you know what's good for you." He kept dropping the "F" bomb. Before I could say anything, he hung up."

"Link?" Jake questioned, his face white as he mulled over the possibilities.

"Had to be. What next?" Jeanne asked, desperation crowding into her voice.

"Part of what's next is this summons to appear at a hearing in Parker. It seems Mr. DA has questions concerning Shark's death."

"What are we going to do?"

"Let's call Poskevich." Jake anxiously rubbed his face. He dialed the Poskevich residence, and when no one answered, he left a message. Fearfully, they called the local state police office, who told them to "call back if Link calls again, and we'll go from there."

"Oh boy," Jeanne said. "Link doesn't need to be a detective to find us. They printed our address in that Scandalizer story. We can't prove he's calling, and the cops won't act without proof. Where does that leave us?"

"There is something we can do if he calls again," Jake said. "We'll record both sides of the conversation on our message center. That should hang his buns."

"You can't believe that, Jake."

"Jeanne, Poskie will use the tapes somehow, even if the information isn't admissible in court. There's thirty minutes on each side, and I have lots of them. We'll take all of the calls on the message center in the family room until this thing is over. Answer the phone, act scared and bait him on. Ask him why he's calling. Figure on odd hour calls, like when the bars close."

Jake answered the phone that afternoon, and it clicked dead in his ear. Later while he was showering, Jeanne received another call. She met Jake while he was dressing. "We got him, but I'm scared. He told me to drop the charges and provided graphic details of what would happen if I didn't. Said he knows where I live. Jake, he may think he has nothing to lose. Shut me up or go back to prison."

"Keep your pistol handy and be prepared to use it. Can you hold out through the weekend so we have evidence for the police?"

"It's the only way they'll get any. What if I record my voice saying "hello" and you play it when you answer the phone, Jake."

"And if it isn't Link?"

"Quickly think up some big BS story. Men are good at that. It's in your genes."

CHAPTER 21

"Jake," the hysterical voice began, "he followed me right into the parking lot."

"Slow down, Jeanne! Who followed you?"

"Link Coleman," Jeanne answered, her voice trembling.

"You sure?"

"He pulled out behind me on Williams Grove Road. Jake, he's come to kill me."

"I'll be right down to get you, Honey."

"I'll be all right," Jeanne replied, sounding like she was trying to convince herself.

"Tell the parking lot guard to watch for Link's truck. Tell your boss too."

"My boss would fire me if she thought there'd be problems, and we need my job."

"Call me at quitting time, and I'll meet you in your office. Jeanne," Jake pleaded. "Please, don't go out until I get there. I'll call the police sergeant Glen referred."

Pheeeewww, Jake sighed as he asked prayer for help and dialed Sergeant Billings, the contact Poskevich provided. The desk officer transferred him to Sergeant Billing, and Jake began, "Sergeant, this is Jake Brewer. Glen Poskevich referred you."

"How can I help you?" the deep voice returned.

Jake explained the threatening phone calls and Link following Jeanne. Billings questioned him in-depth, suggesting that a frightened woman might make an identification mistake. The sergeant agreed to look into things and said he'd contact the Parker substation and ask them to check on Link.

The parking lot was mostly empty when Jake arrived to meet Jeanne, and he parked beside her Buick. After knocking gently on her locked office door, a muffled voice called, "Who's there?" After Jake identified himself, Jeanne opened the door.

She was traumatized, her face white. She collapsed in his arms, trembling, and began to cry. "He called a few minutes ago and said 'Be very scared' and am I ever. He said he came to get me. Oh, how I prayed that was you knocking on the door."

"Let's get out of here," Jake said, shaking his head.

Jake held her trembling hand as they walked to her car. He opened her door, and after a short embrace that witnessed her fear, she got in. The trip home proved uneventful. Jake followed her into the garage, and together, they entered the house, where Jeanne insisted Jake inspect it before she moved from the entryway. When it was clear, Jake called the state police and learned the sergeant had departed for the day. The desk officer agreed to report the problem but reminded him there wasn't much they could do until they proved Link did something illegal.

"Jeanne, I have that hearing in Parker tomorrow morning. Please call off and come with me?"

"We're getting ready for finals. I'll be okay."

"Honey, I can't make you go, but I'm worried. Come with me. Please."

"Jake, I can't. They count on me, and I can't let them down."

Realizing he wouldn't change her mind, Jake retrieved his camera and a motor drive. He mounted a telescopic zoom lens on the camera, inserted new film, and fastened it to a tripod. After attaching a remote unit and flash on the camera to test the operation, he placed the camera in the window focused on the stop sign across the street, then walked across the street and fired the camera three times by remote. Each time the flash went off, indicating everything worked.

Jake instructed Jeanne on the remote operation and had her fire from the stop sign. It worked perfectly.

"It's set to fire, Jeanne. Use the remote to fire it when you stop at the stop sign in the morning and continue every second. Watch your mirror to see if he's behind you. If he is, take off."

"I think I have it," Jeanne agreed, repeating the process to be sure.

"Remember, if you're followed, drive to the Silver Springs Police Station instead of the school. Blow your horn until a cop comes out. They'll notify Sergeant Billings. Don't take chances, and don't stop along the highway. If you have problems, drive into a driveway and blow the horn until someone comes out." After pausing a bit, he pleaded, "Honey, please come to Parker with me."

Jeanne gripped Jake's hand, looking into his eyes, the controlled fear evident. "I have to do this. He can't stalk me and get away with it. The law needs proof and can't seem to get it."

The following morning, Jake tried once more to get Jeanne to go with him, and when she wouldn't, he swung through the neighborhood. With no sign of Link, he apprehensively headed north. Worry climbed as the miles passed. What if he attacked her along the highway? He should reach Parker about the same time Jeanne arrived at school. He'd call before the hearing. Minutes crawled by. Thoughts of the hearing ate at him. Memories of Gus' mutilated body and Shark's laughter flooded back. Maybe he should feel remorse for Shark's death, but there was none.

Surely the Lord understands. Let's hope the justice system does.

He stopped at a payphone in Parker and called Jeanne's office. Fear engulfed him when she hadn't yet arrived, and he called the Silver Springs Police. Patrolman Murphy answered the phone and said, "Yes, your wife's here. She's scared but otherwise fine."

Jeanne's terrified voice came on the line. "Oh, Jake, he caught me at Route 114 and the Carlisle Pike and kept ramming me."

"You hurt, Honey?" Jake asked, his stomach rolling.

"He tried to kill me. I should have listened. He skidded me right into the car in front of me."

"Screw this hearing. I'll come get you."

"I'm going to work. Officer Murphy said he'll take me over."

Jake sensed Jeanne was gaining control as the pitch of her voice changed and some of her spunk returned. "Did they catch Link?"

"No. When I turned toward the police station, Link skidded sideways into the Carlisle Pike traffic. Tires squealed, and vehicles slid around him, but he kept going."

"Don't leave school until I get there. I'll get through this hearing and pick you up."

Glancing at his watch, Jake realized he was already a few minutes late. It was no way to start a meeting that could have dire consequences. Wounded legs throbbing, he took the courthouse stairs two at a time to the hearing room where Justice Jacobs, DA Pennington, Johnston, Poskevich, O'Keefe, the coroner, and a stenographer waited. After duly reprimanding Jake for his tardiness, Squire Jacobs introduced the coroner and the stenographer. The coroner was a middle-aged man with a round head sparsely covered by long reddish hair. Sunken eyes rimmed with dark circles suggested an ancestor might have been a raccoon. Pennington's perpetual scowl and heavy breathing coupled with red, weepy eyes and continued sniffling proved an ongoing distraction that questioned his lifestyle.

Questions flew. The DA was after more than information; he wanted Jake's butt. Although the police and coroner reports stated Shark's death was accidental, and their opening statements supported Jake, Pennington's questions signaled he wanted Jake found guilty. After Jake ran through a brief of the incident, and the police and coroner added their findings, the DA snapped, "You're telling me that man sicced his dogs on you without provocation?"

"On my dog and me. They've attacked many others."

Johnston agreed. "They attacked me last winter, and Shark laughed. Shark was attacked and feared them."

Ignoring the trooper, the DA asked, "Mr. Brewer, why would you walk up to get your watch and ring when you had to drive by there on your way to the doctors? And when you had to drive out, why would you put up that cable?"

"Maybe I wasn't thinking clearly after those dogs mauled us. I wasn't planning anything other than burying my dog. My wife was the one who suggested the doctor."

"You didn't hear his machine?"

"Wasn't listening for it."

"What were you listening for?"

"Peace."

"Don't get funny with me," the DA warned. "Why didn't you have warnings on the cable?"

"He did," Johnston said. "Coleman must have knocked them off."

"Let's see, the cable was marked, but Shark didn't see them. What would distract him?"

"A guilty conscience?" Jake questioned with a shrug of his shoulders.

At that point, the justice interrupted, cautioning the participants that the hearing was not a criminal trial, it was a fact-finding effort, and the growing hostility wasn't necessary. In the way of an answer, the DA continued. "This confrontation appears to be much more sinister than the version presented by Mr. Brewer. There are too many unanswered questions."

"I'll tell you what's sinister. Link Coleman attacked my wife and continues to threaten her. His brother oversaw the murder of our dog." Jake clenched his fists so tight the nails dug into his palms. Struggling to maintain composure, he took a deep breath. "This attack happened on our land. We wouldn't be here if Shark hadn't been trespassing against police orders. For sure, if he hadn't chosen to tear up my yard, he wouldn't have been near that cable. And if he were jailed for any of these recent problems, he'd be alive. Why aren't we addressing those things?"

"Could these conflicts be episodes in a long-running feud?" the DA asked, a snide look of power on his face.

"Where'd this feud idea originate? All we want is the peace we pay for. This unending nightmare won't go away until the law does something about it. My wife was attacked in Mechanicsburg this morning."

"Mr. Brewer, I find this supposed attack to be another hard to believe, unprovable complaint designed to thwart justice, and it isn't going to work. This hearing is about one man's hanging death on a cable you intentionally put across his path of travel. That's what we're addressing."

Jake shuddered with the cable-hanging comment; it had spread. Anger rose, asserting its power over him. "Dammit, call the Silver Springs Police Department. Link Coleman attacked my wife this morning."

"I said we aren't discussing this morning!" The DA Hammered Jake. "You're explanations to this point do nothing to expel concerns that you deliberately caused Mr. Coleman's death. Now let's go over this event one more time. Hopefully, we can understand why you acted with such reckless disregard for the life of another. I cannot put the facts together as I see them and develop a logical reason why a rational person would behave as you did."

"We aren't sitting on the sidelines speculating; we're living the problem. Look at my legs," Jake snapped angrily, sliding away from the table and exhibiting the purple lacerations. "Those wounds might make anyone irrational. Look at the doctor's pictures of my wife after she was assaulted a few weeks earlier," Jake said, laying the pictures on the table. "Link Coleman beat her, tore off her clothes, and would have raped her if I hadn't stopped him. Shark and his brother were waiting outside to join in the fun."

"Yeah, right. You stopped three men all by yourself. Maybe you killed Mr. Coleman to get rid of a witness?"

"Hold it," Jake demanded. "You have no right to make that statement. Everything suggests otherwise. Do you have reason for supporting the Colemans?"

"Don't question me on how to do my job, Brewer. You need to be more forthcoming with information."

"I've answered every question asked of me. It's beginning to look like there's something more sinister than the Colemans attacking us for the pure hell of it. Maybe some official is teaming up with them for some reason. Someone should follow up on that angle."

"Let the law take care of the law's side of things," the DA responded as he returned to asking questions. When the same questions were asked over, the Squire suggested adjournment, his dark eyes made it plain the meeting was over.

It became apparent that Pennington was upset with the meeting's outcome, but he concurred, informing Jake he would let him know how the law would proceed in a matter of days.

Out on the sidewalk, Jake paused to talk with troopers. "Jake," Glen said, "the DA carried that 'I hold all the cards look,' and he's gunning for you. The deck's stacked against you. You need a good lawyer."

"I know that, but with no job, I was trying to save a few bucks. You can't believe we want this to continue, but I'm not running. I'm living what we learned in the Corps. It isn't so much the number of men that come but did they come to fight. And I believe Pennington's involved with the Colemans in something illegal."

"Jake, you have to know it looks like a feud is brewing that you may be fueling. There's a lot of talk going around that doesn't support your cause," Glen reminded him. "The DA asked tough questions that beg answers. A smart man would be searching for answers that a jury could buy."

"Do you see this going to trial?"

"It will if the DA has his way, and you know what he wants for an outcome."

Jake knew, and he believed this was bigger than the Colemans. They might be just a destructive diversion. In a hurry to get home and check on Jeanne, he departed. The trip home seemed never-ending. He met Jeanne in her office, and she grew fighting mad as she provided Jake with the details of the morning's events.

That evening Glen called. "Link made his scheduled parole meeting this afternoon, and we couldn't get his bail revoked. He denies making calls to you or your wife and swears he never left the county. His truck doesn't show signs of damage that would suggest he ran into anything, but his bumper is a heavy steel one and appears freshly painted."

"What happens if we can prove Link is lying?"

"That could change things."

Jake explained they taped Link's threatening calls for several days and how the undeveloped and dated film would show Link's truck in their neighborhood before he rammed Jeanne.

Glen was ecstatic. "Man, you did good. I need those tapes, and it'd be better if the State Police lab developed the film. Noone could say you altered them."

"I'll leave the film in the camera and copy the tapes."

Just after nine P.M., a young trooper from headquarters arrived to pick up the film and tapes.

He asked how the pictures were taken, and Jake showed him the camera poking through the drapes. They talked while Jake removed the camera from the tripod and rewound the film. He handed the film canister to the trooper and then took him to view their answering machine. After asking a few more questions, the trooper departed with the tapes and film.

Saturday morning, the Brewers sat drinking coffee when the phone rang. Jeanne hit the record function. "Good morn . . ."

"Listen close bitch," the chilled voice threatened. "Call off the dogs while ya can. I know where you live, and you know friggin' well what I'll do to you if you don't cooperate. Yer luck ran out yesterday."

Jeanne stood fearful and angry, looking at a dead phone. Her expression told Jake who had called. He removed the receiver from her hand, replaced it in its cradle, and held her. "Jake, this is driving me nuts. You should have taken care of business when he assaulted me."

His heart plunged. He tried to soothe Jeanne, but a vicelike crushing smothered him. His mind snapped back to Vietnam Hill 861A, and he remembered the helpless feeling that ate into Marines as they were pounded by NVA artillery, waiting for the ground attack. Relief came when the fight began.

"It's not going to happen here," Jake murmured, his mind lost in another war.

"What's not going to happen here?" Jeanne asked, wiping her eyes with her hand.

"I don't know what I was thinking," Jake lied in a quiet voice.

CHAPTER 22

The Brewers sat discussing the problems engulfing them when a late evening phone call produced an official-sounding female voice. "Mr. Brewer, this is Allison Carver of the Mountain Sentinel."

"What can we do for you?" Jake answered, mentally picturing a chisel-faced man-hater. "I'm investigating charges made by Mr. Hurwitz, attorney for Lester Coleman. He contends his client is being harassed because lies concerning attacks on your wife are fueling this feud your family is perpetuating."

"Perhaps you should ask how Link Coleman got this high-priced out-of-town lawyer to represent him and who might be paying his fees."

"Mr. Brewer, can you shed light on this feud situation, or can't you?"

"Ms. Carver, where did you dig up this feud idea?"

"It's common knowledge. Since —"

"Knowledge," Jake asked. "The first mention of a feud was in your column."

"My sources report this feud spans several generations. Our DA has expressed considerable concern after the murder of a Coleman on your property and another had a new truck destroyed."

"Did you question what they were doing at our place, Ms. Carver?"

"Perhaps you could enlighten me."

"The Colemans ignored the State Police issued "No Trespass" order and wrecked their truck escaping an attack on my wife. That assault didn't end in another gang rape for one reason; I arrived home on time."

"You ran off three grown men by yourself?" Carver asked scornfully.

"Me and the good Lord," Jake angrily replied. "In the other incident, Shark Coleman was trespassing and sicced his dogs on me. His dogs killed our dog and tore me up. Coleman hit my cable after tearing up our place with his four-wheeler."

"I can't believe Mr. Coleman encouraged his dogs to attack for no reason?"

"Maybe you can't," Jake said through clenched teeth. "Then you're writing about it, and we're living this mess."

Without comment, Carter changed subjects. "Mr. Hurwitz reports you told the police Mr. Coleman made threatening phone calls and attacked your wife on the highway in Mechanicsburg."

"I did, and he did."

"Come now! Mr. Coleman has no phone, and he swears he hasn't left Sterling County. Your answers don't square with information I have from reliable sources."

"Would you believe there's proof Coleman made those calls and stalked my wife?"

"The DA has none."

"Maybe you and the DA don't want proof. Truth might not sell as many papers as this feud baloney. Talk with the cops. You may uncover something closer to reality."

"Thanks for your time Mr. Brewer." With that, the phone went dead.

"Aren't you hospitable tonight?" Jeanne chided when Jake hung up. "I could only hear one side of the conversation, but —"

"Let me play the tape back for you."

"You recorded her?" Jeanne queried.

"It's getting to be a habit," Jake answered with a smile.

After listening to the conversation, Jeanne said, "Two things are evident, she may get to eat her words, and there are very biased people in Sterling County. Let's pray you don't go to trial before a Scandalizer influenced jury."

*   *   *

Brewer could screw up everything, Pennington thought, mopping his brow with a wet handkerchief. He has to be found guilty. He punched

142

the numbers in his phone and snuffed heavily. After a brief discussion, Pennington got to the point. "Judge, this Brewer-Coleman case must go to trial. The district justice won't send it up to me. Brewer murdered a man."

"Maybe. Maybe not, but my career is over if I make the wrong call. Coleman was guilty of criminal trespass, and he assaulted Brewer through his dogs. He'd be alive if he obeyed the 'No Trespass Order.'"

"That's for a jury to decide," Pennington snapped. "Brewer is a dangerous man. Until he's off the street, the violence will continue. He must stand trial."

"Two problems, Harlon. You have historical reasons to hold a grudge in this case, and I talked with Justice Jacobs. He finds no basis for a Brewer trial. Coleman trial, yes."

"Screw Jacobs. You have to go over his head and get this case to the grand jury. Look, Digger, I know you want to go to Congress, and I know the people who can get you elected. My grandfather was a congressman, and my family has had a major part in picking every member of Congress since. I'd consider this Brewer trial a personal favor that would be well rewarded. If you don't do what's needed here, the seat you want in Congress could be out of the question. You have other things to worry about too. We both know what I'm talking about."

"I'm not sure the evidence supports a trial," Paladino answered.

"Digger, hear me out." Pennington's voice took on a threatening tone. "You get this case to trial, and I'll make the evidence stick. Brewer will hang. What potential juror in Sterling County is going against me? And remember this, you're a stakeholder in The Business. You better take care of your end of it."

*   *   *

Two nights later, Glen called to report he received the prints and tapes. "If they're not incriminating enough to revoke bail, I don't know what would be. Jake, be careful until we get this under control. Link and the DA are threatening to make you pay for Shark's death."

"He called and threatened Jeanne again. That tape and another Ms. Allison Carver call are in the mail. Question Glen. How can we win when the legal system, Sentinel, merchants, and criminals seem to be on the same side, and it's not ours?"

"Hang tough and be watchful. Things will turn out right."

"I pray for that. Can you call me if you hear anything about a grand jury? The stress has us hauled uptight."

Mac called the following day busting with information. "Word's out Carter from the Sentinel gave you a chance to tell your side of the story, an' you gave her a hard time."

"She already had her mind made up."

"She's spendin' a lot a time lookin' into stuff. Visited Link in jail. Ya know what a convincin' liar he is. They say she's been to the Coleman shanty. Saw her at the Chat N Chew with the DA's secretary. And get this. Carver had lunch with Link's attorney. Link's back in jail. Somehow the cops got tapes of Link calling Jeanne and pictures of him stalking her too. Man, how do the cops get that kind of stuff?"

"They have their ways. Probably got stuff on you too."

"Not likely, Brewer. I ain't feuding with anyone."

CHAPTER 23

Smoke smells jerked Jake awake. Flames leaping off the barn roof pulled him to the window. "Damn!" he screamed, jerking Levis over tender legs. He slipped into boots and raced for tools, climbing on the garage roof carrying a heavy tarp from inside the building. He quickly spotted the fusee that set the fire, tossed it into the yard, and smothered the burning shingles with the tarp.

Turning, Jake saw the house roof fire and rapidly growing blaze. He grabbed the tarp, jumped off the garage, and tore through the house to the front bedroom. Slipping the screen to the side, Jake climbed out on the porch roof and threw the tarp up on the main roof. Struggling up behind it, he kicked a fusee free of the fire and threw it into the yard. Snapping the tarp open, he flipped it over the flaming shingles.

The barn burned with fury. Spark showers shot into the night sky, setting additional fires. Jeanne met Jake as he climbed in the bedroom window. She was dressed and scared. "Climb out on the roof, and I'll get the garden hose up to you. We'll lose the house if we don't."

"Jake, let's get out of here before we die," Jeanne pleaded, but Jake ran down the steps.

Jake turned on the hose and fed it up to Jeanne. The barn burned with fevered intensity, long past the time it could be saved. Drought-dried brush fueled the blaze. A fire-induced updraft carried ever-bigger pieces of flaming debris aloft with fires erupting where they fell to earth.

Blazing refuse burned blisters on Jake's bare arms and neck. He ran into the house, grabbed a pair of jackets and two towels, and soaked them in the toilet tank. Running upstairs, he crawled out on the roof and gave

Jeanne one of the jackets while he slipped into the other. "Put this towel over your head!" he shouted above the din. "It'll protect you from the heat."

Fires encircled Hill Place burning night into day. The roar drowned out their voices making communication difficult. "I'm losing water pressure," Jeanne yelled.

Jake grabbed the hose that trickled to a stop. "We're in trouble. The spring pumped dry."

"What'll we do?" Jeanne shouted over the inferno, opening the towel just enough to see Jake.

"There'll be water left below the pump intake. I'll soak those old quilts in the attic. You spread 'em over the shingles."

"Sure," Jeanne replied, trying to show confidence with fear riding her face.

Jake grabbed the quilts out of a chest and tossed them to the ground. Returning, he emptied the other chest. Jake took the stairs two at a time and quickly stood the garage ladder against the sun porch. He snatched an armload of quilts and ran for the spring house. Two feet of water remained below the suction pipe. Fighting against time, he soaked all the quilts he could carry, shouldered them, and trotted up the steep hill with lungs begging for air. Climbing the ladder, he handed them up to Jeanne.

Jake slid down the ladder, scooped up another load of quilts, and soaked up the remaining water, then soaked his towel in the wildlife overflow tub. Climbing the hill, a doomed feeling fell over him; they were trapped. He waited too long to leave. Death would follow failure. Lungs burning, he climbed the ladder and placed the quilt load on the roof. He hurriedly exchanged his wet towel and jacket with Jeanne.

"You okay?" Jeanne screamed, fear riding her reddened face.

"Hotter'n hell," Jake yelled over the tremendous roar. Tree sap heated to steam exploded, ripping the air, scattering showers of sparks. The acrid smoke made it difficult to breathe.

Jake fought back fear. Scooping up the earlier discarded tarp, he threw it on the garage roof and climbed up to spread it out. Jumping down, he grabbed another load of quilts and sprinted down to the spring. He sopped the last of the water out of the wildlife tub, and not knowing what else to do, he took the quilts over to the overflow pond and soaked up water, mud, and all. This load staggered him. A ladder rung snapped from the weight barking his shins as he slid to the ground. Gathering his load, he carefully climbed past the broken rung, placing his feet close to the rails to reduce further breakage.

"There's mud in these, but it's all the water that's left," he shouted to Jeanne as he struggled to get the load on the roof.

"Both roofs are covered, Jake. Maybe we don't need them."

"Hang 'em off the sides. It'll protect the eves," he said as he climbed back down the ladder, his shins painfully reminding him to be careful.

Jake grabbed bedding and sleeping bags from the house and labored two more trips with the last of the mud water mess. One load went to the roof, where Jeanne spread them over the eves. Jake spread the remainder on the garage roof. Finished, he motioned Jeanne to come down and ran inside. Looking around, he scooped a wool blanket off the back of a couch and soaked up the last of the toilet water before rejoining Jeanne.

"C'mere! Crouch on the porch! I'll fill buckets in the rain barrel."

In what seemed like an eternity, Jake met Jeanne with the last water available. He carefully soaked the blanket, got Jeanne to sit by the buckets, and covered her with the blanket. "Pray, buddy!" he said, crawling in beside her.

The blanket soon dried out from the heat, and they sopped the last of the water in the first bucket wetting their blanket and towels. Jeanne sagged, sobbing into his aching arms. The fire raged around them, consuming years of underbrush, the thunderous noise blasting them from all sides. The blanket grew hot to the touch, and Jake soaked it with water from the second bucket. "It's over, Jake. You know it too. That's the last of the water. Just remember, I always loved you."

A mile and a half across the ridge, as the crow flies, two rough-looking men sat at a picnic table. Off to the side, a big, heavily-muscled man and an attractive, red-headed woman sat in lawn chairs watching the fire burn across the mountain.

Two men roared in on four-wheelers and took places at the table. They whispered something to the others in hushed tones, laughed a bit, and then opened beers from a cooler. "What's so upsetting about the Brewers?" the redhead asked.

"Everything," the big man sitting beside her answered. "Them an' the Vances stole over 600 acres from my granddaddy. Grandaddy was one of them Christians, and they took him bad. That lands worth a fortune now with the timber an' gas leases. Things are gonna be different when we get 'em outta here an' get our land back. They ain't screwin' us no more."

"You act like they caused all your problems."

"It's fact. Things get done, an' we get jailed. We can't even run a business without everyone getting their noses outta joint."

"What kind of business are we talking about?"

"Any business. I'm sicka everyone tellin' us what we kin and can't do. They either tax ya outta business or jail ya for runnin' it. Been that way forever. They jailed my grandfather an' two uncles when both Judge Clements and Bucky Thornton, the sheriff, was drinkin' Gramp's stuff."

"What kind of stuff?"

"Best corn likker that ever came outta these mountains. I know. I drank my share when I was firin' the still. We'd catch it in a tin cup when it was comin' outta the pipe steamin' hot."

"There's your problem. That's illegal."

"It ain't fer Jack Daniels."

"Jack Daniels is a legitimate business. They —"

"Legitimate 'cause they bought off some politicians. Same with drugs. Doctors can get 'em for anyone an' half them sawbones is usin'. Lawyers too. Them an' all their uppity friends. They're dealin' an' lettin' poor folks go to jail fer it. I know that fer fact. I lived it. I'm tellin' ya, Red; it's gonna be different now. Hear my words!"

"What are we talking about, Link?"

"We're talkin' about a real profitable business. I tol' you there was a story up here. Hide an' watch. Yer in fer a good 'un. It jus' better read right when yer done, that's all."

The redhead carefully crafted mental notes for a story on this place and these rowdy men, at the same time wondering how she could cover the story without self-incrimination. *Man, I could go to jail as an accessory,* she thought.

CHAPTER 24

Dawn caught the Brewers surveying the devastation from their badly blistered swing. Exhausted, they huddled under a blanket for warmth against the cool morning air. Scattered logs and stumps still burned; the remains of the barn smoldered on. Scorched pine needles rained down with the slightest breeze.

Their charred home stood against the steel-blue morning sky; long mud streaks ran down her white sides. The blackened mountain stood as stark testimony to the disaster that nearly ended their lives. Unlike most mornings, a deathly silence ruled; wildlife was gone. A vehicle traveling toward them became visible through the leafless forest.

Jeanne leaned against her man as the truck rolled to a stop. Dean and two passengers, Hanratty and a fireman, climbed out and looked the place over until the Brewers were spotted. "Man, it's good to see you," Dean said with disbelief. "We thought . . . well, we were worried."

"We made it," Jake softly answered.

"Not by much," the fireman announced, wide-eyed, looking over the remains of the barn and fire-blackened home.

"How'd you fare, Dean?"

"Blistered the paint on my truck. My well gave enough water to wet down the house until the fire burned past. The Laceys lost their outbuildings. Firemen saved their house."

"Any idea how this started?" Hanratty asked.

"Some unknown and innocent until proven guilty party torched us," Jake tersely replied.

Hanratty reddened under the insinuation. "You think someone deliberately set it?"

"Started on our roofs," Jake said, his voice strained.

"The evidence is in the yard."

The visitors walked where Jake pointed and discovered the remains of the fusees. Dean started to pick up one, but Hanratty stopped him. "I need them for evidence."

"There's a towel under my seat," Dean said. "Put them in that."

Hanratty searched for clues while the fireman climbed the ladder to look over the roof. The trooper surveyed the skeletal remains of the burning barn, where some of the building's chestnut log walls stood against the stark, cremated forest. Pungent smoke wafted skyward from the smoldering ruins with an occasional outbreak of fire that burned with the morning breeze, flickering out as the breeze died.

The fireman climbed off the ladder and introduced himself as Gary McNeil. "Folks, you survived a close one. The quilts hanging over the sides have holes burned in 'em. They couldn't take much more heat."

"Neither could we," Jeanne somberly replied.

"Lucky you had the quilts. Where'd you get them?" McNeil asked.

"My great-grandmother," Jake answered. "My great-grandfather ran logging camps when they cut the virgin timber in these parts. My great-grandmother made quilts for their loggers. They saved one of their logging camps from a fire using wet quilts. I got the idea from listening to their stories."

"They saved your buns today," Gary admitted.

Hanratty walked up and listened for a lull in the conversation. "Any idea what time the fires started?"

"The fires didn't start; they were started," Jake snapped. "Probably wasn't more than an hour after the Pandemonium Bar closed in Parker."

"Why didn't you get out when you discovered the fire?"

Jake glared at the officer, his mind sorting through the question posed. "Officer Hanratty, my family came to stay. So did we."

"We'd better go," Dean said, ending what promised to become a difficult situation. "Fires still burning. It's maybe two miles wide and burned to the road between the Griffith place and Wheatons. Burned out the Holloway place. House, barn, the works. Ben was working. Dottie got the kids out. Ballards lost their barn and three horses. Willy Whiskers saved his place by cutting a fire brake with his dozer. They got three helicopters out of Pittsburgh hauling water."

Gray ash swirled behind the departing truck. The old barn smoldered on, standing defiantly against the fire that had gutted it. Looking at it, Jake whispered to Jeanne, "I've been meaning to clean the barn. The fire took care of that job for me."

"You're sick, Brewer," Jeanne replied without raising her head. "I'm thinking about all the fun we had in that barn, and you're laughing about it getting burned."

"Have to laugh when you're too depressed to cry."

"Jake," Jeanne began in a pleading voice, "where are we headed? How much more . . ." She allowed her thoughts to drift off with the wind when she caught the sound of another approaching vehicle. "Bet it's that newswoman Hanratty mentioned," she remarked disdainfully.

"She needs a closer look at one of our parties. Might see things differently."

Jeanne rose to depart as the car approached, but Jake held her. "Let go!" she protested. "I have to clean up."

"Whoever's coming should see us this way."

The car drove slowly into the yard and stopped. The occupant sat looking around, staggered by the surrounding spectacle. After a bit, she spotted the Brewers and strode toward them. "Oh great," Jeanne whispered sarcastically. "She has a camera."

"Good morning," the young woman greeted in a subdued voice. "I'm Allison Carver of the Sentinel."

"Gathering material for another feud article?"

"I endeavor to be an accurate, unbiased reporter."

"I couldn't tell from your previous articles."

"I used the available information." She looked away, gathering her thoughts. "You've had a trying experience. How did you survive?"

"Wasn't much choice," Jake responded without emotion, carefully looking over the attractive young reporter, her bright eyes meeting and holding fast.

"You're very brave," Carver said, looking at Jeanne.

"You fight when you're cornered."

"Folks, I hate to ask, but may I take some pictures?" she asked, readying her camera. "I was afraid of this," Jeanne answered.

"Please," Allison requested. "This could be important. I'll get you copies."

Jake shrugged, "okay," and she took pictures of their blackened faces and burned clothing from several angles, some closeups, others with Jake holding Jeanne with their home in the background. The young woman then walked about taking pictures of the house and garage draped in the old quilts and the remains of the barn. When finished, she returned with questions. All went well until she mentioned talking with the Laceys, and Joe Lacey had mentioned the Brewers had a brush pile to burn, then asked if the fire started from burning brush.

After thinking through several mean answers, Jake softly answered, "Miss Carver, that may be the dumbest thing anyone ever asked me. For sure, it ended our conversation."

CHAPTER 25

The blazing fireball reddened clouds the evening the Brewers arrived home from a weeks vacation at Ocean Beach. The blinking phone recorder beckoned with five bleeps indicating calls without a message before his sister's angry voice announced, "Link Coleman mauled Mac at your place. He's in intensive care. Call me if it matters." The second angry message from his sister followed a few messages later. "Jake, this is Sis again," emphasizing the again. "Mac's out of intensive care. Link broke his arm, collarbone, and leg and he has a concussion. The doctor says he'll heal in time. I guess expecting a return call from you is too much."

Several calls later, an Allison Carver message concerning the fire article requested a call after the Brewers read her fax.

Jake dialed his sister's number, and after two rings, she answered the phone. "Sis, this is Jake. We just got back from —"

"Another vacation. We should all have it so nice that we can make life a constant vacation."

Jake overlooked his sister's angry rhetoric. Growing up with Sis and his mother made it an expected part of both relationships. "When did Mac have the accident, Sis?"

"It was no accident, and it happened Thursday," Sis snorted. "Mac ran out to check your place and got his butt beat. I told him to stay off the hill, but he won't listen. You men think you know it all."

Sis is Sis, Jake thought. Refusing to be drawn into an argument, he asked about visiting hours and asked Sis to call if she needed anything.

"Yes, and leave a message. You may or may not call back," Sis replied.

"I'll try to get up to the hospital during the week."

"Right, and I'll hold my breath," Sis said indignantly and hung up.

"Do you think it's wise to drive up there and back in one day, Honey?" Jeanne asked when Jake hung up the phone.

"I owe it to him. He got hurt looking out for us."

"Maybe I can take the day off from work and help you drive," Jeanne volunteered.

"I'll be okay," Jake hedged.

"It sounds like you don't want me along."

"No, that's not it at all," Jake replied as he snatched up the fax from Allison Carver.

Raging Fire Sweeps Hill Country

By Allison Carver
Sentinel Staff

Spawned by a drought that has seen little rain since early May and driven by a volatile mix of high temperatures, low humidity, and gusting winds, a fast traveling fire ravaged the woodlands of the Hill Country, burning homes, outbuildings, cabins, and livestock across the mountains. Crews evacuated residents in the fire's path until the fire came under control late Wednesday.

"We've feared this hazardous situation all summer," Parker Fire Department Chief Foster Lewis reported. "A forest fire couldn't have come at a worse time. The forest is a tinder box, and little water is available to fight fires. We were lucky to contain it."

More than 200 firefighters from surrounding counties answered the call to fight this blaze. Facing 40 mph wind gusts, they battled the flames across the mountain. This massive fire burned for five days and consumed everything in its path. The fire charred over three thousand acres of parched woodland and fields before it was brought under control. The Holloway family lost everything, and several residents were burned, some badly. Trees and crops, tinder-dry from lack of rain, were rapidly consumed.

Firefighters reported problems with rattlesnakes and bees as they struggled to contain the wind-fanned blaze. Two firefighters from Parker were hospitalized for heat exhaustion and another due to a rattlesnake bite.

This destructive blaze apparently began on the Brewer place and spread from there. It is unknown at this time if the fire resulted from careless burning of brush or other negligence. The Mountain Sentinel staff will follow the continuing investigation and report the results as they become known.

Fire Chief Lewis issued a stern warning against unsafe burning practices. He said the foolish actions of a few inconsiderate people caused millions of dollars of damage and considerable **See Fire - Back Page**

Note: The editorial staff added the underlined words!!!

"A lot we don't understand," Jeanne said as she reread the underlined part. "I'll call Ms. Carver when I'm not so upset."

Exhausted from the trip, Jeanne showered and was asleep when Jake slid into bed. Worried about Mac and the war they faced, sleep would not come. Maybe it was time to give the Colemans reason for concern. A plan took shape calling for explosives but getting them without drawing attention would be tough. Thoughts of his Marine contacts carried serious risks.

Searching for ideas, Jake remembered the notebook he created during his military career. He eased into Levis, fished a key ring from its hiding place in his topcoat pocket, and made his way to the attic. The summer-driven heat quickly increased as he climbed into the no-mans-land of boxes.

Jake reminisced as he worked through his war chest past the black Vietnamese clothes, a small felt pouch containing bullets a doctor removed from his shoulder, his locksmithing tools from security school, and finally, the notebook. He leafed through material on edible fruits and vegetation, animal trapping, navigation, and booby traps until he came to a section on explosives that could be manufactured from common household chemicals. Plastics offered the best remedy; procuring blasting caps the first problem. He remembered the blasting caps he had seen in Forrest Denton's engine shop when he visited last fall, holdovers from his coal mining days. How to get some of those caps, he wondered. He looked at his lock picks, but remembering the Denton's dog; he decided there had to be a better way.

With plans forming, Jake left the notebook open for use in the morning and returned to bed.

Morning finally arrived. Eager to begin, it seemed that Jeanne would never depart for work. He waved as she drove down the street, then retrieved the lock picks and notebook from the attic. After placing the lock picks in his suitcase, he opened the notebook and began listing the required equipment and supplies needed to make plastic explosives, checking off equipment that he could use in this process. His darkroom photography scale was precise, the antique beaker his father gave him was ideal for cooking off the mixture, and his battery tester was an acceptable hydrometer. Their three-burner camp stove was the needed heat source. With the equipment accounted for, he began work on the supplies, making a two-column list, one of the materials on hand and the other things that had to be purchased.

He soon returned from the mall with large jars of petroleum jelly, several gallon jugs of bleach, and salt substitute for the potassium chloride. He put on safety glasses and went to work in his darkroom where the exhaust fan prevented odors from smelling up the house. Jake carefully measured bleach, the required potassium chloride, and other ingredients in the beaker, cooked them off, and while one batch cooled, he started another. He repeated the process several times during the day, working on his book as time allowed. When Jeanne went to work on Tuesday, he would complete the project.

Remembering Allison Carver, he called. Jake agreed to her request to discuss the matter in person and returned to work on his manuscript until Jeanne arrived home. They kissed before discussing the day's events. "How'd the book go today?"

"A fair amount of editing and seven pages in the computer."

"Jake, what's this book about?"

"Some author wrote, 'It's only when you open your veins and bleed on the page a little that you establish contact with your readers.' I'm bleeding."

"Jake!"

"Trust me."

"I can't."

Jake was signing off the computer when Jeanne returned to the office. "What are those jugs of stuff in your darkroom?"

Panic struck. "What were you doing in the darkroom?"

"Turning off your exhaust fan. I could hear it from the bedroom. What is that stuff?"

"Photo chemicals that are past their useful life. I have to dump them." The outright lie issued as an explanation seemed to satisfy Jeanne, but it left Jake stewing over his mistake. It could have prompted questions he would find difficult to answer. Better get my act together, he told himself. Mistakes get you killed.

The following morning Jake began work as soon as Jeanne departed for work. He retrieved the container of potassium chlorate crystals and mixed it proportionally with distilled water. This mixture was boiled on the stove and then allowed to cool. This fractional crystallization process produced crystals of nearly pure potassium chlorate that were ready to powder. Jake dumped the crystals into a Pyrex mixing bowl and used the base of a drinking glass to crush them into a powder that resembled corn starch. Spreading the powder evenly on cookie sheets, he dried it in the oven to remove all moisture. He moved his operation to the back porch and used white gas to dissolve equal parts of vasoline and wax. He added the potassium chlorate powder and kneaded the ingredients like a meatloaf. When it was thoroughly mixed, he spread it out to set while the gasoline evaporated.

With his materials for the plastic put away, Jake went to the barn and started his chain saw, allowing it to idle until the engine warmed. After noting its position, he turned the fuel adjustment screw until the saw stalled. Thus adjusted, he returned the saw to its case and placed it in his pickup.

After a quick lunch, he located a bag phone salvaged after an ESI service crew discarded it. Like many other things, Jake, the packrat, set the malfunctioning phone aside for repair. He removed the phone mechanism from the canvas bag and disassembled the handset. He soldered a length of thin wire to one end of the antenna clip and a flexible antenna on the other. The extension soldered to the handset lines would activate when they received a call. He connected the negative side of a six-volt lantern battery to one line from the handset and soldered extension wires with quick connect couplers on the ends to a battery-powered timer he used when printing large murals. He finished by connecting the battery to the positive terminal of the timer and the negative terminal to the bag phone. Jake was about to pack the device in a box when he remembered the lessons of yesterday. Sloppy efforts provided Jeanne with clues that he was up to something. A mistake with plastic explosives would be fatal. He set his multimeter to read DC volts and connected it to the leads where he would attach the blasting cap wires. It read six volts! Jake's knees jellied. He had come close to committing his final error. The explosives would have blown the moment he touched the wires to this device, thus ending his life.

Summoning courage to continue work, he drew the electrical circuit on paper. The design flaw became painfully evident. As constructed, the phone didn't control the system; it was fully energized with power to the blasting caps when connected to a battery. He redrew the circuit the way it should be and changed the wiring to match his schematic. With this modification, the phone should have to ring to activate the timer, and the timer would run to zero before it powered up the circuit to the blasting caps.

He reconnected the voltmeter. It read zero volts, and the timer wasn't running. Great, he thought as he set the timer for five minutes. Another snag developed; he didn't know the phone number for the bag phone. Locating an old ESI phone roster, he dialed the number. The phone's ring provided ground for the timer, and it began running. When the preset time elapsed, it closed the switch that would set off the explosives. For the test, it read six volts across the blasting cap leads. Bingo! Jake smiled with relief.

He tested the system two more times to ensure it was correct, and when the timer worked perfectly, he dialed again and listened to understand what would happen when he called. The phone rang once and stopped when the timing device made the connection. With the soldered joints taped, he reset the timer for thirty minutes. This allowed thirty minutes to elapse from the time the phone rang.

He carefully packed the mechanism in a small box, poked two small holes in the side, and passed the quick connects through for blasting cap connections. He then sealed the completed unit in a heavy-duty trash bag and stored it in the tote box he carried in the back of his truck. Returning to the shop, he put things away. There could be no evidence left behind to alert Jeanne.

With sufficient time passed, Jake checked his plastic. The gasoline had evaporated, and the mixture stiffened. He divided the completed explosive into three square loaves and coated them with wax to waterproof them. Each finished bomb was wrapped in wax paper, placed in a plastic bag and taped, then placed in a cardboard box in the back of his truck. He cleaned up his mess and went to his office to resume work on his book.

CHAPTER 26

Five A.M. Wednesday morning found Jake headed for Parker. With little traffic, he pulled in front of Forrest Denton's place three hours later and carried his saw in for repairs. The place was empty, and he seized upon the opportunity to stuff three blasting caps that he spotted on an earlier visit in his pocket. He returned to the truck and pretended to search for something while sliding the caps under the seat.

"Brewer, is that you?" Forrest Denton called from the porch. Jake waved as he backed out of his truck. That was close. Forrest added, "Good Gawd boy, I was just being polite when I told ya to come back. Stoppin' twice in a year's a bit much?"

"I can take my saw somewhere else if being here again is too much," Jake returned, knowing Forrest enjoyed all the company he could get. "You get a late start in your old age."

"I was up half the night. Somebody broke into the Danning place across the road. Probably her idiot son Roger and them druggies he runs with. His mama should a throwed him out an' kept the afterbirth. Cops were there most of the night talking loud like everyone in the county was deaf. Overslept 'cause a them. I otta bill 'em for the work I lost."

"Come on, Forrest; I'm the first sucker that drifted in here this morning."

"You are, but the cops don't know that. Now, where's that saw?"

"On your shop floor," Jake answered.

"Homelite junk," Forrest said, kicking the saw with his toe to show his disdain. "Your old man know yer usin' cheap Mexican junk?"

"Are we going to stop jawing and start fixing my saw? Some folks have places to go and people to see."

"Ain't you somethin' boy. I'd boot you outta here if you weren't Jackson's kid," Forrest snarled. "Bet it needs a new air filter; that and a shot of carb cleaner otta do it."

He tossed the old filter to Jake, "Clean this up. Never hurts to have a spare. What happened to your brother-in-law? Heard he's in the hospital?"

"Link Coleman got him. I'm on my way to see him."

"They should put the Colemans, Carlin, and Danning in jail and throw away the key. Might otta throw the DA in and blow up the place while they have 'em rounded up. None of 'em fit to be around decent folks. Them druggies is responsible for Bob's death, them an the kids they got usin' the stuff."

Forrest had the saw back together and jerked the starter rope a dozen times without success. "Damn," he said, now breathing hard, sweat popping out on his forehead. Jake volunteered to try it, but Forrest refused. "Not by a damn sight. No jarheads gotta start a saw for me." He grabbed starting fluid, shot ether into the air cleaner, and began yanking on the starter. "Help me," he gasped and slumped over on the floor. Jake hurriedly rolled him over and loosened his coveralls. Forrest's face was ashen, his breathing shallow and labored.

Jake rushed to tell Mrs. Denton. She replied in a frightened voice, "He has a heart condition and won't take it easy."

Forrest was sitting on the floor holding his head in his hands when Jake and Mrs. Denton hurried into the shop. "You okay?" Mrs. Denton asked, placing her hand on his shoulder.

"Why wouldn't I be?" Forrest lied. "Just got a little lightheaded, that's all."

"Maybe you better lie down for a bit," Mrs. Denton gently suggested.

"Can't do it, Mom," Forrest answered as he struggled to his feet. "Got this saw about fixed, and I don't want to miss out on any of this flatlander's money. I'll be along directly." Realizing there was no changing his mind, Mrs. Denton departed, shaking her head.

While the Dentons talked, Jake placed his saw on the bench and quickly readjusted the carburetor to the point where it would run. He pulled on the starter rope a couple of times, and "VROOM," the saw started. He gunned it a few times before shutting it off.

"Must a been the filter," Forrest said, but without the strength of voice he had earlier. "Man gotta be careful with ether. That stuff nearly killed me once before."

"It can get you," Jake agreed. "How much do I owe you?"

"Gimme maybe eleven bucks for the filter, an' that'll do it," Forrest returned. "I couldn't even get the thing started."

Jake fished a fifty-dollar bill out of his wallet and handed it to Forrest. Seeing what it was, he said, "I'll see if Mom has change. I don't have it yet today."

"Keep the change, and we'll make it even later. I have another saw that needs work," Jake assured him, endeavoring to pay for his time and the stolen blasting caps.

"If you got work, we can do it that way, but I don't want no charity," Forrest said. "Me'n Mom are doing just fine all by ourselves."

Jake agreed and carried the saw out to his truck. Before departing, he walked to the porch and yelled goodbye to Mrs. Denton.

It was a thirty-six-mile trip over crooked mountain roads to the hospital from the Denton place. Jake's mind raced from one incident to another as the miles melted away; remembering Forrest fainting, he felt ill. Nearly killed him just to steal a few blasting caps, he thought.

In the hour it took to reach the hospital, Jake mentally worked through the situation he faced at Colemans, knowing he had to come up with some way to work without interruption. Jake stopped in the lobby, where a hospital volunteer gave him a pass and directions, reminding him that visiting hours didn't begin for another half hour. Killing time at the cafeteria, he purchased a sandwich and a newspaper. He discovered a nearby lumber store advertising a major tool sale while browsing through the paper.

With the sandwich devoured, Jake caught the elevator to the second floor and walked into Mac's room. His friend lay sleeping, one leg in traction, an arm in a cast, and his head bandaged. Jake sat in the chair next to his bed, his resolve stiffening.

Mac finally stirred himself awake, fighting the sedatives he took. "Jake?"

"How you doing, Mac?"

"Look at me! How do you think I'm doin'?" Before Jake answered, Mac continued, "I got careless. I was unlockin' the gate when Link rolled up with dust flyin'. Pissed me off, an' I steamed back to give him a piece of my mind. He stepped out with a tire iron and swung at my head. Broke my arm when I covered up. Broke my collar bone with the second swing. That finished me. He whacked me across the head when I bent over, and the lights went out. Dean was cuttin' grass when Link tore outta there. Wondered why Link was leaving with his fanny on fire, so he came to investigate an' here I am."

"What upset Link?" Jake asked, hoping that it wasn't because of him.

Mac exhaled like air rushing out of a giant balloon. "Said I shouldn't hang around you, Brewers 'cause things was gonna get real ugly." Mac continued on a different track. "Hanratty investigated. I tol' him no investigation was needed; someone needed killin'. He warned against retaliating. It's more'n a police matter now. Ain't none of them cops layin' in here with me."

"I wouldn't think you'd want them. Not a woman among 'em."

"C'mon, Brewer," Mac pleaded. "Ya know what I meant. Someone has to stop this stuff, and who's better suited than us, Dean and a couple of his brothers, and maybe Lane Kirkwood. He has no use for Colemans since those drugged-up idiots sideswiped his wife's car an' put her in the hospital. Johnny Ballard's more'n ready too. And ya know I can shoot so —"

"You never could shoot?" Jake kidded.

"Says you," Mac refuted angrily.

"Yeah. Remember that time Jeanne and I were shooting tin cans with my new pellet rifle. You challenged us to shoot for money. Being the good guy I am, I let you go first - remember?"

"Oh man, like it was yesterday. I missed the first shot and never got another. You guys cleaned me, an' I was s'posed to take Sis to the movies. When I told her about losing the money, she went from talking my ear off to giving me total cold shoulder in zero seconds. She said, "Robert, why can't you mind your own business? You know Jake cheated you.""

"Sis wouldn't say that about her big brother," Jake said.

"She surely said it. You went to the movies on my money. Then the next day, you kept tellin' us about the movie and how good it was, how ya had popcorn and how good that was, an' how ya had a couple glasses of pop to wash the popcorn down and how good that was too. Sis got mad and stormed into the house."

"I never knew if she was mad at you or me."

"Both," Mac angrily answered. "Me for a loosin' our movie money and you for settin' there telling how much you and Jeanne enjoyed yerselves on my money."

"Jeanne felt bad, you losing your money and wanted to give it back. Said it wasn't right after you planned on a movie. I told her you'd be upset if we didn't go, fair or not."

Jake allowed the bait to hang out for Mac to look over. "Whataya mean fair or not. It was fair, wasn't it, Brewer?" Mac asked, now wondering if he had been taken. "It had to be fair. You ain't smart enough to rig that contest. And anyway, the next day, I aimed at that catbird knowin' I couldn't hit it, not after the way I shot at them cans, so I squeezed one off. That bird came somersaultin' out of that mulberry tree an' just when ol' Jackson came walkin' out on the porch. I thought he was gonna kill me. Jackson called me an idiot for shootin' songbirds. I tried to explain it was an accident, but he said, 'It ain't no accident when a man takes aim and kills a bird; it's just plain murder. Mac, I don't need that kinda' guy hangin' around here.' Man, he was angrrrryyyy."

"You looked like you swallowed a toad when that catbird dropped. Dad never liked people shooting songbirds. Said they needed their butts kicked."

Mac detected the smile creeping across Jake's face. "Damn you, Brewer, I know I was screwed, but I can't see how you did it. Let's have it?"

"Since you're in traction, I guess it's safe. Dad stopped at the Parker Hardware to buy shells for his revolver. I saw that pellet gun and bought it. Dad was against it, said you couldn't use it for hunting, but he soon discovered it could murder songbirds. You showed him that. Anyway, when we got home, Jeanne and I tried it out. It shot off to the left, but after a few shots, we learned to compensate. We got where we were hitting pretty good when you showed up. I made the rule you had to start on the left side and shoot cans in rotation so you wouldn't make any lucky shots. Jeanne came over Sunday after church, and we sighted in that gun. Dad saw the pellets in the back of the barn where we hung the target and was still upset when you shot the bird."

"Man, Brewer, why didn't ya keep me from shootin' that bird?"

"How was I to know you would do something dumb?"

"'Cause I'm always doin' dumb things, that's how," Mac replied indignantly. The statement hit Jake's funny bone, and he chuckled, angering Mac. "Don't laugh, Brewer. I'll get even. Man, that jerks my chain, me going all them years thinkin' it was fair."

"If it makes you feel any better, the movie wasn't all that good. Jeannie went on all night how bad she felt because I cheated you out of your movie money. That isn't all. I've had to tell this story a lot of times over the years when people got to talking about shooting. You should feel sorry for me."

"Sorry, my pained fanny. And to think you've been braggin' behind my back all these years."

"I told you not to get in on a contest with a gun you didn't know."

"Ya can bet I wouldn't have shot for money if you'd a tol' me the gun was shootin' off. You sucked me in good. Once I started, I couldn't quit. You had the money I needed for the movies an' I knew Sis would kill me if I didn't get it back."

"You have the classic gambler's syndrome. You gamble with money you can't afford to lose until you lose it all, and then you cry in your milk. Besides talking bad, this anger thing can't be good for your head."

"Screw my head; I'm frosted. You would be too if yer best buddy screwed ya. That wasn't gamblin' neither, that was cheatin' an' they ain't the same. If I —"

"Is everything all right in here?" the nurse questioned, walking into the room. "I heard angry voices and thought I'd better check."

"One angry voice, miss, and I'm glad you came along. Mr. MacFarland's making threats on my life," Jake said innocently.

"Mr. MacFarland gets a little uptight."

"You'd get mad too. He cheated me when we was kids, an' he's been braggin' about it behind my back ever since. Then to make matters worse, he waits until I'm all crippled up and comes in here crowin' about what he did. I could kill him."

Mac was steaming, his face flushed. The nurse walked to his bedside, shook down a thermometer, inserted it under his tongue, and took his pulse and blood pressure. "Mr. MacFarland, it isn't good to get all worked up." Turning to Jake, she said, "Please don't argue with him, or we'll have to ask you to leave."

"His name is Jake Brewer, and he's a cheat," Mac retorted around the thermometer. "An' I'm not Mr. MacFarland, I'm Mac, an' he ain't steamin' me; I'm doin' it all by myself. He ain't smart enough to steam me. An' I'm sick a being here, an' I told ya that before too."

"Mr. MacFarland, you're at it again," the nurse warned.

"Didn't I just tell you my name is Mac, an' all I want is out of here," Mac stormed?

"Any more outbursts and Mr. Brewer must leave," the nurse said as she departed.

"Man, ya breeze in here, rile me up, get my butt chewed, an' then sit there smilin'. What else ya gonna do to me today, Brewer?" Mac asked, smiling as he now saw the humor. "Mark my word, I'll get even."

"Vengeance is mine sayeth the Lord," Jake uttered without thinking.

"Oh, shove it, Brewer. Anyway, I'm glad you told me about that gun contest. I thought ya beat me fair an' square all these years, an' now I know better. You couldn't beat me now."

"I'm willing to go again as long as you don't get mad when you lose. You're such a sore loser."

"Loser my stinkin' butt. An' we're way off track here, Brewer. The real shootin' contest should be at Link an' his idiot brothers."

"Let's let the legal system do the job. It'll work out all right."

"Work out? Look at me. If you was layin' here all beat up, you'd be thinkin' different."

CHAPTER 27

Jake departed the lumber store with a Ryobi battery-powered drill, a box of three-inch deck screws, and three sheets of plywood. He parked at an unoccupied roadside rest and cut plywood with his chainsaw to produce two door and two window covers. He placed the tools and boards in the truck and returned to scatter sawdust and wood scraps.

Needing gas, Jake pulled into an Exxon station and country store with outside entrance restrooms. He filled up and pulled around to the side for a nap. He took the drill's battery charger and one battery into the bathroom, where he discovered an old medicine closet with an outlet on the side. He placed the charger on top of the medicine closet, plugged it in, and returned to the truck to rest. After an hour passed, he exchanged batteries in the charger and returned to the truck for another catnap.

An elderly couple talking their way toward the bathrooms snapped Jake awake. He glanced at his watch and noted that the battery should be fully charged. He waited anxiously for the man to exit, and when he did, he retrieved his equipment. After placing it in the truck, he returned and washed his face. When he opened the door, the attendant stood waiting. "Can I help you?" Jake asked innocently.

"Yeah, did you see anything strange in there?"

Jake knew the question might come and had an answer ready. "I had my razor charging if that's what you mean. I need to knock back my whiskers before I visit the hospital. Didn't think you'd mind."

"Thought it was something like that, but I had to check. That guy reported a bomb."

After thanking the attendant, Jake headed north. He parked in the empty overflow lot at the hospital and headed up to find Mac entertaining a roommate. "Good evening, guys," Jake said as he walked in.

"Jake, meet Ralph. Got hit by a car while he was ridin' a bike. I told him 85 was too old for bikes, but he says it keeps him young."

Jake shook left hands with Ralph; his right was in a cast. "It's hell," Ralph said. "I fought through two wars and three wives without getting hurt and then wind up here because of a hit and run accident. Japs couldn't kill me in the big war, and the Gooks couldn't do it in Korea, but a damned Toyota rice burner got me right here in town. How do you figure?"

"Guess the Good Lord knew Mac needed mature company," Jake answered.

"Ralph beware," Mac said. "He'll get in yer knickers too."

They made small talk until 9:00 P.M. when Jake checked his watch and prepared to depart. "You stayin' on the Hill tonight?" Mac asked.

"Heading home. Have things to do in the morning," Jake said as he departed. There were few vehicles in the lot at this time of the evening, so he took the drill and started screws along the sides of each plywood sheet. Facing the screws in, he lashed the plywood together with a length of nylon rope he carried to secure things on his truck rack. He took another length of rope and fashioned a harness to carry the sheets.

Stepping into the truck, he heard sirens approaching. Trying to stay calm and hoping someone didn't report him, he pulled the truck into gear and moved toward the street. With sirens howling and lights flashing, a squad car pulled off the road with two ambulances following. Led by the squad car, they raced off towards the hospital emergency entrance leaving Jake shaking.

Within the hour, Jake sat on his haunches in the dark running through his plan, his truck hidden off the road. Satisfied, he slipped the plywood harness over his head and grabbed the drill and screws. Night sounds engulfed him as he headed through the woods to the Coleman shanty, where he placed his load in a ditch. He then returned to the truck for the explosives. Hearing nothing at their shanty, he carefully shouldered his first load and eased across the road. He ran a screw through the front door into the jam to temporarily hold it closed and ran around to screw the back door. The drill roared like earth-moving equipment in the quiet darkness. He ran four corner screws in on the board covering the first window. Inside, a muffled voice hollered, "What's that noise?" Unintelligible mumbling followed.

Jake eased the plywood against the building at the opposite window and began running in screws. Lights came on, but he was far enough along now that no one could see outside. Jake eased back along the side of the building and twisted the electric meter out of its base, causing the place to go dark.

"They cut the damn power," a mean voice complained.

Another deeper voice yelled, "That you out there, Danning? Ya better let us outta here, Danning, or you'll get what Carlin got. I swear I'll kill ya, Danning."

He arrived out front as someone smashed against the door. Jake slammed the plywood against it and began running screws home. The door buckled under the force of a hurtling body. The door wouldn't hold another ram. Working feverishly, he ran in screws around the door until the drill battery died. Desperately, he inserted the second battery. Another charge inside. This time with the screws in, the plywood held. Jake ran around back and drove in the screws until the futile ramming ceased. Additional screws followed into each window as the occupants threatened him with every evil punishment known to humanity.

Jake was recrossing the road with the explosives when a car approached, its spotlight flickering about for deer. The light caught him momentarily. He melted into the grass, his heart banging. The vehicle stopped while a spotlight danced across his hiding place. A female remarked, "It was a bear. It ran right in there."

"Wow, look what they did now," the male voice said. "They boarded their house."

"Let's get out of here. If Rob finds out I was with you, we're both dead meat."

Jake recrossed the road with the explosives and began work. The smell of human waste hung heavily under the shanty, pushing Jake to quickly wire the explosive packages together. He placed them on the building sill plate and ran the thin antenna wire through the weeds and up the backside of a close-in pine tree.

Running the first wire to the timer, he breathed heavily before connecting the wire. *If this thing's going to blow prematurely, this one* will do it; he thought as he wiped the sweat off his forehead. Jake's heart pounded remembering the basement incident. Touching the second wire, he considered a thunderous explosion, the last sound of his life. Relief flooded over him as quiet prevailed. Working rapidly, he completed wiring the devices and hung each wire out of sight.

Slipping back away from the shanty stench, he breathed deeply of the clean air. Looking the place over, he realized anyone checking under the building might see the explosives. An idea hit him as he grabbed his rope and tools. The first truck was locked tight, but the second truck's door was unlocked with the key in the ignition. Link's truck. The arrogant bugger figures no one dares fool with his vehicle, Jake thought as he placed his stuff in the back. He fired up the new Dodge, and the big Cummins diesel purred to life. He drove around the first pickup, stopping when he neared the end of the shanty. Slipping into four-wheel drive, low range, he crept against the building, increased throttle, and pushed it off the blocks. It crashed with a "THUD." Nothing was visible now.

Easing back, Jake turned up the road. Swinging around at the top of the hill, he locked the emergency brake. Looking around, he found a music tape case lying on the seat and a pair of sneakers on the floor. He took the shoestring out of a sneaker and looped it over the emergency brake release. He wedged the fuel peddle down, holding it in place. The emergency brake held the truck while Jake stepped out. He picked his stuff out of the back and pulled the shoestring through the window. It's only neighborly to return what you borrow, he thought and gave the string a jerk. The big diesel crawled down the hill in low range as Jake ran to retrieve his truck. The crash of twisting metal shook the night as Link's truck smashed something.

Jake thought through questions as he drove along in the dark, disturbing thoughts with disastrous conclusions. What was the connection between Roger Danning and Link, and what had happened to Carlin? "I guess the best part of the night is Link thinks Danning got him. And if he's upset now, how will he feel when he sees his truck?" Jake wondered aloud.

Jake grew ever more apprehensive as he considered the events he started in motion. Someone would surely die if anyone dialed the bag phone number at the wrong time of the day. And what if the timer failed? What then? It could go off at any time. "Why'd I do this?" Jake chastised himself, worrying if there might be some way the cops could trace this episode to him.

CHAPTER 28

Jake packed the truck to go north and had a light meal ready when Jeanne arrived home from work. After picking up Pappy, they headed north with Jeanne driving and talking with her father while Jake sat in the back seat thinking through their situation, wondering what had happened on the hill in the week since he had last been there. He was on edge. Too much could go wrong.

Jake discovered a new phone in their mailbox when he stopped for mail. At Hill Place, they found a note on the window explaining Adelphia telephone linemen spent Thursday running cable along the power line poles bringing phones to Hill Place. The message contained their new phone number, explained their phone was tested, and said they could use the box on the back porch for emergencies. They'd be back Saturday to run the lines into the home.

After they unpacked, Jake plugged in the phone and tested it by calling home while Jeanne created a light supper. After eating and talking for a while, they went to bed, where Jeanne asked Jake what was bothering him. "Nothing, Honey. I'm just uptight about Mac getting hurt trying to help us."

"Jake, nightmares eat you alive, and you have night sweats. I should have listened to you and called it quits when we started having problems. But no, I had to talk tough until Link beat the tough out of me."

"No, Jeanne, you were right. I was born and raised here, and it holds special memories for us.

Things will work themselves out if we hold on. Poskevich finally seems to be getting on top of things."

"We'll get a chance to talk with him when he brings Sue to dinner next Saturday."

Pappy slept in on Saturday morning, and after eating a light breakfast, Jake prepared to visit Mac at the hospital. "I wish I could go with you, Jake, but I hate to leave Pappy alone."

"I know, Jake said. He kissed Jeanne goodbye and headed for their truck. When he arrived, he parked away from the hospital, where the truck was visible from Mac's room and went upstairs where Mac waited. "Hey Brewer, do I got news for ya," Mac greeted excitedly. "Ya ain't gonna believe it."

"You always have news," Jake replied, waving a greeting to Mac's roommate Ralph as he sat down on the window sill, "and most of it is somewhat unbelievable."

"C'mon, it's about the Colemans. Somebody wrecked their place the night you were here."

"The cops called me at home. I can't figure out why none of them woke up," Jake replied innocently. "They had to hear all that pounding."

"Wasn't any poundin'. They used screws and worked fast. Screwed plywood boards over the doors and windows. Then they used Link's new truck to push the house off the foundation. Dumbo musta left the keys in it."

"Their shanty didn't have a foundation; it sat on cement blocks," Jake said in an informed manner, further agitating his friend.

"Okay, okay," Mac stammered. "So it wasn't much of a house, and it sat on cement blocks. What does that have to do with anything?"

"Facts are facts," Jake replied naively, goading his friend.

"Can I go on?" Mac asked angrily. Without waiting for an answer, he continued. "Anyway, they drove off in Link's truck and —."

"It should be easy enough to find the truck. The cops have pictures of it from when Link was stalking Jeanne. They'll find that truck and catch who's driving it. Bingo, they got their culprit. Case closed."

Mac's aggravation mounted with the interruptions and dumb detective-type suggestions. "Stop. Jake, yer way ahead of me again," Mac said disgustedly. "The truck wasn't lost. They drove to the top of the hill, turned the truck around, and sent it back toward Coleman's place. Lucky it smashed into a tree' fore it got to the house. Link's upset an' makin' threats."

"Threats are his life's work. Remember how —"

"Hold it," Mac shouted, holding his hand out like a cop stopping traffic. "There's more. They were boarded up the next day in that heat until Ol' man Corbett walked his dog by an' called the cops."

"Well, I'll be," Jake exclaimed with a shocked look.

"Who'd do that?"

"Roger Danning an' friends is everybody's guess. Link told 'em that."

"I wouldn't want to be old Roger," Jake said, shaking his head.

"Fred said they're still living in the house an' they ain't got no power."

"The health department should condemn the place. That's the only way they'll move."

"Fat chance that'll happen," Mac chuckled. "They call the guy headin' the department Chick for a reason; it's short for chicken. It fits too."

"You probably ain't got any idea how Mac got knobbed up," Ralph butted in. "Know what he told me?"

"That'd be hard to tell," Jake answered.

"Mac was at choir practice," Ralph began, "and when the choir stood, a fat woman in front of him had her dress tucked into the crack of her fanny. Mac knew she wouldn't like that, so he pulled it out. She turned around and slugged him good. That's when he got his first black eye. Sunday morning when the choir stood up, the woman's dress was stuck in her fanny again. I know what you're thinking, but Mac didn't pull it out. He learned his lesson, but the guy next to him hadn't been to choir practice, and he pulled the dress out. Mac knew how mad that made her, and as he was gently tucking it back in," Ralph said, making a tucking motion with his hand, "she mauled him all over that choir loft. They had to rush him here in the ambulance. He said he's giving up the choir altogether when he gets out. Can you believe that?"

"I believe the part that Mac told you that," Jake said with a smile.

Mac quickly moved to another topic. "We had visitors. You won't guess who."

"Wasn't Link, was it, him in here feeling sorry, apologizing and all? Maybe he got religion."

"No, it wasn't Link, an' before ya rain on a guy's parade, let me tell you. First came Crow and Buzzard, an' they went on about this feud thing, how you better lay off while ya can. Then Bailey Donahue walked in big as you please. Yes, Bailey. She walked right in and planted one on me. She was all ears listenin' to the Laceys. Spurred 'em on some too. Crow said him and the Buzzard are stayin' clear of you, yer a lightnin' rod fer trouble. They went on a bit and then left. I asked ol' Bailey how she's doing, an' she said, "Nobody's complainin'." I bet they ain't, neither. Ask Ralph. She's one foxy lookin' lady. 'Member, I went with her in high school? What in the world did I ever give up on that stuff for?"

"If I remember correctly, Bailey threw you over for that fat, little pimple-faced kid who played the flute in the band. Said she wanted somebody a little more exciting. The two of them used to go to the library and read poetry together."

"Oh bull, she moved to Pittsburgh."

"Why was Bailey here? She couldn't have been up here looking for you."

"Said she's writing stuff and has a story here. She stopped at the building supply and bought herself a battery-powered stud finder. She had that gadget on when she came to the hospital, and it went off when she went by our room like it found a stud. She just followed the buzzer. It got ever stronger as she got closer to me."

"And it led her right over to Ralph's bed, and that's when you spotted her."

"Oh, sit on it, Brewer. I don't even know why I talk to you."

"Maybe Ralph got tired of you, and I'm all you have left."

"BS Brewer. Anyway, Bailey was in rare form. You can ask Ralph," Mac said, stopping for Ralph to confirm his story.

"Oh ya," Ralph agreed. "Man, I'd like to cozy up next to that sex kitten for a year or two."

"That could be hard on a person's health," Jake replied with mocked concern.

"She'll have to take her chances. A man my age can't be worrying about the welfare of every woman that comes down the pike, not and look out for his own needs too."

The three snickered until Mac added, "Bailey ain't changed much. Still has that sexy voice and wild laugh. That red-haired Irishman —"

"Irishwoman Mac," Jake corrected in a serious manner. "Either you're blind, or she's lost that figure she had in high school."

"She ain't lost nuthin' Brewer," Mac snapped.

"Probably all make-up and plastic now, Mac," Jake countered.

"So what if it is," Mac said. "She looks good, an' them green eyes still grab me. Still got that nice chest too."

"I'm surprised you'd notice Mac, you with your disabilities and advancing age. Be careful; you could have heart problems and a rapid loss of manliness. The two go hand in hand."

"I ain't losin' my manliness, not one bit. I'm as good as I ever was."

"Yeah," Jake agreed, "but how good was that. Bailey threw you over for a pimply-faced —."

"Just take my word for it, Brewer," Mac injected. "I don't have any agin' problems."

"How old are you, Mac?"

"Same as you."

"Somebody must have left you out in a lot of bad weather."

"Go to hell, Brewer. Now, where was I? Oh ya, I was fixin' to tell you Bailey said she was in for a checkup after her operation. She had a hysterectomy and was out of business for two or three more weeks. Said she got bad news and good news. The good news was the doctor found my high school class ring during the operation. Then she laid her head back and gave one of them belly bustin' laughs. Man, it was just like old times."

"She's a freelance writer now workin' on a series of articles for the Country Journal Magazine," Mac began. "They print stuff about people in rural areas, how they live, and like that. She said it gives readers a look into 'The way it was' as she put it."

Ralph spoke up. "Bailey's coming by to take pictures of Mac. Said she'd get one of me too."

"Maybe she can get a picture laying beside you, Mac, kind of consoling you, and they could print it. Man, Mac, the guys at the Chat N Chew would have something to talk about."

"Ya, my funeral if Sis saw them pictures."

"Mac, think on it. Do you want to love up on old Bailey and get your picture taken, or are you gonna let a little fear ruin a great story?"

"I ain't gettin' a picture taken in bed with nobody. How dumb do you think I am?"

"Don't ask!"

"You twisted a legitimate picture into a dirty little scene. See how you are?"

"You loved it, Mac. Truth be known, you're probably all hot and bothered right now thinking about cuddling up to old Bailey. I'll stop and tell Sis she better be nice to you if she plans on keeping you."

"Mind yer own business, Brewer. I got more'n enough problems already."

"Don't say I didn't offer," Jake returned. "Consider this; Sis might get a little jealous over Old Bailey and decide you were worth fighting for. Who knows what that could do for a marriage, the marital bliss kind of thing."

"Ya, right, Brewer," Mac sarcastically returned. "Marital bliss is mostly a marital blister at my place. I could end up dead, or worse yet, nutted."

A bright flash of light surprised them. When they looked toward its source, the light flashed again. "Smile pretty boys," a husky voice called from the doorway as the men struggled to see through the light patterns dancing before their eyes. The camera flashed again, followed by husky laughter. "Told you I'd be back," Bailey said and kissed Mac.

"Wow, Bailey, yer something," Mac managed to say as he glanced at Jake. "I tol' Jake, you're in town."

"Jake Brewer, I didn't recognize you," Bailey said as she whirled around. "Man, you're looking good," she added, starting to kiss Jake on the mouth. He turned his head slightly, offering his cheek instead.

"Bailey won't rape you, baby," she chided as the color rose on his face. "Not with witnesses."

Mac took the conversation in another direction. "I tol' Jake about yer writing."

"Great!" Bailey said. "I'm endeavoring to capture the feel of mountain life, the wild freedom, hell-raising attitude that's prevalent in Sterling County. You know Jake?"

"I'm not sure what we're talking about," Jake softly replied.

"Your feud with the Colemans, for example," Bailey explained. "Conflict sells."

The comment infuriated Jake. "Bailey, you're hard up for heroes if you're championing the criminals tearing the county apart?"

"I've considered several story angles - the Hatfield and McCoy hillbilly feud thing or maybe a backward family standing bravely against oppressive outsiders, that or land thieves who force people to take drastic measures to get their property back, those twists or —"

"Or maybe the truth Bailey, maybe that would work for a documentary," Jake growled.

"It would seem that you're trying to eradicate them single-handedly!"

"Where'd you get that idea?" Jake flashed.

"Buster Coleman was killed on your property. I've already sold the story to a publisher. Add the fire you set, and there's a real story here."

Fighting back angry rhetoric, Jake rose to depart, "Well, Mac, Ralph, it's been good talking to you guys. Bailey, you take care."

Bailey's voice called, "Nice seeing you, Jake," as he walked out. Then she turned to Mac and innocently asked, "Who stepped on his tail?"

"That Coleman crap," Mac angrily replied. "Look what Link Coleman did ta me. Jeanne's been beat to hell an' almost raped. They killed Jake's dog an' tried to burn 'em out. You're way off base on this one, Bailey."

"Ah, Mac, it isn't all that bad. Somehow I find the Colemans exciting in a strange sort of way. You might think this is crazy, but Link is somewhat handsome, a kind of young Ernest Borgnine. Those strong, white teeth and huge muscles. You and Jake may be more than a little jealous."

"He ain't nothin' but trouble Bailey. Be careful!"

"The Colemans have rights too and no spokesperson."

"Bailey, you can't shine dog crap like the Colemans with smooth words. The best ya can do is buff 'em to a high gloss for a short period of time. You may fool some bleeding heart flatlanders with a bunch of BS, but you can't believe it yerself. You ain't that dumb."

Jake's trip home was a mixed bag. Bailey's arrival added another twist that worried Jake. He was still thinking about her when he arrived home, and Jeanne met him at the truck.

"Jake, you're not going to believe what happened now," Jeanne said excitedly.

"Come out on the deck so we can tell you."

When they reached the deck and sat down, Jeanne began again. "Dad and I were sitting out here when we heard a WHOOMP WHOOMP sound. It was one of those little helicopters, and it came right in close and looked at us. You could see their faces, and they were anything but friendly-looking. Dad waved at them, and they flipped him the finger. It looked like the passenger had one of those automatic weapons you see in the movies. After they looked us over, they disappeared over the hill to the west of here. After a while, we heard them heading south toward the state game lands. Think we should call the cops?"

"Let's save it for Glen."

CHAPTER 29

"Blue Birdie . . . This is Angel Ops."

"Go ahead, Angel Ops."

"You want to record this! There's a lot to report."

"Roger Angel Ops. Go ahead with your report."

*"Checked out the Brewer digs. Jake's truck wasn't there. His wife was sittin'
on their deck with some old man. He waved at us. Wife ran into the house.
Possibly saw our weapons. Not —"*

"Dammit, Labrozzi, I told you to be careful!"

*"I believe that's Angel Ops to you. Anyway, the three pot fields you wanted
checked out are all there, and they are big, big, big. Have to be worth millions
on the market. Like your informant said, they're all in elk food plot clearings,
and they planted the pot on the remote sides of those plots. Someone's taking
care of them, but we didn't see anyone. Did see a couple of biiiiggggg bull elk
in one of them. Wrecker wanted to dust them off with his pea shooter."*

*"You make sure what Wrecker might want to do and what Wrecker does
are different. Got it?"*

"Got it."

"See anything that connects those plots to Coin Man?"

"I take it Coin Man is worth a Penny?"

"Close enough. Maybe not quite a penny now if our Intel is correct."

*"Coin Man's Mercedes is parked in front of the shanty you wanted checked
out. There were four people in the car. We didn't get close enough to be noticed.
Just flew by."*

*"When you finish your report, I have assignments for you and Wrecker.
Hope he's listening?"*

"*He's hanging on every word. You wanted to know about access to the pot fields. They're Game Commission roads, and they're gated. You could walk by on the roads that lead into them and not notice anyone was growing anything. Someone's putting a lot of work into them.*"

"*Roger that. Anything else to report?*"

"*No. You don't seem too interested in wildlife stories.*"

"*No interest at all. Angel Ops, I need you to fly past Coin Man's car with Wrecker taking pictures.*"

"*Anything special you need in the pictures?*"

"*Shoot everything you see. Don't get too close. I don't want that ass to get suspicious until he gets his package.*"

"*Next, I need you to get a stem of pot from each of those plots without putting chopper marks in those fields. Can you do that?*"

"*You're talkin' to a dust-off pilot who —*"

"*What's a dust-off pilot?*"

"*Chopper pilot that picked up the wounded in Nam. I did it for two tours. We'll get your pot samples. But why three? They're all the same.*"

"*I want you to tear off the samples so whoever is tending those fields will notice someone knows you were there. I don't want them to know it was someone with a chopper. Got it?*"

"*Got it. Is that all?*"

"*No! I want you to drop Wrecker off near town without him being seen. Tonight when it's dark, I want Wrecker to run eight or ten gun rounds into the driver side door of Coin Man's Mercedes. Put three more through the windshield in front of the driver's seat. Put a stalk of Mary Jane in each hole. Then I want you to pick Wrecker up where you leave him off and come home. Just don't be seen. I'll leave the details to you two. Any questions?*"

"*Angel Ops looked at Wrecker with his palm up to see if he had questions. After Wrecker shook his head, he replied. "No questions on this end. I'll have to sit the bird down somewhere until it's time to pick him up. State College isn't that far away, and they have an airport. I'll refuel too. Any questions or problems with that?*"

"*Got a comment I almost forgot. Wrecker, use a .380 caliber gun. That way they can't know what gun you used.*"

"*Roger. Blue Birdie. Over and out.*"

As soon as Angel Ops signed off the air, Wrecker hit him. "Where do you plan to dump me off, flyboy?"

"It'll be your choice, but your choices are limited with ninety-five percent of this county forested."

"I can just quit."

"Right! You know what happens when folks don't listen. You killed Lonestar for not listening. Could happen to you too."

While Wrecker got the camera ready, Angel Ops swung over Hill Road and headed to photograph the Mercedes. Two men headed for their shanty while Coin Man stood talking with another man.

"Run that damned camera," Angel Ops yelled above the chopper noise.

"It's running! Not sure why this is so freaking important."

"There's a lot of money involved and maybe a double-cross. Glad we aren't those boys."

"Won't be much of a loss. Look where they live."

With that part of the assignment complete, they headed south to the first pot plot, where they hovered just above the patch. Wrecker bent low off the skid and jerked off the first sample.

Climbing back into the cabin, he remarked, "I mangled the plant as Blue Birdie ordered. The grounds soft and with no tracks, someone is going to wonder how that happened."

"A little mystery is good for everyone."

They took off for a drop site after collecting the final samples. The fire tower was five miles from town, while well sites were closer. They chose a close-in well site with a good road out to the road to town.

Heading to the tower site, Angel Ops remarked, "You may want to leave your .44 magnum here in the bag. It doesn't fit Blue Birdie's orders for this op."

"How will he know?"

"Look, I don't know how he knew about the pot fields or how he's going to use the info we're gathering or why he wants you to do the job you're pulling off. But you can bet there are going to be surprises for somebody. Maybe a lot of somebodies."

CHAPTER 30

The Sunday morning sun climbed into view as the Brewers headed out with Jake's camera gear, binoculars, and revolver in a backpack. Fog hung like a glacier field over the valley below. Their boots kicked up fire ash puffs with the smell of burnt forest riding their tongues. Taking care not to be seen, they dropped off the ridge that ran past the Laceys and walked down the gated game commission road. Hearing an approaching vehicle, they worked their way up a small draft and hid behind a fallen tree where they could watch the road. Jake shrugged off the backpack and glassed the truck coming into view. "Link," he said, handing Jeanne the binoculars, "and he has himself a new truck. Wonder where he's getting the big bucks."

With Link disappearing around a bend in the road, Jake decided to see how he got past the Game Commission gate. They worked their way up the side of the mountain until they could see the gate standing open. "Gates aren't open to the public," Jake remarked as a heavy-caliber rifle shot rang out in the valley and echoed back. BAWHAAAAM. A second shot followed the first one. Then silence.

"Probably shot a deer," Jeanne replied.

"Let's give him a challenge," Jake said, handing her the binoculars. "I'll be right back." He ran toward the gate and soon emerged from the woods where Jeanne could see him. The open lock hung on the gate post with the key in it. "No, no Link. You always lock up and take the key with you," Jake said as he swung the gate back in place. Slipping the keeper in place, he snapped the lock and placed the key in his pocket. He found small sticks and jammed the keyway full.

After pounding them in with a flat rock, he smashed off the excess so they couldn't be pulled out, wiped off the lock with his handkerchief, and headed for Jeanne.

"Phew," he said, breathing heavily. "It's a hot one today."

"Gives you an idea of what hell might be like if you don't mend your evil ways. Pray tell, what were you doing."

"I closed the gate for Link."

Come on, Brewer," Jeanne said. "I watched you."

"It's called adding a challenge to his life. Unless Link can fly, he's walking home."

Soon Link drove into view. Jeanne glassed his truck as it passed. "He shot a deer all right," she said, handing Jake the glasses.

"Uh-huh," Jake agreed. "Hey, that's not a deer; it's a young elk."

Jake handed Jeanne the glasses so she could confirm his discovery. Link was now out looking at the gate. "He can't find his key, and he's cursing too," Jeanne said gleefully. "Now he's returning to his truck," she said, maintaining a running discourse of what was occurring. "Looks like he has a flashlight. He's trying to see what's wrong with the lock. Oh man, Jake, you missed a good one. He jumped up, cursing, and banged his head on that gate. He's mad. Here, look!"

Jake took the glasses and watched Link standing in the road, kicking stones and cursing while holding his head. "He knows he's licked. He threw the flashlight in the truck's window and started walking up the road. Swearing like a jaybird and kicking rocks too."

"Let's get out of here," Jeanne said.

"There's a steel mirror in that survival kit. If you see anyone coming, flash it back and forth in the sun to get my attention. I'm going to take a picture of that elk for the Game Commission."

Jake soon stood on the bank taking pictures from the truck's rear end with the license plate visible in the foreground and the gate in the background. Finished, he slipped the camera back into the backpack and placed it on the bank where he could quickly retrieve it.

Opening the truck door with his handkerchief, he searched through the truck. He discovered a handgun under the driver's seat and pulled it out with his handkerchief exercising care not to leave fingerprints. It was an older model Smith and Wesson 38 Special with a familiar look. He ran the gun across the road, slipped it into his backpack, and returned to the truck. "Never leave keys in the ignition, Link," he muttered as he pulled them from the ignition and threw the keyring up into the woods. Glancing up the mountain, he caught the mirror flashing wildly in the sunlight. He waved his arms over his head indicating he saw her signal. A four-wheeler roared toward him as he ran up the bank, snatching his backpack as he raced into the woods and out of sight. The engine went quiet.

He couldn't find Jeanne. Many places in the woods tend to look alike, but he was sure he was near the right place. Panic set in. What if they had her? He slid down to catch his breath, and something hit him. He jerked around, scanning the forest above, finally seeing Jeanne's hand waving cautiously.

Jake picked up his pack and carefully moved beside her. "Man, you scared me when I couldn't find you and again when you hit me with that stick."

"Sorry, Honey," Jeanne whispered back. "I flashed the mirror when I first heard the engine. When you didn't seem to catch it, I moved up here."

Jake nodded understanding without saying anything.

"What did you put in the backpack?"

"My camera."

"The second time." When Jake didn't answer, she continued. "I'm scared. He knows we're close."

"Let me see the binoculars," Jake said without answering her question.

Link was lying on the ground on his back holding a propane torch above his head, burning sticks out of the lock. He protected his face with his bandaged hand as the flaming material burned out. Finally believing the lock was free, Link shut off the torch and tossed it in the truck. When he reached in the truck to retrieve his keys, they were gone.

"Man, he's storming," Jake relayed. "He discovered his keys are misplaced."

Link jerked the door open, looking through the truck for his keys, then fished through his pockets. Nothing! He slammed the door with enough force to rock the truck and then kicked the door. He grabbed his rifle through the window and fired the four remaining rounds into the woods. His threat followed, "You bastard, Danning. I'll kill you."

After Link roared off on the four-wheeler, the Brewers headed out across the top of the mountain to the closest elk clear cut. These fields were seldom visited except for deer hunting season and then only by a few hearty individuals. Dragging an elk out would be a chore.

They stayed back in the trees while Jake carefully glassed the field. The vegetation was darker green and taller than the natural grasses along the side of the field farthest from the road. After studying it for a bit, he handed the glasses to Jeanne. "Look at this side of the field. What's that look like to you?"

"I don't know . . . weeds of some kind."

"Could be, but I think it's what that helo was checking. Link might have been down here checking on it when he ran into that elk. Bet it's pot. Let's slip down for a closer look. Be careful. They could booby trap the place."

The Brewers made their way back along the hillside toward the vegetation. Jake took the camera out of his backpack and cautioned Jeanne to wait while he got a closer look. He proceeded carefully, looking for tripwires hooked to explosives or cameras. He caught sight of a wire just off of the ground as he approached the field and carefully eased by it. His hunch was correct. Someone was using this remote field to grow acres of marijuana. He took several pictures and then moved to the field, where he cut one stem for future use.

Retreating, he found Jeanne waiting anxiously. They discussed what he had discovered and then headed out across the mountaintop for Hill Place.

CHAPTER 31

"BAAAWHOOOM." A powerful explosion-generated fireball sucked the wreckage of the Coleman shanty up in a mushroom cloud. The concussion rolled through the mountains. As the force of the explosion waned, gravity pulled pieces of burning debris earthward. Fire consumed the remains of the shanty.

The shock wave slammed Clyde and Lu Coleman's mobile home. Bewildered, Clyde angrily asked, "Can't a body get a little sleep without you bangin' around?"

"Keep yer mouth off me. Somethin' blowed up."

Lu picked her way across the darkened bedroom. In wide-eyed amazement, she asked, "What've them boys done now?" She answered herself, her voice high pitched. "They blowed up their house; that's what they done."

Fire illuminated the Coleman bedroom with grotesque flashes. Secondary explosions cracked like fireworks. An enormous blast sent showers of sparks and blazing material skyward in a rainbow of destruction.

"I better git down there," Clyde said, his eyes glued to the inferno.

"An' git yerself killed. Ain't nobody there. Trucks are gone."

"I tol' 'em not to keep chain saw gas inside. That's what blowed up, that an' all them shells.

Maybe dynamite too. They always got some."

"Hard to tell what they had. For sure, whatever they had, they ain't got no more."

A police vehicle approached, siren blazing. Flashing lights illuminated the night. The cruiser stopped on the road above the shanty fire, and the driver played a spotlight around. The car inched forward, then back as the driver searched the area.

"It's the cops that's camped out behind Lacey's place," Clyde muttered. "Took 'em long enough," Lu added. "Prob'ly up there sleepin'."

Finding nothing, the police vehicle approached the mobile home. After running his spotlight over the mobile home and the surrounding weeds, he got out with his gun drawn. Clyde pulled on a pair of pants and shuffled out the door. Lu stood behind him in pajamas, her hair in curlers. "How about turnin' off that siren!" Clyde irritably ordered. "Don't need the lights neither."

"Oh yeah," the young trooper said, and he silenced the siren, explaining he had to leave the lights on at a crime scene.

"Ya might put away that cannon. Ya ain't catchin' no bad guys tonight."

"What happened?" the trooper asked, holstering his weapon.

"You been sittin' up there spyin' on everything we done. You tell us."

"Yes, sir," the trooper apologized, realizing the police weren't popular with this family. "Any idea what caused the explosion?"

"They prob'ly fergot somethin' cookin' an' went ta town," Lu said. "That'd be our guess, a cookin' accident that touched off chain saw gas and shells."

"The building wasn't occupied?" the trooper questioned.

"It's Friday night," Clyde answered. "You'll find 'em down to the Pandemonium."

The trooper's radio cracked alive, and he hurriedly climbed into his car to answer the call. "Schmidt here," the trooper answered in an excited voice.

"This is base. Your backup and the fire department should be there momentarily. What's your status? Over."

"Base, fires are burning all over. They hit the woods, and we're in deep trouble."

"What did the explosion look like? Over"

"A fireball shot up like a nuclear weapon went off."

"Did you see anything suspicious? Over."

"Nothing," Schmidt replied. "Over"

"Any traffic in or out of the Brewer place tonight?"

"None," Schmidt confirmed.

Sirens became audible and grew louder as the emergency vehicles raced toward him. Two volunteer fire crews quickly had hoses out, spraying the remains of the house while large and growing grass fires burned. Clyde ran to the fire lieutenant. "You in charge here?"

"I am."

"Let that shanty burn," Clyde snapped. "Get them grass fires' fore they burn us out."

The fire lieutenant stomped off to talk with the crew hosing the house remains. "Ain't nobody left alive in what little's left. Let's get the grass fires."

A fireman moved the truck and began spraying fires dotting the field. A third fire truck arrived, and everything was soon under control. Darkness settled in except for flashing emergency vehicle lights. Police officers strung crime scene tape around the perimeter of the burned shanty. Officer Schmidt returned to his position on the mountain; another trooper sat in his vehicle waiting for daylight when they could inspect the ruins.

*   *   *

Worried, Jake Brewer fast-forwarded through a part of the Forest Gump video and began watching at what he estimated to be mid-point. The phone rang, and Jeanne answered. "Jake, it's Hanratty."

"Yes, sir." He was nervously anticipating the call, his mind running through disaster scenes. "Good evening. What can I do for you?"

"Where have you been this evening?" Hanratty calmly asked

"Is there a problem, officer?"

"A fire and explosion at the Coleman place."

"I suppose we're suspects," Jake said sarcastically, forcing anger into his voice. "Where have you been this evening?" Hanratty calmly asked.

"We went to Trawler John's for a fish fry. I'd guess we left there around nine. Drove home and packed our clothes. I've been watching a video since then."

"What video Jake?"

"Forrest Gump," Jake answered.

"Can you describe the scene you're watching?"

"Gump's woman died." Jake held the phone by the TV until Hanratty could get an idea of what was happening. "Did you get that?"

"Where will you be if we need to talk with you?"

"Here tonight. Plan to leave for Parker in the morning," Jake answered innocently.

"Thanks, Jake."

"What was that about, Honey?" Jeanne asked as Jake replaced the receiver.

"There's been an explosion on the hill, and Hanratty wanted to verify where we were. I told him about going to Trawler John's, but I didn't tell him we rode up along the river because we can't account for that time. If anybody asks, we came straight home from Trawler John's. We packed clothes. I watched a video. You paid bills. That's all they need to know."

Jeanne nodded, a concerned look shadowing her face. "Is this tied to the truck stop phone call?"

"We came directly home, packed clothes, paid bills, and watched a video! That's all anybody needs to know."

CHAPTER 32

Crow met the Brewers excitedly spitting out the news. "Had an explosion down to Coleman's while you was gone. Looked like one a them 'tomic bombs. Never saw nuthin' like it," Crow said, his eyes big. "They can't find Punk, but them hogs never left him in the shanty. Link walked in on us this mornin', and made Maw say "Grim Reaper" and Big Bang" two three times. Had me say it too. Listened real careful, then shook his head an' said, "It ain't you." Hands shaking, Crow continued. "He said, 'I know who done this' an' took off madder'n a baptized cat. Threatened to kill us if we talked. Them boys gotta be big into drugs - sellin' 'em an' usin' both."

"Who'd you tell about this?"

"Just Hanratty. We need pertection. It's all we got." Fear rattled Crow. "For god's sake, Jake, don't tell anyone I tol' ya. Link'd kill me sure."

"Won't say a word, Joe. Is Bea okay?"

"We know how you guys feel now. You gotta be on the short end of the stick to 'preciate the problems of others."

"You're a lightning rod for trouble too?"

"Ah Jake, ya know I didn't mean nuthin' by that, don't ya?" Crow didn't stop for an answer. "Link got hisself some other problems too. He was poachin' down in the game lands an' shot him an elk. The game warden had to get him outta there."

"When's this gonna end, Joe?"

"Can't be too soon. We got us other problems too. Our spring gave out. Not enough water left to water a cricket. Could ya spare some drinkin' water?"

"This won't get you in the feud thing, will it, Joe?"

"Ah, Jake, I never meant nothing by that." Crow tried talking past his comment. "Man, it's been drier'n a popcorn fart. We're up agin it with no water."

"We surely are," the Buzzard added, joining them. "We'd appreciate you bringin' water 'cause we can't leave. Cops are goin' through the Coleman place with Willy Whiskers' backhoe, an' we gotta be here."

"Keep me posted," Jake said as he eased out. "We'll bring water."

"What do you know about the Coleman place?" Jeanne asked when they drove away. "It wasn't worth much, just an old —"

"Brewer, you know what I mean," Jeanne said, an edge in her voice.

"They had an accident. Nothing we want to talk about. Not ever!"

Near supper time, Jake filled four buckets with spring water, clamped lids on to keep out dust, and headed for the Laceys, where Jake carried in the water. "Oh man Jake, they found a body." Crow greeted without taking the binoculars away from his eyes.

Jake nodded and walked out for the remaining water, struggling for control as his mind rushed through worrisome possibilities. Who was killed in the explosion? Could he be tied to this mess?

"Ya gotta see this," Crow said, still peering through the glasses as Jake walked by. "They got a black thing down there now, but I can't tell what they're doing with it."

Bodybag, Jake thought without answering. Nothing brought the realities of war home more than the noise of a zipper closing a friend into one of those bags. Sweat formed on his brow as he sat the buckets beside the first two he carried in.

Bea watched him wipe his forehead with the back of his hand. "Can you stand something cold?"

"I'd better go," Jake said, wanting to get outside and witness what was happening.

"Ya missed it, Jake. They put what was left of that body in that bag. That's a terrible way to go, blowed up and on fire."

A siren marked the approach of an emergency vehicle. The attendants pulled out a gurney and loaded the body. From the trooper's actions, it appeared as if their search was complete.

"Man, Jake, I forgot to tell ya what else they found. They pulled a bunch a wires out of the ashes, an' they was talkin' about explosives on their radios. Then someone tol' 'em to get off the radio when they was discussin' evidence."

Sunday afternoon found Jake sitting on their swing; a gentle breeze whistled through the remaining needles of the giant white pine tree that stood watch over him. The sound of a vehicle coming in their lane caught his attention. A white Jeep Cherokee with a Pennsylvania State Police logo on the front door soon appeared. A trooper stepped out of the vehicle and strode toward the front door. "Over here," Jake called, waving his arm.

"Looks like you're going somewhere," Poskie remarked, looking at his clothes and the open Bible.

"Just got back from church."

"Hope you learned something," the trooper said with a slight smile. Poskie then walked through a status summary of the recent problems. "It's difficult to put some of this together. We dug through that rubble when we couldn't account for Punk. Found a body," Glen said, carefully searching Jake for a tell-tale response. There was none.

"Oh," Jake replied, fighting to steel his emotional control. After investigating many things in the Corps, he knew the ruse, pass on partial, disturbing information, and watch for reactions.

"The Colemans aren't talking, but you know they could think you had something to do with the explosion."

"Link made a lot of enemies."

"How about you, Jake? Link considers you his enemy. Knows you're tough and capable."

"What reason could I possibly have? Assault, rape, arson, stalking, and ongoing destruction. Nah, that shouldn't upset any right-thinking American."

"I didn't mean to offend you. I want to be your friend, but you're walking a thin line. Couple of things you should know. Someone shot up the DA's new Mercedes. Nine holes .357 caliber. Hanratty said you own a .357." I'm worried about you, Jake. Did Jeanne tell you I called when you weren't home?"

"Yeah. Said you asked how I was doing and did I have medical problems. Real nosey stuff. It frosted me off."

"Jake, I'm trying to help you. The call was prompted by the sudden cancellation of our dinner together. When I asked about nightmares or sleepless nights, she acknowledged you suffer both. Jake, please consider a trip to the nearest VA Hospital. Vietnam vets with much less combat exposure than you had experience PTSD problems. You don't need to face this alone."

"I don't have combat problems; I have Coleman and DA problems," Jake said in a voice loaded with anger.

CHAPTER 33

Poskevich listened to Sergeant Ristine, leader of the investigative team from state police headquarters, who was conducting the evidence review of the Coleman explosion. Poskevich was uneasy, wondering if he should volunteer some of the hunches he held. Motive and opportunity were important, but capability added another dimension. Jake Brewer was undoubtedly capable. His inner conflict derived from more than friendship. He had suggested the law can't always protect those it should, and if Jake had pulled this off, he could have acted based on that comment. That statement could have legal ramifications, perhaps the straw that ended his career without a retirement. And he worried that Jake suffered PTSD and all hell could break loose.

"— the blasting caps found wired together were of an older vintage than some others we discovered. Lab reports show traces of dynamite, petroleum distillates, and plastic explosives, and comments by the elder Colemans accounted for all but the plastics. At this point, we have no suspects with access to plastics. The body discovered was killed with a .357 caliber bullet, most likely a .38 special or a .357 magnum, but we have no murder weapon or apparent motive. The coroner is sure the body was under that building for a while. What other facts do we have?" Sergeant Ristine asked.

"Many people include the Brewers, the Vances, Mac MacFarland, and others hold motives to go after the Colemans," Hanratty said. "Link recently harassed the Laceys. Placing anybody at the scene of the explosion has been impossible to date. I sense that the explosion and the incidents where someone boarded Coleman's windows are tied together. That would seem to suggest several people might be involved."

"How's that?" the sergeant asked.

"The Colemans are positive more than one person was outside their place when they boarded it. If that's true, we should hear something. People talk. Those most likely to pull this off appear to have rock solid alibis. I also believe the body is part of something different, not tied to the explosion. The body would still lie buried if we located Punk after the explosion."

"That's a valid assumption," the sergeant agreed.

"One last thing, Jake Brewer carries a .357 magnum. His wife has a .380. Both have permits. We're checking their guns now."

"What's your take, Glen?" Ristine asked.

"I don't think we'll find a bullet match with Brewers. I agree they're two separate incidents. I believe the killing points to Link Coleman who may have a motive related to the drug traffic problems. Many people fear Link would kill anyone who could finger him. We can't find any record showing he has a .357 caliber handgun. Being a felon, he'd be in deep trouble if we found one in his possession. Brewer is a retired combat Marine who has experience with explosives. We can't find any information that indicates he had access to explosives. His phone records contain no suspicious calls, and we can't find where he's been near any military units."

"Brewer has sufficient motive, but he also has a solid alibi," Hanratty agreed. "I checked." Poskevich breathed easier. He offered valid input, and Hanratty took the focus away from him.

Knowing Jake Brewer and his record indicated he could have pulled this off. He wouldn't overlook any evidence, but neither would he . . . There he stopped, not wanting to consider what he might or might not do.

"We're investigating several other unexplained incidents," Hanratty said. "Someone recently shot up the DA's car. Nine holes in the door appear to be .357 caliber. Same for the three in his windshield. Pennington didn't report it; his wife did. She said the windshield holes had pot in them. She's worried about her husband. Says strange things have been happening, late-night calls, strange cars driving slowly by, things like that. The DA provided very little information that can be considered helpful. He states it was probably some kids screwing off. Consider this, after they wrecked Link's new truck, he had another new one hauled in and the old one hauled out. He also had the mess cleaned up where their house sat and brought a new mobile home. Someone paid cash for all of it. We can't find where Link or any of his brothers had savings accounts, took out loans, or borrowed money for any of this. How does this figure?"

"It doesn't. Do you think these incidents can be connected?" Ristine asked.

"Maybe, but it will take time to put it all together," Hanratty answered.

"Time is something we're growing short on," Ristine countered. "People are being killed."

*   *   *

Late Saturday afternoon, Jackson Brewer arrived at Hill Place to talk with Jake. The two of them sat on the deck with cold Straub beers. "Jake, what are you doing with your life now that you quit that factory job?"

"Trying to write a novel."

"Why don't you move back here and become my partner? I've been thinkin' on this for a while. I ain't getting any younger, and I worked too hard to let Brewer Logging get sold for nothin' when I kick out of here. It'd be good for both of us. I could use that industrial engineering degree of yours to update our sawmills. And if that book is important to you, you can work on it nights and weekends.."

Surprised, Jake wondered what Jeanne would say? Jeanne was working on retirement from the school district. Would she want to move back here, where Link attacked her? He had no idea of the financial status of the company. His mother seemed to have all she wanted. But was that an indicator of what the company was worth?

"Mills? I thought you only had the Two Mile Run mill?"

"Got two more. One over in Forest County and one just past Mansfield off route six."

"I didn't know that."

"No, and neither does your mother, so please keep that information to yourself."

"Dad, we don't have the money to buy into that size operation. Jeanne's job and my Marine retirement are all the money we have coming in."

"All the more reason to come back here. Jeanne can be our bookkeeper and secretary. She's an intelligent woman and will catch on to everything quickly. Maude Zimmer is still working for me, and she's well past the social security age. I begged her to stay on until I found a trustworthy replacement. Her and Jeanne would be a natural fit."

"I'll have to talk this over with Jeanne. What kind of a business deal are we talking about, and what will it cost me to get in."

"Jake, I'll make this right for you. You never got college or much of anything else from me. I always wanted you as a partner. Told you that more'n a few times."

"I dreamed for years about working with you. I need to know what kind of deal you have in mind so I can talk this over with Jeanne."

"I got two new Kenworth tri-axle logging trucks ordered. They'll be coming in here in the middle of September. I could use some help with the down payments."

"Those trucks must cost $150,000 each. What is it that I'm not seeing?"

"The trucks as ordered are just shy of 200 grand each. There's a lot you don't need to know until you're a partner. You know you can trust me, Jake. You get me thirty grand to throw toward the down payment on the trucks, and that will be your buy-in."

"What kind of a percentage will I own? A couple percent? I might as well be your employee."

"I don't need you as an employee Jake," Jackson snapped. "I'm talking about a fifty percent share. And I'll make it, so you have sole ownership when I'm gone. I'll get insurance coverage to buy my share, and it will be in your name. This ain't no spur of the moment thing. I talked it over with Bear Mihalovich, and he's fine with this."

"I'll have to talk this over with Jeanne. Why don't you stay for supper, and we can —"

"You two need to be alone to talk this over, but let me add a little something more. That boy of yours loves these mountains almost as much as you two do. He won't make the military a career. It ain't in him. He'll need a job, and a third-generation Brewer Logging guy would be great. Like to see him learning the trade while I'm still alive."

"I can't speak for Trey."

"Course you can't. I just threw that in the mix for when you were doing your discussion. Don't screw around making a decision. I need to know soon. A lot depends on your answer."

CHAPTER 34

The Brewers grew ever more edgy with so much at stake. Jake suffered through problems he neither understood nor acknowledged, and Jeanne hurt for him, fearing his actions. The Coleman problems wouldn't go away. Jackson's partnership offer required Jeanne to give up her job, a job that meant a lot to her. And they would have to sell their home in Mechanicsburg and move here where there was a never-ending string of troubles that bought marital stress that wasn't present before the Coleman mess. This morning, they argued because Jeanne refused to attend a meeting with the DA, confessing she was finding it difficult to keep going. "We're in a prison we can't escape," she said in a hushed voice. "Everything we try makes the situation worse. Pennington's pushing us into a criminal trial over the Shark mess. How did we earn this, Jake?"

"Everyone thought I had to be involved in this war. I'm in for the duration. I lost one war, and I'm not losing another. Maybe you want to hear this call," Jake snapped as he punched in the phone number.

"Good mornin', health department."

"This is Charles Coleman out on the hill," Jake began with his voice changer. "We got us a new trailer house right beside our old place. We need a sewer inspection. It shouldn't take too long. Ain't much to see."

"Let me check our schedule." The line went silent for a moment. "How does Thursday morning look for you??"

"Thursday's fine. Can ya get here early?"

"Thursday it is. Let's put you down for eight."

"Just blow the horn, so we know yer here and go about yer inspection. We'll be out directly." Jake smiled after he hung up the phone. "Well, did I sound like Swifty?"

"Why would you set up their inspection Jake?" Jeanne wondered.

"Because they don't have a septic system. They ran flex pipe down over the hill and dump raw sewage in the beaver dam behind their place."

"How would you like to be the inspector Thursday morning?"

"He'll earn his pay this week."

"Why report a sewage violation when they do nothing about serious problems?"

"We're bringing all possible heat to bear. The feds never charged Al Capone for murder, racketeering, booze running - nothing. He went to prison for income tax evasion. Wouldn't it be great if these guys got jailed for an unapproved septic system?"

Later that morning, Jake's meeting with the DA brought him through millionaire's row and the mansions of lumber barons past before wheeling in behind one of the larger homes where three generations of Penningtons had their law offices. He parked next to a black Mercedes noting the primer paint covering recent bodywork. In the office, he took a seat and looked about. High ceilings, ornate woodwork, and expensive furnishings spoke of generations of wealth.

High heels clicking on the tile floor alerted Jake. A glance into the window reflected a young woman approaching. She paused where visitors couldn't see her, straightened her clothing, carefully checked the buttons on her blouse, and patted her hair before proceeding. The heel clicks commenced, and an attractive brunette rounded the corner. "Oh, I didn't know you were here. May I help you?"

"Jake Brewer. I'm early for a ten o'clock appointment."

"It's nice to meet you. I'm Karen. I'll let Mr. Pennington know you're here."

Karen soon escorted Jake into the DA's office. "Good morning Jake," Penny said with put-on cheerfulness. Pennington exuded affluence with his hand-tailored suit and a silk shirt accompanied by gold jewelry. His high school good looks were slowly eroding. Standing, Pennington offered a well-manicured hand. His soft, clammy handshake felt like fish bait, contradicting the image he wished to portray. Jake resisted the urge to wipe his hand on his pants and took the empty chair in front of the handsome cherry desk.

"Let's get right to the point of this meeting," Penny began. "I don't have a hearing decision on the death which occurred on your property. I'm doing all I can to get that behind us. There's been a date change for the Coleman cases; the judge is ill. However, the Colemans pled guilty in both cases. They won't require trials."

"We wish to make public statements before their sentencing."

"Is that necessary?"

"After all that's happened, yes, it's more than necessary."

"I read your letter to the probation department and share your concern," the DA sniffed. "I'm just not sure how it will bear on the judge's decision."

"Shouldn't we have the opportunity to find out? Jeanne was assaulted, stalked, and almost raped. Our home's repeatedly vandalized, Mac was badly beaten, and there's the arson fire."

"The problem becomes proving that these incidents occurred and, if they did, who may have perpetrated them," Penny said, shaking his head, sniffing again. "Knowing things and proving them in court are two different beasts. In one case, it would be impossible to prove anything other than assault, so we plea bargained. The stalker thing in Mechanicsburg is out of our jurisdiction and won't have any bearing on this case."

"Some of Link's actions may have been out of this jurisdiction, but the threatening phone calls came from here."

"It must be proven that the phone calls occurred, and if they were, who made them."

"You waiting for us to get killed?"

"I understand your concern," Penny said in a caring voice, sniffing once more, rubbing his nose with a monogrammed silk handkerchief. "However, the State Commission on Sentencing Guidelines provides a very narrow range of sentencing possibilities."

The sniffing irritated Jake. The DA's red eyes appeared to be more than an allergy, perhaps a coke habit. "What do those guidelines mean to us and our problems?"

"With the trespass charge, trespassing on your property would be strictly forbidden. We'll go for probation with time served and strict guidelines that mandate no further contact with you or your wife," Penny said, sounding tough.

"Probation should motivate them to turn their lives around, and it should give Jeanne the reassurance she needs to feel comfortable again," Jake said mockingly. "Link's on parole from prison, comes here and gets probation for breaking parole. They should study this case in law schools."

"We'll get a restraining order. It'll be a parole violation if they even walk on your property."

"That should strike fear into the heart of a multiple convicted felon. Mr. Pennington, I'll go forth brimming with confidence that this course of action will end our problems. We'll be able to live out our lives in peaceful tranquillity."

"Your sarcastic concern is noted, but this gives us additional leverage. We're trying to get them to relocate, perhaps to Indiana County, where they lived one other time."

"I don't see you slapping your hands."

"Slapping my hands?" Penny questioned, his irritation growing.

"As if this problem is finished, and the Colemans might move."

"It may not seem like much, but my hands are tied. You don't understand."

"Now we're getting somewhere," Jake snapped angrily. "I don't understand. Do you think the people in Indiana County want someone sentencing criminals to move there so they can put up with their never-ending problems? Come on, Penny, Link's a hardened felon," Jake said disgustedly. "What happens when he busts probation the next time?"

"He'd be in deep trouble. Of course, there would be an investigation; it's the way the law works. The accused have rights too."

"Link's out on parole. Has the parole board been advised of this mess? And what about victim rights?"

"I can't change the constitution."

"Do you think as our founding fathers were constructing one of the greatest documents in history, they held the mindset that criminals and thugs had all these rights, while law-abiding citizens were kept around so criminals would have someone to prey upon? Please help me understand, Penny. Do you have a personal interest in the Colemans?"

The DA ignored the second question. "The most we can give them is time in the county jail, and we have to pay for that. We're a poor county with a limited criminal activities budget."

"Oh, so it's a matter of economics. Crime pays because there's no money for punishment."

"You make this sound worse than it is. Rehabilitation is in order. These boys might be different if they were in different surroundings."

"There's the answer," Jake injected. "Are there any empty homes in your neighborhood? Move them into your home until a place becomes available nearby. You could become their mentor."

"Jake, I'm trying to work with you on this thing. I'll talk to the judge about public statements. Do you have any other concerns?"

"What happens to Punk? This mess began with him."

"Vincent is a problem," Penny agreed. "There's little that can be done with him. He's so —"

Jake cut Penny short. "Severely retarded. His brothers drink up his social security assistance checks and beat him routinely. He should be in a home to get the help he needs."

"There's only so much I can do," the DA pleaded.

"Maybe you should look for another line of work," Jake suggested in a low voice, "something you can handle. You shouldn't be forced to do all these things you disagree with when there isn't anything you can do about anything."

Pennington was showing anger. "Look, when Mr. Coleman and his brothers agreed to plead guilty, they saved this county the spectacle of a long court trial. They also spared your wife the embarrassment of testifying."

"Mr. Pennington, Jeanne's ready to testify today."

"Maybe you don't know what kinds of questions she would face."

"She doesn't care about the questions! She's not guilty. She's the victim."

"Believe me, I understand your frustration," Penny began, searching for another ploy that would relieve the tension. "There is another matter to consider. A jury might be more lenient on the Coleman family after losing a brother in this —."

"—feud. Just say what you're thinking."

Refusing to say it, the DA continued, "There's also the explosion of Coleman's home and the body found at the scene. Their lawyer swears someone planted the body, and they blew up their home to frame his clients. It won't be easy to make a case against them."

"If it's as hopeless as you make it sound and you're as helpless as it appears, it's time to divorce yourself from the DA position. Who could blame a fearless crime fighter such as yourself whose hands are tied? I'd support your decision to resign."

"I guess we don't have anything else to discuss, Jake."

"Mr. Pennington, I see no effort to prosecute these crimes to the level they deserve, and I won't be satisfied with no punishment," Jake said in a chilling voice as he jumped to his feet.

"Don't threaten me, not yesterday, not today, not tomorrow." Without thinking, a now angry Pennington continued, "You think the world owes you because you're some war hero. You got paid for your service, and you get a fat retirement for your efforts. Now —"

WHACK! Jake's fist slammed the desk. "My friend," Jake followed in a low, strained voice, his ice eyes boring in, "Don't let your alligator mouth write a check your chicken ass can't cover. Good day."

As Jake turned to leave, the DA hustled around his desk and grabbed Jake. "Wait just a —"

Jake grabbed Pennington's arm and jerked downward, slamming him face-first into the floor. In one fluid motion, he straddled the DA's back, forcing Pennington's arm up behind his head, making him scream with pain. With the other hand, he pulled his head back to slam his face into the floor again. Thinking better of it, he let go and allowed his head to drop forward. "Mr. DA, keep your hands and mouth off of me and mine! Your family won't recognize your body if you don't."

CHAPTER 35

After his DA visit, Jake sat on the deck reading the Mountain Sentinel and sipping ice tea. "Hey Jeanne, look, an autopsy reveals the body discovered at the Colemans was shot twice in the face and twice in the back at close range, and they haven't found the murder weapon."

Jeanne accepted the paper, read for a bit, then looked at Jake, "We need to be careful. The state police have a special investigative team in here." After a few minutes, she added, "Geez, Jake, Link's out on $20,000 bail. What'll it take to keep him off the street?"

"Death."

"Don't get any ideas," Jeanne replied with concern. "The law doesn't coddle law-abiding citizens."

The following morning, hot from the steep climb, the Brewers perched on a rock outcropping overlooking Coleman's new mobile home. The mountains presented a tranquil scene in a world turned upside down by ever-increasing violence. Jeanne shook her head as she considered what was about to happen. "Jake, I've known you for a long time, and you were always a great guy, but lately, you've become devious beyond description."

"Let's call it the ingenious pursuit of victory."

"I'm worried, and I may not know everything."

"Folks assured me war was the only way out of this insanity."

"Yes, but what are we going to accomplish with this inspection thing?"

"These guys feel secure because they're never held accountable. That ended with Gus's death. I intend to draw attention to these birds any way I can."

Several cars went by before the septic inspector's arrival. True to his directions, the driver blew the horn, got out of his car, and walked around the mobile home. A few minutes later, a man emerged walking faster to catch up with the inspector. The resident approached the inspector and began shaking his fist at him and pointing to his car. He was upset.

Jake handed Jeanne the binoculars. "I think Coleman is telling the inspector to get back in his car and get going," Jeanne suggested. "I wish I could hear what they were saying."

"I can give you a rough translation," Jake volunteered. "You —"

"Don't bother!"

Swifty grabbed the inspector's arm. The man shook loose and hustled around to the rear of Coleman's new home. He crossed his arms and looked over the pipe that carried raw sewage into the stream. "The inspector is shaking his head in disbelief. He can't believe his eyes."

Swifty stepped in front of the inspector, cutting off his view, shaking his fist at him, and pointing in the car's direction. Swifty physically jerked him around to face his car when the man didn't move. Placing his hands on the man's shoulders and hopping along on one leg, he booted him in the butt with the other. The inspector reached the relative safety of his car and jerked the door open. Swifty slammed him into the car and then took another swipe at him with his foot. In desperation, the inspector yanked the door closed on Swifty's leg. Hopping on one leg, Swifty jerked his leg clear, skinning his shin. Upset, he began kicking in the side of the car until the man spun off down the hill road.

"I hope you're satisfied, Mr. Brewer," Jeanne stated in a subdued voice.

*　　*　　*

Shortly before dark, the Brewers hauled fresh drinking water out to the Laceys. The land begged rain to quench its summer-long thirst. Feathery wisps of clouds stretched row-on-row in long pink bands across the evening sky. "Sure is a pretty evenin'," Bea called from the porch.

"Ya can't drink pretty," Crow sardonically reminded her.

The Brewers walked across Lacey's yard, the brown, tinder-dry grass cracking under their feet. "There's one benefit to the dryness, Joe; I haven't had to mow grass for a while," Jake said.

"Ya, but it's so dry it hurts to spit. I'd rather be mowin' a little grass."

"'Cause you never mow it, Joseph, I do," the Buzzard reminded him.

"Guess it's time to pray for a good soaker," Jake said.

"Past time," Crow agreed. "I bin askin' for other help too. I'm afraid the Coleman boys will come up here after us. Got my old Noble .22 ready. It's a shooter."

"How would you know that, Joseph?" Bea countered. "Forty years ago, you couldn't live without that miserable gun, an' the only time it's been moved since you got it is when I moved it to clean."

"Sounds like a lot's been happening," Jeanne said, changing the subject.

"More'n enough," Bea said sharply. "A red-headed chippie in a skimpy dress stopped by. She kept sayin' how hot it was and slidin' that little dress of hers further up her legs. I knew what she was doin' ta Joseph; she was primin' him for information. Between them ugly brown legs and big breasts hangin' out, Joseph got looked tight to that woman. That little set-to ain't over yet, Joseph Lacey."

"It wasn't all that bad," Crow complained. "Her name's Bailey Donahue, and she's originally from Parker. She's back here doing a documentary. Been down ta Colemans too. She has this Coleman mess figgered wrong, and I told her so. Bailey said she thought maybe they was gettin' blamed for things they didn't do. I about threw her off the porch, didn't I, Maw."

"Ya didn't seem angry, Joseph," Bea said. "Ever' time that little hussy crossed her legs, yer eyes crossed too. I never saw you drool so."

Crow's face turned beet red to match the dazzling sunset behind his head.

"She has gorgeous legs. Is that what you're saying, Joe?" Jake asked. "No wonder Bea's upset with you."

"Joseph better be careful. I ain't sharin' no man with a trollop from the city."

"Let's go, Brewer," Jeanne said disgustedly and began walking toward the truck. "As I said earlier, Brewer, you're getting to be a real prince," Jeanne said as Jake opened the truck door for her.

"I don't understand, Honey. If it's Bailey, forget it. I only have eyes for you."

"Stuff that innocent crap, Jake. You love to stir."

CHAPTER 36

One morning not long after the big fire, Allison Carver and Bailey Donahue arrived unexpectedly at Hill Place. Seated on the deck in a revealing summer dress, Bailey complained about the health department visit at the Colemans. "People should mind their own business. It's no wonder these men are angry."

"Bailey, I was born and raised near this family," Jake said. "They've experienced considerable difficulty, and they earned most of it. Their poor choices are responsible for the lives they live."

"That attitude fosters problems," Bailey said in an accusatory tone. "I might be just like them if I got treated that way."

"That's noble-sounding, Bailey, but not accurate."

"There isn't much to gain by arguing," Jeanne suggested. "We have photo albums and dated journals that list the problems we've experienced and the subsequent retaliation after our problems. Would you care to look at them?"

Although Bailey sniffed at the offer as one-sided, Allison eagerly accepted. The albums contained dated pictures of every destructive act showing the extent of the damage.

"Could a third party be behind these incidents, someone trying to fuel conflict?" Allison asked.

"Anything's possible," Jake said. "Some think it could be connected with the local drug problem because the Colemans and others have unexplained money. Were they doped up when they beat Punk half to death, and he broke in here? It was cold with a couple of feet of snow on the ground. He could easily have frozen to death if we hadn't come here."

"Did you catch Mister Coleman in here?" Bailey asked in a discrediting way.

"If you mean Punk, yes, we did. We tracked him, and his tracks led straight to Coleman's place," Jake coolly answered.

"That wouldn't stand up in court."

"Maybe not in Parker," Jeanne agreed. "Punk walks duck-footed, and they were duck-footed tracks. The police followed them to the Coleman place, where they found Punk unconscious. They discovered stolen items with Punk and found his fingerprints throughout our home. That suggests he had some part in the break-in here."

"Oh yes," Bailey sneered, "that's the incident where that boy was lured in and poisoned."

"No, Bailey," Jeanne corrected, "he was beaten, broke in to survive, stole rat poison, and ate some because he can't read."

"The police have his fingerprints?" Allison asked incredulously.

"Yes," Jake answered, looking at her with steely eyes. "We've allowed the law to handle our problems, but that hasn't worked very well."

"How do you take this?" Allison asked Jeanne as she looked at the pictures taken at the doctor's office after the assault.

"With twisted emotions and terror. Troopers are actively pursuing this problem now because we wrote the State Police Commissioner, and he ordered an investigation."

"That's one side of the story," Bailey said.

Jake continued with Allison, "You can't blame the police for not wanting to tackle these birds. You've covered some of their crimes. They get arrested, and the DA doesn't press charges. No cop wants to get killed arresting criminals when they know nothing will happen to them."

"They've had their problems too," Bailey said, her face a wrathful red. "Rusty's trucks destroyed, their home was blown up with a body planted under it, and let's not forget Buster's beheading on your property. Who's keeping score for them?"

"Us," Jake answered.

"And how might I ask, are you doing that?" Bailey demanded.

"By keeping newspaper clippings, logbooks, and a running list of hearsay information. Somewhere in all that lie answers that eluded investigators."

"Have you stopped to think some of those incidents could point directly to you, Jake?" Bailey asked angrily.

"Yes, Bailey, or to you," Jake replied evenly.

"And what would my motive be?"

"Your documentary. You said conflict sells. I wonder if the cops considered that possibility? The only person I can see benefitting from all this is the person writing the documentary. We certainly have nothing to gain."

"You must be nuts," Bailey snapped.

"Could be," Jake said with a cold smile. "You saw those pictures. Would you like those problems?"

"I'm sure we wouldn't," Bailey agreed, "but then we haven't treated that family like some have. Maybe it's "the 'walk a mile in my shoes' sort of thing."

"Bailey, if you came here to upset me, you're succeeding," Jake angrily replied. "Try as you will; you can't remake them into choir boys."

"What do you expect, Jake Brewer? Your family and the Vances stole their land."

"Where would you get that idea?"

"You gave them a few horses for all this land."

"Bailey, there's a lot you don't know. My great-grandfather traded two teams for land Colemans were letting go for taxes. That's when men worked for pennies a day, and horses cost a thousand bucks or more each. Check the deed transfers. Their great-grandfather, Jacob Coleman, left several thousand acres go to the state for taxes. Loggers considered the land worthless once they cut the timber. People ridiculed my great-grandfather for giving too much for land he could have had for nothing. He and Jacob Coleman became fast friends. They built the Hill Church and served there as Deacons together."

"That's not the story I got."

"Consider your source."

"I am," Bailey said, chilling the conversation. She excused herself to use the bathroom, and while she was gone, Allison returned the subject to an earlier discussion. "I'd like to review your logs if it wouldn't be an infringement. Could we set up a time?"

"So you can write more one-sided journalism?" Jeanne asked.

"I understand how you both must feel. I never considered that I may not have had all the facts until this morning. It's strange too. Outside newspapers have covered some of the same stories, and I thought they were incorrect."

"Allison, we can work something out," Jeanne said as Bailey approached. "Our number here is 386-0697. It's unlisted."

"It sure got quiet when I came out, guys," Bailey remarked when she returned. Then looking at Allison, she said, "We better go."

"Yes, thanks for the coffee and the conversation," Allison added, and the two departed.

"Well, they're gone," Jake said in a relieved way.

"I quickly got sick of Bailey."

*   *   *

Late Sunday afternoon, the Brewers departed. Hanratty drove by and waved as they pulled onto the state road. "Jake, promise me you won't go hunting trouble while I'm gone," Jeanne requested.

"I just don't want anything more happening to Hill Place."

"I'm trusting you."

Jeanne stopped for a deer killed by a vehicle along the hill road, and Jake drug it off the road. They traveled on, soon reaching Jake's drop point, where Jeanne pulled to the side of the road for their goodbyes. Jake kissed her before disappearing into the fire-blackened woods to return to Hill Place.

He walked swiftly across the mountain top on long-familiar trails. The hectic schedule he planned forced him to hustle to complete everything within the four hours it took Jeanne to reach home. At Hill Place, he changed into camouflage clothes with gloves and retreated to the garage, where he retrieved five Coleman blue fletched arrows and his bow and wiped them down to remove fingerprints. Armed, he headed out; his first destination was the deer he had pulled off the road.

CHAPTER 37

A chorus of songbirds tattooed the silence as waves of pink rippled across the early morning sky with Jake anxiously waiting for Allison Carver to arrive. Within minutes, he caught glimpses of her approaching through the laurel and hemlocks. She wore a yellow blouse with jean shorts and carried a blue backpack. Jake whistled, and Allison stopped abruptly looking frightened. As she locked on to Jake, she waved, then began climbing the mountain toward him.

"Morning, Miss Carver," Jake said with a smile. "You're early."

Allison readily returned the smile, "Good morning Mr. Brewer; you're early yourself. I had trouble sleeping. What's your excuse?"

"Same," Jake sheepishly replied. "I tried to call and cancel. You must have departed early."

"I want to review those logs. Some things no longer fit together. I believed there was a feud, and now I don't know."

"There's no feud Allison," Jake said as he led off toward Hill Place. Arriving, he carefully surveyed the area with his binoculars before leaving the security of the woods. Satisfied no one was watching them, he climbed the steep hillside using the house to block the view from above. Opening the back door, he stood aside and allowed her to enter the dimly lit interior. She stopped dead when the door closed, and the lock snapped shut, her fear evident. "Nothing sinister, Allison," Jake assured her, his hands up, pleading, "We don't need visitors."

"You have the blinds drawn," Allison questioned in a fearful voice as if she had incorrectly read this man and his intentions.

"We're not supposed to be here."

"Oh," she replied with a hint of relief. Her face was a fine one, thin, straight nose, a friendly mouth with a shyness that became her, brown eyes, eyes that seemed strangely alive yet sadder than they should be, and olive skin nicely tanned by the sun.

Jake retrieved logbooks, picture albums, and various police reports for Allison's review.

Returning, he found her looking at two pictures of an old building and a framed key that aroused her curiosity. "What are these pictures?"

"My grandfather's camp. It was a two-mile walk up a long hollow near the top of the mountains. We walked in on an old railroad grade used to haul out logs. Gramp and I spent a lot of time there. I earned my way to hunting camp cutting firewood with that cross-cut saw.

"You the boy on the porch?"

"I am."

"Was Jeanne ever there?"

"Once. We walked in after my first trip to Vietnam. Both the place and me were in poor shape, but we shared an unforgettable day. It was peaceful there, and I badly needed peace."

The rest of the story was no one's business. That day they began the process of piecing their marriage back together. They had held hands quietly searching for answers, letting life sort itself out. After a while, they kissed and held each other tightly, releasing the unspeakable pain they suffered.

Allison understood the private nature of his thoughts and remained silent. Without expressing themselves, they turned to their projects. She studied through journals and picture albums while Jake continued typing, fighting to keep his thoughts ordered. Occasionally he chanced a glance at Allison, twice their eyes met unexpectedly, and they shared a smile. Each time he remembered Jeanne's parting words. "I'm trusting you."

Mid-morning, a noise alerted him, and Jake peeked through the blinds. "A trooper's coming in. Grab those books and run upstairs."

Without hesitation, Allison followed directions. Jake quickly saved his work and shut off the computer. Upstairs, he discovered her sitting in a chair with her head in her hands. Looking up, she whispered, "Are we caught?"

"Routine. They checked yesterday too. He won't come in," Jake assured her.

Rap. Rap. Rap. Silence followed, then another series of raps. When no one answered, the trooper worked his way around the house, checking doors and windows for forced entry.

Satisfied that everything was as it should be, he returned to his vehicle. Jake quietly moved to the front bedroom window, where he watched through the curtains as the trooper drove off. He soon reappeared at the top of the hill and took up a position that looked down the power line to Hill Place.

"What's wrong, Jake?" Allison asked, her worry showing in her eyes.

"Just stay away from the windows."

"Why did I insist on coming here?" Allison nervously questioned, her face ashen white.

"It'll be okay," Jake assured her, but he didn't like the feel of things. They returned to work with an uneasiness settling over them.

Around noon, Jake made sandwiches, and they ate while listening to the news. One story concerned the gruesome murder of a female hiker, which prompted Allison to ask, "Can I share something without upsetting you?"

"Give it a try."

"When you locked that door behind me, I was terrified. I can't even describe how frightened I was. I was sure something terrible was about to happen, something that would land me on the evening news."

"Remember that feeling. Now picture yourself in Jeanne's shoes when Link broke in here and attacked her."

"I could never stay here alone again. What did Jeanne do?"

"She fought him until he beat her unconscious. I showed up before he could carry out his plan."

Jake stopped there, and they returned to their work. After studying the journals and taking notes, Allison remarked, "I've had things figured so differently."

"Oh?" Jake questioned, turning to look at her.

"My investigations . . ." Allison began, then stopped. "A serious journalist must know the people she writes about well enough to feel how they feel and think the way they think, or the story is just so many words."

"Tell me about your investigation."

Allison hesitated, embarrassment flooding across her face. "After I talked with you on the phone, you seemed so hostile, which fit the description I had pieced together."

"What's that?"

"A warped, half-crazy Vietnam vet with a chip on his shoulder. These logs say that's not you."

"I hope not."

"I sense a bigger story in this mess, but I can't put it together yet."

"There's something much bigger than the Colemans driving this problem. Many believe it's the drug problem tearing this county and perhaps much of the Eastern USA apart. And the people driving the drug trade could be political leaders."

"You mentioned you had a score sheet of some kind."

"Look in that brown envelope. It lists problems with newspaper clippings and personal notes concerning what we know about the incidents. You'll find questions Jeanne and I developed about these incidents and the potential people who could be involved. Bailey's listed."

"You don't think Bailey. . . I guess one can't overlook anyone," Allison said.

"Please keep this information between us. Corporal Poskevich has been researching the Coleman family and their illegal shenanigans for several generations. Link's grandfather had a still in his cellar and another one in the cave they used for storing food. They began before prohibition started, and the congressman for this area, the county sheriff, and the DA bought their booze from him. Link and his father helped run the stills and took over the business. Word was the DA, sheriff, and congressman went out of their way to protect the Colemans and may have benefitted from their moonshine sales. That DA was the grandfather of the current DA, who may be involved in drug trafficking. Many believe some Colemans hopped from moonshine to drug sales. Be aware, your boss at the paper is the DA's sister."

"Oh my. That explains the call I overheard with my boss talking with the DA. She was angry and warning him about something. I —"

"I don't need to know about it."

"Thanks, Jake."

It was late afternoon when Allison finished working through Brewer's material. After eating a leftover lasagna dinner Jeanne prepared, Jake and Allison prepared to leave for her car. She slipped into her backpack as dusk descended over the hills. Menacing clouds accompanied by lightning flashed across the mountains tops with rumbling thunderclaps. The wind built as they slipped out the kitchen door into the gathering darkness. They hustled into the woods at the top of the hollow, where Jake took out his flashlight and helped Allison down the path. Half trotting, they were soon at her vehicle. Jake waited until she drove out before heading up the trail accompanied by a building wind and driving rain.

CHAPTER 38

Jake hunkered against the hillside waiting for Jeanne's arrival after an eventful week. Memories of earlier years ran through his mind as he looked down on the streets of Parker, virtually the same scene he shared with Jeanne the night he proposed marriage. His pulse quickened when he heard a vehicle laboring up the mountain. It slowed to maneuver the tight curve, then sped off. Time crawled. It was getting darker, and his stomach began to knot. Jeanne could have encountered situations that would need his help, and he had been out of touch since early afternoon. Man, where is she, he wondered, trying not to worry but failing miserably. "She should have been here an hour ago," he muttered, throwing a stick down the hill in frustration.

Dusk was closing in when the next vehicle approached, slowing for the horseshoe curves, taking what seemed to be forever to reach the lookout corner. This better be her, he thought as the vehicle slowed for the turn. His heart sank when kids pulled into the lookout to watch the sunset over the mountains. Jake worried. They could ruin everything if they saw Jeanne pick him up.

He struggled to his feet, his back hurting, and moved stiffly down the mountain toward the curve below. He saw lights and struggled up near the road as total darkness closed in. It was Jeanne, and he stepped out, waving his arms.

"You scared me, Jake! We're supposed to meet at the lookout," Jeanne exclaimed as he slipped into the passenger seat.

"Two love birds pulled in just before dark. Had to move," he replied as he leaned over and kissed her, moved away and smiled, then kissed her passionately.

"Well, Mr. Brewer," Jeanne teased, "either you're delighted to see me or have a guilty conscience."

"We'd better get going," Jake said without answering. "We need to stop at the Lacey place and get water buckets. I want them to see us arriving together."

After a mile or so, Jake said, "Jeanne, we need to talk. You know that state land that begins about a mile past the backside of the Cold Springs Gorge?"

"You mean down where Jack got the big twelve-point buck with a bigger rack than any his father shot?" Jeanne teased.

"Yeah, down there. Two elk plots are planted full of marijuana just like the one we saw in the hollow behind Colemans."

"Really?" Jeanne asked, surprised and a bit shocked.

"Yeah. I figure that's where the helo went when it left you and Pappy. Maybe he was checking his crops. Few people ever visit there except during hunting season. By then, any trace of a pot crop would be long gone."

"We have to report this, Jake."

"I agree, but how? Might open questions we don't want to answer."

Jeanne turned off the township road and stopped to retrieve their mail. Crow waited with water buckets when they stopped. "Got a lotta news, Jake," Crow said excitedly. The good news is we had a monster rainstorm while you were gone. It gave us back our spring, so I'm returning yer buckets. The bad news is the Colemans went on the warpath and shot up the hill with arrows. Hard telling what you'll find at yer place. That new cop, Poskevich, is collectin' information and says he won't reveal the names of who tol' him what."

"Poskevich is a good man," Jake agreed.

"Somethin' else. Me an' Bea put together a list of all the Hill problems. We're figgerin' out who done what in this —"

"Feud."

"It ain't a feud; that's as plain as the nose on your face. I need you to look at the list real quick."

Crow quickly returned with a handful of papers. Jake wondered why he was wasting his time waiting, but he changed his mind after looking over the list. "Man, Joe, you folks spent some time on this. Poskevich needs a copy."

"Ya think Jake?" Crow asked excitedly.

"I do." Getting in the truck, Jake said, "Crow and the Buzzard have been playing detective. Made a list of the hill problems and who did what and maybe why. They created a timeline and have information we couldn't even guess. Crow's calling Poskevich."

"Wondered what made him hightail out of here. Usually can't get rid of him."

Jake nodded.

Night was upon them when Jeanne backed in. Jake got out of the truck, walked around the house with the flashlight looking for fresh signs of entry, and when he saw none, he went in and turned on the lights. Breezing through a quick inspection of the place, he returned for Jeanne, and they quickly carried in their things.

Jeanne was tired from her work week and the four-hour drive alone from Mechanicsburg. As they were getting ready for bed, a car drove in and turned around. "It's Glen," Jake said, looking out the window. "Don't wait up for me."

Glen sat waiting for Jake in his patrol car. "Good evening, Jake. Saw you drive by and thought I'd drop in for a minute. Get in. Let's talk."

Jake climbed in, wondering what happened that brought Glen in at this time of night. "Crow had a list of things for me and asked me to stop by. He seemed anxious to get it to me, so I came out before my shift ended."

"He showed me the list when I stopped to pick up my water buckets."

"Something strange occurred while you folks were gone. Someone shot up a bunch of stuff with blue arrows, and the store in town only sells those blue arrows to the Colemans. Colemans claim they don't know anything about it."

"I wasn't here, so I can't help you with this one."

"Something highly unusual occurred while you were in Mechanicsburg. Troopers spotted someone moving about inside your place. Might have been two people."

Jake felt a sinking feeling coming over him, and he fought to retain facial control. "What are you suggesting?"

"Mean things are happening, and your record suggests you could pull them off."

"As long as we're pointing fingers, let's look at you. You have the proven capacity too. Remember, that's how you got stationed here."

"Come on, Jake, I'm trying to tell you something."

"And I'm telling you something too," Jake snapped. "Firemen get caught setting fires to fight, rogue cops set up crimes so they can become heroes. Like I told Bailey Donahue, it could be a journalist creating writing material. Anything's possible."

"Be careful, Jake. You're writing a novel too. Let's explore some of these things. First, there's the Coleman shanty blowing up. That wasn't an accident. They had gasoline and dynamite inside, but plastic explosives were also present, and the Coleman boys didn't have plastics. It was most likely set off by a timing device, which changes parameters."

"What are you insinuating?" Jake asked in a voice that carried a measured hardness.

"I'm telling you to be careful. Things are happening that take a lot of planning and more than a little intelligence."

"This mess is ruining my relationship with Jeanne. That's a steep price to pay for a game I didn't want dealt into. I shouldn't admit this to an officer of the law, but I quit running when Link brutalized Jeanne. When they killed Gus —"

"Be careful, Jake. I don't need to hear this," the trooper interrupted. "You lucked out when Johnston was assigned to investigate Shark's death. Johnny hated Shark. The embarrassment of Shark pounding him was compounded by a slug of racial slurs in front of Hanratty and others. The DA's asking questions, and he's out to get you. Don't run yourself out of luck," Glen admonished. "Let's be honest. Somebody has pulled off some cute capers, and when I consider motive and ability, I gather conclusions that are difficult to dismiss. It's easy to get caught up in stuff like this. People get away with things for a while, think they're invincible, and blow it. Don't let that happen to you. You deserve better."

Jake sat collecting his thoughts, wondering how much Poskevich could prove. "We're searching for a stop sign. Maybe the sentencing does that."

"Maybe, maybe not, but you're creating enemies you can't afford. Your letter to the State Police Commissioner has Troopers upset. They're standing a lot of extra duty watching Coleman's comings and goings. The game warden is catching all kinds of crap. Somebody sent pictures of Link's truck with an elk in the back on the wrong side of a gated road to Game Commission Headquarters. Add the health department inspector called out to the Colemans for a sewage inspection and got his fanny kicked for his troubles. There's also the Grim Reaper's call to the Pandemonium. These pose questions not yet answered."

"Maybe if people did their jobs, we wouldn't have all these problems," Jake replied flippantly.

"Stop!" Glen interrupted, obviously displeased with the implication. "Troopers have presented substantial supportive evidence in these cases. I can only guess why the DA doesn't pursue them."

"You can bet your fanny if a trooper's wife experienced Jeanne's attack, or if someone systematically destroyed their home, they would do more than present evidence to the DA."

"Dammit, Jake, listen! I've uncovered a lot of stuff. You had a rough problem with Mr. DA in the long ago, and that score may not be settled. His secretary recently called in a report and said you were pounding Pennington in his office. Penny called back before we could dispatch a car and said it was a mistake. Someone recently shot up his car. Is that an open sore being scratched?"

Jake looked away, and it was quiet for a time. "Wounded pride heals a lot slower than a wounded body, but if you're asking if I shot up his car, the answer's no."

"There were nine closely spaced .357 caliber holes in his door and three more in his windshield."

"The .357, .380, 38 special, and 9 millimeter are all .357 caliber. Add an Uzi. Many big-time criminals have access to them. Mister Pennington could be in trouble with someone, and these were his warning shots."

"Man, Jake, that slipped past me."

"Glen, you suggested this could be a much bigger problem than it appears. I think that's a fact."

It was quiet for a bit while both men thought through the situation. Finally, Jake spoke. "Glen, I realize I can trust you as a friend. I have information that confirms some of what you think you know."

"Such as what?"

"When I was down buying Jeanne's .380, Barry Dixon informed me that a new tough-looking, no-nonsense kind of cop bought some topo maps. Have you looked at them?"

"Yes, and I've used them too."

"Here's an opportunity to use them again. The last time Jeanne's father was here, a helo flew right close to the deck where Jeanne and Pappy were sitting. Jeanne looked at them with her binoculars as they hovered right next to the deck. She said they were a couple of mean-looking dudes and swears one had an automatic weapon."

"How does this tie into my topographic maps?"

"That helo left our place and flew due west. A while later, Jeanne heard it flying south over the mountain in front of this place."

"I'm not sure what's west of here, but one would fly past the Colemans by going south."

"There are three elk clear cuts down that Game Commission road behind Colemans. The road is gated, so you'll need a key. Two of those fields are growing large plots of pot. Other pot crops exist on state land west of our place. All of those elk fields will show on your topo maps."

"Man Jake, if they're as big as you say they are, they're worth millions. This could be the break we're looking for."

"Glen, please don't use my name in conjunction with this information."

"Jake, I also have news you need but can't say where you heard it. You weren't here when their shanty went up, but you're on the list of suspects. We hit a snag when the investigation team discovered the body. We think we have a motive, but there's no murder weapon."

"Hanratty picked up my revolver and Jeanne's pistol for testing. He won't find anything."

"He doesn't want to, Jake. He's a good trooper covering his bases and not your enemy. There's more. Hard drugs are involved. A lot of them. The Colemans may be bit players in a big operation. Be watchful! It could get nasty."

"Don't worry, Glen, they won't catch me asleep on watch."

"I wouldn't think so," the trooper agreed. Then with a slight smile, he added. "This mess could provide some interesting plots for your writing efforts. Don't get into creating real-life situations to generate writing material."

"Please, Mr. Trooper. I'm a peace-loving man."

CHAPTER 39

Jake awoke Saturday morning after a fitful night of drifting in and out of nightmares past, worrying through the latest information Poskevich provided. Pain stabbed through his back making breathing difficult. Fully awake, he struggled out of bed.

Jeanne woke while he struggled and sleepily asked, "Your back bothering you?"

"Yeah," Jake softly answered.

"Oh my. Why didn't you say something?" Jeanne asked as if she felt the pain herself.

Jake held on to the bedpost and fished his pants up one leg at a time. Ready to struggle into his shirt, Jeanne was there holding it in the proper position, knowledge gained from longtime experience.

Jake took a pain pill and then struggled through shaving while listening to the news. Jeanne took two calls while she prepared breakfast; the first was Allison Carver, who was calling to make sure her invitation was still good; the second was Mac, who was out of the hospital with a walking cast and raring to share the latest gossip. When Jake learned of the impending visits, he immediately began worrying about Allison. What if something went wrong and Jeanne discovered her previous trip?

It wasn't long until Mac arrived and sat with Jake on the deck. A few minutes later, Allison drove in and joined Jeanne in the kitchen.

"Word has it Link will walk away from this mess with me," Mac bitterly complained.

"Did you file charges against him?"

"The DA said there was no use. It's just my word against Link's."

Jake looked at his friend, shaking his head. "Mac, you said Dean saw Link tearing out of here and came to your rescue. You have a valid complaint and refuse to file it. Help me understand."

"I tol' ya what the DA said. Besides, too damned many people are sidin' with the Coleman bunch. She's one of 'em," Mac said, thumbing over his shoulder in the direction of the kitchen. "I wouldn't think Miss Carver would have the guts to come up here after some of her articles. Did you ask her about 'em?"

"Some."

"Let me do some asking," Mac suggested.

"We'll take care of her."

"Ya, I bet you'd like to be alone with that little honey," Mac retorted.

"My friend," Jake warned, "leave it alone," his guilty conscience slapping his face.

Mac knew Jake, and the warning upset him. "Screw you, Brewer. You ain't got a corner on problems. Yer gonna need friends, an' ya ain't gonna have any." With that, he thumped across the deck and departed, stones flying as he sped away.

Jeanne heard him leave and didn't ask questions. It was apparent there had been a problem of some sort. Jake would tell her when the time was right. Instead, she busied herself with breakfast, and within minutes, the three of them were seated around a table of steaming food. As they held hands around the table, Jake prayed. With the last echo of "Amen," Jake squeezed Jeanne's and Allison's hands in unison, taking care to hold Jeanne's after he let go of Allison.

When they had eaten for a bit, Allison said, "I know you both must question the slant of past articles with my byline. I would."

"We have concerns," Jeanne agreed.

"I'm dedicated to discovering and writing the truth. Our conversations have opened questions about the people I was assigned to interview and the information they provided. I also have heartburn concerning editorial changes made to my work, edits over which I have no control. I brought copies of my work and the changes so you can understand what I'm talking about."

After finishing breakfast, they reviewed the samples Allison presented. Jeanne asked, "Why Allison? The changes appear to turn your articles from fact to fantasy?"

Allison hesitated, ordering her thoughts. "I owe you answers, but I don't have any," Allison said, obviously embarrassed. "I submitted two separate articles that gave this feud thing a rest. They were combined and changed. It ticked me when they kept my byline. When I asked about it, the answer I received was 'editorial privilege.'"

"All you can do is report what you see or know. The rest is up to the editor," Jeanne said in an effort to set her at ease.

"I discussed the situation with our editor. If things don't change, I'll resign."

"Don't do it because of us."

"Not because of you, because of me. It's a matter of trust." Looking sad, Allison added, "This has me down. I enjoy working here, and there aren't other journalistic opportunities available."

The conversation turned to other areas, and Jake excused himself to retrieve logs and picture albums. Jake slipped Allison notes she forgot on her previous visit and began going through the material. "Allison, this chart may help you sort out things. Each incident is recorded by date, what occurred, the damage that took place, follow-on incidents that may be related, and anything else tied to it. Stop at the Laceys on your way out. Ask them to see the record they're developing on this mess. They have ways of piecing together information that would make most detectives envious."

Allison read through the charts, jotting notations in her notes for later questions. Some time later, she said, "Three different conclusions could be made of this Coleman situation. These could be the random actions of hell-raising hillbillies, or there could be a feud going on. Then there's the possibility this could be a conspiracy for some larger purpose, such as a drug war. Maybe it's a combination of all three."

"All we want is peace," Jake answered, knowing the state police were working all three possibilities.

CHAPTER 40

Jake's thoughts on the destructive acts he engineered made concentration on his writing efforts difficult. Those acts produced little change while the power of the pen, some pictures, and a few phone calls stirred considerable activity that proved unpopular with public servants but brought action on their problems. Game commission letters and pictures put them in action. The state attorney general's letter concerning the various investigations started a review with the Sterling County authorities. In return, the DA furnished the attorney general with information concerning the problems, with a copy to the Brewers. After reading the DA's letter, Jeanne said, "If you had to describe a worthless incompetent, all you would have to say is DA Pennington."

Jake focused on related problems. The letter to the state office of mental retardation explained Vincent "Punk" Coleman's severe retardation, that he lived in a chicken coop, and on occasion, Mister Coleman ran afoul of the law after family members seriously abused him. The DA's hands were tied because Vincent was incompetent to stand trial, and he couldn't be institutionalized because Sterling County couldn't afford the associated costs. Therefore, Vincent was released on his recognizance. Jake ended by requesting information on state-run programs that could provide Vincent Coleman with the assistance required to achieve some semblance of a quality life.

They sent variations of the letter to the Mental Health/Mental Retardation offices in neighboring counties that shared tri-county responsibility for this program. Another letter went to the area Social Security Office which maintained regional responsibility for Sterling

County. It explained Vincent received a monthly SSI check, but his brothers reportedly took the money for their use, and he was improperly cared for and often beaten. Jake noted that Mr. Coleman's retardation made the Sterling County DA powerless to act.

With the letters mailed, he called the IRS 800 fraud line number, suggesting they review recent year tax files for the Coleman brothers and provided the names of their various employment and their logging operations. The eagerness of the investigator taking the call told Jake he never wanted to be on the wrong side of the IRS.

*   *   *

"Corporal Poskevich, we have problems. Bailey Donahues significant other reported her missing."

"Did he seem worried, sergeant?"

"She, Corporal, and she's as masculine as it gets. That good-looking woman is a lesbian. She was last seen Monday afternoon driving into the Brewer place. We need to interview Brewer."

"Brewer wouldn't kill her. It isn't in him."

"Corporal, he has capability written all over him."

"Oh, he's capable, more than you might guess, but he didn't harm her." Poskie searched the sergeant's face, wondering how much he could tell him without being in trouble. "Can I trust you with something you won't like to hear?

"There must be a reason why you ask."

"Sitting up behind Lacey's place had to be my most boring, unproductive assignment since I was a rookie road patrolman checking vehicle inspection stickers. I took it upon myself to do some investigating while my car remained parked on assignment. Bailey Donahue is at least bisexual or an excellent actor. And I saw her late Wednesday night after she left Brewers."

"Let's hear it."

"I've eavesdropped on her and Link using audio enhancing headphones they sell for hunting. It ended with sex at least twice. She began the relationship using Link for information on some stories she is writing. It became clear the worm had turned; Link's using her."

"Is that it?"

"For now. I'll get my notes together for you. Now, what are you withholding from me."

"Looks like the DA twisted Judge Palidino's arm to the point where he's convening a grand jury to determine guilt in Swifty Coleman's death. We better be clean."

"Does Jake know this?"

"No, and I don't want you to tell him. Let the court do that."

*   *   *

"Jake, we need to talk. I never understood the baggage you carried from Vietnam until Link attacked me. Since this mess began, I keep wondering what you haven't told me. Even more, I'm afraid of what you might do." Tears formed in Jeanne's eyes. "Oh, Jake, I love you so much. I don't want to lose you."

"Nobody else would have me," Jake whispered.

Jeanne leaned back, teardrops sliding down her cheeks. "I know two women who would take you right now," Jeanne said, sobbing softly.

"And who might that be?" he asked, straining to maintain his composure.

"Try Allison Carver."

"Why her?"

"Jake, I should lay out that 'Does Macy tell Gimbell' line of yours. When you called from the hill the night of the storm, you said 'We' when you talked about something, so I thought someone else might be there. Woman number two could be a real problem. The state cops called. Bailey's missing, and they said the last location they can place her is Hill Place. They know you and her have not been all that friendly."

"Bailey came uninvited. She said I was the only one that could help her. She's suddenly afraid of Link, and maybe she has reasons. Nothing happened with her and me."

"I believe you, Jake," Jeanne said, her eyes tearing heavily. "When I needed compassion for the problems I caused us, you were there for me. I know that's what real love is all about. And Jake, I do love you so."

"Oh Jeanne, I love you too. More today than yesterday."

"Less today than tomorrow."

226

CHAPTER 41

"I don't hear a clickety-clacking keyboard in here," Jeanne remarked as she walked behind Jake and placed her hands on his shoulders. Then in a concerned way, she asked, "Are you having problems, Honey?"

"Welcome home, Jeanne. And yes, I have writing problems. I can't find an ending."

"Have you prayed for guidance? That's one of the first questions you always ask me."

"I pray continuously, but that doesn't mean I received an answer. The longer I work on our book, the more I'm mentally getting real-world occurrences mixed up with incidents I'm creating. I find myself entering conversations from the viewpoints of characters I created."

"They say successful authors must live the parts of their characters to bring them to life. Then too, there's that thin line between the sane and insane. You've always been a borderline case, my dear husband. Perhaps this book has pushed you over the edge."

"What is it you say to me, something like 'Ah stuff it, Brewer.' Yeah. I think that's it."

"I think I may have said that on occasion when the situation called for it, Jake. There's something else we need to discuss. I've been thinking a lot about the business proposal your father proposed. I have concerns."

"Likewise. Let's hear yours."

"Jake, I've been praying on this ever since we first discussed it. We have thirty thousand to invest. It seems like a great chance for you to start a new career that you would love, and you'd be working with someone that means a lot to you. The first question is, why would he ask so little if the business is solvent? The second concern is the problems we currently face up there. I know we have to decide soon, but do we have to move back the day we buy in?"

"I wouldn't think so, Jeanne. I can clear that up before we make a decision. As for the first question, I strongly believe the business is financially secure. When we discussed the whys of this deal, dad said he had paid for the other kid's education and provided other financial support over the years. He asked them if they were interested in buying into Brewer Logging, and they laughed at him, which was the reaction he hoped for. He wants the company to go on after he's gone, and he mentioned Trey might like to get in when he leaves the Navy. I'm convinced he wants us in to help us and continue the company. The thirty grand is just a token to say we bought in if Mom or the other kids ask. He even said he has insurance to cover estate taxes, and he'll make me the sole beneficiary of that policy. I can't see a downside other than the current problems. Now, what are your other concerns?"

Jeanne was quiet for a bit, trying to find a way to phrase what she had to say. Finally, she began. "Jake, I love you and only you. I love you with all that is in me. I don't want anything to come between us, not ever again."

"I can't see why working with Dad would cause us a family problem. Nobody cares more for us than Jackson Brewer. And you know he was my best friend until we married, and you took over that spot."

"Oh, Honey, I hate to bring this up. It sickens me so every time I think of it. I'm talking about our early marriage problems. Can you live there without being continuously reminded of that? You had a problem not long ago with —"

"Jeanne, that problem came because Pennington grabbed me. We've built a strong, loving marriage that others envy. I love you and trust you."

"I'm ready for a change. I worry that one of these days some drugged up kid will walk into school with a gun and —"

The phone interrupted their conversation, and Jake answered. His sister immediately nailed him. "Don't good evening me, Jake. My boss threatened to get rid of me this afternoon if you don't stop harassing everybody. You're going to cost me my job."

"What are you talking about?" Jake asked, baffled by the conversation.

"I work for the county commissioners. Luigi Muscarella is a county commissioner. He had a call from Harrisburg concerning our mental retardation program, budgets, and policies. He doesn't like State people nosing around up here. Then Luigi tells me the DA had a call from Harrisburg concerning your problems with the Colemans. Luigi doesn't like that either."

"Why would your boss care about the DA's problems?"

"He cares about the DA's problems because his sister Carmen is married to the DA. Brothers and sisters talk, you know."

"I guess they do, Sis. After all, we're talking."

"You're such a smart ass. You can't continue to make enemies of everybody, and I can't afford to lose my job. Mac's just getting back to work, and we're in a financial bind. Everybody can't afford to lazy around causing problems while their wife supports them. You should get a job and quit messing with people."

Jake felt a deep urge to lash out, but his sister needed understanding. "How can they fire you for something I did, Sis?"

"You can't be that naive. Luigi didn't say he would fire me; he said my office would be eliminated. That's what they do to prevent legal problems. Harrisburg faxed a copy of your letter to Luigi. And you were so proud of your letter to the attorney general's office that you sent the DA a copy. Luigi is furious. Jake, if I lose my job over you, I'm going to . . . , oh what's the use, you don't care."

The phone cracked in Jake's ear, and he hung up. "I never thought my letters would hurt Sis," Jake said, shaking his head as he explained the situation his sister reported.

"Honey, we may have received another piece to the puzzle, the Muscarella connection. We know the DA's wife and the head county commissioner are Muscarellas. And doesn't the newspaper in Parker have a Muscarella connection?"

"Two connections," Jake said. "Baker's the Scandalizer's publisher. His mother owns the paper. She's a Muscarella. There's another connection. The DA and the editor of the paper are brother and sister. Hard to beat that team."

"Poskevich needs to know."

The phone buzzed a few evenings later, and Jake muted the late news while he answered it.

Sis laid into him like an upset drill sergeant. "Well, Jake, you had to do it. When the Social Security people came snooping around to see what our office knew about Vincent Coleman's social security check, it cooked my goose. I just got home from the monthly commissioners' meeting. In the open forum, they announced my position was being eliminated. I was fired, and just in time for winter too. Thanks, Jake, we needed this."

"I'm sorry, Sis, I didn't think —"

"No, Jake, that's your trouble," Sis screamed, cutting him off, "You don't think. We don't know how we'll get by without my job. Even worse, nobody else will hire me because my brother has the entire world stirred up. In case nobody told you, let me. You aren't the most popular person in Sterling County. You aren't one of us anymore. Why can't you forget that old shanty?"

"It's home. We're not going to abandon it."

"That's fine for you, Jake, but what about the rest of us?" Sis screamed, and the phone went dead.

The next afternoon Jake returned from a four-hour interrogation by the state police concerning the disappearance of Bailey Donahue. He answered all questions thoroughly and honestly, yet they remained skeptical. It was understandable; they had a missing person report, no leads, no body, and Bailey's last provable stop was the Hill Place.

At home, he picked up the mail and noticed something from Pennington. Jeanne arrived with coffee refills while he read the contents and watched Jake angrily shaking his head. He reread the signature line, and a deep-seated hatred fueled his anger. Handing the letter to Jeanne, he muttered, "Don't read this if you want to keep your lunch down."

Dear Mr. and Mrs. Brewer:

This letter serves as a follow-up to our telephone conversation regarding the Coleman sentencing matter for the trespass case. As you can see by the enclosed copies of the Court Orders in the matter of the trespass case, the Coleman brothers were sentenced by Judge Henry Paladino.

At the suggestion of Lester and his mother and her assertion that Lester and Charles could find work in Morgan County where they have stayed out of trouble and were gainfully employed in the past, Lester and Charles were ordered to relocate for the purpose of finding employment.

Melvin has official permission to remain in Sterling County; however, as you can see from the Order, he must refrain from any contact whatsoever and wherever with you or your family. Additionally, none of these brothers may come onto any of your property, wherever located. If they violate these conditions, please advise my office at once, and I will deal sternly with them.

Finally, I understand that Vincent will also relocate to Morgan County and be enrolled through their Mental Health System. Accordingly, because of his incompetency to stand trial or plead guilty, we will delay further prosecution until we have a clearer picture of Vincent's behavior and competency.

I truly understand your frustration and your wife's concerns. As we discussed, those of us in law enforcement experience the same frustration when we have to deal with sentencing laws.

Unfortunately, such sentencing laws saddled us regarding incarceration for crimes against your property. I hope this takes care of your problems "on the hill" and that you and your family can enjoy Sterling County again.

> If you wish to discuss this matter, or if my office can be
> of further help, please advise. Sincerely,
>
> Harlon C. Pennington IV
> Sterling County District Attorney

Damn you, Pennington, Jake thought as he read through the accompanying court orders. You promised we could provide statements before sentencing. There will be a day of reckoning.

"You knew it was coming, Jake."

"What upsets me is I can't do anything until the assault case is sentenced. How can they do anything but put Link back in prison for a parole violation on that one? They won't do anything with Punk because he's incompetent. Such a revelation. He was born retarded, and he'll die retarded. That didn't stop him from breaking into Hill Place. The list I gave the DA itemized more than $12,000 in damages with the last incident when they vandalized the place, and that's not counting the labor to repair the place. The DA and judge have to be sitting in Parker just roaring over this, and I bet they're naive enough to believe we think they struck a blow for justice."

"Don't have a coronary, Jake. I can't fight this alone."

CHAPTER 42

With no movement on Jeanne's assault case, summer slid into fall. One morning after a difficult night loaded with Jake's nightmares, the Brewers received a phone call that set them on edge. "Are you sure, Allison?" Jeanne asked incredulously as she gripped the phone in anger.

"Positive," Allison assured her, hesitant to pass along unwelcome news. "At the end of the court session, They heard your assault case. It had to be planned. The Colemans were there.

Rusty received probation, and Link received 60 days to two years in jail; he'll serve all but 60 days on probation with time served counted toward the 60 days. In my interview, the sheriff said Link would do about another month. He's to turn himself in to the county sheriff on December 11 to begin serving his term. The judge gave him time to get his business in order. No one even questioned that he was out of prison on parole and had no job."

"That says something for American justice," Jeanne said. Silence followed. In a calmer voice, Jeanne began, "I'm sorry, Allison, I had no right to go off on you like that. Pennington assured us we would be able to have input, but that no longer matters."

"I hesitated calling."

"This is maddening. The judge and DA haven't walked in fear after an animal like Link attacks and continues to stalk you. Every unknown sound becomes a challenge for emotional control. The night becomes hell, and it won't go away. Oh Honey, why am I burdening you?"

"Please. It's okay. Something else you should know. The autopsy results are back on the body found at Colemans. It's Jake Carlin. Someone shot him four times, and they recovered at least one bullet."

"They tested Jake's revolver and my pistol. We knew they wouldn't get a match. ."

Jake arrived home soon after Allison's call, and when Jeanne relayed the information she provided, he flew into a rage, something that was growing ever more common. When he finished berating the authorities and the system, he questioned God. Then in a calmer voice, "We had to know Pennington wouldn't call; he didn't want us to make a statement. You can bet Poskevich is also wondering what is going on."

"Please don't go up there and do something foolish. It's over."

"No, it's not over. Keep blowing the trumpet," Jake challenged with a sarcastic grin, one that masked feelings of deep anger.

"Trumpet?" Jeanne asked with a puzzled look.

"Yeah, like Joshua marching around the walls of Jericho blowing his trumpet until the walls came tumbling down."

"And, where are our trumpets?" Jeanne questioned, depression evident in her voice.

"Our writing campaign would have brought walls tumbling down if some well-placed people weren't propping them up." Jake shook his head, wondering what would happen next in this battle. A sudden thought struck Jake. "Jeanne, this war is closer to an ending than I realized. I told Poskevich about the marijuana farms. That bulldog is on to a lot more than people realize. Now I'm going to drop an anonymous letter to the Pennsylvania parole board concerning Link's activities since his release. I'll write it as a concerned citizen from Sterling County and mail it in Parker."

"Are you sure we shouldn't just stay away from up there until this clears up?"

"The Colemans aren't dumb. They know the cops are watching them." After careful consideration, Jake confessed. "You're gonna be upset, Jeanne. I may have the evidence to connect Link to Carlin's death."

"You what?"

Jake retrieved the Bible his grandfather gave him when he enlisted in the Marines and the revolver he found in Link's truck. "Gramp said his

Bible had his notes that would help me understand God's word, and it has. And this is my grandfather's revolver, Jeanne."

"I thought it disappeared when they killed him."

"It did. Link had it hidden somewhere after he killed Gramp. I bet he used it on Carlin, too, and God only knows who else."

"Are you sure it's the same gun? There must be lots of guns that look like that."

"I already checked," Jake answered as he turned to the twenty-third Psalm. "See these numbers; they're Gramp's guns with their serial numbers. The SW38 stands for Smith and Wesson 38 special, and the numbers that follow, 1-7-3-9-5-4, are its serial number. The other numbers are for his Winchester model 70 30-06, his Winchester model 12 pump shotgun, and his Winchester 22 rifle. He loved Winchesters and wrote down their serial numbers in case someone stole them. Gramp said no thief would steal his Bible, so he'd have that record. He used the page of the twenty-third Psalm because it was his favorite passage."

"How'd you get the gun?"

"Under Link's truck seat."

"Down at Whiskey Springs?"

"Yeah."

"Turn it over to the police. That should clinch it for Mister Coleman."

"Problem! How do I explain how I got the thing? The cops can't know I'm connected with that trip. Too much is riding on it. The game commission pictures, screwed up gate lock, and more."

"You can't let Link get away with this."

"I have to get the gun back in Link's truck in a way that gives the cops reason to search that truck before Link does. I wish now I had let it be."

"So Link could get rid of it?"

"You're right," Jake agreed. "If anything happens to me, you know where the gun and Bible are. Turn them over to the cops and tell them how I got the gun."

That weekend the Brewers went north with Jake's plan, a $30,000 cashier's check which eliminated their savings, and the letter to mail to the Pennsylvania Parole Board. Saturday night after supper, Jake used his voice-changing box to make a call, knowing Link wasn't following orders. "Pandemonium Pleasure Palace, this is Ivory. How may I help you?"

"Good evening. Is Link Coleman there?" Jake whispered into his voice apparatus.

"How'd you know he was back in town?"

Without answering, Jake asked, "May I speak with him?"

He listened to the jukebox roar and rowdy bar conversation while Ivory called Link to the phone. "Some sweet soundin' woman wants ya on the phone." The next voice he heard was Link saying, "Ya dumb bastard Ivory, you didn't have to tell the world I'm in town. Link here."

"Hi Link, it's me. I wasn't sure you'd be there. I didn't see your truck."

"I parked on the top of Spring Street so the cops wouldn't see it."

"Man, have I missed you. I couldn't stay away. I'm at the Sunrise Motel. Can you meet me at the bar? I'll be dressed by ten."

"See ya at ten, Baby, ya know I will," Link replied enthusiastically, the lust lowering his voice to a husky growl.

"Do me a favor, walk up here. I don't want anyone to see your truck."

"Okay," Link agreed, sounding excited about the prospects."

Jake slipped into a black wool sweater, black ski cap, and a pair of latex gloves when Jeanne walked in and spotted the canvas case on the bed. "What's this, Jake?" Jeanne asked inquisitively, "Please don't tell me it's nothing."

"A lock picking kit."

"You planning on becoming a cat burglar?" Jeanne asked, a frown forming as she talked.

"They're for just in case," Jake answered without further explanation.

Jeanne opened the little pouch and looked over the metal tools. "What are all these things, and where did you get them?"

"Well, my curious little cat," Jake answered, "I came about them legally in the Corps. Security school. That's enough to know."

"Can any lock be picked with these?" Jeanne asked as she inspected the tools.

"Most locks are pickable," Jake answered.

"What would we do if everybody had these? Nothing would be safe."

"Everyone can't get them, and most home burglaries happen by force. If the burglars can't find unlocked windows or doors, they break in, work rapidly, and leave. Professionals are different. They break into places for a purpose such as stealing security info, trade secrets, formulas, documents, those kinds of things. They use picks because they don't want anyone to know they were there."

They ran through the plan for the evening and the pick-up point on the way to Parker while Jake put on rubber gloves. He took his grandfather's revolver still wrapped in the rag and a Coors Silver Bullet beer can wiped free of fingerprints and stuffed them in his pouch. Jeanne drove up Spring Street until they spotted Link's truck. In the next block, Jake jumped out when she stopped at the intersection. He was letting himself in Link's truck when a voice called, "Nice truck."

"Thanks," Jake mumbled back in the deepest voice he could muster. He opened the door with his head turned away from the porch so that he wouldn't be recognized when the truck's dome light came on. Link never learns, Jake thought when he spotted the key in the ignition. As he was easing away from the curb, he spotted the person watching leave the porch. Just my luck, Jake thought. I look suspicious. "Oh well, such is life," he said aloud. At the stop sign where Spring Street intersected Main Street, he slipped the gun under the seat while waiting for a truck to pass. He then turned left and headed out of town toward the Sunrise Bar and Motel.

On the highway, Jake nervously searched for a man walking. He rounded the curve north toward the Sunrise Motel. Still no Link. Finally, he spotted a person almost to the motel. He pulled the hat down close to his eyes and slowed to see who the person was. It was Link. "Unbelievable!" Jake said to himself as he slowed the truck. He blew the horn when he passed Link, watching for a reaction in the mirrors.

Link recognized his truck and yelled, "Hey you, where ya goin' with my truck?"

Jake gassed the vehicle just as Link reached it and shot up the highway. He slowed again until Link almost caught up, then gassed it again. As Jake swung into the parking lot, a police cruiser with its siren wailing and lights flashing rounded the corner, speeding toward them. Link ran toward him for all he was worth. A deep ditch dropped off just past the Sunrise parking lot. Jake slowed the truck, cut the wheel down over the bank, and slid into the ditch, laying the truck on its side. The police cruiser was closing as Jake shook the can of beer and let it spray. With Link racing across the Sunrise parking lot, Jake dropped the beer, climbed out, and disappeared into the night.

The following morning the Brewers skipped church and went for an early morning walk. When they returned, Jeanne caught the tail end of the local news report. "... and they quickly extinguished the fire. In an unrelated incident, State Police report Lester Coleman of RD 2, Parker was arrested last night at the Sunrise Motel for driving under the influence after his truck left the road and slid into a ditch. Coleman was remanded to the county jail following an altercation with the arresting office. Investigation of this incident continues." Jeanne shot a dark, how did you arrange this look at Jake, and he just shrugged his shoulders.

A little over an hour later, Mac called with the latest gossip about the incident. "Just in case you didn't catch the news, they arrested Link last night. DUI. He wrecked his truck up by the Sunrise Motel. Hanratty caught him at the truck, but he swore he didn't drive it there. Claims someone stole the truck. Link said he was meetin' someone at the motel bar but wouldn't say who, and no one in the bar would admit to meetin' him there."

"Guess nothing much changes," Jake answered.

"They jailed him too. That ain't all. They found a revolver under his seat. Convicted felons ain't allowed to have 'em. That's what fired Link off. He swore he didn't have a gun but couldn't explain how Hanratty found it. He punched Hanratty three or four times' fore it was all over."

"Link did?"

"Yep."

"Will those guys never learn?" Jake asked, feeling like there might finally be a little light at the end of the tunnel. Then he added just to gore Mac, "Punching a cop could get Link in real trouble. Somehow you have to feel for him."

"You gotta be nuts, Brewer," Mac snapped, and the phone went dead.

CHAPTER 43

"Jake! A lumber truck wrecked, and there's gonna be hell to pay. You can't believe what —"

"Hold it, Mac. I'll turn on the radio."

After a brief time, Jake returned to the phone call. "I'm back, Mac. I got the radio on just in time to hear them announce they'd be back after a brief intermission. What's happening?

"What ain't happening? One of Parker Sawmill's lumber trucks wrecked. Hit an elk and ran through the guard rails an' down the hill. Lost its load. They got two wreckers to pull it back up on the road. Cops found drugs that came out of a box on the bottom of the trailer. A van load of FBI agents arrived just before this news break. The truck driver said he was headed for a Johnson City, Tennessee furniture factory with a load of cherry boards. Claims he don't know nothin' about drugs 'cause that box is always locked, and he ain't got keys. None of the drivers do. The news guy said there are four metal boxes, and the driver only has keys for two of 'em. Poskevich is there. Said he doesn't know any more than the radio guy trying to interview him. The radio guy said they haul lumber to Norfolk that ships haul all over the world. He speculated that the drugs could be coming into Norfolk on ships, picked up by lumber trucks, and brought back to Parker, where other lumber trucks are redistributing it. FBI is down checking all the trucks at the mill.

Can you believe this?"

"Have to believe it. Maybe Parker will become famous as America's drug distribution center.

Wouldn't that be —"

"Gotta go. News is comin' back on. You can listen yerself."

Jake finished his supper listening to the news. Newspaper, TV, and radio news personnel were now on site. Their interviews with the Parker Radio Person went over the information Mac covered earlier.

Jake tried TV news, but they reported nothing on the wreck or the drugs. Tired from a day of hunting with time spent writing, Jake turned in early wondering what would happen at the mill.

Dawn slipped in on cat's feet Saturday morning. The overnight snow hung on the hemlocks and mountain laurel, deadening the forest's sounds. Winter was venting her fury, and most living things were waiting for the storm to work itself out.

As he thought about the truck wreck and drug news, he wondered if this somehow figured into the Coleman problems and the pot plots discovered during the summer. He hunted earlier in the season by those plots, and the pot had either been harvested or destroyed.

Jake swept snow off his truck after breakfast and threw the broom in the back of his truck. He carried his suitcase, the manuscript, computer disk, and mini tape recorder to the truck and packed them in the back seat in preparation for leaving at the end of the day. After rechecking the fire, he turned out the lights and locked the door behind him.

He was on his way before he could legally shoot, finding it challenging to concentrate considering what happened with the lumber truck. As the day wore on, the wind picked up in intensity, and the temperature plummeted. Jake made his way up through the boulders that made up the backbone of this ridge towering over surrounding mountains. A face-eating wind now raced unimpeded across these high places making him pull his hat tighter as he climbed up on a boulder. Hill Place now stood in view on the other side of the hollow. Glassing the old homestead with his binoculars, he noted how much the place reminded him of a Currier and Ives painting. The old log cape cod with green shutters, the stone chimney with wood smoke curling skyward, and the American flag flying in the breeze painted his picture of home. All that was missing was the old chestnut log barn, now little more than a memory of the fire that almost ended their lives.

While he watched, a vehicle rolled into view, turned around, and backed in front of the garage. The driver got out and approached Hill

Place, walking out of sight on the front porch. Jake visualized the person knocking on the front door. Finding no one home, the person returned to the truck, and a passenger got out to meet him. The passenger picked two bundles out of the truck, handed one to the driver, and they walked back to the house. Moments later they returned to their truck and drove away. Jake sensed something vulgar was happening, and there was nothing he could do about it.

Flames ripped skyward from the front of Hill Place, followed by a blaze that climbed up and around the back porch. Jake sprang into action, running out along the ridge toward Laceys. It was too late to rescue his home. The fire company couldn't save the place now if they were sitting in the driveway running out hoses. Filled with gut-searing anger, he screamed at the sky. "What did I do, God? Is this how you treat your faithful servants?" Second thoughts took over. Feeling sorry for himself wasn't going to stop his problems.

Jake scrambled across the boulder-strewn summit. Hot and breathing hard, he discarded his hunting coat on the crest of Fox Ridge. Frigid air burned its way down his throat and into fiery lungs. He struggled with his heart pounding and chest fighting efforts to suck in enough air. He tripped over a buried obstruction and pitched headlong into the snow. Defeat rose within him. Fighting back the give-up temptation, he crawled to his feet and in a staggering gait, trotted down the ridge.

Burned out jack pines from the summer fire were now just so many flame blackened toothpicks poked holes into the bright, blue sky. Running was difficult. He struggled along in a half trot - half stumble. The truck that torched his home approached after its trip around the hill. He had a chance, but it would be close. The old sergeant major willed himself on. He ran out of the pines and flopped across an old elk trail. Pulling the rifle to his shoulders, he slipped his eye to the scope. Nothing. Jerking the gun down, he frantically dug the snow from his eyepiece. The truck came into view below him. He had it in his scope. One chance, he thought, thumbing off the safety. Fighting to control his heavy breathing for accuracy, he mentally calculated the distance between 300 and 400 yards. Squeezing off a shot, the .270 jumped in his hands. The muzzle blast reverberated through the mountain tops. The truck disappeared around the bend.

"Damn," he cursed, lying there in the snow straining for air. The depth of his loss struck him.

Family antiques, old pictures, and much of what was dear to him in life other than Jeanne and their kids were now gone. Tears wet his eyes.

Anger followed. "Why God? Why me? What did I do to deserve this? Oh Lord, we have a new career here, put our home up for sale, and invested our savings in this opportunity. I prayed and thought our coming home was your will. Jeanne did too. At least Jeanne wasn't there when they torched the place."

A deadly chill overcame Jake. The cops couldn't stop the violence, and the legal system seemed invested in it continuing. Standing, he brushed off the snow. The memory of flames licking up the sides of Hill Place dumped his emotions down a mine shaft. Drained, he slowly eased back up the hill to retrieve his coat.

The pungent smell of his destroyed home drifted up to him long before he could see the burned log cabin where he was born. Coming out of the hollow above his field, he caught the first glimpse of the remains of the old homestead. Smoke from the cellar wafted into the frosty air where smoldering logs and oak timbers continued to burn. The scorched American flag flapping in the breeze stood watch over the pitiful remains. The stone fireplace chimney still curled smoke, the refrigerator and the old wood cookstove poked out of the rubble where they had fallen into the cellar.

Grief crushed him as he looked over the smoking rubble he had called home. He walked to his truck, slid his loaded rifle into his truck barrel down on the passenger side, and climbed in. Pulling his revolver from under the seat, he checked the loads and laid it on the seat beside him. "Oh Lord, I'm gonna need a ton of forgiveness, but this won't go on."

Jake took one last look at the smoking remains, allowing the scene to burn hate into his heart. He climbed into his truck and drove off, carefully staying to the side of the other vehicle's tracks in the fresh snow.

He met a surprise as he entered the bend before Laceys. Swifty's truck slid over the bank and hung there. Seeing no occupants, he eased out with the revolver. Legs stuck out from under the truck on the far side.

"Help me," someone gasped from under the truck.

Ya, right, Jake thought, thumbing the hammer back on the big revolver. Kneeling, he could see under the down side of the truck. The man was pinned. Jake approached after scanning the truck and not seeing the second occupant. Fresh tracks led away from the passenger door and across the field.

Gun ready, he peered underneath. A small tree bent over as the truck slid past, wedging against the drive train. The truck had been jacked up but slipped, pinning the man underneath when he tried to remove the tree.

"That you Swifty?"

"It's me," Swifty gasped, the axle across his chest squeezing the air out of him. "Jack this thing up before it crushes me."

"That's just what I should do," Jake replied in a strained voice.

"Ya got me in this fix," Swifty gasped in a hoarse whisper, the smell of whisky strong on his breath. "Ya shot at us. It scared me. Ran off the road," Swifty uttered between breaths.

Sensing an opportunity to gain valuable information, Jake returned to his truck and retrieved his tape recorder. Swifty called after him, "Don't leave me."

Jake rummaged in his glove compartment until he found a new tape and replaced the one in the recorder. Chilled now, he shrugged into his hunting coat, returned to Swifty's truck, started the recorder, and propped it in the snow. "You still under there, Swifty?"

"Where'd you think I'd be?"

"Just making sure. Where's Link?"

"He took the stuff and left." Swifty gulped air. "Now jack up this friggin' truck."

"You're in no position to be barking orders. You got yourself a bad situation here. What I should do is blow you away for torching my home," Jake replied, showing Swifty the cocked handgun. "Now, what was the stuff Link took?"

"Some bagged stuff. That's all I know." Swifty said, struggling to breathe."

Jake fought back fury and slipped the revolver into his waistband. He maneuvered the jack in place and gave it a few clicks up, relieving some of the pressure on Swifty's chest. "That better?" Jake asked in a controlled voice.

"Little more. Maybe I can get loose." Swifty uttered, obviously relieved. Jake gave it another click and asked, "How about now? Can you get out?"

"A little more otta do it," Swifty said eagerly, breathing easier now. He was going to survive.

Jake flipped the direction switch on the jack and gave it an ever so slow click. "Hey, yer going the wrong way," Swifty howled as the axle tightened against his chest.

Jake lowered the jack another click. Swifty's air supply became more restricted, his chest crushing under the truck's weight. "That's for my house and barn, Swifty." Another click. He stopped and looked underneath, "That's for what you boys did to Jeanne."

"I didn't do anything ... to your woman," Swifty gasped. "That was Link. Please let me outta here."

"Got a question, Swifty. What's your tie to the DA?"

"Ain't none," Swifty gasped. "He's Link's friend. Link sends us away when he comes around."

"You're in a bad fix Swifty." While Swifty fought for breath, Jake took another click down. "Guess it's time to end this if you won't talk."

"I don't wanna die," Swifty said, as he alternately gasped for breath and wheezed information.

"You worked at the Parker sawmill. What do you know about lumber trucks and drugs?"

"Link knows stuff, but he won't talk about it. Tells us to mind our own business."

When he stopped talking, Jake asked another question. "Who was growing the pot in the elk clearings?"

Swifty didn't answer. "Don't make me let this jack down, Swifty. I'm in no mood to fool."

"Belonged to some guys outta Erie. We was watchin' it for 'em. They came in an' worked on stuff now and then. They got contacts in town. Not sure who." Swifty gasped a bit to get air before continuing. "Link knows more about everything. That's how he gets the money for trucks and stuff."

"Is pot all they're into, Swifty?"

"There's two groups. Pot in Erie and ... drugs from Newark. Help me. I can't breathe," Swifty gasped.

Jake jacked it up two licks. "Talk or the jack goes down."

"Between them two, they got anything you can use. I did a little experimentin', but I quit after wrecking my snowmobile."

"What do you know about Bailey Donahue's disappearance."

"Nothin! All I know is Link said she couldn't keep her big mouth shut. Please jack this up like ya promised."

"Swifty, I never promised you anything. The last problem we had, I told myself it would be a cold day in hell before I helped you. It isn't cold today."

"I'll talk. Just don't leave me here."

Swifty began answering questions and provided a level of information beyond Jake's belief.

Satisfied he had all the facts he would get, Jake lowered the truck to finish the job until he remembered Jackson's words. "You can't kill every no-good jackass that needs killing; you'd empty half the county. And remember, son, some folks believe we should be among the dearly departed."

Jake looked under the truck and softly said, "Swifty, I'm not setting you free because I don't know what you'd do. Be sure of this! You fool with me again, and you're a dead man."

Jake started to leave and thought better of it. He jacked the truck up enough to allow Swifty to breathe a bit easier. Swifty pleaded, "Get me outta here. I swear I'll never bother you again."

"Lord knows I'd like to believe you, Swifty, but I can't. I'll send help from town."

Jake picked up the recorder, walked back to his truck, and laid his gun on the seat, wondering if he should set the man loose or let him be. Swifty was dressed warm enough to make it. He took the broom out of his truck to brush out his boot tracks. Satisfied the wind would finish the job, he departed for Parker. As he came to Lacey's place, he considered telling them to call the cops to rescue Swifty. Crow's car was gone. Reporting Swifty's problem would have to wait until he hit Parker.

CHAPTER 44

Jake fought with himself all of the way to Parker and finally decided to call the state police and report the incident when he arrived at the Handee Mart. His Christian beliefs required it, and Swifty had provided considerable information, albeit forced. Abandoning Swifty to the elements wouldn't feel good discussing it while standing before God.

When he pulled in, the payphone was busy, and he waited impatiently, wondering about Swifty. When the phone became available, he quickly called the police with his accident report and Swifty's location. It was clear the duty officer felt questions remained unanswered. Jake resolved it by promising to come to the barracks to make a complete report when he finished fueling.

Jake started his pump and then grabbed the windshield cleaning tool. "WHACK" A thudding blow struck the back of his head, slamming him face-first into the side of his truck. Dizzying lights flashed before his eyes. A second blow struck his left shoulder as he fell. Somewhere a woman screamed. Warrior instincts took over as he snake crawled away from the impact that flattened him. A boot caught him in the ribs knocking the wind out of him, forcing a curse from his lips. Desperate, he gathered will and pulled himself under the truck.

The follow-on kick missed. The kicker cursed when his shin struck the truck. "Come outta there," a nasty voice snarled through the fog of his mind. Looking back, he glimpsed Link Coleman looking under the truck. "I'm gonna burn yer ass to a cinder."

Jake struggled out on the opposite side of the truck, pain shooting through his head and shoulder. Something splashed on his truck. Gasoline fumes washed over him.

"Come out, or I'll torch ya, Brewer." Link laughed his contemptuous, trademark mocking laugh.

Painfully, Jake worked into a crouch behind the rear wheel. Link knelt again to look under the truck. When he couldn't see Jake, he screamed, "Brewer, ya better come back. I know where ya live, an' I'll be coming for ya."

Jake formulated an attack plan as he fought to gain control of the pain and his senses.

Quietly, he retreated to the rear of the truck. Chancing a peek through the rear window of his truck cap, Jake located Link slowly easing toward the back of the truck, a butane lighter in one hand and the gas pump nozzle in the other. Oh Lord, he's going to torch it, Jake thought, fighting back the temptation to run. He gripped his left hand and had little feeling other than stabs of pain as he edged closer to Link's approach. Crouching, Jake waited for Link's body to slip into view. Turning his back to Link's approach, he swung around where Link's head would appear with all the force he could muster from his 223-pound frame. Jake's fist slammed home, crushing Link's lips against his teeth. Link fell backward between the gas pumps, his hand instinctively grabbing his wounded mouth.

Jake's combat-trained killing instincts raged. Link crawled to his knees. Jake kicked him full in the face, slamming him back against the concrete. Jake kicked again. Link grabbed his foot.

Jake grasped the gas hose swinging in front of him, swung it back over his head, and delivered a crushing blow to Link's head, smashing him down between the pumps. He tried to swing the hose with both hands for more force, but his wounded arm refused. Jake raised the hose over his head and slammed Link again, knocking him back against the concrete. Again Jake hammered him, venting hatred. Link rolled on his stomach to protect his head with his hands as the blows rained down. Jake threw the hose aside and walked around the pump island. He jumped astride Link's back and jerked him up where he could get at him. Pinning him against a pump with his knee, he smashed him in the face with his good fist. Link tried to get away but was too near unconscious. Jake pulled his knee out and allowed Link's face to splat against the concrete.

Straddling Link's back, he grabbed his hair, pulled his head back, and slammed his face into the concrete island with a bone-crushing thud that sent teeth and blood flying.

He jerked Link's head back, but hands prevented him from slamming Link into the concrete.

"It's over, Jake," a voice said. Reluctantly, he let go of Link's hair and collapsed against his truck. Arms under his shoulders, Trooper Johnston helped him stagger to his feet. A crowd gathered. Sirens and flashing lights surrounded them.

Hanratty arrived, saw Link's condition, and called an ambulance to the scene. He covered Link with a blanket, stopping sightseers from gawking at his destroyed face. While he waited, Hanratty tried unsuccessfully to disperse the crowd.

Lightheaded, Jake leaned against his truck for support. Hanratty and Johnston stood beside him. Pain coursed from his head and neck down into his shoulder. Broken ribs made breathing difficult. Blood ran down his face. "What happened?" Hanratty asked.

"I can tell you," a blond woman with a shrill voice volunteered. "That guy standing beside you was pumping gas," she said, pointing to Jake's pump, "and I was using this one over here. The man on the ground slipped out of his truck and hit this man on the back of the head with his fist so hard it knocked him down. He hit him again with a tire wrench thingy. Blood splattered when he slammed into his truck. Then the man that's down kicked him and sprayed gas all over the truck. Somehow that man," she said, pointing to Jake, "got away from this other guy. Then he got him on the ground and pounded him good."

"That's what happened, officer," a gray-bearded man agreed. "The guy down started it."

"Got to sit down," Jake said as he struggled to get in his truck. Severe pain shot through him, and he almost blacked out.

Johnston gently assisted Jake into his truck, noting the handgun and rifle. "These loaded," he asked.

"Can't do much with empty guns."

"You better turn them in for safekeeping," Hanratty demanded.

"Those guns had no part in this fight," Jake said quietly, the fury still in him. "Had they,. . ." and his voice trailed off.

A woman arrived from the Sentinel newspaper and began asking questions. The ambulance arrived, and EMTs slipped Link on a gurney. Another trooper pulled in while they were loading him. Poskevich stepped out, talked to Johnston quietly, and then stepped aside to allow him into his vehicle to escort the ambulance. With siren blazing, the ambulance raced off toward the hospital.

Hanratty returned to Jake's truck with Poskevich. "You almost killed him, Jake," Hanratty said as he mentally pictured Link.

"You calling me a failure, Officer?" Jake asked, looking Hanratty a bone chiller.

"What do you mean by that crack?" Hanratty demanded.

"Officer," Jake began through clenched teeth, a fit of overpowering anger evident, "he's lucky Johnston came along. He'll be back at me as soon as he heals."

"Nobody deserves a beating like that," Hanratty said.

"You heard the witnesses. It was self-defense," Jake said softly. "You cops should have stayed out of this. Now the finish will wait for another day, but it'll come."

The external speaker on the police cruiser cracked alive, and Hanratty ran to silence it. Another police sedan arrived, and an older trooper Jake didn't know stepped out and began interviewing witnesses. Many now told second-hand stories as if they were somehow involved.

"Guess I got here a little late," Poskevich said as he looked in at Jake. "Can I get in your truck so we can talk privately?" When he closed the door, Poskevich began. "This has to remain between us." With the nod of agreement, the trooper continued. "I was on my way with a pickup order for Link when this problem came on the radio. I'm thinking your letter to the parole board resulted in Link's parole termination."

"I watched Link and Swifty torch our home while I was hunting," Jake angrily injected.

"You're kidding me."

"No. It's gone."

"The DA might have given Link a heads up about returning to prison, and Link was getting even. Question. Is this mess hooked up with the Swifty problem you called in?"

"It is. Link and Swifty."

"Link has real problems. We got the ballistic tests back from Carlin's murder. The gun we found in Link's truck killed Carlin, and Link's fingerprints are all over it. Strange though, Link swears that revolver wasn't in his truck. Said he didn't drive his truck to the motel either."

"You know what a liar he is."

"If I were a betting man, I'd bet there could be some truth in his claim."

"Kind of hard to fake fingerprints."

"It's impossible," Poskevich agreed. "His fingerprints were on an open can of beer too. He was legally drunk, but he swears that beer wasn't his. There's a mystery about this case we may never unravel, that is, not unless somebody gets careless and talks." Jake understood the veiled warning and let it go without comment.

Hanratty finished his business and returned to Jake's truck, knocking on the window. With it down, he asked. "Where were you headed before this incident?"

"To the police station," Jake weakly replied. "I have a crime to report and an accident report to complete. Then I'm heading home."

"You're in no shape to travel," Poskevich said, looking at his bloody face, now white from the loss of blood and the shock of the fight. Better stay in the area until we sort out this mess."

"No place to stay."

"No?" Hanratty asked with a puzzled look.

"Colemans torched our place a couple of hours ago. That's what this is all about. All that's left standing are two chimneys, parts of the log walls that are still burning, and the flagpole with Old Glory burned but still flying. My lifetime home is gone."

"How do you know it was the Colemans?" Hanratty asked, now on the defensive.

"My friend," Jake said, his anger evident, "I watched them set the fire. Swifty's pinned under his truck on the road out of our place. I called in a report when I got here."

"You left him there?"

"His truck is in a precarious position. I tried to jack it up but was afraid the truck would slide and kill him. Got enough problems without going to jail for being a good Samaritan."

An unsettled Hanratty looked at Jake. This man was capable of great violence, and now the revelation about Swifty. "You can't leave until —"

Jake cut Hanratty short. "Link started it, and I protected myself," Jake said in a nasty tone. "And you know where to find me if you want me."

"You can't beat a man to death," Hanratty said. "That's —"

Before he could continue, Jake interrupted with a raised palm and a steely-eyed stare. "My friend, maybe you couldn't kill him. I would have." Jake added, "Arson's provable if someone gets out there and checks for gasoline where the fire started. Note the tire tracks on my road and boot prints in the yard before the wind erases them. They have Coleman written all over 'em. A blood test will prove they've been drinking against court orders. You heard the witnesses. Link tried to kill me with a tire iron." The emotional surge made him lightheaded, and he fought to remain sitting upright. "You know, the DA will be disappointed. He knew Link would behave like a model citizen if given a chance."

CHAPTER 45

Understanding the problem between Jake and Hanratty, Poskevich suggested Hanratty check for fire evidence at the Brewer place. Hanratty looked at him, understood, and departed. After his departure, Poskevich said, "I've been thinking a lot about your DA problem Jake. What am I missing?"

Jake looked out the side window, wondering what Glen knew and what he should tell him. Thoughts of problems past boiled his stomach. "Can this be forever between you and me?" Jake asked as he turned to face the trooper.

"Jake, you gotta know that's the way everything is."

"I don't know why I'm telling you this. I've never talked about it before. Jeanne and I had a problem, Glen. I thought I lost her to Pennington when I was in Nam." Jake looked out the window, having difficulty facing Glen. Finally working up the courage, he began again. "Jeanne and Pennington dated in high school. They broke it off when he went to college. I joined the Marines, and we hit it off when I came home on leave. I was crazy about her. We got married. She came home when I went to Nam the first time. I got badly wounded. I didn't think she'd want me that way, so I wrote her a letter and told her our marriage was over. Didn't tell her why. Came home on leave and found she had been back with Pennington. We got back together and never discuss the Pennington situation. She told me she was afraid of what I might do to him. That's about it. I'm crazy about her."

"I can understand why Pennington might want you out of the way. Did the fight in his office have anything to do with past problems?"

"None. Pennington grabbed me when I was leaving his office after he frosted me off."

"You sure you won't stay with us for a few days. You look rough."

"Been worse a few times," Jake replied, struggling to hide how miserable he felt.

"You gave Link one helluva pounding."

With a wry smile, Jakes replied, "I prefer to think of it as a laying on of the hands ministry."

"Jake, how are you doing . . . personally?" the trooper asked with deep sincerity.

Jake studied his face, understanding where the question came from. After struggling for a place to start, he began. "Glen, until a few hours ago, this was the best week I've had in a long time. Things seemed to be calming down. I have a new future with my father's logging business. I've been writing, and that seemed . . . well . . . seemed to be writing the anger out of my life. I hunted mornings and evenings and wrote during the day and at night. I was getting something accomplished that I'd put off for a long time. You were right when you questioned my anger and asked if I had nightmares. It's yes in both cases and hard to handle. These constant problems are eating me alive. I'm past tired of being pissed on by the DA and being told it's raining. I can't look at old uniform pictures. The medals represent the death of many good men and the death and destruction on both sides of that damned war. Then there's the personal side of it all."

"Jake, you don't have to face this alone. Help's available for PTSD."

"I don't want to talk about it, to relive this . . . this hell."

"Jake, we're far enough along in this relationship that you know you can trust me. I can go to the VA with you. It'll stay between us."

"I came to realize I scare Jeanne. That's the last thing I want. I love her so. It was getting better until this morning. I'm running out of . . . out of about everything."

"You know Sergeant Major Ambrose Mitchell better than most and know that tough shell he walked around in. He came to the point of nearly self-destructing before he got help. He's getting better now.

"That's hard to believe. Like those who know him say, 'He's one tough S.O.B.'"

"He's no tougher than you. Mitchell said we could all stand to be more like Jake Brewer. Don't lose it, Jake. A lot of us gather a special something from you."

Embarrassed and not knowing what to say, Jake muttered, "I better get on the road."

"Stay with Sue and me tonight. We'd love to have you."

Head in hands, Jake leaned on the steering wheel, considering the offer. "I'm a mess and not much for company. I better go home. Don't want my problems screwing you up."

"You won't."

"Grab your notebook. Swifty provided information you need."

"You heard the parole board revoked Link's parole. Like I said earlier, I believe the DA may have tipped Link about the parole board decision. I also believe Mr. DA fears what could be coming for his part in this drug mess and wanted Jake Brewer to make Link gone because he's a witness."

"Glen, this tape talks about the drug problems, the Colemans, and more. It should help you. Penny kept telling me I didn't understand the problem. After talking with Swifty, I have special new insights and understand things more clearly than he wants me to."

"Is that all?"

Jake sat quietly, deciding how much more he wanted to share. "No, that's not all. Swifty believes the hard drug and pot operations are two separate operations controlled by two different parties, which could be coming to blows. Pennington is involved in both, and his shot-up car served as a warning from the hard drug folks. The three holes in his windshield each had a pot stem in them. I think one came from each field. Swifty believes Penny is funneling cash to Link to keep him quiet."

"You sure?"

"As sure as Swifty is. You're sitting on my tape recorder."

With an embarrassed look, the trooper leaned over and pulled it out. "You'd have felt the recorder if you weren't getting soft from all those donuts you eat," Jake said with a wry smile.

Jake took the recorder in his good hand and hit the play button. They listened to the exchange for a few minutes, and then Jake cut it off. "Sounds like you two had quite a scuffle."

"We had an information exchange. There are holes in what Swifty knows. I doubt parts of his story, but there's plenty on that tape to lead you to the rest of the story. Do you have a cop named Perato at the barracks?"

"We do. He's the guy out there interviewing witnesses. Why?"

"He came from Philly, and he's dirty. Works with the drug boss headquartered in Philly. They're dealing about every drug imaginable. The Philly guys don't run the pot farms you discovered, and Pennington's car is evidence they're upset about that. They run the pot out of Erie. The DA is involved in both operations, but Swifty isn't sure how it all fits together. Those log transfer trucks haul veneer cherry boards out of Parker to Newark, where they load the lumber on ships bound for Germany, Japan, and other places. On their return, the trucks haul drugs back to Sterling County."

"You're kidding me?"

"No, Poskie, I'm not. There's more. In addition to Newark, the rigs hauling lumber out of the mills in Sterling County are carrying drugs to Johnson City, Tennessee, Buffalo, New York, a couple of places in North Carolina, and other places where they make high-quality furniture. Swifty doesn't think the drivers know they're hauling drugs. There's a lot more on the tape. Use it with discretion."

"New subject Jake. Anything on the tape concerning Bailey Donahue?"

"Not much that can help, but there's talk of her on there. Apparently, Link was upset with her. Remember Poskie, I'm trusting you to keep my name out of all this stuff. You'll have to find ways to verify everything because that tape was made under duress."

"Knowing the players, I would bet it was a high level of duress."

A goofy grin spread across Jake's face. "Funny thing. When I can get a quiet moment to myself, you know, a little time when cops and bad guys aren't harassing me, I'm going to thank the good Lord for this day."

"You got burned out and half-killed. What's to be thankful for in that?"

"There's your answer; I was just half killed. Jeanne wasn't there alone, so she wasn't cremated. We're planning on moving back but not sure when now that we don't have a place to live. I'll be working with Brewer Logging. Jeanne too. Strange how God works things out."

"You believe God's for real, Jake?" Posky asked in amazement.

"I believe it with everything in me. A few times in my life, I've been where I had nothing left but the Lord through prayer. I prayed, and my prayers were answered, maybe not the way I wanted, but better. I try to follow God's perfect plan for my life. It isn't always easy, and this mess on the hill has stretched my Christian walk to the breaking point. Vietnam did the same. The longest hours of my life were flying back to the States trying to remember who I was, the person Jeanne loved. I realized being a good Marine seemed to be at cross purposes with the Lord's plan. I'm a long way from perfect, but with the Lord helping me along, I grow stronger in my daily walk with Him."

"I wish I had your faith, Jake," Glen said.

"The Lord has a plan for Glen Poskevich. You have a Bible?"

"No, I don't."

Jake struggled out of the truck with Poskevich asking, "Hey, where are you going?"

"Clear to the back seat." Jake opened his suitcase and fished out his study Bible. Struggling back into the front seat, he handed it to the trooper. "Take this one! I got another one at home. There are many notes in there about things I came to understand. Start in the New Testament book of John. It's all about love and the Lord's love for guys like us. 'For God so loved the world that He gave His only begotten son, that whosoever believes on Him will not perish but have everlasting life. For God sent not His son to condemn the world, but that the world through Him might be saved.' That's John 3:16 and 17. I hang on those words. Throw in a chapter of Proverbs each day for a daily face slapping. When you get done with John, go back and start with Matthew and read through it until Revelations. That's pretty tough reading, so skip it for now and reread the New Testament."

"I can't take your Bible, Jake."

"You can't turn down a friend's gift."

The trooper handled the Bible as if it were hot. "I'm not sure I'm ready for this."

"Maybe not ready, but you need it. It's written all over your face."

"Sue's been telling me that for a long time."

"Glen, it should be obvious that I care about you. Please get started. Stay in touch. We both need that. There's a letter and some Bible verses in the front that I hope you'll read from time to time. Now let's pray together. 'Oh Lord, our God, be with me and my friend Poskie. Help us come to an understanding of Your will for our lives. Lord, please work with us and help us as we journey forward. Please support Glen as he works to clean up this Sterling County mess. In Your Holy Name, Jesus, we pray. Amen.'"

"Amen," Glen answered, surprising Jake.

"Now, back to the present," Jake said. "You might want to radio the troopers who are going out to get Swifty and suggest an in-depth interview as they work to get him out from under his truck. He should be cold and glad to talk. Then they'll be better able to understand what's driving problems on the hill. Link should be jailed for a long time and may have some important cellmates from here. Even more, you're reading God's word. And on top of all that, I've been handed the ending to my book. This has been a great day for me."

"Jake, it's hard to believe this is a great day for you, but I came to an understanding today," Poskie said with an easy smile. "Sergeant Major Mitchell said to be very careful around Jake Brewer, that you would get in my knickers. I can now see what he meant."

"Oh?"

"Bet he has one of your Bibles too."

"He does, Glen. He got it with Gramp's advice, the advice I received as a questioning teenager when Gramp gave me his Bible. It contains important Biblical notes throughout. But the advice Gramp gave me proved to be much more important. He said 'Many find the Bible difficult to believe. Try this. Read and reread Isaiah 53 until you feel you understand what it's telling you. Then begin reading the last chapters of Matthew, Mark, and Luke, remembering what Isaiah predicted 700 years earlier. Watch it come true. Then decide whether or not you can believe.' I believe."

"I'll do that, Jake. Something tells me I'll find what's missing in my life."

www.ingramcontent.com/pod-product-compliance
Lightning Source LLC
Chambersburg PA
CBHW072104300726
48975CB00003B/690